C000152684

WARM PEARLS
AND
PAPER CRANES

WARM PEARLS
AND
PAPER CRANES

by E.V. Bancroft

2021

Butterworth Books is a different breed of publishing house. It's a home for Indies, for independent authors who take great pride in their work and produce top quality books for readers who deserve the best. Professional editing, professional cover design, professional proof reading, professional book production—you get the idea. As Individual as the Indie authors we're proud to work with, we're Butterworths and we're *different*.

Authors currently publishing with us:

E.V. Bancroft
Valden Bush
Helena Harte
Karen Klyne
AJ Mason
James Merrick
Robyn Nyx
Simon Smalley

For more information visit www.butterworthbooks.co.uk

Warm Pearls and Paper Cranes

© 2021 by E.V. Bancroft. All rights reserved.

This trade paperback original is published by
Butterworth Books, Nottingham, England

This is a work of fiction: names, characters, and incidents are
the product of the author's imagination or are used fictitiously.
Any resemblance to actual persons, living or dead, business
establishments, events, or locales is entirely coincidental.

This book, or parts thereof, may not be reproduced in any form
without express permission by the author/ illustrator.

Cataloging information
ISBN: 978-1-915009-02-9
CREDITS
Editor: Nicci Robinson
Cover Design: Lucia Morgan
Production Design: Global Wordsmiths

Acknowledgements

I had no idea just how many people can be involved in producing a book, and I am so grateful to all of those who have given of their time and expertise.

Firstly, I'd like to thank Nicci Robinson from Global Wordsmiths/ Butterworth Books for putting up with various edits and a couple of shit sandwiches, for sharpening up the whole manuscript, and for leading me through the whole process through to publication. I'm sorry that I still haven't ironed out all the dialogue misattributions, despite attending Global Wordsmiths training. Clearly, I'm a slow learner!

Secondly, I'd like to thank my sensitivity readers, who answered a strange call on Facebook and gave their time and experiences to a complete stranger. I'm touched and honoured. Thank you, Mildred, Wynne, Catherine Butler, and Ayaka Katsube. I'd also like to thank Geoff and Wal for their war stories, even though I know neither of them will read this.

I'd like to thank my awesome ARC team and my beta readers, Annmarie Llewellyn and the Swallows critique group: Joey Bass, Valden Bush, Jane Fletcher, Lee Haven, and AJ Mason. I know the book is so much stronger because of all your input. Thanks also to Emma Nichols for comments and support, and Sue Llewellyn for marketing help.

I am grateful to Lucia Morgan for designing the book cover, despite having other commitments. I know it's so much more professional because of it.

Em and Mairi have been unstinting in their support and putting up with me having strange queries and conversations and disappearing to scribble, and I couldn't have done it without them. I'd like to thank Jerry for his fleeting support but really, I could have done it a bit quicker if he didn't walk all over the keyboard, demand his quota of strokes, and stick his tail in my face at inopportune moments.

Finally, I'd like to thank you, the reader, for taking a chance on me and giving me such wonderful feedback. It's been such a thrill, and it provided encouragement that I'm not completely off base. Thanks.

Dedication

To all my wonderful and quirky aunts and uncles,
wherever they may be, who enriched and informed my
values and outlook on life from a very early age.

And to Em, for being here and challenging
and critiquing even if you probably got fed up with it.

...And I lie here awake,
knowing the pearls are cooling even now
in the room where my mistress sleeps. All night
I feel their absence and I burn.

Warming Her Pearls
Carol Ann Duffy

CHAPTER ONE
Staffordshire, present day

"THERE YOU GO, Auntie, you're all set." Amanda tucked the plaid blanket around Maud's knees.

When had Amanda perfected the art of being patronising? If she expected a reward for coming with her cousin to settle Maud in her new home, she'd wait a long time. This wasn't where Maud was expecting to be. A bubble of anger rose through her body. Why couldn't they follow simple instructions? She could not have been clearer. "Where's Bea?" Maud caught a glance between the cousins.

The hint of a frown flashed on Amanda's finely Botoxed forehead. Then she smiled affectionately and knelt beside the wheelchair. "Bea's not here."

Amanda patted Maud's hands, hands she no longer recognised as her own. She had such large powerful hands, not these shrivelled, liver-spotted pieces of leather stretched taut over gnarled knuckles. She looked up. "Where is she? When she came to the home, I promised I would join her." Maud attempted to glare in the way that had stilled so many rebellious employees over the years but had now lost its potency and was merely a brittle hint of what once had been.

Amanda frowned at her cousin Matthew. He looked as uncomfortable as he had when he'd broken Maud's window with a loose stone when he strimmed her lawn. What weren't they saying? What was going on? He too bent over so she could smell their breath, like dragons about to devour their prey.

He cleared his throat. "Now, Aunt Maud, we talked about this, remember? Bea isn't at this home. We had to find you somewhere that specialised in Parkinson's that would give you the progressive care you'll eventually need. When you can't look after yourself properly, they'll move you to the other wing where they have twenty-four-hour nursing care—"

"We promised we'd look after each other." Maud raised her head, tears prickling the back of her eyes, but she wouldn't let them see. She wouldn't give them the satisfaction of seeing her break down. All the hardships and obstacles she and Bea had overcome, to be thwarted now after she had promised Bea on her life that there would be no more separation.

Amanda patted Maud's hand again. "You can't look after each other. Bea is virtually deaf and almost blind, and you've got early onset Parkinson's—"

"I am fully aware. That's why we arranged to come into a home." Why did the damn girl keep on about the disease? She wanted to forget it, and why wasn't she obeying instructions? They'd been very clear.

"Bea's not family. We can't pay for her out of the family trust." Amanda's grip tightened on Maud's hand.

"But she's family to me." And Maud had set up the trust fund initially, which Amanda had clearly overlooked.

Amanda huffed with the apparent exasperation of one whose patience was stretching so thin, it was almost translucent.

"We already discussed this. The trust fund is for family members only. This is a lovely home, but it's very expensive. It's got tennis courts, a bar, and a swimming pool, and I must show you the library. It reminds me of the library in Heaston Hall. Floor to ceiling books, light and airy, and the carers have promised to wheel you down there whenever you want, if you can't walk down. It's more like a five-star hotel than a home, and the staff are lovely. Lorraine, the manager, is a real sweetie, and she said we can contact her if we're worried about anything at all."

Maud thrust up her shaking hands. "How can I play tennis with these? And I don't want the library. I'm in the wrong place. I want Bea." And much to her chagrin, the tears dripped down her face and onto her lap.

"Please don't cry. We can't afford for Bea to come here." Matthew patted her shoulder.

Sometimes he wasn't very bright. Of course there was more than enough in the trust fund. Especially if Bea shared her room, like she had for many years. But they didn't know that. Maud placed her hands on the sides of the wheelchair to control the shaking. She sighed.

It was payback time for all the secrets she'd kept, all the lies she'd told over the years, too old, too cold to unravel now. They just expected her to accept it. Maud had only herself to blame. She had wrapped the cloak of status and duty around her so tightly it became her strait jacket, because of what? Cowardice? She had given away the family jewels when

WARM PEARLS AND PAPER CRANES

she thought she was placing them in safe keeping. She stared at Amanda, whose smile was tight.

"I'm not sure Bea would even know where she was, anyway," Amanda said, as if she thought that made it better.

Maud's knuckles tightened to white on the wheelchair. How dare she insult Bea? "There's nothing wrong with Bea's mind. She's one of the most intelligent people I have ever known. She worked at Bletchley Park during the war, you know."

Amanda rolled her eyes at Matthew. Did she think Maud was blind too, or dumb? Amanda patted her hand again, as if trying to placate her.

"We know, Auntie, you told us."

Her tone was sharp, as if to say "and we don't want to hear it again." Perhaps it was a mistake making these two the trustees of the trust fund. She hoped Hannah would be able to keep them in check. "Where's Hannah?" Maud asked.

The cousins shot a glance at each other. Maud clamped her mouth into a thin line. They were clearly keeping something from her.

"Auntie, Hannah isn't coming. She's busy writing up her PhD," Matthew said and patted her shoulder.

What was with all this patting? She wasn't a pet dog. If she was a pet, they would have put her down by now, no doubt. Where was Hannah?

"You chased her away, love," Bea had always said. "You're too hard on the poor girl."

"I only want the best for her," Maud had replied, so many times. "How will she get a decent job with all those tattoos and piercings and spiky blue hair? No professional organisation will ever take her seriously."

"Maybe she doesn't want a professional job," Bea said.

Maud fingered her pearls, barely containing her own fear. "But she needs to be financially independent. It's crucial she's not owned by anyone."

Bea had cupped Maud's face in her hands. "Life is different now, my love. I'm sure even accountants have tattoos. And maybe she'll change when she gets older, when she's less angry with the unfairness of the world." Bea had stroked her cheek and kissed her on the nose.

Maud put her hand up to her face as if she could still feel where the caress had been.

"Auntie?"

Amanda's voice was like old glass ready to shatter into a thousand shards, as if she was doing her best to keep it all in one piece and resented every minute of obligation. That was all Maud was to them now, a duty. What a trap, and yet if people hadn't done their duty in the war, what would've happened to the country? To their lives? Maud felt like King Lear banished in the wilds after giving his kingdom to his daughters. Was Amanda Goneril or Regan? "You've done your duty now. You can go." Maud tried to affect the tone of dismissal she had used when Amanda had first worked for her.

Amanda's shoulders relaxed, and she wore the polite smile she adopted with clients, then kissed Maud on her forehead and picked up her bag, ready to leave.

Matthew kissed Maud. "Do you want to stay here, or would you like me to take you to the library?"

Maud surveyed the strange room. Her room, for now. "No, I'll stay here. I'm sure the nurses will take me to the library if I ask."

"Of course. You know you just need to press the buzzer, and they'll come."

Will they? Or was it just one of these homes where the staff are all pleasant when the relatives are around but neglect their charges when they're out of sight? Maybe she should write down her thoughts before she was reunited with Bea. Was it too late to change the terms of the trust? "Matthew, will you get in contact with Katherine and ask her to see me, please?"

Matthew frowned. "Katherine?"

"My lawyer. You should have her details."

"Yes, of course, Aunt Maud."

Duty completed, Amanda and Matthew left. Would they contact Katherine? Katherine could find Bea and sort out this mess. She should write Bea a letter. It would be like before the war, if she wrote it in Morse code, maybe someone, Katherine, would tap it out for her?

Maud reached out to the photograph of Bea in her Wrens uniform on the bedside table under her favourite Tiffany lamp. She looked so smart and beautiful. It had been hand-tinted to show her golden locks and pink cheeks. With a trembling finger, Maud traced the face she knew so well. *I love you, Beatrice Williams. Will you think I've failed you?* After all the promises she'd made that they would never be parted again.

4

Maud fumbled at her cardigan and pulled a worn handkerchief from her sleeve and blew her nose. A violet had been embroidered on it in childish stitches. "One Violet, by Violet, so you will never forget me," she had said when Maud left, though Maud could never forget her little sister. Violet, poor Violet. She sighed and tucked the handkerchief back in her sleeve. All the people who have died. What would Violet have thought about Hannah? She would have been so proud of what her granddaughter had become: bright, articulate, working on her PhD. Soon she would be Dr Hannah Jones, the first doctor in the family. Maud sat up higher in her wheelchair.

Maybe she would explore the library and see if they had Shakespeare. She wheeled the electric wheelchair to the wall and pressed the buzzer. She checked her watch to time them. *Don't worry, Bea, we'll sort this.*

CHAPTER TWO
Bristol

HANNAH'S MOBILE RANG at 7:31 a.m. She dragged her eyes open and stretched over, groaning when she saw the caller ID: Amanda, her second cousin. What did she want? She rubbed her eyes, needing to be awake for whatever she was about to be volunteered for. "Amanda."

"Hannah. I need you to sort through some boxes."

"What?"

"Gammy went into the home yesterday, so we're clearing her house out before the builders come in on Monday. You did remember, didn't you? Have you sent her a moving in card?"

She'd already said she didn't have time to help with Gammy. Typical Amanda to disrespect her wishes.

"I thought if you weren't doing anything else this weekend, you could come and help. There's a train from Bristol Temple Meads at 9:32. We could use some young arms and legs."

Hannah inhaled and counted to three. "This young *brain* is occupied this weekend writing up my thesis." She swung her legs out of bed, fumbled her way to the kitchen and filled the kettle. The noise of the gushing water wasn't quite loud enough to block out Amanda's shrill tones.

"You weren't writing when I called. You were asleep."

Amanda was always so precise. No wonder she'd been Gammy's favourite and taken over the business when she retired.

"That's because it's early. I finished writing at two this morning... But I don't have to justify myself to you. Sorry, I'm busy." It sounded harsh, but she was only doing what Gammy had told her to do: *"Take care of yourself, because no one else will."* She switched on the kettle.

"You can't even be bothered to help your great aunt after all she's done for you, how she took you in after—"

"Yeah, I know. I don't need a lecture. I need to finish my thesis. My supervisor's breathing down my neck." She really didn't want to think back to the worst time of her life. Thanks, Amanda, for taking all of two minutes to go there, and then trying to guilt trip her. Gammy made it very clear she didn't like Hannah's tattoos or hair, and she certainly wouldn't approve of Hannah's lifestyle if she knew about it, so why would Hannah voluntarily subject herself to a ritual humiliation and dressing down?

"Gammy was insistent that you have all her old diaries, letters, and papers. There's probably two or three boxes' worth."

Wasn't it bad enough having had to listen to Gammy's xenophobic opinions for years without having to give them house room? Hannah walked back into her bedroom and sunk onto the bed. Her head was throbbing, she needed her caffeine fix. "I don't want them. Burn them."

"I thought you were doing a PhD in International Relations? This could be valuable research."

Hannah was about to correct her but caught herself. She never had told the family she was studying gender and international relations in case Great Aunt Maud put two and two together and concluded she was a lesbian as well as a feminist. That would be totally against her religion and stir a shit storm. And honestly, it wasn't worth the argument. Better no one knew. "I don't have space. I live in one room in a shared maisonette; there's not enough room to swing a *domus cattus.*" She surveyed her bedroom. Research books were scattered on every available surface, bristling with yellow Post-it notes. Definitely no room.

"They could be valuable social history—"

Hannah snorted. "So bigoted comments about the war and her complaints about the Japanese can be preserved for posterity?"

"Well, if you came up this weekend and searched through them, perhaps you could find the diamonds in the rough."

Hannah sipped her coffee, and the caffeine hit her system, kick-starting her awake. "Amanda, I'm on a really tight deadline for my thesis—"

"Surely you have flexibility for one weekend?"

"No, I don't. Sorry." *Hash tag sorrynotsorry.* There was no way she was going to pay a fortune for a train ticket to the middle of nowhere to be her family's gofer all weekend. Hannah held her breath, waiting for the lecture about how ungrateful she was *blah di blah.*

"Fine, I'll just get the boxes couriered to your house. Are you still in that place in Bristol?"

Hannah grinned and notched that up as a victory. She wouldn't have to waste the weekend now, and she could just recycle the paper. "Yeah. As long as it's no more than two boxes."

***

A week later, Hannah arrived home from a meeting with her PhD supervisor to be confronted with two large removal boxes sitting in the middle of the lounge. Her flat mate's boyfriend, who Hannah dubbed Farty Boy, had received them during the day. What was he doing here anyway when Suki wasn't home? She saw the paused screen of the game *Battlefield* on the Xbox and their TV: Hannah's Xbox. She gritted her teeth, about to ream him out for using her things.

"Dunno what they are, but Suki's gonna go ape if you don't move them."

"I imagined they'd be shoebox size."

"Giant's shoes, maybe."

Farty Boy returned to his game, and the soundtrack of rapid fire and radio calls of "enemy trooper spotted" made it difficult for Hannah to think. "I can't have them in my room. There isn't space."

He grunted as he released another round of ammunition. "She'll hate them in here," he said, not taking his eyes off the game.

Hannah looked around as if seeing their small living room for the first time. "Maybe we can put them behind the sofa?"

"She'll notice in a nanosecond."

Hannah waved her hand at the boxes. "But at least they won't be so obvious. Come on, Connor, give me a hand, will you?"

The clatter of the key in the lock made her jump. *Shit.* A bike ticked and purred as Suki wheeled it into the downstairs hall. Footsteps up the stairs forewarned of her arrival. Hannah did a double take at Suki in her uniform. She was stunning: petite and feminine with clear Asian features. What did she see in that douchebag? She said she was going through a straight phase, but honestly, even if she didn't want Hannah, she could have had someone else. Almost anyone else.

Today, though, her features drew into a scowl as she pointed at the bulky boxes. "What are those?"

Hannah noticed that the game had been paused on the TV, presumably so Farty Boy could witness Hannah being chewed out. "The boxes I told you about, from my Gammy."

"Your great aunt who you're too scared to come out to?"

Hannah wouldn't have put it quite like that, but yeah, it was an accurate description. The sound of *Battlefield* started up again. Hannah turned to Suki with her full-charm smile. "That's the one. She's moved into a home, and her house is being cleared."

Suki tapped her foot and signalled towards the boxes. "So all her shit is being dumped in my house?"

Technically it was her house, Hannah supposed. Suki's parents had taken out the lease, and Suki sublet to Hannah to supplement her radiographer's salary.

"We thought we could put the boxes behind the sofa," Farty Boy said.

Him siding with her was a first. Or maybe he felt guilty using her Xbox without her permission. Hannah smiled. "Only until I have time to go through them—"

"When you finish your PhD? No, I need them out before then."

Hannah raised her hands. For someone so tiny, Suki could be terrifying. "Okay, I'll get started on them when I've redone this chapter. Old Matthews isn't happy with what I've done so far. Says I've gone overboard on the cultural chauvinism—"

"Tell me after my shower." Suki bustled towards her bedroom but turned back at the door, as if for dramatic effect. "Do what you can to hide them from view, so our lounge doesn't look like a parcel office."

Hannah sensed Suki was fine with the arrangement, she just needed to establish she was queen bee. That was okay with her; she was happy to be a worker bee tending to the queen, even if the honey was forbidden.

CHAPTER THREE
Staffordshire, 1939

MAUD SKIPPED INTO the library to join her younger twin brothers and their new tutor, just down from Cambridge for the summer. She stopped in the doorway and suppressed a gasp. The tutor wasn't a man but a blonde woman with mid-length hair that curled away from her face and the most startling blue eyes Maud had ever seen. She was probably only a couple of years older than Maud, maybe nineteen, but she was so much more grown up and sophisticated, making it difficult not to gawp. Bubbles of delight percolated through her body. She had never seen anyone like her.

The woman smiled and paused for a beat too long before stretching out her hand. "Good afternoon. You must be Miss Heaston. I am Miss Williams. I'm delighted you're able to join your brothers in the afternoon classes."

"Good afternoon." Maud's tongue clung to the roof of her mouth, unwilling to cooperate. Her brothers Jack and Joe mocked the "Miss Heaston" and sniggered. Maud glared at them. They wouldn't be this rude in front of a male tutor, but before she could admonish them, Miss Williams had turned her gaze on them.

"Misters Jack and Joseph Heaston, is that appropriate behaviour for young gentlemen?"

They cast their eyes down and muttered an apology, but Maud knew it would only be a short while before they got up to their usual tricks and practical jokes. If only they realised what a privilege they had, being able to study all day. They weren't expected to do charity work or look after little Violet, adorable though she was. Realising Miss Williams was still holding out her hand, Maud shook it. "Please, call me Maud."

The handshake was firm but not bone-crushing like some men Maud had encountered. Miss Williams' hands were smooth and small. Maud studied her own long fingers, which were great for spanning an octave on the piano easily but little else. Miss Williams wore a cotton print dress with a pinched waist that accentuated her slim frame. How Maud wished she had a waist like that and her petite features, rather than her tall, "big-boned" self as her elder brothers often called her. Even Miss Williams' canvas two-tone blue and cream Oxford shoes looked sporty, not drab. Maud brushed down her slacks. She wished she'd worn a pretty dress today, although dresses always looked wrong on her.

Sunshine streamed in, casting a halo around Miss Williams' hair as she stared across the boys' heads to Maud. It caught Maud's breath.

"Shall we start?"

Miss Williams smiled, and it was as if the warmth reached all Maud's hibernating senses, unfurling feelings she didn't know existed.

"Now, boys, I want you to find out the names and dates of all the kings and queens of England since 1066. The answers are all to be found in those books in front of you. You just need to do some research. In the meantime, I'll set your sister a test. No noise, please, so she can concentrate."

Miss Williams may as well have asked the earth not to turn. Her brothers were never quiet. Maud nibbled at her bitten-down nails, then remembered young ladies didn't do that. She would never be the lady her mother wanted her to be. *"The trouble is, Maud, you are so tall, it will put off a lot of eligible men. Will we ever find you a suitable husband?"* was her mother's constant complaint.

Amazingly, the boys opened their books and remained relatively quiet. Maud gulped as Miss Williams approached with a sheet of paper and some scraps to write on.

"Don't look so scared. This is just to find a baseline so we can see what we need to work on."

Maud took the paper with a trembling hand and pushed her glasses up her nose before reading the paper. It seemed to be a test in English, maths, and Latin. Maud rattled through the maths test and wrote out the English in her neat copperplate handwriting, as she had been taught, and dabbed at the ink with her blotting paper. She swallowed hard when she arrived at the third part of the test and wiped her hands on her slacks. How humiliating. The words in front of her mocked her in their gibberish, and there was nowhere to hide. She put her hand up as she'd done at school, which elicited a slight twitch from Miss Williams' lips.

"Yes, Maud?"

Maud fidgeted on her wooden chair, her cheeks burning. "I'm sorry, Miss Williams, I don't know any Latin."

The twins glanced up at her and recited what sounded like gobbledegook. "Well done, boys, maybe you can teach your sister Latin? How are you getting on with your history? Have you found out the dates of all the kings and queens of England yet?" She moved to peer over their shoulders.

They groaned and put their heads down, pretending to study. Miss Williams turned to Maud, her lips quirking upwards. How could someone smile that much? Was she really enjoying teaching them all? Tentatively she returned the smile and handed up her paper to be marked.

While Miss Williams skimmed over her answers, Maud looked around the library. This was her favourite room in the house, and when she had time, she would sneak in to pick out a Jane Austen or Anthony Trollope. There was a small pile of books on her desk. She inhaled the delightful mustiness of them and luxuriated in the texture of the red leather covers beneath her fingertips. With its two floor-to-ceiling windows, the library was always light, even on the murkiest days, and today the sun made the dust motes glisten.

Maud chewed her lower lip, waiting for the verdict. She was awarded by another wide smile.

"This is excellent, Maud, and you clearly have a penchant for Maths as you got one hundred percent correct, even with the two tough questions I threw in. Those were at university level."

Maud's cheeks burned again, this time with pleasure, and she ignored the sarcastic comments from her brothers.

"You like maths and puzzles?" Miss Williams asked.

"Oh, yes." Maud was sure her own eyes reflected the glint she saw in those of her tutor.

"Well, maybe when we have your brothers settled, we'll go through some other exercises. I love them too."

The boys ducked their heads again, and Miss Williams turned to Maud. "I know you only have the afternoons free because of your other duties, so how about I set you a puzzle you can think about overnight? My father taught me Morse code. Would you like to work out the message if I give you the code sheet?"

It sounded like fun and relief from the boredom of preparing to catch the perfect husband or caring for her younger sister. Maud pushed her thick glasses up her nose and nodded.

Miss Williams handed over a book of war poetry, with a black and white cover of rows upon rows of graves from The Great War. Maud shuddered as if someone had walked over hers.

"Read the poem on page forty-three and write in your own words what you think it means."

While reading the poem to herself and her brothers got up to whatever mischief they were engaged in, Miss Williams scribed out the code sheet in small, neat handwriting and a brief message on a scrap of paper.

"Can we learn Morse code too, Miss Williams?" Jack asked.

"Would you like to?"

Both boys nodded.

"Okay." Miss Williams took a slate and repeated the process, standing by their desks.

As the chalk scraped on the blackboard, scratching out the dots and dashes and grating slightly, Maud considered the poem she had been set: Wilfred Owen's *Dulce et Decorum est*. She wasn't really sure what it all meant, except it was horrific. She looked up to ask a question and saw what the boys had done to Miss Williams.

"Watch out," she said as the boys sniggered.

Too late. Miss Williams attempted to stride, but her shoelaces were tied together. She stumbled but stopped herself from falling by clutching at Maud's desk. Maud caught a whiff of lily of the valley and a glimpse of Miss Williams' heaving chest. A thrill of excitement shot down her spine, quickly covered by shame that she was looking, followed by a blanket of concern.

"Are you all right?"

How could they do that to the beautiful Miss Williams? Maud turned on her younger brothers, goaded to distraction. "You stupid boys."

The twins' eyes shined with mirth as they desperately tried not to break into laughter. Maud's heart beat faster, excitement and anger competing for dominance, but Miss Williams' chest had slowed, and she seemed unfazed.

"I see you've tried to trick me, boys. That shows me you haven't been doing your exercises as requested, so you'll need to complete the whole of pages thirty-two and thirty-three of your history books before tomorrow, so we can be sure you've learnt the lesson."

"But, Miss, that's not fair," Jack said.

"That'll take us ages, Miss."

"Maybe you should have thought about that before playing a trick on me?"

Miss Williams raised an eyebrow, clearly unmoved by their pleading. Maud glared at her brothers. They squirmed.

"Sorry, Miss Williams," they said in unison in that fake singsong way. Maud mouthed "Sorry," but Miss Williams shrugged and retied her shoelaces.

"Tomorrow we will read a play about sprites that can fly and a man named Bottom."

The boys giggled, clearly thinking Miss Williams had said a rude word.

"Midsummer Night's Dream?" Maud asked.

Miss Williams entire face glowed with delight, and it was as if she outshone the sun.

"Spot on. Do you like it?"

Not wanting to disappoint, but not wishing to tell a lie, Maud said, "I think so, but I don't really understand Shakespeare."

The twins groaned.

"Shakespeare?"

"Boring."

"If you understand the words, it has all life and death in there. Acting it out will help. I love it. Now, boys, how are you getting on?" Miss Williams asked.

Maud yearned for four thirty when the twins would run off to play on their bikes, so she might share a minute or two with Miss Williams alone. Finally, the twins escaped, banging their desk lids, and slamming the doors behind them.

Miss Williams sat at her desk, collected her books, and placed them in a battered satchel. How Maud would love to have a satchel like that. She approached and was tempted to touch the leather. It would probably be soft. She dreamed of having an existence where she would need such an article, a proof of intellectual pursuit, of challenge, of being something more. Maud stood upright, as she had been told to do when addressing a teacher. "Please, Miss Williams, could you teach me other things?"

Miss Williams met her gaze, her eyes glinting, and her mouth tweaked up at the corners. "What other things?"

"I know I'll never be able to go to university, like you are, but I want to use my brain."

"For university, you need Latin and algebra. The algebra won't be a problem, but have you studied any classics?"

Maud's shoulders sagged, and she picked at the blotting paper on the desk, unable to look at Miss Williams. Would she think Maud was stupid, or ignorant, and not worth associating with because she'd never studied the classics? For one moment she hoped they could become friends and talk about intellectual things that Maud had no knowledge of, but that would never happen once she admitted her position. But she couldn't lie; she hated lies. "No, I left school at fourteen. I wanted to go on, but it's not safe to go to finishing schools in Europe at the moment. I want to do something useful." Not just get a husband and be a baby factory. "I want to help the war effort." How could she admit she wanted freedom and independence? Was that selfish and ungrateful? Eventually, Maud raised her head and kind, blue eyes met hers.

"I could help you with the classics and algebra, or if you want to use your maths skills, maybe you could explore an apprenticeship for accounting. There are a few women doing that now. Or teaching?"

Maud shook her head, acknowledging the truth of what was planned for her, the same as it had been for her mother and her grandmother. To be the scabbard, not the sword. "I'm not sure I'd be allowed. I don't even get to see the newspapers until after my father and brothers have read them, sometimes never, if they're used for spills."

Miss Williams put the last of her papers into her satchel and fastened the buckle. "But you're interested in world affairs?"

Maud stood straight again. "Yes, and not just for the royal visit to America. I'm concerned about what Japan is doing in China and Hitler in Germany."

Miss Williams's brows knitted as if she was trying to find a solution. "Do you have a wireless?"

Maud shook her head, desperately wishing she could provide a favourable answer, but that was as much to please Miss Williams as herself. "There's one in the drawing room, but that's where the men go to smoke and drink after supper."

Miss Williams nodded. "I'll see if I can get you access to the papers, and we can discuss them, if you like?"

"Yes, please. I'd love that." Maud glanced at her watch. "I'm sorry, Miss Williams, but I need to pick up Violet and fix her some tea."

The handle of the library rattled as the double doors opened, and Maud's mother entered, dressed in the old-fashioned, Edwardian style with large puffy sleeves and wearing a wide-brimmed hat. Five-year-old Violet unhitched herself from her mother's grasp and ran to Maud, flinging herself into her open arms.

Miss Williams's blonde hair bobbed as she stood to attention. "Good evening, Lady Heaston. I was just about to ask if Miss Heaston would like some help with young Violet."

"How do you do, Miss Williams? No, no, I won't hear of it. I'm sure you have more pressing matters. I trust you find your lodgings suitable. Have you had the opportunity to go to any of the dances in town yet? Have you met my two eldest sons? Of course, Bill has volunteered for the Royal Engineers so he's waiting for his call-up, and Harry will probably do the same. I'm so proud of them, and I'm sure they'll look so handsome in their uniforms. I'll ask Harry to escort you to the dance. They've got a car they've been tinkering with, so they could take you there. Much easier than trying to catch a bus."

Maud scooped Violet into her arms to hide her burning cheeks. Her mother could not have been more obvious if she tried, pushing Miss Williams into Harry's embrace. But when she cast a glance at her, Miss Williams didn't seem embarrassed at all.

"That's a very kind offer, and I shall bear that in mind. Thank you, Lady Heaston. And my lodgings are just fine. Miss Talbot is very accommodating."

Maud stifled a snort. Miss Talbot was a skinflint busybody. Maud would be surprised if she was feeding Miss Williams properly or heating the room. She decided she would give her some of their homemade gingerbread biscuits and one of her hand-crocheted blankets to help keep her warm at night.

Before she said her goodbyes, Miss Williams fixed Maud with an intense gaze that caused Maud's heart to race. Warmth seeped through her, like a candle melting wax with its bright flame. It was as if she was trying to tell her something. Maud would need to learn this Morse code pronto.

CHAPTER FOUR

A FEW WEEKS AFTER Maud started her extra tutoring with Bea, as she was allowed to call her when they were out of the classroom, she approached Maud's desk as she finished her exercises.

"Do you have some time now? I'd like to show you something," Bea said.

Maud cocked her head on one side, her curiosity piqued, then checked her watch. "Daisy leaves at five, so I have to look after Violet then."

Bea was standing over the desk, and Maud could feel the warmth of her breath as she spoke.

She closed Maud's exercise book. "Enough for today. And Violet can come, she'll love them. I see them most afternoons on my way back to my digs."

Maud was curious. What did Bea mean, "them"? "Shall I fetch Violet, then?"

Bea nodded. "I'll tidy up here. Meet you by the back door."

A tingle of anticipation shot down Maud's spine as she made her way up to the nursery. She tried to imagine what the surprise was as she strode down the dark corridors. She patted the wooden rocking horse that had been their father's. It now lacked a mane and had a permanent list to the right, where the twins had tried to practise Western-style shoot-outs, hanging off the side.

"Can I help you, Miss Maud?" Daisy asked, trying to bob a curtsy as she wrangled with Violet, who was stubbornly refusing to put her hand into a cardigan.

Vi struggled free and ran to Maud, her hands raised for a cuddle.

"I thought I'd take Violet, Daisy, so you can go now."

Relief washed over the maid's face. For one just turned fourteen, she looked so tired. No doubt having spent all day cleaning, scrubbing, playing nursemaid, and chopping wood, she would go home now to do exactly the same.

Daisy bobbed her head a few times. "Thank you, thank you, Miss Maud. Mam will be really pleased."

"How is your family?"

Daisy stretched as if her body was twenty years older. "Good, thank you, Miss, but my mam's finding it hard this time round."

Another baby on the way when there were already nine mouths to feed couldn't be easy. Poverty was such a terrible depletion of the body, and a diminisher of opportunities. Maud was so grateful they were more than comfortable. She dreaded never having enough to live on. Mother made it very clear that Maud needed to marry well, as Heaston Hall would go to Bill when they died. She always thought if she was destitute, she would live with Harry; he would never turn her out of his home.

Maud determined to pick Violet up when she could, so Daisy could go home earlier, as long as her mother didn't dock Daisy's wages, of course. "Does your mother need any more baby clothes? I'm sure I could ask Mother if she has any of Violet's left over."

Seeing Daisy look uncomfortable, and not wishing to embarrass her, Maud spun Violet around, then blew a raspberry on the little girl's palm.

"That's very kind, Miss, but please don't go asking Lady Heaston. I don't want to be any trouble. I need this job."

"I'm sure Mother won't mind."

Daisy nodded and curtsied again before grabbing her embroidered bag and disappearing through the door.

Maud knelt so she was at Violet's height, hardly able to contain the thrill of anticipation herself. "We're going on an adventure. What do we need when we go on an adventure?"

Violet cocked her head on one side. "A sword?"

"You're right, a sword might come in handy to chase away dragons, but I was thinking we need explorer clothes." She held up the cardigan Violet had refused to put on earlier. "This is the perfect explorer's jacket, and maybe we need to find some wellington boots to protect you as you wade through crocodile-infested waters."

Violet squealed and pushed her hands into the sleeves, then pulled away to patter downstairs to the back door and the boot store. She put her boots on the wrong feet in her haste. She could probably have gone in her shoes, but Maud didn't really want Daisy to have to clean them again. She helped Violet to put her boots on correctly.

"Where are we going?" Violet looked up as she stood in her wellingtons and cardigan, all enormous eyes and innocence.

"It's a secret, Vi. Even I don't know." Maud tied her own shoelaces and looked up as Bea's distinctive cream and blue shoes padded into view. She smiled at the sight of Bea in her pretty dress, her curls bobbing as she breezed along the dark hallway. "Say hello to Miss Williams, Violet."

Violet grabbed onto Maud's long legs and hid behind them, peeping round the side.

"Come on, silly, she won't bite. Do you bite?" Maud asked and grinned.

Bea raised an eyebrow and shook her head. She crouched to Violet's height. "Do you want to see the secret?" she whispered and glanced to make sure no one was looking.

Violet blinked and nodded.

"Come on, then." Bea put out her hand and stood.

Violet looked up at Maud, who nodded to reassure her it was okay. Violet took both of their outstretched hands, and they ambled down the lane towards the village where Bea had her digs. As they approached a field of grass and buttercups, Bea put her finger to her lips.

"We need to stay downwind and be very, very still."

They all lay face down on the grass by the gate. A breeze ruffled the flowers, scattering pollen particles. Maud held a finger under her nose so she wouldn't sneeze. At first there was nothing other than the warmth of the sun on their backs, the light wind rustling their dresses and the poppies, buttercups, and wild oats bowing on the field fringes like ladies at a dance.

"Keep your eyes peeled to the far part of the meadow over there," Bea whispered to Vi, then turned to Maud.

They held a steady gaze, and Bea's lips parted as if she was about to say something. Maud felt a surge from her core up her body, and her heart opened and blossomed like the poppies. Violet tugged at Maud's sleeve. Reluctantly, Maud averted her gaze towards the close-cropped grass. Five rabbits peeped out of a burrow, their ears twitching. Not sensing any danger, they hopped onto the grass, and nibbled, played, and chased each other in the sunshine.

"Aren't they great?" Bea whispered and leaned closer to Violet and Maud.

Violet was mesmerised. Bea was so close that Maud could feel the warmth of Bea's legs near her own. Bea flashed her a secret smile over

Violet's head and tilted her foot towards Maud's calves. A delicious thrill of daring shot through Maud as she lolled her leg to rest against Bea's. She held her breath, excitement bubbling up as their legs touched.

Behind them, a loud honk of a car horn made them jump. Harry laughed as he pulled up beside the gate in his Austin A7. The rabbits scattered, and Maud scowled at him. She shot a glance at Bea, who looked as disappointed as she felt. Bea cast her a wistful smile as if to say, "Thwarted again." But they both turned to face Harry as he clambered out the car. He approached them with a broad grin and an unlit cigarette dangling from his lips.

Maud couldn't stay cross with him for long. "Harry, you spoiled it. We were just watching a family of rabbits."

They all stood, and Maud brushed down her clothes then Violet's.

Harry spun round as if he was going back to the car to collect something. "Rabbits, yum. Show me where, and I'll get my gun."

Violet squealed.

"Don't tease her," Maud said. "It's okay, Vi, he doesn't mean it."

Violet clung to Maud's legs again, so Maud swung the girl up in her arms to comfort her.

"Isn't Harry horrible? Horrible Harry," Maud said. Violet giggled.

Harry leaned against the car and lit a cigarette. He inhaled and puffed the smoke to the side away from Bea. "Well, Horrible Harry was going to ask if you would like a lift home, but Horrible Harry might not ask now."

He turned to Bea and bowed. "Miss Williams, lovely to see you again. I apologise for my little sisters; they can be so rude and uncouth. Can I give you a lift to your abode?"

Bea laughed. Why was she laughing at Harry when he was mocking them, mocking Maud? Maud turned away, seeking to control the spike of jealousy so they wouldn't see. She couldn't be this vulnerable, not in front of the people who meant most to her in the world.

"No, thanks. It's such a lovely day." Bea pointed at the blue sky. "I'd like to get some fresh air, and it's only half a mile."

Harry sighed, defeated in his conquest. "If you're sure. Any time you need a knight in shining armour, call my brother Bill." He laughed at his own joke. "Oh no, he's signed up, hasn't he? Well, it better be me then." He flashed her a cheeky grin.

"I'll bear that in mind, kind sir. Thank you." Bea mock bowed.

Harry returned the bow and gestured to his sisters. "I suppose I'd better get these scallywags home. Hop in."

It was as if he still saw Maud as a child. He was barely a year older than her, but he'd been more emotionally remote since he'd been at Manchester University, like he was too grown up to mix with her. Maud hated being too old to be a child and too young to be an adult.

Reluctantly, she climbed into the front seat and put Violet on her lap, so she could see outside. Harry cranked the starter handle, and the motor roared into life. Her eyes met Bea's, trying to convey her frustration that their time was cut short.

"Thank you for showing us the secret," Maud said, hoping Bea could pick up on her sincerity and maybe her desire. She focused her attention on her sister and pulled her close. "It was lovely to share the secret, wasn't it, Vi?"

Vi nodded. "Go, go, let's bumpity bump."

Harry laughed, waved his hand out of the window at Bea, and drove them away. Maud twisted in her seat to watch as Bea made her way back to her digs. Bea's step was light and dainty, as if she didn't have a care in the world.

For the first time in her life Maud really understood, at a visceral level, what the romantics wrote about. The yearning for a look, a touch that was almost painful. That evening she dug out Elizabeth Barrett Browning's *Sonnets from the Portuguese* from the library. This time, as she imagined reading it out to Bea, she breathed the words, inhabited the emotions, and let them pump around her body like oxygen.

CHAPTER FIVE
Bristol, present day

FOUR WEEKS AFTER the boxes arrived, Hannah's curiosity won out and she rummaged through them. The envelopes were yellowing, and the ink bleached to sepia. She started by picking them at random but found herself fascinated and pulled in like a vortex, so she organised them chronologically to read from the start. The lounge door opened, and Suki caught Hannah sitting cross-legged on the floor, surrounded by piles of letters and diaries.

"What happened here?" Suki gripped her bag.

She hadn't even heard the front door open. Where had all the time gone? "Sorry, I'll clear it up but look at this. It's my gammy's letters and diaries. This is interesting; can I read some out to you?" Hannah asked, unable to keep her enthusiasm out of her voice.

Suki look down at her uniform, shrugged and smiled. "Sure, I'll just take a shower. Can you put the kettle on?"

Hannah stood up on stiff legs, having been by the boxes for longer than she realised. It was great Suki wasn't on her case for the mess in the lounge, she mused while the kettle boiled. She tossed a matcha tea bag in Suki's "I can't fix stupid but I can X-ray it" mug, a present from Hannah the previous Christmas, and made a builder's tea in her own pride flag mug. She sniffed the milk, decided it was just about passable, and poured it in.

When Hannah returned to the lounge area, Suki was dressed in jeans and a Greenpeace T-shirt, curled up on the sofa with her legs tucked under her. Hannah handed her the tea and placed her own mug on the side table, before kneeling by the boxes. The contents were now ordered into neat piles on the floor, with Post-it notes denoting the month and year.

"It's taken me most of the day just to sort them into a semblance of order. And there are also a host of slips of paper with code written on them. They were great ones for codes and riddles. Gammy's personal assistant, Bea, worked at Bletchley Park during the war, but she never talked about it." Hannah stretched over and extracted the frail paper from a blue envelope. "It's dated August 1939 and seems to be a poem," she said before beginning to read it out loud.

To M
You said you couldn't see
How 'someone like you' could appeal to me.
You said you couldn't understand
The allure of a 'clod' with 'a jaw like a man.'
The someone I see is striking and tall,
A thoughtful, gentle soul,
Going beyond for charity,
The way you love and care for V.
I admire your wonderful brain,
Quick to learn, so keen
To challenge again.
I love your generosity,
Your loyal, kind sincerity,
And delectable androgyny.
I want to get to know you.
I hope I did not misconstrue,
Please tell me that you feel it too.

"She signed it 'B.' What do you make of that?"

Suki took a sip of tea then eyed Hannah over the top of the mug. "That sounds like more than friends, doesn't it?"

Hannah sipped some tea and returned Suki's gaze. "Yeah, my thinking too."

Suki frowned. "But I thought you said she was homophobic, which is why you haven't come out to her?"

Hannah threw her hands up. "Exactly. You wouldn't believe it; she's so into religion and the church, quoting from the Bible. She's the typical English lady of the manor, arranging the flowers, and getting everyone else, mainly Auntie Bea or me when I lived there, to polish the brasses. She was domineering, judgemental, and always interfering in everyone else's business. Or she was. There is no way I would tell her my secrets for her to pick over and criticise, and I hate lying."

The gammy from the letters didn't mesh with the old woman she knew and avoided. A cloak of guilt weighed down Hannah's shoulders. She should have sent her a card. Gammy must have found it hard moving out of her lovely home and into care. And why was she in there? Couldn't she look after herself anymore? She made a mental note to ask Matthew, her favourite, or the least obnoxious, cousin.

"That poem could have been written about you," Suki said as she placed her mug on the side table. "Tall, handsome, kind, quick minded, and androgynous."

Hannah felt the blush rise to the top of her head, glowing in the admiration. "Thank you," she whispered, not daring to hope it could signify anything more.

"What else is in there? This is exciting." Suki clapped her hands together.

She was so cute when she did that and looked so much younger than her nearly thirty years. She's going through a straight phase, Hannah had to remind herself, and she's with Farty Boy.

As if on cue, the doorbell rang, and Suki dashed off to welcome him in. Hannah towered the piles of papers back into the boxes in order and pushed the boxes back behind the sofa when Farty Boy entered. Talk about bad timing. It felt as though the shell had been cracked, and Suki might open up more. Doubtless, now Suki would scurry back into her shell. Hannah resented his intrusion and grimaced in an imitation of a smile.

"I come bearing gifts." He held up some bento boxes, oblivious to the tension. "Shall we just split the cost in three?" he asked.

Hannah wasn't falling for that again. Farty Boy devoured most of any food presented but only expected to pay a third. Suki hardly ate anything, but she still paid her third and never complained. "No, I'm good, thanks."

"Hey, do you mind if I use your Xbox, Hannah? My TV isn't working at home, and I'm just levelling up."

"Be my guest." Hannah retreated to the kitchen to grab some snacks and escape to her room. There was no way she wanted to play third wheel while they made out on the sofa, seeing him put his sausage hands all over Suki's petite body. If Hannah sifted below the jealousy and snide comments she aimed at him, the nugget of truth was that he didn't love Suki the way she deserved to be loved. He wasn't harsh but seemed self-absorbed, as if Suki was merely a way of meeting his needs. He didn't see below the prickly exterior to the hurt young woman who wanted to be loved for who she was. Hannah caught glimpses of the vulnerable, romantic Suki who yearned to be loved. She sighed. It wasn't going to change anything, and the uncomfortable truth was that Suki had chosen him, not Hannah.

Maybe it was time to look for another apartment. Hannah powered up her laptop to distract herself on her thesis. Weighing up the pros and cons of moving, she wasn't sure she could cope with seeing them together much longer. On the plus side, at least she got to see Suki every day, and even if she couldn't be with her the way she wanted, she could laugh, and chat, and admire her from afar, squashing down her feelings for her into the just friends bento box. Besides, Suki was impeccably clean, and the place was reasonable and not too far from the university buildings. That didn't make it easy though.

CHAPTER SIX
Staffordshire, 1939

THE SUMMER DAYS clicked on, like the ticking of a clock. More rumours circulated about an imminent war, and the Government made hurried preparations.

"Too little, too late," Harry said.

On Saturday night, Bea was invited to join the family for supper. Maud and Bea sat beside each other opposite Harry and Bill. Harry gazed at Bea with moon eyes, his adoration obvious. Maud would never be so stupid as to look like that, would she? But maybe she did. Bea's knee brushed against her own. Maud didn't dare glance at her. The warmth from Bea's body matched her own. It couldn't be the warm summer's evening, as the windows were open, and a slight breeze whispered through. That probably accounted for the goosebumps spreading down Maud's arms.

Harry leaned across the table. He ran his fingers through his slicked-down hair. "We're going to the hop in the town hall. Do you want to come, Miss W?"

"Please call me Bea," she said and rubbed her knee against Maud's.

Maud stifled a gasp of pleasure and snatched up a forkful of potatoes to distract herself. Harry smiled at Bea, picked up the salt and pepper silverware, and pretended they were doing the waltz. At the end, he tipped the tops together as though they were kissing.

Maud glared at her brother. *He can't woo her. She's mine. She's my Bea.* A pain burned in her chest, just as Bea's hand settled on her thigh. A tingle of excitement shot from that touch and dissipated the discomfort. She risked a glance at Bea, who indicated her left hand resting on the table to the side of the plate. Maud followed the gaze with her own.

With her index finger, Bea tapped out a word in Morse. Dah dit dah dit: C. She spelt out the remainder of the word, COME. Their gazes locked, and Bea's head tilted, as if in question.

Bea looked at Harry. "Can Maud come too? It would be fun. I'm sure she'd love to go dancing."

"I don't think they provide a nursery."

He looked up to see Bea arching an eyebrow at him and raised his hands in surrender. Maud sat up in her chair. She had just turned seventeen and desperately wanted to go to her first dance with Bea. Maybe they could dance together if there was a shortage of men. She longed to hold Bea in her arms, with a yearning that almost hurt. She could imagine how it would be: they would waltz around the room as if no-one else was there, and they would smile at each other, and maybe in the dark, they could steal a kiss.

Harry glanced at Bill, who nodded in agreement. They all looked to the far end where their father sat. Silent as always, their father read his paper and slowly chewed his way through boiled potatoes, lamb, and kidney beans. He never ate mashed potatoes on account of that's all they'd been given in the prison camp in the Great War. He still had respiratory issues after they'd been caught in a gas attack. As if on cue, he coughed behind his paper.

"Sir, can Maud come to the hop with Bill, Miss Williams, and me?" Harry asked.

Their father lowered his newspaper and looked over at his elder children with a frown on his face, as if trying to decide what mischief they were up to. Maud bit her lip. Speaking up would elicit an immediate refusal. When would her father ever consider her an adult? If they knew what she had dreamed about Bea, they would have proof she wasn't a child anymore.

Her father exchanged a glance with their mother, who smiled at him.

"I'm sure Maud would love to go. She deserves a bit of fun," she said. Maud could hardly believe her ears, her formal mother encouraging her to have fun. Or maybe she thought Maud might meet a young man there. That was more likely. But she would take it, whatever the motive.

Their father grunted. Clearly girls should not have fun, certainly not his daughter. Maud held her breath.

"Come on, John. Who knows what will happen with everything going on in Europe? Let her have a little pleasure. She's seventeen now, and she's not going to be silly," their mother said.

He grunted again and folded his newspaper beside his plate. "Bill, will you drive and chaperone her the whole time? And I mean the whole time?"

Bill winked at Maud. "Yes, sir, I'll do that."

"And mind you drive Miss Williams back to her lodgings too. She can't be walking out alone."

"Yes, sir, it would be my pleasure." Bill nodded to Bea, who inclined her head in response.

A flutter of butterflies took flight in Maud's stomach, like the meadows filled with colour, red admirals and cabbage whites, common blue and painted lady. She was going to the dance with Bea. She could hardly keep the joy from her smile. "Thank you, sir."

Their father nodded, then waggled his index finger at Bill and Harry. "No getting drunk. I don't want to pull you out of a ditch at two in the morning."

"No, sir."

"Do you need to change into anything else, Miss Williams? I'm sure I could find you something appropriate to wear?" Their mother seemed to show genuine concern.

Harry disguised a snicker as a cough, and he shared a sly grin with Maud. Clearly, he also considered their mother's taste in fashion too dreary for Bea.

"No, thank you, Lady Heaston, that's very thoughtful. I'll freshen up but go as I am."

Maud's food sat heavily in her stomach, quelling the flutter of butterflies. The reality was more nerve-wracking than the anticipation. How confident of Bea to wear whatever she liked. What would she wear? Dinner finished quickly, with the party requesting to be excused before drinks were served.

Harry checked his watch. "Maud, you have fifteen minutes to repair seventeen years of neglect. Go and change into a sack or something." He grinned.

"Would you like a hand to get ready?" Bea asked.

Maud just nodded and fled upstairs, desperately trying to work out what in her wardrobe would be suitable. She entered her room, grabbed her diary and slipped it under the pillow, as if she thought it might pop open and announce her inner desires to the world.

Bea followed her into the room and opened the heavy wardrobe door to search through Maud's meagre collection of dresses. To hide her shame at the lack of style, Maud concentrated on pouring water from the china jug into the basin on the chest of drawers. The cascade of water sounded like a fountain as it splattered onto the porcelain. She splashed her face, the water cooling her heated cheeks.

"Maybe this one?" Bea held up a simple dress in cream with embroidered pink flowers.

Maud snatched the dress and turned away to slip it on, grateful she had on her newer underwear. Meanwhile, Bea reviewed her collection of jewellery of mainly old-fashioned heirlooms from her grandmother and Aunt Elsie. She fingered a necklace of rose-tinted pearls and warmed them in her palms, while Maud zipped up her dress. Their eyes met. Bea's flashed darker, so there was just an aura of blue around her shining pupils.

"Shall I help you on with these?" Bea asked, holding out the warmed pearls.

Maud nodded, not trusting herself to speak and spun around to sit on the chair, making it easier for Bea to reach.

"They say that pearls retain body heat."

Bea's breath felt warm on Maud's ear as she fastened the clasp. Her fingers smoothed over the nape of Maud's neck, causing a shiver, then lingered on Maud's shoulders for a few seconds. Their eyes met in the mirror. Maud's gaze dropped to Bea's lips, poised in a perfect Cupid's bow. She was so close. All Maud needed to do was twist around and pull her into a kiss.

What was she thinking, straying into her dreams and the secrecy of her journal? A strange sensation stirred below her belly, uncoiling from her core and slipping up her spine. No, she had to stop.

Maud bent down to tie her laces and give her heart time to slow. They would have to be her flat shoes. She didn't own delicate heels, and she was too tall for most men as it was. Bea renewed her lipstick in the mirror and indicated the same bright red lipstick to Maud. She gulped and nodded. As Bea applied it, their breaths mingled. Maud was fascinated by the look of care and concentration on Bea's face, her tongue tracing over her bottom lip as she worked. When she finished, Bea cupped her jaw and trailed her thumb over Maud's chin. Her hands were so smooth and soft. She could lose herself in those hands. She met her gaze, and their faces were close, so close, just a whisper away from a kiss.

"Oh, Maud," Bea said as though she wanted to say more, but she pulled away. "We need to go." Bea spun around and headed towards the stairs.

Maud followed, grateful for the distraction from her heart pounding and her face glowing bright enough to light up the night sky. As they exited the porticoed front door, Bill was already in the driver's seat with the engine running, and Harry leaned against the car, taking a drag of his cigarette.

"You sit in the front, Maud. I'll go in the back," Harry said and pushed the passenger seat forward for Bea to climb in the back, before following her in.

"Push the seat forward, Maud," he said, obviously struggling to squeeze his knees in.

It was probably the first time he had ever ridden in the back. Given how uncomfortable he looked, it would probably be the last. Maud turned her head to hide her smile. Served him right. She breathed in the aroma of wood, leather, and engine oil: the smell of her brothers and the freedom of their exciting world outside the wheel of domesticity and duty.

Bill pulled away down the lane, and Maud wanted to ask him if he was scared about joining up, but he seemed completely focused on driving. Maud stared out of the window and strained to hear what Harry whispered to Bea, who laughed and swatted at his arm. He was probably being inappropriate, as usual. Maud bit down on her lip, attempting to hold down the jealousy.

CHAPTER SEVEN

THE TOWN HALL buzzed with the music played by a live band. "They're playing Glenn Miller's 'Moonlight Serenade,'" Bea said and rushed ahead of the small group.

It was smoky, very unlike the atmosphere when the hall was used for the flower and vegetable shows Maud attended with her mother. They were genteel country pursuits. This was raw, frenetic, exciting, and desperate. Strong perfume mixed with sweat, and a hubbub of people talked and shouted over the band playing. Bodies swayed and crushed round the bar. The men lined up against one wall, the women against the other.

They found a place to sit at the edge of the dance floor. Bill had been given the short straw of chaperoning Maud, so he stretched out his legs but hurriedly withdrew them as dancers came perilously close. As soon as Harry went to get them all drinks, Bea was asked to dance by a tanned man whom Maud didn't recognise. He must be from out of town. She glanced an apology at Maud and accepted his offer. Maud tried to smile, to hide the disappointment, but really what had she expected? Bea was incredibly beautiful. They looked good together, like Fred Astaire and Ginger Rogers except everything was in colour, not black and white. Jealousy buzzed about Maud's heart, or was it envy? She wanted to hold Bea and feel the warmth of her hands around her waist, to drown in the sparkle of her eyes, and move around to the music. Maybe later.

The sting of jealousy in Maud's chest became a hornet's nest of anger as Bea was immediately asked to dance again when the track finished. She hadn't even made it back to her seat before she had a third request for a dance. Most of the other women were snagged for dances too, leaving Maud rejected. She felt like an oversized book, rarely taken down from the shelf, dusty and overlooked because she didn't *fit*. It was very clear she would not be dancing with Bea this evening. The thrill of anticipation she had at coming to her first dance crumpled like a discarded piece of paper. How naïve she had been to think she would get to spend some time with Bea, dance with Bea. She wanted to go home, but that wasn't going to happen for a long time, so she decided to sit back and enjoy the music.

Through the swirl of legs, arms, and laughing faces, Maud tried to follow Bea's progress as she was twirled and spun around the dance hall. Finally, Harry returned with the drinks and placed them on the table. The bar couldn't be seen beyond a seething mass of bodies; no wonder it had taken so long. Harry followed Maud's gaze to Bea, then back to Maud. He took a swig of his beer and replaced it on the small foldable table.

"I'll toss you for who gets the short straw." Harry jerked his thumb toward Maud.

"Tails," Bill said and slurped his beer.

Harry tossed a coin, caught it deftly, and slapped it on the back of his hand before checking it. He grimaced. "Damn, tails it is. Right, Maud, look lively."

He held out his hand to her. Although he was probably only teasing, it was humiliating. Maud rubbed her fingers over the pearls, thinking back to Bea's hands warming them earlier. How she would love those hands to be fondling her now, not wrapped around the waist of some overconfident man.

"It's all right, you don't have to ask me out of politeness or to fulfil your promise to Father," she said.

"Come on." He hauled her up with the same finesse as he would use to remove a car engine.

Being on the dance floor was like being caught in a fast-flowing river; she had to move with the current or cause a dam. Harry set his position and gave her a grin before launching off. Having always been the tallest in the dance classes, Maud was forced to lead and had never learned how to follow, so she pushed forward with her left foot. "I'm not very good," she said and trampled on his toes.

"You need lessons," Harry said over the music. "Can't you get Bea to teach you how to dance rather than waste your time on maths and algebra? She's a superb dancer."

Tempting though it was to tell him that no time spent with Bea was a waste of time, she followed his gaze towards Bea, who twirled her way across the floor. The expression of longing on Harry's face was probably reflected on Maud's. She trod on his foot again, this time deliberately.

"Ow. You did that on purpose." Harry limped exaggeratedly.

"Serves you right. You're just envious because I'm much better than you at maths."

"I'm not sure I'll ever walk again," he said.

He grinned and spun her around the floor anyway until the music stopped. They rejoined Bill, and Bea made her way back, shaking her head at another potential dance partner and pointing at their table.

"Would you care to dance before I'm too battered and bruised by my sister to ever dance again?" Harry asked Bea.

Bill nodded as if to say he was now on sister duty. As she was led away to the dance floor, Bea glanced across her shoulder at Maud. She imagined it was an apology. Harry whispered to Bea and even in the dim light of the dance hall, Maud saw Bea blush.

Ethel Porter came across to talk to Bill. She fussed around him, trying to encourage him to dance. He mumbled something about Maud, but when George Waites, the solicitor's son, came towards their group, Ethel grabbed him.

"George, you want to ask Maud to dance, don't you?"

He made an exaggerated move of elongating his neck as he looked up to Maud, his lazy eye following the rest of his movement. "Sure. Maud, would you like to dance?"

"Um." She didn't want to say no and be rude, but she didn't really want to dance with anyone who wasn't related to her or who wasn't Bea. She glanced across at Bea and Harry, jealousy buzzing in her heart at how closely Harry held her. Coming to the dance was such a stupid move.

She looked back to see George holding out his hand. He was kind and a gentleman, and she was well brought up, so she smiled politely, and they weaved their way to the middle of the dance floor. Maud was conscious of how ridiculous they must appear with her two inches height advantage. But he didn't seem bothered.

"I want to be a pilot. I've signed up for the RAF, and my dad's pulled a few strings," he said.

She squirmed a little when he held her too close, his body rather too near her breasts. She tried to move away slightly. He wasn't Bea, and his hands were clammy.

"I'm just waiting for my papers and medical to come through."

Was he allowed to fly with a lazy eye? She didn't like to ask. Someone kicked her foot from behind. "Ow." The pain radiated from her heel, and she wondered if she could slip away. All the seats were taken by other people where they had been sitting. Her heart beat faster as she cast around the dance floor and saw Ethel getting rather close to Bill, and Harry was still clinging on to Bea. There was no escape for a while, so she turned back to George. At least he seemed harmless.

She remembered him in primary school standing up for Ethel when she had peed in her pants when the teacher made her recite a poem. She glanced over to where Ethel was dancing with Bill. She imagined Harry relating that story at Bill and Ethel's wedding, not that he had witnessed the original incident but that never stopped Harry from telling a great yarn.

Maud's foot landed with a crunch on George's foot. He winced but continued to smile up at her. She stumbled as she tried to regain her balance but instead of complaining as Harry did, he caught her in his arms and laughed.

"Whoops-a-daisy, Maud."

The song ended, and she saw Harry and Bea making their way to the side. She gravitated towards them, but George pulled at her sleeve.

"Will you...?"

Maud's eyes blinked in frustration, but she leaned down to hear what he was saying. The dim lights showed the glitter of fear in his eyes.

"I don't want to go to war and never have kissed a girl. Will you kiss me?"

Maud felt sorry for him. He seemed scared. No, she wanted to say, she wanted to kiss Bea, but Bea was probably kissing Harry by now. She relented and nodded. Relief flooded his face, and he grabbed her by the neck to pull her down and pressed his lips against hers. His mouth stayed closed, thank heavens, but his moustache scratched. He smelled of beer and sweat mixed with aftershave. She tried to pull away, but he was surprisingly strong.

"Will you dance with me again?" he asked.

The increasing smokiness in the hall made it difficult to see the others, but she could see no way to ever getting a dance with Bea. She nodded. Better the devil you know. They propped each other up for the rest of the evening, like two pillars of a bridge, not wanting to let go in case they collapsed. Balanced and brought together by fear: George of going to war, and Maud of never getting to dance with Bea and not encouraging George.

Finally, the band played the last song, an Al Bowlly number, "Blue

Moon."

"Can I see you again?"

"I'm sure we will, George. Thanks for dancing. Now I need to find my brothers. Night." Maud cast around to find her group in the mayhem and shot off when she spotted Harry.

When they eventually got back into the car, Bea announced she would ride in the back with Maud.

Harry climbed in the front, then turned to Maud. "I saw you kissing George Waites. He likes you."

Maud's cheeks burned, and she caught Bea's gaze. "He kissed me. It's not like that. I don't like him," she said. I like you, she wanted to say but was silenced by the gag of societal acceptance. The fear in Maud's expression must have shown as Bea leaned against Maud as the car bounced over potholes. She found Maud's hand in the darkness and interlaced their fingers as if to ground her in reality and truth. Bea stroked Maud's palm with her thumb and a circle of fire followed her fingertip.

Harry started talking with Bill about the mighty Wolverhampton Wanderers—his definition, not Maud's. She wasn't interested in football.

"Sorry if it was awful," Bea whispered. "I hoped we might dance together."

Maud shrugged and opened her palm so Bea had easier access. All that was right with the world could be felt by the simplicity of Bea's skin on hers. The soft caresses caused fireworks that seemed to reach every cell in her body. She turned in her seat to face Bea.

The lights from an oncoming car lit up their faces, and Bea's expression was one of joy as she gazed at Maud. It was the same for her, but what about Harry? She glanced to the front seat of the car, conflicted by her feelings for Bea and her love for her brother. Had he and Bea come to an arrangement? He certainly seemed in good spirits, but that wasn't unusual. Harry was always the life and soul of the party, and she loved him for it.

He continued to chatter, teasing Bill who had kissed Ethel Porter and danced with her for the rest of the evening. Bill said nothing, just concentrated on keeping the Austin 7 on course and peered at the road ahead, lit by the dim headlights. Then the car lurched to one side, throwing Maud into Bea's chest. She inhaled soap, lily of the valley, and perspiration. It was heady and warm, and Bea's chest heaved up and down, fast. If only Maud could put her arms around Bea and kiss her, not as George had kissed Maud, all scratch and slobber, but soft and passionate. "Sorry," Maud said.

Bill swore. "Puncture. Everyone out."

They swarmed out of the car, and Harry and Bill gave Maud and Bea their jackets to keep them warm while they changed the wheel. Her brothers lit their cigarettes before cranking up the car.

"Make yourself useful, get the spare," Bill said to Harry, who laughed and whistled between his teeth as he removed the good tyre from the rear of the vehicle.

Maud shivered.

"Come over here. It'll be warmer by the hedge," Bea said, pulling Maud away from the car.

She wrapped one arm and Bill's jacket around Maud. She tucked her head down, and all she heard was Bea's heart beating fast. "Thank you." Maud shivered again, although she wasn't sure it was the cold this time.

"You're welcome. Come closer. Keep warm."

Maud tried to see Bea's face in the gloom as her brothers knelt by the wheel, but the only light was Harry's cigarette casting a tiny pinprick of glow. Bea wrapped her other arm around her. Where her hand held Maud's arms, heat expanded and radiated. Then she noticed Bea was tapping out Morse again, and she screwed up her eyes as she tried to remember it.

I will miss you, Bea tapped out on her hand. Maud leaned into her and wrapped her in her arms tightly, with her head resting on Maud's shoulder.

"Me too," Maud whispered into Bea's hair that smelled of shampoo and cigarette smoke. She hated to think of Bea leaving at the end of the summer. She couldn't go back to how it was before. Bea had changed her, opened her eyes, her mind, and her heart. Being together like this felt so right, like a jigsaw slotted into place. As her eyes had adjusted to the dark, Maud could sense that Bea was smiling.

"Look up," Bea said.

The clouds parted like curtains on a stage, revealing the moon. Silver settled on trees and distant houses, highlighting the backs of her brothers as they bent over the car. The planes of Bea's face were cast in blue light and shadow, surreal and beautiful.

She stretched up to caress Maud's cheek. "I feel like the moon, orbiting around you," she said.

Maud laughed, not sure what Bea meant. Was she referring to her height or did she mean more than that?

"No. You're the sun, not the moon; you're all heat and light." Maud pulled her closer.

"Thank you," Bea murmured and brushed her finger along Maud's bottom lip. She dipped her head and could smell the port on Bea's breath. They were just a few inches apart. One small stretch and their lips could meet, and everything would change.

"All done." Harry stood.

Bea pulled away. Cold crawled down Maud's body, and she was left with an unshakeable feeling of loss. Harry rubbed his oily hands on his handkerchief as she and Bea returned to the car. She gave Bill his jacket.

"Your jalopy awaits." Harry bowed and opened the door for Bea.

"Thank you, kind sir," Bea said in the same mocking tone as she climbed in the back.

Maud scrambled in on the driver's side behind Bill and pulled the front seat up. The leather was cold as she sat back and snuggled next to Bea. She was enveloped in the smell of leather, oil, and cigarettes, although they would never smoke when there were women in the car. Bill toed his cigarette out on the gravel, fiddled with the mix on the dashboard, then cranked the handle by the radiator. The engine caught, then revved too high. He patted the vehicle's bonnet, hopped in, and put the car in gear.

Bea reached for Maud's hand and held it in hers in the darkness. Maud's fingers were still so numb that it took a few moments before the blood returned, stinging and tingling. She leaned into Bea, not wanting this evening to finish. The horrors of the dance hall, of George Waites and being unable to dance with Bea, all receded like a nightmare on waking. She could sit in this car, behind her brothers, with her hands in Bea's forever.

CHAPTER EIGHT

A FEW DAYS LATER, at the end of their lesson, the twins ran off after an empty thank you to Bea.

She laughed. "They're really not interested in studying, are they?"

Maud shook her head, although she couldn't begrudge their haste as it gave her extra time with Bea. "They don't realise how lucky they are, but I guess that's always the way."

Bea perched on Maud's desk. "Very true. And with the imminent war, we need to snatch whatever happiness we can, wherever we can."

She held Maud's gaze. Her words didn't seem to refer to making the most of education. Maud gulped, and her heart leapt as she remembered last night's dream, where she had awoken, all agitated and horrified she'd had her monthly. She'd rushed to the toilet, but no, she was wet for a very different reason. "I'm not sure what's happening here, Miss W, Bea. I—"

"You and me both." Bea tucked a stray hair behind Maud's ear. "But it feels right?"

Bea stroked Maud's cheek, causing tingles beneath her skin. Maud nodded. "Oh, yes." Her face was so close. Drawn into Bea's blue eyes, Maud's gaze strayed to her lips. Bea's hot breath mingled with her own. She leaned in.

"Maud! Where are you?" Faint footsteps echoed down the corridor outside, along with the sound of doors opening and closing.

Maud jumped back. "I'm in the library finishing my lesson with Miss Williams."

Bea hitched an eyebrow as she closed the exercise book they had been using. "Finishing a lesson?"

Maud stifled a giggle. The handle turned, and without waiting for a reply, her mother entered with Violet in tow. The temperature in the library dropped, like a freezing fog obliterating the sun. It seemed her mother had reverted to her usual rigid self. Perhaps it was too much to hope that her relaxing of the rules would last.

"Come and take Violet. I need to get to the annual show committee meeting."

Maud opened her arms to her sister, who skipped to join her. She ran her fingers through the young girl's hair, her chest heaving, unsure whether it was because of Bea's proximity or their narrow escape.

"I assumed you'd finished ages ago. The boys have already disappeared into the village on their bikes." She turned to Bea. "Good evening, Miss Williams. How are you? I do hope Maud is not taking up too much of your spare time."

"Not at all, Lady Heaston. It's always a delight to tutor Maud. She's so keen and has a real aptitude for mathematics."

Her mother sniffed. "I'm sure she has, but that won't help her find a good husband."

Bea straightened to her full height, at least three inches shorter than her mother. "With the upcoming war, everyone will need to use all their skills, irrespective of age or sex."

Maud admired Bea standing up to her mother like that. If she did that, she would be punished, and she wasn't sure she was too old for her father's belt. Violet clung to her legs, probably sensing the tension in the air. Wanting to hide from the conversation, Maud crouched down to give her sister a hug.

"She can get a job as a nursery nurse. Children seem to like her," her mother said.

If she had said she can pretend she's helping until she gets married, Maud wouldn't have been surprised.

"With respect, Lady Heaston, Maud can do anything the boys do," Bea said.

Didn't she realise she was playing with fire now? Her mother would not take kindly to being contradicted.

"Unfortunately, Miss Williams, opportunities are not open to girls. It's all right for bluestockings such as yourself—"

"I planned we'd take Violet out for a brief walk, Mother, before giving her some tea. It's such a lovely day." Maud had seen Bea visibly stiffen and felt the need to cut in. Whilst Bea might be a bluestocking—an intellectual with an intellectual father—the tone her mother used was not one of approval.

Her mother blinked as though she was still processing whether Bea had been intentionally rude. Then she broke into her public-awards-presentation smile, wide but false. Maud had seen it on display at so many garden shows and coffee mornings.

"Good idea, Maud. I'm sure you all need some fresh air. It's not good for you to be cooped up inside all day. Make sure you're not late for supper. You know your father gets anxious if it's not on the table when he gets home. And he has more than enough to be anxious about at the moment."

"Of course, Mother," Maud said.

"Be good." Her mother waved her hand in dismissal as she left.

"I see where the twins get their disdain for education from now," Bea said, collecting her books together and setting them neatly on the desk. She picked up her satchel and rummaged around until she retrieved a folded piece of Basildon Bond. "Here's your puzzle for tonight."

Maud tucked the slip of expensive blue paper into the pocket of her slacks without looking at it. She was still burning up with shame and embarrassment. "I'm sorry about Mother. I hope you're not offended. She has such fixed views of how things should be."

Bea placed a hand on Maud's arm. It was as welcome as a warm sun after a cold shower.

"Not at all," Bea said. "But we will need all the skills we can get."

Maud swept Violet into her arms and turned to Bea. "Perhaps we'll accompany you some of the way back to your digs and see if the rabbits are still there."

"Rabbits," Violet shouted. She struggled to get down and rushed to the door.

Maud changed Violet into her wellingtons, although she didn't expect any mud, but it was easier to keep her clothes clean. The best walking route was over a rough path passing an open meadow and through a small wood. Late summer flowers scattered their fragrance about them, and a lonely blackbird chirruped with tweets and whistles that sounded like a monologue. Maud closed her eyes to try and fix this moment in her memories, like exposing photographic film to sunlight. She never wanted to forget the surge of joy, all the more precious because it would pass so soon.

Violet walked between them both. Bea and Maud swung her between them.

She squealed as her feet left the ground. "Again, again."

"One, two, three," they said in unison.

"Violet, can we find any acorns?" Maud asked as they approached the wood. Violet slipped their grip and scrabbled on her hands and knees. So much for keeping her dress clean.

Bea dropped to her haunches and turned over leaves to assist with the search. Her hair fell forward into her eyes. Maud reached out and brushed Bea's locks behind her shoulder. At her touch, Bea rose and linked their fingers. Without a word spoken, they finished what they started earlier. Bea's lips were soft and warm. Gentle and delicious, tender and tentative. A thrill shot down Maud's spine and excited heat glowed at the junction of her thighs, as it had in her dreams. This seemed so right. Maud licked Bea's bottom lip, and her mouth opened. Their tongues touched, exploring, desperate.

Bea pulled away. "Wow."

Maud nodded, not trusting herself to speak, her chest heaving. In her peripheral vision, she noticed a movement. Violet stood watching them, holding out a green acorn, her mouth open. Maud crouched to Violet's level. "Have you found that for me?"

Violet nodded. Her head bobbed from Maud to Bea and back again. "Are you going to get married?"

They both laughed, but it was embarrassed, brittle as a pane of glass. It felt like all the breath had been sucked out of her and blood rushed in her ears. Violet mustn't say anything.

"No, we were just practising," Bea said.

Maud managed to recover her breath. "For our boyfriends—"

"So we know what to do."

"Have you got a boyfriend?" Violet asked Maud.

Maud flicked a glance at Bea, then focused on Violet. "Well, I had a dance with George Waites on Saturday, and Miss Williams danced with Harry."

Violet toed the dusty ground, seeming to consider this. She cocked her head to one side. "Is Harry your boyfriend?"

"No, he's a friend, and he's very funny. Does he make you laugh?"

Bea's tone was all sunshine and rose petals, covering their indiscretion well.

Violet stamped her foot. "He calls me Sprocket, but that's not my name. I'm called Violet."

"Yes, and it's a lovely name," Bea said.

Maud glanced across at Bea before turning her attention back to the little girl with a smudge on her face. "Should we let Miss Williams go back to her house now? Then we can get some tea."

"Can we have jam sandwiches?"

It seemed as if the danger was averted. Surely it was better not to draw attention to it, so Violet wouldn't think to discuss it at home. "Of course we can, and there's some cake left from yesterday. Say goodbye to Miss Williams."

Violet put out her hand, a serious frown on her face. "Goodbye, Miss Williams. Thank you for having me."

Bea laughed and shook her hand. "Goodbye, Miss Heaston, it was a pleasure."

The girl looked up with enormous eyes. "Would you like Harry to be your boyfriend? He really likes you, he told me."

The slightest dusting of pink touched Bea's cheeks. "Well, I like Harry, but—"

"Come on, young lady, that's an impertinent question to ask." Maud pushed Violet's shoulder, gently. "Will you give your acorn to Miss Williams, or do you want to keep it?"

Violet opened her hand and offered the acorn to Bea.

"Thank you, Miss Heaston, I shall treasure this," Bea said, and wrapped it in her handkerchief.

"'Bye," Violet said, her head crooked to one side.

Bea rewarded her with a full dazzling smile and turned to Maud. "Goodbye, Miss Maud Heaston. I'll be interested how long you take to work out your puzzle this evening."

She twitched her eyebrow, spun round, and followed the path in the opposite direction. She didn't glance back, even though Maud waited till she was out of view. She put her hand in her pocket and pulled out the puzzle as Violet skipped along the path. The message was much longer than normal, but even the thrill of anticipation couldn't quell the anxiety that Violet would say something. Her heart thumped in her chest like an over-revved engine, and she wasn't sure whether it was the excitement and desire or disbelief and fear.

CHAPTER NINE
Bristol, present day

"HEY, SUKI, GUESS what I've found today amongst the papers?" Suki threw down her bag. "Let me take my shoes off, I'm knackered. It's been a hard day." She untied her sensible shoes and placed them neatly by the lounge door, straightening up Hannah's Converse as she did.

Hannah almost asked if taking lots of photos of people's bits was hard, but she caught sight of Suki's face. She was grey and blinking back the tears. "Hey, are you okay?" Hannah unfolded herself and stretched.

Suki leaned against the doorjamb. "There was a lovely lady today who reminded me of my gran. Very chatty, came in for just a routine MRI scan, but she was absolutely riddled with cancer. When we'd finished, I couldn't face her, and it was obvious something was wrong by my reaction. The question was in her eye, but I couldn't say anything. It's not allowed. I just told her that her doctor would be in touch."

"Oh, Suki, I'm sorry. That's hard." She wanted to hug her, but Suki didn't like physical contact. "Can I get you anything?"

"I'm just going for a shower. Can you order a takeaway? Maybe pizza."

"Vegan mushroom?" It was Suki's favourite from the "proper" Italian pizzeria that now delivered.

"Great."

Suki closed the bathroom door, creating a barrier a chasm wide. Hannah sighed and returned the frail folded paper back to the box and to the back of her mind. She would try to cheer Suki up. Tea was always a good start, and chocolate. She opened the fridge. *Damn, no chocolate.* She could run out and pick up some and still be back by the time the pizza arrived, if she was sharpish.

The corner shop was stuffed with sweets but had yet to stock vegan chocolate, and Suki was an avowed vegan, aside from eating fish, but that didn't seem to deter her. It was an eight-minute walk to the independent supermarket, so Hannah would need to be in and out without a hitch. She sprinted as long as she could, but her wheezing and cramped chest forced her to stop and lean against a gatepost. Damn her damaged knees. She'd become so unfit and needed to get back into training for Ultimate Frisbee. She arrived home just as the pizza delivery guy stepped away from the door to their maisonette.

"Hi," she called out. "I'm just coming."

The guy noticed her. "Great, I was about to give up. Or leave it on the step."

"My flatmate is probably still in the shower." Hannah hoped Suki hadn't just dragged her butt out of the shower, otherwise she wouldn't be happy.

Hannah took the pizza inside, clambered over Suki's bike in the hallway, and ran up the stairs. She was confronted in the lounge with Suki wrapped in a towel. It would have been cute, except her scowl would have curdled milk.

"Sorry, I guessed I'd be back in time. I got you chocolate." With a grin, Hannah presented Suki with her offering of chocolate and pizza.

"Oh." The scowl lightened but didn't disappear completely. Suki snatched the chocolate and spun around. "I'll dry off then." Suki's door shut with a click.

Shit. Hannah twiddled around one of her piercings. That plan backfired a little. She strode to the kitchen area separated from the lounge by a breakfast bar, which doubled as a table, desk, and general clutter gatherer until Suki insisted they organised it. She rummaged around in the kitchen drawer and found the pizza cutter. When she pushed in the drawer, the front panel fell off again. They'd complained to the landlord, but he did nothing about it. She banged it in with her fist and promised herself she'd re-glue it at the weekend.

She plated up the pizzas and poured out tea, placing everything on trays so they could sit in front of the TV and watch *Friends* reruns, Suki's favourite. Hannah sat in the small Ikea cloth recliner to give Suki space to stretch out on the sofa.

When Suki returned, she curled up on the sofa with her legs tucked underneath her and patted the seat next to her. "Tell me what you found from your Great Aunt Maud."

Her smile reached her eyes, more dazzling for the storm before, and Hannah basked in the sunshine as she lifted the lid off the box. "Are you sure? You don't want to talk about your day?" Hannah asked.

Suki shook her head. "No."

"Sure." Hannah put down her slice of pizza, placed her tray on the floor, and wiped her hands on her T-shirt before picking up the fragile blue paper, so worn away that tiny holes had appeared along the lines where it had been folded.

"This is a code written by Bea, I'm guessing, with the deciphered translation by Gammy. It was dated August '39 on the back."

"Just before the second world war?"

Suki leaned over to read the neat handwriting. Her shoulder brushed against Hannah's arm, warming her. Suki smelt of Ghost Sweetheart with the citrus, pineapple, and mint mix. Hannah inhaled. It reminded her of sunny afternoons lying in the Royal Fort Gardens when they were supposed to be revising. "Exactly. From what I gather Bea was employed to tutor Gammy's younger brothers, and Gammy sat in during the afternoon only. From a gender studies perspective, it's interesting social proof that talented women were held back, rather than be allowed to reach their potential."

When Suki's eyes glazed over, Hannah focused on Gammy's translation.

"'M, time is short, precious. I think of you constantly. In the morning, I strain to hear your voice or search for you, returning from your visits to the sick. In the afternoon, I wish the boys would play outside and leave us so I could drink you in. Afterwards, when V is our childish chaperone, I am so tempted to touch you, kiss you, and take you in my arms. I realise a tutor should not feel the way I do about you, but I consider myself not as your tutor, but as a friend. I would like it to be more. If this offends, please say, and I will go to war and come you not so near, as Shakespeare says. If this resonates, tell me and I can leave, treasuring the bubble in my heart until we can meet again. Love B.'"

Suki snuggled up to Hannah, who was careful not to move a muscle. When Suki showed her softer side, Hannah felt honoured to be trusted with her vulnerability. She also needed to keep her libido in check.

"That's so romantic. What a wonderful love letter. How exciting it was all in code. Can you imagine uncovering it word by word? I wish we had those nowadays, rather than a 2am 'U Up?' text," Suki said.

Hannah shrugged. She hadn't had a text like that since Megan left her for a man, and she slept her way through a series of one-night stands in her undergraduate days. The one-night stands scratched an itch but left her even more lonely and bereft.

Suki cuddled closer. "So, Bea loved your Gammy. The plot thickens. I would love for someone to love me like that."

Suki placed an arm around Hannah's waist. The touch was what, friendly? More? Suki was impossible to read like this.

"Have you decided to see your Gammy in her home? I'm guessing she's there because she can't care for herself anymore. You should see her while you can."

Hannah sat up, pulling away from her touch. She didn't need to have the lecture from Suki about her duty; she'd had that all her life. But she didn't want to argue, so she avoided the conversation. "I've bought a card to send her. More pizza?" She jumped up to pick up the pizza box on the breakfast bar, waiting for the scolding that a card was not the same as going up there.

When Hannah turned back, Suki was reading a text on her phone and frowning.

She looked up. "Huh?"

Hannah pointed at the pizza box, but Suki shook her head.

"No, thanks, but don't chuck it out, because Connor's coming around."

Hannah sighed, placing the box on the breakfast bar. "What'd he say, 'U up?'" she asked before she thought it through.

Suki's eyes widened. "I...no... Shit."

A jagged flash of hope blinded Hannah as realisation seemed to pelt Suki. If Suki could see Farty Boy for what he was, just interested in her for sex and whatever else he could get, maybe Suki could also see that Hannah cherished her. Not responding to Suki's touch was getting harder, when all she wanted to do was run her fingers through Suki's glossy hair, hold her close, and love her. But Hannah was not and never would be a homewrecker, so she needed them to work things out and let it play out. She couldn't be involved, and it was best to be out of their way. "Sorry, I didn't mean to startle you. I might just take some more of these papers and head off to bed. I've got a meeting with Matthews first thing tomorrow. Night."

"Night, Hannah. Sorry if I've chased you away from the lounge again."

Hannah raised her hand in acknowledgement and entered her bedroom. She prayed they wouldn't be as noisy as normal in their lovemaking. But around midnight, instead of the usual frantic thudding of the headboard and grunt as Farty Boy came—God, she hated these plasterboard walls—she heard raised voices. The words were indistinguishable, but the tone was unmistakable. Hannah rammed her head under the pillow, debating whether to plug in her music, when the front door slammed. Farty Boy had left, but was it for now or for good? A thrill shivered down her spine. Would Suki finally see that he wasn't good for her and wasn't really interested in her for anything other than free food and sex? Was this her chance? *Don't be stupid. Suki's told me very clearly that she's going through a straight phase.* But Hannah couldn't squash down the bud of hope pushing into her heart.

A few minutes later, when she slipped out to the bathroom, she heard snuffles from Suki's room. Compassion flooded her. She paused by the bedroom door and knocked. "Hey, Suki, are you okay?"

The crying stopped, and there was silence.

"Suki, do you want to talk?"

There was a rustling and the sound of a nose being blown.

"Come in," Suki said quietly.

Her bedside light was on, casting an eerie gloom. Suki had the covers pulled up, but her shoulders and arms were bare. Oh God, she was naked under the sheets. *Stop it. Focus.* "Hey, you all right?" Hannah mentally kicked herself for such a stupid question.

"I guess. I broke up with Connor, and I'm feeling a bit down." Suki wiped her eyes.

"Why? I thought you liked him?" Hannah flashed a sympathetic smile. She hated seeing Suki like this, her eyes red and tissues strewn over the floor where she'd missed the bin. All she wanted to do was take Suki in her arms, hold her tight, and make it okay, but Suki had made it very clear she wanted no touching, or none that she didn't initiate anyway.

Suki gulped and shuffled over to one side of the bed, tucking the duvet under her armpits. "He didn't see *me*. I was just a way for him to have sex. It wasn't going anywhere, and I didn't love him."

Hannah stepped further into the room, and Suki patted the edge of the bed for her to sit. Hannah did so, being very careful not to touch any part of the lump in the duvet that would be Suki's body. This was exquisite torture. Her body thrummed to be so close to Suki, but her mind screamed at her to back away. Hannah took a calming breath as Suki pulled a tissue from the box on the duvet.

"I kept pondering that letter you read out from Bea declaring her love for your Gammy. It just spun around my head that I don't love Connor. He's a nice enough guy, but I don't feel that strongly about him."

She blew her nose into a tissue, and Hannah passed her the waste bin. Suki pulled the duvet up. "I suppose it was easy, expected. Everyone at work talks about their husband or boyfriend, and I just wanted to be normal and accepted."

"Why wouldn't you be accepted?" Hannah asked.

Even in the dim light, Suki's lips curled in a look of incredulity, as though Hannah had just said something stupid, and it should be obvious.

"I already get enough from the public because my dad is Japanese, I have a Japanese name, and look foreign. I don't need to add in homophobia from my colleagues."

If Suki had added "duh," Hannah wouldn't have been surprised. "Surely a lot of the staff at the hospital are queer, or at least allies?" Hannah asked.

Suki bolted upright, heaving the duvet to cover her dignity. "Some are, but we also have a number of very religious staff who don't approve. Not to mention the gays and lesbians who don't understand bi or pansexuals. We're not all the same, you know."

Hannah raised her hands, palms up in supplication. "Sorry, I appreciate that. I assumed that—"

Suki pulled the duvet tighter around herself. "That's your trouble, Hannah. You make assumptions all the time. Like with your Gammy. Why don't you go visit her?"

"I'll think about it, okay?" Hannah rose to go. She didn't want an argument, and they were teetering on the precipice of another disagreement.

"Wait." Suki sunk her face in her hands. "Sorry, I don't mean to be a bitch. Stay awhile and hold me?"

Hannah sunk back onto the bed, lying outside the covers, and held her arms out for Suki to shuffle into, being careful to maintain her dignity.

"Thanks," Suki whispered and snuggled into Hannah.

Hannah sighed. *Like I'm her giant teddy bear, used only for comfort.*

CHAPTER TEN
Staffordshire, August 1939

IN CHURCH EVERY Sunday, all the Heastons sat in the family box at the front. It had a little wooden door painted with the Heaston crest, a way of excluding the congregation and an assertion of privilege, the Heastons having paid for the church a few centuries ago. It was not intended for a family of eight, so Vi sat on Maud's knee. To Maud's right, the twins shuffled around, pinching and nudging her at any opportunity. Harry sat next to Maud, Bill to his left, and their parents to Bill's left, closest to the aisle. It was always the same, in the strict hierarchy of age. Both her parents knelt in private prayer. It was like any Sunday for her entire life.

Maud and Harry turned at the same time to gaze around the church. Bea was sitting beside Miss Talbot, her landlady. Bea smiled, and both Maud and Harry waved back in unison.

"Pay attention." Their mother's whisper would have commanded a battlefield.

As they turned to the front, Harry's expression lit up with pleasure. The same delight was probably showing on her own face. Her stomach roiled. Harry was in love with Bea, and so was she.

She pulled Vi closer on her knee as the girl was straining to reach the common prayer book on the pew ledge. Bea had said she would like more than friendship. But what did that mean? They could not live together as a couple, like man and wife. She scanned the church again. Everyone was in couples or family groups consisting of one man and one woman. A few widows who hadn't remarried after their husbands had been killed in the Great War still wore black twenty-one years later. How could Bea be anything more than a friend? Maud stroked her silk gloves, the material cool to the touch. She wished her ardour could be as cool, and her understanding sharper. It would all be so much simpler. But she loved Bea and would do what she could to be with her.

Harry nudged Maud, and she angled herself towards him.

"Say nothing, but I'm going to ask Bea to marry me."

Hot and cold swept over Maud, and she faced him. *No, no, no.* It was one thing suspecting something, quite another to have it confirmed. Her stomach twisted into a knot. He was looking at her eagerly, watching for a reaction. "Shh." She frowned at Harry and gestured at Vi, who was stilled, as if holding her breath listening to the conversation.

He shrugged. "I don't care," he whispered, then mouthed 'I love her'. He must have seen the horror on her face as he leaned in. "Don't worry, we'll try to get you a nice young man for a tutor next time. I'll put a friendly word in with Mother. He'll need to be tall, though. Giant needed to teach bespectacled freak."

"Hey!" she whispered back with a false lightness in her tone and elbowed him.

"Hush, Maud," Mother said from the other side of Bill.

Maud wanted to protest that Harry started it but realised it would do no good. She sighed.

"George Waites is looking at you. No, hang on, it's difficult to tell with his lazy eye. No, he's watching the choir, or it could be the altar, or maybe the vicar." He rolled his eyes.

Maud poked him in the ribs in his ultra-ticklish spot, and he leapt in his seat.

"Maud, I won't tell you again."

Her mother's hissed rebuke was loud enough for half the church to hear. Maud snapped to the front, burning from the neck upwards. Oh Lord, is Bea going to marry Harry? Nausea clawed up her throat, and she swallowed. She must have been holding Vi too hard as the little girl wriggled and pushed away at Maud's hands. "Sorry, sweet pea," Maud whispered and unclenched her fingers, smoothing Violet's dress to give her something to do.

The vicar droned on about the "evil over the Channel" and how it behoved every man, woman, and child to do their duty. Maud looked at her brother in profile. Handsome, in a kind of tall and sticking-out-ears way. He was funny and she supposed, with others, he could be charming. Surely it was good that Bea married Harry. At least she would be her sister. Maud unclenched her fists again. She didn't want Bea as her sister; she loved her. She didn't dare glance back and face another admonition from Mother. A man had the right to marry, garnering the church and society's blessing. A woman, none. The answer was inevitable; Bea would marry

Harry. The certainty felt like a punch in the stomach, so real it was painful. The woman she loved was going to marry someone else. The strength of her feelings for Bea was as clear as a frosty night, and now when she was able to articulate them, Bea was about to be snatched away from her.

Vi wriggled on her lap and trod on Maud's thigh as she turned and stood up facing the rear. "Ow, jiggle bottom, be careful."

Vi waved at people she recognised in the pews behind.

"Maud, will you please control Violet?"

Maud sighed and turned Violet to the front where the vicar was still talking. She played pat-a-cake silently with Vi to keep her amused, but her head shot up when the Vicar said, "This week in our prayers, we will say a special thank you to Mister William Heaston who is answering the call of duty and is waiting for his call-up any day soon."

"More like call of nature," Harry whispered, but Maud didn't reply.

Bill was going any day? Her blissful summer, her entire life was shifting and recalibrating. Maud glanced over at Ethel Porter, who sat chewing her bottom lip. She looked as anxious as Maud felt. Why did life have to change? How long could she cling on to the last battlements of denial? Like a sandcastle washed away by the incoming tide, water was rushing in, obliterating the ramps and turrets, pools and caverns, and consuming all the spilt ice creams and dropped wrappers of life.

And still the vicar pontificated. Sunday lunch would get cold or burned. Maud dropped her gaze as her joy and hope eddied and was sucked away.

CHAPTER ELEVEN

H<small>ARRY KICKED</small> M<small>AUD</small> under the table. "Can I talk to you afterwards?" he whispered.

That was strange. He wasn't normally that polite, and he was fidgeting in his seat. Discomfort crept over her like a November fog. This had to be to do with Bea. His comment in church had been serious then. Part of her hoped he was just trying to wind her up. She gulped and nodded, no longer wanting the blackberry and apple crumble, even though it was her favourite.

"Thank you for our meal. Please may we get down?" the twins asked as soon as they had scoffed the last of their dessert, and there was clearly no opportunity for seconds.

Their mother looked to her husband, who nodded.

"Don't go setting fire to the hay ricks again. We'll need all the food we can get in the war, including animal feed," their father said before Joe could quibble.

"But it was an accident. We were seeing if it was possible to start a fire using a magnifying glass," Jack said.

"If that's the magnifying glass from my study, you'll get the back of my hand, young man."

"No, sir," they answered in unison.

Maud realised it was probably hers. They must have "borrowed" it from her needlework box. Not that she ever did any embroidery. The entire family rose, and Daisy entered to collect all the dirty crockery.

"Thank you, Daisy," Mother said, "and will you thank Mrs Baker for a lovely meal as usual, despite us being delayed half an hour at church."

"Yes, m'lady." Daisy curtsied and towered the plates on a huge tray.

Harry grabbed Maud by the sleeve and dragged her into the library, her sanctuary.

"Maud, Maud, tell me. I'm going to drive over to ask Bea to marry me. Will she say yes?"

Maud clutched at the desk to steady herself. He had such an earnest expression, not the usual cocky brother she was used to. Inside she was screaming, no, no, she's mine. She picked up a book to have something to hold and give her time to consider her response. It was the mathematics textbook they'd been looking at on Friday, which seemed a lifetime away. Maud cleared her throat and willed herself to sound normal. "I'm not sure. Have you asked her father?" It sounded squeaky, but Harry didn't seem to notice, probably because he was emotional.

"The Cambridge Don? That would be scary. No, I figured I'd ask her first before I face that. What'll she say? You're very close to her..."

If you had any idea. But would that be enough for Bea? Hiding what they were, Maud wouldn't cope watching as all the men buzzed around Bea like bees around a honey pot. Did Bea even want to be with Maud in the long term? Subconsciously, Maud's fingers slipped in her pocket for the folded paper that she had reread umpteen times. It was a talisman. Bea said she wanted more than being friends.

"What aren't you saying? Is there someone else? Has she mentioned me? Does she even like me?" Harry checked himself in the mirror over the fireplace and smoothed down his hair.

Maud noticed he had liberally splashed himself in cologne. "I don't know, but she'll be asphyxiated if she gets within two steps of you."

Harry punched her on the shoulder, hard enough that she might have a bruise the following day. "Come on, don't make this harder than it already is."

Maud inhaled and chose her words carefully, counting down on her fingers. "I guess you're handsome and will be an engineering graduate one day so you have prospects. You can be funny when you're not being obnoxious and underneath it all, you are kind and generous, so I'm sure you're a real catch."

Harry raised his hands and huffed out a breath. "Yes, but does she like me?"

"I can't answer that. She seems to like you, but I don't know what plans she has for when she goes back to Girton. You must ask her."

Harry snorted. "But there's a war about to start. It's all so uncertain, and we need to snatch what happiness we can, when we can."

Maud shrugged. Bea had said that to her recently too. It was as if everyone was desperate to squeeze a complete life into a few days in case that was all they had. "Ask her then." She felt she was signing hope's death warrant, and the knot in her stomach that had started at church twisted itself tighter.

He must have picked up on her mood because he spun away, his shoulders sagging. "You're no help. Thanks a bunch." He pulled a cigarette from his packet and clamped it between his teeth.

"Your breath will stink if you smoke."

"Yeah, but I need one. I expected you to be supportive."

"Harry." But he had gone, banging the library door behind him, fluttering the loose papers on the desk. Maud collapsed on the nearest chair and rested her head in her hands. Bea was going to marry Harry and leave, Bill was off to war, and the entire world was changing. The tide was threatening to overwhelm her, and she couldn't cope. She wanted to hold back the waves and protect her sandcastle. Feeling numb, she searched the shelves for Jane Austen as she needed a comfort read.

Maud settled herself on the overstuffed leather armchair, her back against one arm and her legs dangling over the other. She kept reading the same paragraph. Would Bea say yes? Of course she would. How could Maud cope? She would, because she'd have to. At least she'd have the chance to see Bea. Who was she kidding? Nausea rose in her throat. She tossed down her book in her lap and stared out of the window without seeing.

A knock on the door startled her.

Her mother popped her head around the door. "Ah. This is where you're hiding."

Maud stretched and stood to face her mother, who fussed over Maud's clothes and smoothed down her Sunday dress.

"Come quickly. Mr George Waites is waiting in the front parlour to see you."

"What? Why?" Now she had to tamp down the nausea. Could this day get any worse?

"Come on."

Dread and fear battled within Maud as she followed her mother down the corridor. It wasn't long enough to settle her thumping heart, even though it was at the far end of the house. It was like going to the gallows.

George Waites stood to attention as she entered. He was dressed in his Sunday best. Her mother clicked the door shut behind her, leaving them alone. In his hands, he held a rather wilted bouquet of wildflowers he must have picked on his way over.

He cleared his throat. "I'm waiting for my medical to join the RAF."

"Yes, George, I know," Maud said, her words calmer than her thoughts. "When will you hear from them?"

"In the next fortnight." He pinched his moustache between his thumb and forefinger. "I was hoping you would do me the favour of writing to me."

Maud let out a breath. Was that all? "Of course. I'd be honoured to write to you, George, you're a good, kind man—"

"Will you marry me?" He thrust the flowers at her, without catching her eye.

Two blooms sagged over his index finger where he must have been clenching them too hard. Maud shook her head to clear her thoughts. "Thank you for asking. It's very flattering, but I don't—"

"You don't need to answer me now. Think about it and tell me. It's just with the war coming, we have to—"

"Yes, everyone's desperate to say or do things or get them sorted."

"But we might be dead next month."

He looked so young; he'd only just turned eighteen. Hope etched lines of anxiety and pleading across his face. "I'll think about it, George," she said, if only to ease his kicked puppy expression.

He whistled through his teeth and bowed. "Thank you," he said and took his leave.

She should be elated, but she felt sick and scared. At least she had bought some time, for now. But what if Bea had said yes to Harry? What a mess. She stared at the fire, trying to realign her world that was spinning out of control.

Her mother entered the parlour so fast after George had exited, she must have been waiting outside, listening in. "Well?"

Playing coy wouldn't help. "George has asked me to marry him. I said I'd consider it, but I don't want to."

"Why ever not? He is a gentleman, from a respectable family."

Maud sat taller, her chin up. "I don't love him."

"Maud Emeline Heaston, how many offers of marriage do you think you are going to get? The Baker son isn't eligible, nor Daisy's brother. George Waites is a nice young man, from an excellent family, and kind to boot. With the war, there'll be a shortage of eligible bachelors, like in the Great War." She lowered her tone as if letting Maud into a state secret. "I know."

Maud had to clamp her jaw shut as realisation dawned. "Are you saying you didn't love Father?" It surprised her that she found the courage to ask, but the words tumbled out without thought. Was she just trying to deflect from having the spotlight on her? Her mother sucked in through her teeth. She must have decided it was time for a heart-to-heart, mother-to-daughter conversation, as she perched herself on one armchair and crossed her legs at the ankles, knees together, like the proper Edwardian lady she was, and everything Maud could never, nor wanted to, be. The only sounds were the clock ticking and the crackle and lapping of the fire.

Her mother folded her hands in her lap and took a deep breath. "I didn't love your father when we were first introduced, but we got to appreciate each other and love each other over time, and now I can't imagine being without him."

"What if I don't want to get married?"

Her mother flapped her hands at her neck. "What else can you do? It was a mistake to let you be influenced by a modern young woman such as Miss Williams. I'm sure she's been putting all sorts of nonsense in your head."

Maud clenched her fists in her pockets but spoke calmly. "No, Mother, I've wanted to use my brain for as long as I can remember. Lots of girls have careers now."

"But Maud, dear, what career could you have? The house and title will go to Bill when we die, and there won't be much left to spread around between the rest of you. I'd hate for you to be destitute and alone. Why don't you give George a chance? I'm sure you will grow to love him over time." She patted Maud's knee. "I'll ask your father to have a word with you; he'll make you see it's your only proper choice."

A shiver ran through Maud. What would she do? She didn't have an education, so wasn't eligible for an office job. She didn't want to be reliant on anyone else, but she couldn't do manual work. Was there any choice? Was her mother right? "No, Mother, please don't."

The outer door opened and closed. Quick footsteps hurried along the corridor and up the stairs, with the tell-tale squeak on the third stair. It sounded like Harry. "May I go now, Mother?"

"Of course, my dear, but do nothing rash. Give it serious consideration."
Maud slipped up the stairs and knocked on the bathroom door. She heard crying, so knocked again.

"Go away," Harry shouted.

If he was angry maybe it meant she still had a chance with Bea. The tiniest crack of hope opened in her heart. Now all she needed to do was let George down gently.

CHAPTER TWELVE

THE FOLLOWING DAY, Harry said he didn't want to talk about it. She hoped she might speak to Bea and talk through their respective days, but her mother said Maud needed to go with her to take food parcels to the sick all day. It was clearly a ploy to keep her away from Bea. She scribbled a coded note, hoping to pass it on, and was pleased that the Morse came to her easily now.

GW asked me to wed. Said I'd think about it. Mother insists I accept, as I can't keep myself financially.

When she returned home in the evening, Harry, Violet, and Bea were in the drawing room playing the gramophone. They had pushed back the furniture, and Harry was taking Bea on a foxtrot while Violet clapped. When they entered the drawing room, her mother surveyed the mayhem, shook her head, and left.

Bea held out her hand to Maud. "Come, let's practise. It's Harry's turn to show Violet how to dance."

"Do you have insurance for your feet, Miss Williams? Miss Long Breeches here has been known to send a man to hospital. I don't want to risk my toes."

If Harry was disappointed, he was masking it well, although by the gleam in his eye, Maud suspected she would be the butt of his jokes for the evening. Harry placed the needle on to the record and whisked Violet into his arms and swung her around. It was Glenn Miller's "Moonlight Serenade" that had played at the dance hall.

"If you want to learn how to dance, I'll lead."

Bea smiled up at Maud, who wanted to sink into her embrace and kiss her soft lips, but Harry and Violet were watching. Their hands fit together, and Bea's hand settled on Maud's back. Warmth travelled from the touch around her body.

"Slow, slow, quick, quick. No, lead off on your right foot, going backwards. Take smaller steps to help you keep your balance. Yes, that's much better," Bea said.

They gazed at each other and as the music played, they found a rhythm. Maud was aware of only Bea and this moment and the counting under her breath. As they moved around avoiding Harry, who danced wildly with a squealing Violet, Bea tapped out a message on Maud's hand with her middle finger. Maud frowned as she didn't pick it up at first. Bea repeated it.

I LOVE YOU.

A thrumming ran throughout Maud's entire body, as if she had been plucked like a harp string. No one had ever said that to her before. She wanted to sing from the rooftops in delight, but there was George Waites's proposal and the instruction from her mother. If she lived with Bea, she could do nothing, she was qualified for nothing, and she couldn't pay her way. Her family and the community would ostracise her. Her heart seemed to burst with joy and pain simultaneously. "Can we talk?" she whispered.

Bea stole a glance at Harry. "Harry's driving me home afterwards, on your mother's instruction."

So much hung in the air, confirmation that they were being kept apart, so much they needed to say. Maud grimaced. "I've a note." Maud dropped her hand into her pocket and passed over the coded message as they continued to dance around the room. Staring into Bea's eyes and feeling the warmth of Bea's hand on her back, Maud felt seen and loved, and every emotion that flowed to her was rebounded back. She would risk everything for Bea. Maud smiled, and they held each other's gaze.

The rhythmic hiss and click of the end of the record pulled Maud out of orbit into their surroundings. Harry stood by the gramophone, his eyes almost as wide and open as his mouth as he gaped at them. He knew. The glow she felt dissipated with his frown, and she tugged at her bottom lip with her teeth. Should she talk to him?

Vi tugged at Harry's sleeve. "Again, Harry."

"What?" He stared down at his little sister as if he was in a trance.

"No," he said, "it's time for your tea."

Then he snatched up the arm of the record player and thrust it on the cradle. He picked up the record and rammed it into the sleeve. Maud hated to see Harry so angry and hurt, but she loved Bea. It was all-encompassing, entrancing, and thrilling. She loved Harry too, and she didn't want to have to choose between them, because she knew she would go with Bea. But she thought she understood how he felt, if it was how she felt when Harry danced with Bea, that raw anger and jealousy. She couldn't bear being the target of hard-eyed Harry.

Violet ran to Maud. "Can we have jam sandwiches?"

Maud reluctantly unhooked her hold on Bea and crouched to speak to Violet. "We've got some strawberry jam I made yesterday." She hugged her little sister as a distraction because she desperately wanted to hug Bea. "Shall we make jammy soldiers?" Maud asked, and an image of bloodied bodies seeped into her vision. "Or maybe just neat triangles?"

Harry glanced at his watch. "I'd better get you home, Miss Williams. Do you need me to check for bruises after my sister mauled you?"

His tone was strained, as though he was desperately trying to cling to his happy, easy-going manner.

"Thank you, Harry, but my feet survived just fine. It was a pleasure." She fixed Maud with an intense gaze, a tiny uptick around her mouth. "Thank you for the dance, Maud. Goodbye, Miss Violet. You're a fine dancer."

Harry opened the door for Bea, and Maud watched them depart, yearning tearing at her stomach. To shake it off, she turned to Violet. "Well, we'd better get you some tea. All that dancing makes me hungry."

Halfway through supper, her father announced, "Maud, we need to see you in the parlour."

Cold clutched her heart. She ignored the sniggers of the twins, who sensed she was in trouble, but what had she done wrong? Maud sifted through her interactions with her parents but came up blank. Unless Vi spilled about the kiss with Bea. Or had Harry said something? She wiped her palms on her dress and tried to slow her heart rate to something more normal.

She followed them into the formal room, and they arranged themselves by the fire that had been made up. Her mother sat in the armchair by the hearth, her knees and ankles pressed together. Her father stood guard behind the chair, his hand resting on the back, as if they were posing for a photograph, except their expressions were stern. Maud gulped.

"Sit down, Maud, we need to talk," her father said.

That was never a great start to a conversation. She slipped onto the edge of the chair on the other side of the fire. The heat made her cheeks glow.

Her mother cleared her throat. "Now I understand why you are reluctant to marry George Waites, and why Miss Williams rejected Harry."

Maud froze. Her heart stopped beating for a second. Everything became muffled, then restarted with a rushing, roaring sound in her ears.

"Violet informed me you kissed Miss Williams, on the mouth. I cannot believe that a daughter of ours would do such a perverse, unchristian act in front of an innocent child."

Any courage she'd mustered seeped out of her body and spilled onto the Chinese rug. There was no point denying it, and she didn't want to deny it, because that would mean denying Bea, and she wouldn't do that. But all her conviction that she and Bea could rush off and be together crumpled into hopelessness.

"It is a sin and abomination in the Bible. You will suffer eternal fire if you follow this path," her father proclaimed, as if he was in the pulpit.

"We have asked the Reverend Davies what to do," her mother said. "He says if you cannot, or will not be cured, you must be abstemious and never act upon your perverseness."

Shame and anger seared her skin, burning so deep she seemed branded from the inside. She hung her head and slumped in her seat.

"I am very disappointed with Miss Williams, and I've instructed Harry to inform her she will no longer be welcome in this house. The twins will have a new tutor as soon as we can arrange it. You will never see her again and should not attempt to contact her."

Maud clenched her fists but didn't look at her mother directly. She didn't want to give her the satisfaction of seeing the tears forming on the sills of her eyes. Maud blinked. She wanted to scream, "I love Bea, I want to be with her," but the words wouldn't form around the enormous lump that had lodged in her throat. What happened now would affect the rest of her life, and she needed time to go through the shreds of her feelings, from her elation when dancing to the ashes of her hopes now. She would never be with Bea. There wasn't really an option. Her parents would never allow it, society would never accept it, and the church would always condemn it.

Her father, normally so taciturn, fixed her with a stern eye. "Look up, child. Your mother has proposed a solution. I understand you young people are in such a hurry to pair up before the coming war."

She willed herself not to blink again, although the stinging in her nose and throat was building as she fought to stem the tears.

"Mother says Mr Waites has asked you to marry him. Do you wish to do that?"

Maud swallowed hard. What was the choice? Maud would never be popular. She was too tall and gawky for that, and she wasn't beautiful or charming like Bea. Harry teased her that she was too grumpy to find a husband, and she had no financial independence. The grandfather clock ticked noisily. She couldn't speak the words.

"You will either marry George Waites and repent, or you will leave this house. I will not have a sinner under my roof," her mother said, clearly impatient with the silence.

Maud was glad she was sitting, as her entire body collapsed as if someone had punched her in the gut. She couldn't stop her hands from trembling, and she swallowed the acid in her throat. Her mind hurtled out of control with erratic thoughts she couldn't grasp. "But what about Violet? I can't leave her." It wasn't what was uppermost in her mind, but she wasn't able to express her conflicting emotions into a coherent argument.

Mother placed her hands in her lap, as though everything was decided. "You should have thought of that before."

A log shifted position in the fire and a single flame curled up, a writhing tongue of yellow and orange. A couple of sparks spat and drifted upwards like fireflies. The clock ticked. What was she supposed to say? What could she do?

Her father coughed, and his chest wheezed as he struggled to catch his breath. Her mother flashed Maud a disapproving stare, as if to reinforce that her father's cough got worse when he was stressed.

"We asked George Waites to come back this evening, and he should be waiting in the drawing room now. Shall we invite him in here so you can accept his offer?"

Her father frowned. "This is important, Maud; this is for life. You are very young. Are you sure you want to marry him?"

Maud opened her mouth but nothing came out, so she cleared her throat. She was sure she *didn't* want to marry him, but what was the alternative? They didn't need to repeat the ultimatum; it was very clear. She was chained by dependence and had no choice. Her dinner turned to lead in her stomach. "Can I think about it?"

Mother's face reddened. "What is there to think about?"

Her father cleared his throat and squeezed Mother's shoulder. "It's a big decision, give her that."

Her father was siding with her? Maud flashed him a look of thanks, and he gave the briefest of nods. Mother's mouth became even more pinched, and she tapped her fingernails on the arm of the wing-backed chair.

"Fine, you have twenty-four hours, assuming Mr Waites is still amenable. You will come with me all day tomorrow to clean the brasses in the church and to allow some quiet prayer and reflection. You will speak to no one, and I mean no one, about this, including Harry."

CHAPTER THIRTEEN

THE FOLLOWING EVENING, Maud once again sat in the parlour, facing her parents. Her thoughts churned like unset butter, and she hadn't slept or been able to concentrate all day. She loved Bea, but she couldn't afford to keep herself, and she loved Harry and Violet and didn't want to leave. She couldn't imagine being here and not having Bea around. Maybe if she had a really long engagement, she could put off marrying until after the war.

Maud looked down at her hands, traces of Brasso evident under her fingernails, and she could still smell the trace of the alcohol and ammonia from the cleaning solvent. Her mother had made flower arrangements most of the day and chatted to her friends while Maud did the grimy work.

"Well?" her mother asked as they settled in their chairs. "Shall I ask Mr Waites to come in?"

Maud picked at the dirt under her fingernails. "Yes, invite him in," she whispered. Her mother strode out with a speed unbecoming of a lady, clearly concerned Maud would change her mind. George accompanied her mother back in the room. He stood stiffly at attention, concern etching furrows in his brows. He tried to catch Maud's glance, but she kept her head bowed, watching him in her peripheral vision.

"Mr Waites, I understand you would like my daughter's hand in marriage," her father said.

"Yes, sir, with your permission of course, sir."

"And Maud, do you consent to marry Mr Waites?"

All eyes focused on her. Oh, how she hated being the centre of attention. She didn't know which was worse, that whatever she said would taste like ash in her mouth, the lies, or the guilt. She cleared her throat and held her head high, staring directly at her father. "Yes, I will marry him."

Relief passed over George's face as he grasped her hand and squeezed hard. "Thank you, thank you. I can go away knowing I have someone at home now, someone to write to."

How strange that he seemed more interested in having a correspondent than a wife. A wall of rejection built up inside her, but she dismissed it as stupid. She would try to explain to Bea. She knew it was the wrong choice, but what were the options? They didn't need to wed until the war was over, and things would be different then. She could only hope that Bea would wait for her.

Maud let George take her hand. He was a good man, but there was no way she could ever love him. She loved Bea, beautiful, intelligent, fun Bea, but maybe friendship was loving girlfriends and tolerating husbands. And who knew what would happen in the war.

"Would you like to take a walk with me, Miss Maud? It's still so light out."

He clearly expected her to accede, as he held out the crook of his arm. She nodded, not trusting herself to speak.

"What an excellent idea. Congratulations to both of you and I'm so glad it has worked out."

Maud tried to respond in kind, but her mouth refused to cooperate and grit filled her eyes. She followed George out in a trance. As they exited the parlour, she caught sight of Harry trying to attract her attention. "Will you excuse me, George, I need to change my shoes. I'll meet you outside the front door." Without waiting for a reply, she rushed back to her brother.

"So, you're to marry Waites?" Harry asked.

"How do you know?"

He tapped the side of his nose, which probably meant he'd been eavesdropping. "And you don't have any thoughts about anyone else?"

Maud felt a blush burn her cheeks and quickly averted her face to avoid him noticing.

"If you're betrothed, there's no harm done in passing on a message." He grinned. "From Bea—Miss Williams. She asked me to tell you 'rabbits,' and she would wait as long as possible."

Her eyes filled with tears. She coughed. "Harry, please will you come with me? I've to go on a walk with George, and I need you to keep him entertained so I can just speak to Bea." She almost choked as she spoke. The look of triumph slipped from his face. Maud bit her lip, her head throbbing and her eyes stinging. "I have to say goodbye...please."

"Sure," he said and tapped the pockets in which he kept his cigarettes. "Let's go."

"I'll get different shoes and meet you out front."

He nodded and whistled as he opened the front door. As she disappeared towards the back door, she heard him greeting George with a teasing tone, commiserating with him for being lumbered with her.

The walk to the rabbit field seemed endless, and George stroked her hand clasped within his elbow. He was a good man, Maud repeated to herself, but prayed that Bea had not left. As they approached, a thrill skittered through her, and she exhaled a breath she didn't know she'd been holding. Bea was there, lying prone, watching the rabbits playing and feeding on the meadow opposite.

On cue, Harry whipped out his packet of cigarettes and offered one to George. George looked uncertain.

"Go on." said Harry. "Do you really want to listen to them prattling about knitting or some such? Which team do you support?" He walked past the field gate, and George followed.

Eager to escape, Maud hurried to Bea and chewed her lip as Bea continued to focus ahead. "May I join you?"

Bea nodded and slowly lifted her head. Her face was stained with tear tracks, and her eyes were bloodshot, the image of misery. Maud's heart bled for her as she crouched and brushed Bea's cheek. Bea clutched at her fingers.

"Oh, Bea, I'm so sorry. I had no option but to say yes to George; they threatened to throw me out of the house and disown me. Unlike you, I've no means of support and am not going on to study. I'm sorry they dismissed you from your job." Maud dropped into a sitting position and crossed her legs, still gripping onto Bea's hand.

Bea shrugged. "It's understandable. I've put my name down for the Wrens and I'm waiting for a call for an interview. My father also said he'd put in a word for me." She glanced at Maud, her fingers tightening around hers.

The touch was warm, soft, transmitting love and hurt, as clearly as if she had tapped it out in Morse code. Maud tried to speak around the lump in her throat. "Aren't you going back to Cambridge?"

Bea studied their joined fingers, and she brushed the back of Maud's hand. "It must wait."

"Will you write to me?" Maud asked, finding the tension between them so difficult to bear.

Bea swallowed hard, unable, or unwilling, to meet Maud's eye. "When

I can."

What did that mean? Normally Bea was so precise. Didn't she get it? "I won't marry George soon, not till after the war, so I can earn some money and work out how we can be together."

Bea nodded but still stared at their interlocked hands. Maud looked up and blinked to stop the tears. On the other side of the field, the rabbits scurried out of their burrow and nibbled at the grass. This would always remind her of Bea, like the wood where they kissed, and the library where they exchanged their first coded message. The library had always been her sanctuary but would now be a sore memento of everything that had been wonderful and would now be gone. Bea would be gone. Maud cleared her throat. "I need to get out of here. I can't bear to be here and see reminders of you everywhere. I love you."

Bea's head shot up, and Maud couldn't help but be entranced by her eyes, now glassy and bloodshot, even though her expression was one of pain and hurt. "Please don't tell me that now. I can't deal with it." Bea rubbed at her cheek with the back of her free hand.

"I also want to be of service in the war, not sit on the sidelines, but I'm too young. And I need to earn my own money, so I'm not dependent on anyone."

"You can join the Land Army at seventeen and a half," Bea said, her voice clogged with emotion.

Maud lifted Bea's palm and gave it a quick kiss, hoping the men weren't watching. Fortunately, the hedge was in full leaf. "Is that what you think I should do?"

Bea sat up facing Maud, focusing on her with an intensity that could burn metal. "I need to know, if you could be with me and we could make a living for us both, would you do so?"

Maud nodded. "In an instant. Even if we go to hell, as my father claims."

"Poor love." Bea cupped Maud's cheek. "I don't believe in hell. Let's write and hold onto the hope of finally being together."

"I'll wait. But what about George, and my par—"

Bea kissed her on the lips with a hunger and ferocity that surprised Maud, and she responded, desperately trying to anchor the moment in her memory to cling to in the weeks and months ahead. Maud pulled away as she heard male voices on the other side of the hedge. "I need to go. Please write. I love you," she whispered.

They both jumped up, and the rabbits scattered to the safety of their burrows. Bea patted down her dress. They reached the gate just as the men approached from the other side.

George Waites bowed to Bea. "Miss Williams."

"Mr Waites. Congratulations on your engagement. You could not have chosen a more wonderful person to be your wife," Bea said.

To the untrained eye, there was no trace she had been crying in the field just a few minutes ago. Maud admired Bea's poise and acting skills.

"Thank you. Good luck with your studies," George said.

"I've signed up for the Wrens to help the war effort. We'll all be dragged in and need to be prepared."

Bea seemed so certain, so clear, it made Maud wilt. Despite all the talk, she hoped it would still be averted, but now it seemed so real. The likelihood that they would all meet up again seemed slim.

"I've signed up for the Royal Engineers," Harry said, looking down as he ground his cigarette butt into the dirt.

Maud shivered in a cold sweat. Her world was collapsing by the minute. "No."

"I'll join Bill. We reckon we can spend the war mending vehicles and won't have to see active service. They'll probably be enlisting men soon, and we won't have a choice anyway. We may as well put our skills to the test. Bill's going to be an officer because he's finished his degree. I guess I must be a sapper. A dapper sapper." He preened his lapels and laughed, but it was mirthless.

Dread spread over her like a summer thunderstorm. *Please don't leave me.* "Is the war really going to happen?"

Harry and Bea both said yes. Maud's stomach churned. "Have you told Mother and Father yet?"

"Not yet. There's been quite a lot of drama in the house already this week." Harry cast a sidelong glance at Bea. "Maud, you must look after the twins and Sprocket, as Mother won't cope."

"But I want to be of service too."

"Hah, you'll never get into anything with those thick glasses you wear. Anyway, you're too young."

"I'm going to apply to the Land Army." It seemed strange saying it out loud, but also so right and solidified her decision. She would pick up the application forms tomorrow. Bea caught her gaze and gave the tiniest of nods.

"We'd best be going. Miss Williams, can I escort you home?" Harry asked.

"Thank you. Goodbye, Maud." Bea stretched up and pecked Maud on her cheek before she turned to George. "Goodbye, Mr Waites."

They spun and headed in separate directions. Maud flicked her head around to see Bea doing the same. Bea blew her a kiss. Not wanting to cry, Maud turned to the front as George rattled on about the planes he hoped to fly in the RAF. She touched the spot on her cheek where Bea had kissed her. When would they meet again? She would wait for as long as she could deflect George and earn enough to live and escape her parents' influence. There were so many imponderables, and now Harry was going away. Maud's world was collapsing, and life would be miserable without them. *Please let them be safe.*

When she finally extricated herself from George at the front door, she rushed away before he could kiss her and ran upstairs to hide in her bedroom. She lay on her back, staring at the ceiling in the dim light of the dying embers, trying to work out her escape plan. She would apply to join the Land Army tomorrow and earn her own money and independence, so she didn't need to return home or marry George. She needed to endure the war. Bea would wait for her, she'd promised, but it was all so precarious. The hopes and wishes of the glorious summer were burnt like a log hollowed out by flames. One touch and everything would crumble to ash.

CHAPTER FOURTEEN
Staffordshire, present day

THE KNOCK ON Maud's door made her look up from her crossword. "Come in." She hated how her voice sounded so weak and vulnerable, like a penny whistle in a brass band. She placed the paper and the pen down carefully so it wouldn't roll off the table. She'd already lost a couple of pens that way and had to wait until a visitor or carer arrived to pick them up for her.

Katherine entered, carrying a box and two envelopes. "Hello, Maud."

Her once-blonde hair was steel grey now, matching her eyes. When did she begin to look older? Maud still recalled her as a fresh-faced solicitor trying to break into the closed ranks of the county set. Maud smiled. "Good morning, Katherine, how lovely to see you." And she meant it.

"I've got some good news," Katherine said.

She settled herself in the second wing-back chair and placed the box on the table between them. She moved the pen and newspaper to the side, and Maud eyed it, checking the pen didn't roll.

"I've seen Bea, and she asked me to scribe a message, but it's all in Morse code. If there are mistakes, it will be my transcription." She shook one envelope. "Would you like me to open it?"

"Please," Maud said. "Damn hands." She inhaled deeply. "How is she? Can I see her?"

"The home she's in is in Derwich, about five miles away." Katherine opened the envelope and handed over the folded paper.

It was written in Katherine's neat hand and was a mass of lines and dots. Maud's lips twitched in anticipation. "I'll read that later." She carefully put the letter on top of the crossword, smoothed down her skirt, and stared at her visitor. "Can I go to that home? Could I stay there?"

Katherine sighed and tapped the other envelope on her leg. She was a great solicitor and good at hiding her feelings, but Katherine tapping with her hands was a tell that she was annoyed or upset. Maud had seen it occasionally over the years. Even before she spoke, Maud suspected the answer was no.

"Unfortunately, Amanda has been very clear about only trustees making decisions or taking you anywhere, even to visit."

Amanda. Maud clenched her fists. The woman's true side was coming out now, like a flag unfurled for the enemy. She had staked her claim of selfishness and greed where before, she was cloaked in concern and deference. A thousand needles of anger and frustration pierced Maud's heart. How foolish she had been to trust this self-serving, ambitious woman.

"So, I'm in prison here. Like Lear, cast out by his relatives." Maud turned to look into Katherine's eyes, seeking the truth. "I wish I'd made you a trustee. Can I change the trust now?"

"Only with the agreement of the other trustees."

Katherine's gaze was filled with sorrow and concern. Her expression showed genuine compassion, unlike Amanda, who was all slick smiles and selfishness. Maud banged the edge of her chair. There was no way Amanda would change anything; it was too settled in her favour. Matthew would never stand up to Amanda, and Hannah was absent. She huffed out a breath. Anger wouldn't solve anything. What would Bea do? "Hatch an escape plan." Maud could almost see the cheeky grin split Bea's face, and her eyes twinkle. She stroked Bea's letter on the table. A clock ticked and outside, the faint hum of a lawnmower drifted through the open windows. "You haven't said how Bea is?"

"Honestly, I think she's bored. It's so difficult, because she's virtually blind and deaf, but I'm going to get her a Braille reader, so she can read ordinary books. She'll have to learn the language and increase the sensitivity of her fingers, but she'll see that as a challenge." Katherine cleared her throat, as if debating how much to impart. "Bea spends her time wandering around the small yard with her white cane, quoting poems or Shakespeare. The carers think she's mad."

"Yard? I thought there was a garden?" Maud cast her gaze to the spring buds and trees as far as the eye could see. How wrong that she had a view of such beauty and all Bea had was a *yard*. If only Bea were here.

"They don't allow residents into the garden without a visitor or carer, and none of them have time. The enclosed yard is mainly gravel, making it difficult to walk on but easier to keep the residents in."

Maud dropped her head in her hands. "Bea, I'm so sorry. You'll think

I've abandoned you." Maud fixed Katherine with her well-practised stern gaze, and Katherine placed her hand on Maud's arm. "We've got to get her in here."

Katherine nodded. "Do you think if I wrote to Hannah?" Katherine lifted the other envelope.

Maud sighed. "Bea said I chased her away. And Hannah's busy; she's got her own life to lead, and she's writing up her PhD." She smiled, swelling her chest out. "Dr Hannah Jones has a nice ring to it."

Katherine handed over the second envelope. "She has sent you a card though, well, I think it's from her. It's postmarked Bristol." Maud clapped her hands together. A thrill shivered down her spine. "Open it, open it."

Katherine handed over the card titled *Moving Home?* with a cartoon snail on it. Maud's hands shook more than normal as she opened it. The written message in Hannah's untidy scrawl (they don't teach children proper handwriting these days) was, "Hey Gammy, hope you're settled in your new home. Love Hannah x"

Love and a kiss. Maud pressed it to her chest. "She wrote. She sent me a card." A tear fell, and she wiped it away with the back of her hand.

"Would you like me to write a reply?" Katherine rummaged through her bag and extracted a notebook and pen.

"Yes, please. And could I trouble you to visit Bea again? Did she know who you were?"

"Eventually. It was a bit like twenty questions. She got me to tap Morse code on her palm, y for yes, n for no." Katherine grinned. "She finally asked if I was the cute young solicitor. I was tempted to disagree—I think young is definitely stretching it—but I knew she was only teasing."

Maud chuckled. "That's such a Bea thing to say. My Bea. Can I send a coded message back? You'll need to tap it out though."

"You'd better give me clear instructions then."

"I always give my lawyer explicit instructions." The shift of her head and sudden firmness of her tone were but an echo of her former self. When she looked at her shaking hands and heard her feeble voice, she couldn't believe she had once established and run a successful accountancy practice, been mayor twice, and previously commanded a room when she entered. Katherine smiled, as if she too remembered how Maud had once been. Maud reflected on the smile, then sighed. "But do you have time, my dear? I've probably taken up too much as it is." Maud hoped she didn't sound desperate.

"The great thing about being the senior partner is I can do this. Besides, I'm visiting my oldest and most important client."

"Oldest is right," Maud said. "In that case, would you mind accompanying me on a tour around the garden first. Today is a good day, and I think I could walk with my stick, but you'd be there if I get into difficulties."

"Of course. It's a lovely day. We'll come back to the letters. Oh, and you haven't looked in the box."

Honestly, Maud wasn't interested in things. She had thrown away an entire lifetime of them in the last few months, but Katherine was looking at her with the eagerness of a child wanting to rip open a birthday present. She smiled at her excitement. "What is it?"

Katherine placed the box on the table further away than the precious letters and cards. She was thoughtful that way.

"I bought you an iPad so you can download books and increase the size of the font. You could also email Bea and maybe Hannah too. When Bea has a braille reader, she may pick up email."

"Bless you, Katherine, and I insist I pay for it all from the trust."

Katherine shifted in her seat. "I'm not sure you have access to funds. But I would gladly fund it all. You've both been so good to me."

Maud's hand fluttered to her chest. How was it that someone outside the family could be so kind and thoughtful, but her family didn't listen or didn't care? The place was luxurious, so they probably thought they were doing the best for her. And if she had been on her own, it may have been the best solution. She had no one to blame for all the secrets and lies but herself. She hadn't even told Katherine. No time like the present. Her heart pounded. How was it so hard to speak to this woman, her friend and lawyer, whom she had encouraged and supported for the past twenty-five years? Maud cleared her throat. "Did you know Bea and I were partners?"

Katherine laughed, a deep, genuine sound. "Oh, Maud, I know you've never said so, but I've guessed as much for many years. Bea was so wonderful, encouraging me when I was coming out—"

"Was she? I didn't know that. She never said. I mean, I knew you were gay, and I thought it was very brave of you, especially as the solicitor for traditional farmers. I could never do that."

Katherine held Maud's hands. "You paved the way, Maud, with your accountancy practice. And now, here you are at ninety-seven, coming out of the closet." Katherine leaned forward and kissed Maud on her forehead. "Now, what do you want to do first: sort out the iPad, write the letters, or go for a walk?"

"Walk, letter, iPad, in that order. I'll do it while my energy lasts." Maud rocked herself upright. She would also check the grounds for an escape route.

CHAPTER FIFTEEN
Bristol

HANNAH'S LEGS BURNED as she cycled up the side of Avon Gorge, along Bridge Valley Road from sea level to the Clifton Downs. Sweat slicked off her back in sheets despite the nip in the air. Why had she agreed to this? Her knee was aching, and she hoped it didn't pop again. This was much harder than frisbee.

"Coming through," Suki called and came up alongside her easily.

She was in a higher gear, Hannah realised, so each downstroke on the pedals took her further and faster. She was obviously not suffering like Hannah was.

"Race you home," Suki said and grinned across at Hannah.

"Yield!" Hannah gasped. There was no way she could keep up.

Suki cycled ahead, making it look so easy. "Get in my slipstream, and I'll tow you home. Keep low though, to reduce the drag on your over-tall body."

Hannah was too exhausted to challenge the quip. Her lungs were bursting, and she tried not to wobble as cars drove perilously close. The last bend came up, and it flattened out past the downs. She wanted to collapse in a heap, but Suki pulled her along. They got separated at traffic lights and when she finally arrived home, Suki had left the door on the latch and already put her bike in the hallway. Hannah hung her bike on the hooks on the wall and stretched gingerly. She dragged herself up the stairs, her muscles protesting. Her bed seemed soft and inviting so she flopped onto it, enjoying the cool sheets against her overheated body. She could stay here all day, but the smell of her own sweat wafted up, and she sat up and unpeeled her cycling gear. She needed a shower pronto, before her legs seized up completely.

"Shower's free," Suki called. "Cuppa?"

"Please." Hannah rolled off the bed and staggered to an upright position to make her way to the bathroom.

When she entered the living room half an hour later, Suki grinned.

"Who's the fittest then?"

Hannah held up her arms in surrender. How come they ached too? And she didn't want to think about her legs and how her thighs had chafed. It wasn't the first time she'd wished she could walk around the flat naked.

"Did you use the chamois cream beforehand?"

"Yes. And the Sudocrem after, but I'm still sore."

"Poor Han."

Hannah raised an eyebrow, unsure whether Suki was being sarcastic, but her face was neutral. She carefully lowered herself onto the sofa. Suki had placed her tea beside her. "Thanks for the tea."

"Sure." Suki put her mug on the side table, picked up an envelope, and waved it at Hannah. "You've got unopened mail. Handwritten, not the usual bills or junk."

Hannah sipped from her tea. "Where's it from?"

"The postmark is Stoke-on-Trent."

A sense of dread and irritation mingled for dominance within her. Her chest tightened, and guilt gnawed deep in her gut. She waved her hand at it, not wanting to read the contents. "It'll only be from Amanda insisting I do something or other for the family trust. I'm thinking of resigning." Her voice sounded lighter than she felt.

"You can't do that."

Hannah pulled both of her legs up on the sofa and wrapped her arms around them. "I think you'll find I can."

Suki handed the envelope over to Hannah, a deep frown carved between her eyebrows. "I don't understand. It's as if your family is dead to you. You're so lucky to have relatives living only a few hours away, not the other side of the world. Do you know how lonely that is? I wish I had family here." Suki sniffed, then shook her head. "You know what pisses me off most about the Connor thing? I turned down a great opportunity in Japan so I could be with him, and now I'm not with him anymore."

Hannah put down the letter and shuffled over to give Suki a hug. "You never have to be lonely. I'm here for you."

Suki sighed and cuddled into Hannah's side. Her body was warm and made Hannah tingle all over, including between her sore thighs. Hannah inhaled the fruity scent of Suki's hair products, and her heart quickened. Her libido was working despite her aching body.

Suki cuddled closer. "I know, but I..."

Hannah waited, holding her breath, but Suki didn't finish her sentence. "You're what, scared?"

Suki nodded. "No. Yes, I'm scared."

"Scared of what?"

Suki pulled away from the cuddle and reached for her tea. She was silent for a couple of minutes as she sipped, as though deciding what to say. "I'm fed up with being different, being the outsider. I just want to fit in."

It must have been hard for Suki to admit that as she looked away, putting her mug back on the side table, and not returning Hannah's gaze. Hannah reached over and gently pulled Suki's chin up with her index finger until their eyes met. "Why do you need to fit in? Why can't you just be your wonderful, unique self?"

Suki shook her head, pulling herself away from Hannah's touch and curling herself up. "You know who you are and where you belong, yet you turn your back on it. Because I'm half Japanese and half British, I always feel I'm an outsider. My family is on the other side of the world and if I tried to get back to Japan, I'd have to redo all my exams in order to practise, and then probably be rejected for being too English."

Hannah shuffled closer and took Suki's delicate fingers in her own, much larger, hands. She expected Suki might pull away, but she didn't. Hannah rolled her hand over to inspect, loving the softness of Suki's skin. She interwove their fingers. "Why does that make you scared?"

"Because I don't want to be judged for being with a woman as well as for being foreign."

Hannah squeezed her hand. "But they're just xenophobic, homophobic bigots—"

Suki let out an exasperated breath. "Who are my patients."

"Do you really think they give a fuck?"

Suki dipped her head, her shiny black mop catching the light. "Yes."

This conversation was getting nowhere, so Hannah decided on a different, more direct tack. "Okay. I get you're scared, but could you be open to being with a woman?" She held her breath.

Suki raised an eyebrow. "With you, you mean?"

"Well, I'd sacrifice myself and volunteer."

Suki punched her lightly on the arm and grinned. "Shut up and open your letter."

Damn, she'd blown it, and the moment was gone. Her shoulders sagged, but maybe she could still salvage something. "You mean you want me to read the boring minutes of the last trust meeting? And was that a yes?" Suki shrugged. "Why not?"

Hannah huffed. "Aargh, you're annoying. Yes to being open, or yes to reading out minutes?"

"Both. Now hurry and read."

Hannah uncoupled their fingers and picked up the letter. Well, that was a start. "I don't recognise the handwriting. It's not Amanda's or Matthew's." She chewed her lip, worrying at the scar where she used to have a lip ring. She withdrew a letter addressed from Gammy's care home.

Dearest Hannah,

Thank you so much for your moving home card. I can't tell you how much I enjoyed receiving it, especially as I know how busy you are with your PhD. I don't know if you remember my friend Katherine Braithwaite, my solicitor. She is kindly writing this out for me as my hands shake too much to be legible now.

The home is very luxurious with vast gardens backing onto farmland, so I can see out and watch the squirrels and the sheep in the distance. It would be lovely to see you if you ever come up this way.

Yours truly,
Love Gammy xx

Suki tucked her legs under her body. "That's a friendly letter. She sounds as though she is settling down okay, and she doesn't sound anything like the dragon you portray."

"Hm," Hannah said. "Maybe she's mellowed in her old age."

"Or maybe you have," Suki shot back. Her eyes fixed Hannah with an intense stare.

"Maybe. Wait, there's another page." Hannah shuffled the page from the back to the front and skimmed it before Suki prodded her with her foot to read it aloud.

Dear Hannah,

I hope you don't mind that I've written a postscript to the letter from your great aunt. Although she is settling in well, she's really upset that she cannot see Bea. Maybe you will understand why. As a trustee, you could authorise her seeing her, and if I may be frank, your cousin Amanda is not interested, and Matthew will only follow what she says. I would do it myself but don't have the authority. I understand you're busy, but it would mean the world to Maud if you could come and take her to see Bea. If transport is an issue, I'm happy to pick you up from the station and drive you around.

Yours,
Katherine.

Hannah put the letter down with trembling hands. How ridiculous, a letter shouldn't scare her, and yet…

"Go," Suki said.

Hannah shook her head. She couldn't go. Every visit was a reminder of the worst time in her life, before she found herself and her tribe in Bristol, academia, and the frisbee team. Every nerve jangled at the thought of the judgement and criticism that all but crushed her.

"She's your family."

"Suki, I know you have a really firm sense of duty and obligation, but she hated me when I was a teenager." Hannah moved to the other end of the sofa and put down the letter, blinking to stop the tears that prickled the back of her eyes. A headache brewed in her forehead. She laid her head on her knees, drawn up close to her chest.

Suki touched her forearm. "She took you in, didn't she?"

Hannah had only discussed this with Jess, and many years before, with Meg. Suki deserved more of the truth. "She was so critical," Hannah said around the lump in her throat. She couldn't quite fathom why she felt so raw.

Suki stroked Hannah's forearm. "Have you thought you might have been really difficult and angry with the world, because you'd just lost your mum and grandmother?"

Hannah jerked bolt upright, her pulse pounding in her head. "So? I was judged the whole time. Just like you hate being judged at work, I hated it at home. I was never good enough. It's not surprising I rebelled." She snatched up her mug and busied herself rinsing it out and leaving it to drain. Hannah breathed in deeply, but the headache was blossoming into a full-blown migraine. She opened the drawer to get tablets and poured herself a glass of water, wincing at the noise.

"If you won't write to her and see her, I will," Suki said.

Heat flared in Hannah's head, and she gripped the kitchen counter. "You can't."

"Why not?"

"She hates the Japanese." Hannah swigged down the pills with the water and placed the glass in the sink. She walked back to the sitting area with one eye half closed. "It's why I had to get out. I couldn't stand her xenophobia."

Suki shrunk into a ball, into what Hannah thought of as her hedgehog pose, prickles to the ready. Hannah braced herself for the onslaught. Maybe she should retire to her bedroom now and sleep off the headache.

Suki shifted and sat up, turning to face Hannah. "All the more reason for you to be the one to put all that aside and see her for who she is now: a lonely old lady. Be open to it and be open to her, just as you want me to be open to you."

Hannah rolled her shoulders and clutched her head in her hand. "I'm going to lie down for a while." She caught sight of Suki's eyebrow raise. "All right, I'll think about it." As she slipped under the duvet, every part of her aching, she had to admit that Suki was right; Hannah had to be the bigger person.

CHAPTER SIXTEEN

A WEEK LATER, SUKI was curled up on the sofa with her legs tucked underneath her. She was reading her precious manga in the original Japanese that her cousin had mailed from Japan. It amazed Hannah how Suki could flip from Japanese to English and back.

Hannah rolled her shoulders to ease the tension built up over too many hours hunched up in the library on her laptop. She flopped onto her favourite spot on the floor and leaned against the sofa, with her legs stretched out in front of her. She picked up her Xbox controller to play and turned the sound down so she didn't disturb Suki. It was comfortable, companionable, and a great way to de-stress from the impending deadline.

Suki ran her fingers through Hannah's hair. She tilted her head to make it easier for Suki to reach. If she could have purred, she would have. She paused her game so she could enjoy the gentleness of touch and its mindless comfort. Who cared if it messed up her hair style?

Suki looked up from her book and stopped stroking. "You okay?" Suki asked softly.

"Always. Tea?" Hannah pulled up her legs, poised to rise.

"Mm, thanks."

Suki resumed stroking Hannah's hair, leaving a thin trail of pleasure. Hannah almost didn't want to get up. She jumped up and tossed the joystick on the sofa behind her.

When she returned a few minutes later, Suki had put down her manga and was staring at the paused TV screen on *Battlefield*. "I don't understand the obsession of the Brits with the Second World War. I was thinking about your gammy's letters and diaries. I get being consumed with it when they lived through it, but now?"

Hannah passed Suki her mug and resumed her position on the floor, placing her own mug on the carpet. "I suppose for most people it was the most exciting time in their lives, frightening but exhilarating." Hannah grinned, knowing she was about to prod the tiger. "And the Brits won."

She snatched up a cushion, ready to defend herself, but the onslaught never came.

"No. The Americans won, and the Russians held up the Germans on the Eastern front."

"I'm only teasing." Hannah sipped at her tea.

"Don't," Suki said and put her tea on the coaster. "I was thinking about your gammy, though. In the letters you've shared so far, she doesn't come across as being the grumpy xenophobe you portray her as. She seems thoughtful, sensitive, and kind."

Hannah winced but didn't admit that she hadn't observed the judgemental woman she'd experienced as a teenager, either. Was there a truth in what Suki said? She put down the cushion and took a sip of tea. "Maybe she was changed by her experiences."

"Where have you got to in her letters and diaries?" Suki asked.

"Still early in the war when she was in the Land Army, and Bea had dropped out of Cambridge to join the Wrens. Do you want to hear some more?" Hannah set aside her mug and turned to Suki, who nodded, inserted a bookmark, and put her book on the side table. Hannah had bundled the letters into months and separated them with elastic bands between those from Bea to Gammy and the fewer letters from Gammy to Bea. "This one is from Gammy to Bea."

Suki clapped her hands together. "Ooh, we haven't heard many of those yet."

"They're not as frequent. I'm not sure if that means she had more people to write to, or she had less time."

"Maybe both."

"This is when Gammy was still engaged to George. It's postmarked Derbyshire, so she must have been posted to a farm there."

August 1940

Dearest B,

Thanks for your latest letter. This will be brief as I'm shattered. This is much harder than the training. Besides getting up at five to start the milking, we've been commandeered to help with the harvest and haven't finished till nine at night, with a break to milk the cows and feed the calves in the late afternoon. At least I can drive a tractor now, so I don't have to spend hours on back-breaking work with the pitchfork, but my eyes sting with the dust and I can't believe how filthy I get.

I envy you lodgings with a bathroom and electricity. We're still boiling water on the fire for the tin bath—the mandatory four inches, of course. How I'd love a nice long soak. Alice and I have to share the same water, although we've got a routine sorted now.

Thanks for sending chocolate. Mother does the same. We're hungry the whole time. Mind you, we're very lucky, some land girls staying in the hostel were getting stale bread and dripping. Their landlady was taking all their rations and selling them off on the black market. Good job they complained to get it changed.

As we thought, George failed the medical for flying in the RAF. His lazy eye means he doesn't have twenty-twenty vision. He's working as an airframe mechanic and says he hates it. He keeps trying to persuade me to take time off to see him, but I've put him off so far. Have you heard from Harry? He doesn't write often. Bill is in London, making houses safe after the bombing. He doesn't say much, but it sounds horrible.

How is the stray settling in; did you call her Lovelace in the end? Or did you decide you couldn't stand at the back door calling Lovie?

I enclose a photograph of me on top of a hayrick.

Good night, my dearest B.
88
M

"Well, that could just be any letter between friends, couldn't it? Especially as she was engaged at the time," Suki said.

Hannah put the letter back into the stack. "Except Katherine's comment about Gammy and Bea implies there was more."

"Have you organised going up to the home?"

Damn. She shouldn't have mentioned the solicitor. "I might go up next weekend. I'll have submitted my next chapter by then. But I'm waiting to hear from Jess whether they need me for the frisbee."

"Can't frisbee wait?"

Hannah flung her hand at her chest in mock hurt. "But we're aiming to get into a higher league next year, so every game is important. And although I'm not the most athletic, being tall helps as I'm a good target to aim for."

"But you said you would be open to going."

Yeah, as much as you've been open to being with me. But this was nice and companionable. Who was she kidding? This was more than a flatmate, friendship thing. The way her body responded to Suki, how her heart stuttered when she saw her in the morning looking cute in her pyjamas, and how she wished she could take away the pain if Suki had a bad day at work. She really wanted it to work with Suki, and if that meant she had to go and see her gammy, so be it. "I said I'm thinking about it, so by definition, I'm open to it." She flashed her cheekiest grin, hoping to placate Suki.

"I don't trust you. Just read another letter."

"Okay." Hannah took another paper from the sheaf of letters. She wrangled her shoulders, trying to get the stiffness out.

"Still sore?" Suki asked.

"Yep." Hannah rolled her shoulders again and stretched her back. She needed to sort out a more comfortable seating arrangement or she'd end up with permanent back damage. There was a clunk as Suki placed her mug on the coaster, and she scooted along the sofa behind Hannah. She placed her delicate hands on Hannah's shoulders. A frisson of electricity sparked from her touch, and Hannah groaned as Suki massaged her.

"Does that hurt?"

Too embarrassed to say the groan was one of pleasure, Hannah lied. "I need to spend less time on those hard library chairs and prop up my laptop, so I'm not bending so much."

"You shouldn't be so tall." Suki pushed her thumbs in hard to work on the knots.

"I'm only five eleven, not a midget like you. Ow!" She rubbed her head where Suki had slapped it.

"You deserve it. Keep reading about Gammy and Bea."

"Only if you continue with the shoulder rub." Hannah pulled the next set of letters she had towards her. Suki leaned over Hannah's shoulder, peering at the handwriting. Her breath was so warm on her ear, it was all Hannah could do not to turn and kiss her. Suki smelt of floral perfume and apple hair products, the scent that was uniquely Suki. Hannah attempted not to be too obvious that she was inhaling deeply and revelling in it.

Hannah had to concentrate hard to continue with the letter as Suki dug her thumbs into the knots of her neck. "This letter is dated March 1941, from Gammy to Bea."

Dearest B,

I see from the postmark that you must have a new posting. I know you can't say what you're doing, but it doesn't sound like you're by the sea. I hope you're not disappointed, as you said you wanted to have a bit of sea air. Are they nice billets, do you have electricity and an inside bathroom? It's been so icy here. The cattle slip and slide on the concrete even though we've put down ashes from the fire. When we're trying to clean down afterwards, the water is freezing over so we have to sweep harder and faster. I don't think I've ever been so cold. We sleep in our clothes, and twice Alice has slipped into bed with me to keep warm. Don't get jealous. Whenever we wake the frost is creeping up the inside of the windows, it makes beautiful patterns, but I dream of being warm again.

Suki leaned even further over. "Did she really say don't get jealous? Do you think Bea was keen?"

Hannah didn't reply immediately as she was enjoying Suki being squashed against her shoulder. *Stop it.* Whatever this was, it had to be at Suki's pace. Hannah inhaled and caught Suki's fruity fragrance. "I guess. Okay, where was I? Oh. yes."

George had time off last weekend. He came up to see me and persuaded Mr Hardy to let me go early. I see what you mean about men. All he wanted to do was get me into bed, even though I kept saying to him I wouldn't sleep with anyone until we married. He was really quite cross. When I told Alice she said I was just frightened about 'it' and said 'you get used to it.' She should know, she's out any opportunity she can, always going out to the cinema in the village hall or the open-air dance on Markeaton Park. I don't know what she sees in it all.

Goodnight, my dearest B.

88

M.

"Well, that's a pretty clear sign she didn't want sex with a man or didn't want sex with that man," Suki said.

"Is that how it was with Connor?" Hannah worried at her lip ring scar, but Suki didn't seem annoyed.

Suki shrugged. "I guess."

She leaned forward again and where her body touched Hannah's, a trail of fireworks shot to her core. It was all Hannah could do to not kiss her.

"What did Bea reply to that?" Suki's eyes shone in anticipation.

"I can't imagine she was thrilled, but I don't see a reply. The next seems to be another letter from Gammy. Right now, I need another cuppa. Chamomile?" Hannah jumped up before she did something she really shouldn't. But oh, she wanted to.

CHAPTER SEVENTEEN
Derbyshire, March 1941

THE LOG SETTLED in the tiny grate and gave out more aroma than warmth, but Maud was thrilled to have some time alone to write her letters. Alice wouldn't be back from the cinema until curfew. She pulled her quilt around her shoulders as she wrote to Harry, trying to think up funny incidents from the farm that would make him laugh.

The knock at the door made Maud jump.

"Are you decent? There's a phone call for Miss Heaston," said Mrs Hardy.

Maud heard Mrs Hardy's footsteps retreat on the squeaky stairs. She scrambled from under the quilt and grabbed a cardigan as the evening chill ran through her. Not Harry, please, not Harry. Maud galloped down the stairs, two at a time after Mrs Hardy, who was taking it more carefully because of her bad knees.

"The phone is in the hall. It's a woman."

Mrs Hardy pointed and returned to the sitting room, closing out the heat and the light from the hallway. A small sliver of light seeped out from under the door. A woman? It could only be Mother. Her heart hammering in her chest, Maud approached the large black telephone, which had pride of place on the hall table, and snatched up the receiver. "Mother? What's happened?" She tried to tamp down the panic rising in her chest.

There was a peal of laughter down the line, accompanied by loud background noises. "I hope you don't ever think of me as your mother. Hello, M."

Maud let out the breath she'd been holding, and a cosy feeling wrapped around her like a warm quilt on a wintry day. The sound of Bea's voice thrilled her to her core. "Bea, is that really you?" Maud's heart hammered now but for a completely different reason. All her cells tingled with excitement to speak with her love again.

"Unless you have someone else tucked away?" Bea's tone was full of mischief and delight.

Guilt nibbled at her a little. She hadn't written to George and let him down yet, as she had promised Bea she would. "I can't believe it's you. It's wonderful to hear your voice. Where are you? How did you find the number?"

Bea laughed again, that delighted laugh that sent goosebumps all down Maud's spine. Maud curled the braided cord around her fingers and wished it was Bea's golden curls.

"All I can say is that I'm in a pub in England. Although you'll probably receive mail posted from everywhere. My father received a letter from the next village along, and he knew I wasn't there. Anyway, it was simple. I know where you are in Derbyshire so narrowed it down to a Mr Hardy based at a farm. Bingo."

She made it seem so easy, maybe for Bea it was, but then she was so much smarter than Maud. "It's lovely to hear from you, but why?"

"I wanted to hear your voice and to tell you I miss you, and I think about you all the time."

Someone must have overheard and made some rude comments because Maud heard Bea say, "I'd have to be desperate to take that offer, Walters...."

"I love you, M."

Bea's words warmed Maud despite the chill nipping at her ankles, and she glanced down the hall to make sure no one was listening. "I do too. I must tell you that I haven't written to George yet."

"Oh."

The joy in Bea's voice evaporated like a light being extinguished. Was that why Bea had really called, because she'd said about meeting up with George? She should have been less cowardly and spoken to him, but he was angry enough as it was and really upset about the flying. Nevertheless, she should have done it for Bea. She thrust her spare hand in her pocket to keep warm, but the cold was seeping through her socks, into her feet, and up her legs. She curled her toes. If Bea had been angry and shouted, Maud would find that easier, but the hurt and sorrow of her simple one-word response was too hard to bear. "But I will. It's just that the RAF rejected him again because of his eye, and he sounds really down at the moment. His dad is hoping to get him transferred into the Air Transport Auxiliary. The timing didn't seem right."

Bea sighed. Maud swallowed, and she glanced at the sitting-room door. It was dark except for a strand of light showing beneath it. "It's hard to talk but I do, you know..."

"Love me?" Bea whispered.

"Yes." This tense conversation was almost worse than not speaking at all. Her thoughts and feelings bubbled to the surface, ones that she'd tried so hard to push down and forget about. Maud pulled her cardigan around her. The door from the sitting room opened, spilling light and heat into the hallway. Mrs Hardy stood, framed in the glow, and tapped pointedly at her watch, then closed the door again.

"I need to go, it's nearly curfew. Thank you for calling. I'll get onto that when I can. Eighty-eight." She referred to the amateur radio code for love and kisses that Bea had taught her.

"Okay, my love. Eighty-eight to you too."

Bea's voice seemed downbeat and disappointed. In the background, the pub seemed to get more rowdy with a rendition of "The Lambeth Walk" being played on an out of tune piano. Maud placed the handset on the receiver. The silence stressed the fluttering of her heart. Was Bea fed up with her? In less than a breath's span, the sitting-room door swung open, and Mrs Hardy came into view again. She must have been waiting for the call to end, listening in, no doubt.

"The telephone is for emergency use only, not for idle chitchat."

"Sorry, Mrs Hardy, it was my friend. My fiancé hasn't got the posting he wanted and is feeling quite down." Maud mentally crossed herself. All the lies that were tripping off her tongue. She prayed she would never be held to account for them at the final reckoning.

Mrs Hardy sniffed loudly. "Well, we all have to do things we don't want to in this war. He needs a bit of backbone. No more calls unless it's an emergency."

"Understood, Mrs Hardy. Good night." Maud fled upstairs, hoping their room would be empty so she could unravel her emotions and examine them in peace, but Alice was lying on her bed, her face ruddy from running to get in the house before they locked the doors at ten sharp.

"Who were you talking to on the telephone? Was it your fiancé?"

For a second, Maud almost told the truth, but it would make it awkward, especially as they occasionally shared a bed to keep warm. "George hasn't got into the flying training in the RAF he had set his heart on." Was obfuscation by deflection less of a lie than a direct untruth? Maud hoped so, as she seemed to walk the tightrope more frequently.

"What will he do?" Alice stepped out of her dress and slip, keeping on her undergarments beneath her pyjamas and bed socks.

"His father is trying to get him transferred into the ATA."

Alice snuggled under the quilt. "I met a real dish. His name is Colin, he works at the airfield. I'm going to meet him again at the dance at the weekend. Will you come?"

Maud's breath caught as she thought back to the last dance she had with Bea, but everything had changed after that. Alice was clearly waiting for a reply. "I don't think so. I'm a rubbish dancer, and the last dance I went to I spent almost all my time dancing with my brothers, because no one else would and they had promised not to ditch me."

"Come on, you never come out. You need to let your hair down and have some fun. Are you ready to blow out the candle?"

"No. Will it disturb you if I continue to write my letters?"

Alice wore a sly smile. "You and your letters. I'll agree if you come on Saturday."

Maud shrugged and picked up a fresh piece of paper and wrapped her quilt around her shoulders as she settled at the tiny desk. She picked up her fountain pen and wrote in her neat copperplate handwriting.

Dearest B,

What a lovely surprise to hear you on the telephone. Not one to be repeated, unfortunately, as Mrs Hardy told me in no uncertain terms that the telephone was for emergencies only. But still it was worth it, if only to hear your voice. Did you join in the singing?

Alice thinks I should go to the dance with her on Saturday, but she just needs a companion so she can meet her new dish, Colin. She only just makes it back in time for curfew. One day she's going to miss it completely!

Nothing will compare with dancing with you to Glenn Miller's record, and I really don't want to go, but Alice can be quite persuasive. I can't believe you found out where I'm living and working. You're so clever.

I will inform G, but please, I need you to trust me as to the timing.

I had better finish now as we have a very early start, as usual.

Goodnight, my dearest B.
88
M.

CHAPTER EIGHTEEN
May, 1941

WHEN MAUD HAD finished the milking, she strode out to the open pastures and joined Alice on the large top meadow. It had an impressive aspect looking across the wide valley towards Derby. The sun was heating up, and as Maud approached, Alice stood and stretched her back as if easing her tender muscles.

"No tractor work today?" Alice asked.

Maud shook her head and handed over a cup of warm tea from her flask. "The tractor needs repairs, so Hardy's not happy. He sent me up here to help you with the thistles."

Alice took the cup, trickles of blood seeping from her palms.

"Where are your gloves?" Maud asked.

"Can't find them. Think one of the men nicked them for a joke."

Alice's curled lip indicated what she thought about that. Maud swigged her sweet milky tea; it was still hot and burned her throat slightly. "I wish they would just leave us be. Is it not bad enough that we get the coldest, dirtiest jobs?" There was no point complaining though. The workers made it very clear what they thought about having women on their farms. But they'd survived one of the coldest winters, and it was supposed to be getting easier now. She looked at Alice's hands, shredded by the thistles.

Out of the pocket of her breeches, Maud extracted the soft driving gloves that had belonged to Harry. *Harry, wherever you are, I hope you don't mind me using them for this emergency.* She stroked the soft leather gauntlet style gloves and handed over the left glove to Alice, in exchange for the cup.

"I can't take that, Maud. Aren't they your brother's?"

"Yes, but he would understand, after he teased me mercilessly." She smiled at that thought, put the flask and cups back in her cloth satchel, and placed it at the side of the gate, so she wouldn't forget it. "Let's get on with it."

Alice put the glove on and stooped to pull the thistles by hand, having loosened the soil with a fork. "If Hardy looked after his fields properly, we shouldn't have to do this. Try to get every bit of them up, or they'll just grow back again."

Alice sang as she methodically pulled and dug. Maud covered a much smaller area than Alice, but Alice was the expert, although she'd envisaged working in greenhouses during the war, growing tomatoes and cucumbers rather than slogging in the fields.

By lunchtime, Maud could hardly stand, and every muscle ached. Sweat poured off her forehead and down her back. She was so glad she was normally on tractors. Despite the glove, she had cuts and scratches all over her arms. She handed over the salmon paste sandwiches to Alice and set the flask of tea down on the ground.

Alice glanced around. "There's no one here, let's take our shirts off. It's so hot."

Maud stared at her. "Are you mad?"

"Come on, we're entitled to have half an hour for lunch, and I don't know about you, but I'm roasting." Alice had already whipped off her shirt and tucked it under her head so she could rest in the sun.

"Okay." Maud unbuttoned her blouse, then saw a dark shape of a plane flying just above the hedgerows out of the sun.

"Cheeky RAF boys wanting to take a closer look," Alice said.

But something about the sound wasn't right. Instead of the continuous roar of the engines, the engine pulsed. "Move!" Maud shouted and dragged Alice into a ditch. Time stilled.

An explosion of machine-gun fire burst, strewing bullets where they'd been sitting, scuffing dust, twirling the makeshift picnic in the air, and lodging in the soil and undergrowth. The noise exploded in her head, and vibrations thrummed down to her toes as the machine roared overhead.

Still shaking and stinging from the nettlebed, Maud peeped over the edge of the ditch. The plane pulled up sharply, sprung by two British planes that chased it across the wide valley. It was like watching a movie reel in colour. They stood and cheered, but the German plane rolled and jinked behind the British fighter and released a torrent of bullets, bringing it down. They watched and waited until finally a parachute opened, as vulnerable as a dandelion drifting in the wind. Meanwhile, the second British plane fired at the German plane that listed earthwards in a plume of smoke and exploded on impact on the other side of the valley. The whole incident had probably taken only minutes. They stared at each other, wide-eyed and shaking. Alice rolled over and reached for her satchel. Maud heard the click of a lighter, which brought her out of her stupor.

"He deliberately tried to go for us," Alice said. She took a long drag then handed the cigarette to Maud with shaking hands.

If they hadn't moved, they would be dead or injured now. It didn't matter that they weren't combatants, and that they were defenceless women. How cruel and random war was. Would anyone have told Bea if she had died, or would Bea just have had letters returned and think Maud didn't care anymore or didn't love her? And could a message have been sent to Harry, wherever he was in the world? Maud tried to inhale but only coughed. "I suppose we're providing food." Maud returned the cigarette, her hands still trembling. "And he got our boy, I hope he survived."

Alice inhaled a drag. "He was going for us," she repeated, her eyes unfocussed, as though she couldn't comprehend what had happened. She blew out a distorted smoke ring.

"I know, that could have been George." Maud's heart rate returned to normal. She wiped her palms on her breeches, the sweat stinging the tiny nicks and scratches from the thistles. "Except the ATA don't carry live weapons." *It makes them sitting ducks, just as we were.* A tremor of guilt swept over her, like a tepid bath on a freezing day. She had written to George to call off the engagement but hadn't had the courage to post it yet. Poor George must be scared every time he took off, and she would compound that by calling off the engagement. He didn't deserve that; he was a good man. She looked across at Alice. She ought to tell her really, but now wasn't the time, and it would mean having to explain about Bea. Would Alice feel differently about their friendship and about sharing lodgings with her? She couldn't risk it. Alice was the only thing that made the whole thing bearable. Maud looked up to where Alice was standing. Her face had lost all colour. She held up her shirt that was ripped in two, presumably by a bullet.

"That would have been me. You saved my life." She fell to her knees and prayed, though she was far from a religious person.

The smell of gunpowder and cordite drifted in the air as innocent as a firework display. Across the valley, a fire engine had arrived at the scene of the impact. Maud looked back at Alice, who was scouring the hedgerow.

"Are there any dock leaves anywhere? I've been stung in all sorts of nasty places."

"Me too. Oh." Maud picked up the flask, knocked on its side and twisted out of shape with a bullet hole that had gone clean through. She traced her finger around the punctured exit hole, bordered by a lace of molten metal, scorched and shiny and still warm to touch. The impact of what almost happened really hit her. She dropped to her knees in the dust and vomited into the ditch with the trampled nettles.

"We ought to get back to work. It's milking soon, and we haven't finished the field." Alice handed over a handful of crushed, vibrant green dock leaves.

Maud nodded and stood up as if in a trance, rubbing the plant over her exposed skin to relieve the bubbling nettle rash. Alice had put the two parts of her shirt back on, but they flapped like sails as she worked, and they didn't cover her bra. She would have to try to mend it this evening given that they didn't have spare uniforms.

Spooked by distant machinery noises, they kept glancing up in case another plane came over. Maud wondered if she could relate the event in her latest letter to Bea or whether it would be censored. About half an hour before it was time to go for milking, young Cecil Hardy came racing into the field on his bike. He dropped the bike by the gate and ran over, his arms outstretched.

"Did you see the plane? I think it was a Dornier Do 17, a flying pencil," he shouted before making engine and machine gun noises and an explosion.

"Shut up, you stupid idiot. He tried to kill us."

Alice was sharper than Maud had ever heard her.

Cecil stopped short and looked aghast. "What?"

"Why are you here, anyway?" Alice asked, clutching the two sides of her shirt together to maintain her modesty.

"Oh." He took out a post office telegram and handed it over to Maud.

She swallowed. A telegram only brought bad news. Even Cecil must know that as his mouth turned down.

BILL KILLED BY WALL IN LONDON BOMBING. SORRY. MOTHER.

Maud slumped to the ground and screwed up the paper into a ball.

Killed by a wall? That didn't make sense. He was supposed to be safe, serving on the home front, not fighting abroad. Alice sat beside her, and Maud handed over the crumpled piece of paper. She read it and murmured something Maud didn't catch. Alice put her arm around Maud's shoulders, and they both stared out across the valley at the impact site of the stricken plane. She wasn't supposed to see this afternoon, to know her brother died. Did Bill die so she should live? But he had so much more going for him; he was a qualified engineer, he would have married Ethel Porter, and they would have had lots of children. Why did Maud live and not him?

Life was rent in two, a torn sail flapping in the breeze. She was untethered, gybing and buffeting in the wind. As the sun shone, tendrils of guilt and grief interlocked and wound around her heart, squeezing and crushing her.

CHAPTER NINETEEN
Bristol, present day

"WHERE ARE WE going?" Hannah knew she sounded grumpy, but the early morning bike ride that had seemed such a good idea last night didn't seem so appealing in the cool morning. At least it wasn't raining.

"It's a secret."

Suki's laugh was full of freedom, such a delight to hear. She pushed harder on the pedals, and the box on the pannier see-sawed from side to side.

"If you pedal much harder the picnic box will fall off."

"And you'll pick it up then."

So much for that ploy to slow her down. That was the difference between Suki, who cycled daily, and Hannah, who was a Sunday cyclist; Suki was exhilarated and speeding away while Hannah was conserving energy, especially as she had no idea of the destination. "Are we going to Ashton Court then?" Hannah asked as she was buffeted crossing the Clifton suspension bridge. She kept to the centre of the lane behind the cars as it was a long way down, and the bridge wobbled with the weight of the traffic and the wind. Suki would have to wait at the far end of the bridge.

She did wait, but the moment Hannah approached, Suki was off again. She avoided going straight on to the parkland and climbed through the woodland.

Hannah gave up trying to guess and decided to enjoy the ride under the trees. Dew drops collected on the leaves until they were heavy enough to sag and spill, cold and refreshing on Hannah's face as she cycled to keep up.

It was about an hour later that Suki paused at the top of a long hill and rather than go down the other side, followed a private road along the ridge lined with huge mansions. Not that Hannah could see more than glimpses through the security gates and established trees.

"We can lock our bikes here," Suki said.

With a tremor in her legs, Hannah eased off her bike and attached it to a railing. Suki had already locked her bike and, with the picnic box in one hand and her helmet in the other, she skipped down a dirt track—actually skipped. Hannah couldn't help but chuckle. She'd never seen Suki like this before, so carefree and joyful. It was contagious, and she started to hum as she followed.

She caught up with Suki, and they made their way over the stones till they came upon the mounds and ridges of an Iron Age fort. Suki crossed to the other side of the wide circle and up to the far outer ridge where it opened out with views to the Mendip hills, the marsh, and flat Somerset levels, and in the distance, the Severn estuary as it became the sea.

Now they'd stopped and a slight breeze wafted against her, cooling her overheated skin, Hannah's heartbeat had returned to normal. She revelled in being here with Suki. "That was worth the ride," Hannah said when she got her breath back.

Suki beamed and laced her hand through Hannah's arm as they took in the view. A thrill shot through Hannah, and she didn't want to move. This was the first time Suki had touched her when they were outside. Okay, there was no one else here early on a Wednesday morning, but it was a display of affection that could have been public. She shivered with delight.

Suki pulled away and undid the lid on the box. "Time for breakfast. Give me a hand."

"Sure."

Suki produced a picnic blanket with a waterproof underside. Just as well because there was still quite a heavy dew.

Suki pulled out croissants and a thermos. "I reckon we deserve a hot chocolate fix after our ride."

She poured out a drink and handed it to Hannah. The sweet claggy taste clung to the inside of her mouth. "I don't think hot chocolate has ever tasted so good," Hannah said and licked the chocolate from her lips. Suki watched her intently, causing a spike of arousal to course around Hannah's body. She so wanted to kiss her right now, open to the breeze, witnessed by the buzzard shrieking overhead.

To cover her desire, she stretched her legs out on the rug, her feet beyond the edge. This was like no other breakfast she'd ever had. Overlooking an open expanse of countryside, the cool breeze was no longer sufficient to regulate her heated skin.

Suki took a bite of croissant, and a couple of flakes broke off and landed on her chest. Hannah almost stretched out to brush them away but resisted, although Suki must have seen where her eyes had alighted because she flicked at the crumbs. She offered a bite from her pastry to Hannah. Their eyes met. Suki's were black with desire. Hannah swallowed her croissant quickly. Suki leaned forward and licked at the corner of Hannah's mouth. She pulled back only slightly, so Hannah could still feel her warm breath on her face.

"You missed a bit of chocolate."

Without waiting for a reply, Suki leaned forward again and grazed her lips against Hannah's, a promise of more to come. Excitement pulsed between Hannah's thighs. Hardly daring to breathe, Hannah responded, but then Suki withdrew and she was left disappointed.

Suki's hand slipped under her T-shirt and Hannah stiffened in anticipation. She traced her fingers up Hannah's torso, scorching a trail of want. Hannah groaned as Suki stroked her nipple over her sports bra. She wanted this, now, outside on the exposed hillside.

Then she was conscious of a snuffling beside her, and Hannah jumped at a Labrador sniffing around the discarded croissant.

Suki leapt away from Hannah and sat up. "I don't think you'd better have any of this, boy. Way too much butter to be good for you. Where's your owner?"

A middle-aged woman struggled up the steep ascent in front of them. Hannah could have shouted in frustration that the moment was broken, but she returned the woman's smile.

"Oh dear, has Caspar been annoying you? What a lovely day for breakfast up here. We don't normally see anyone this early. Enjoy your morning."

"Thanks," Suki said and wrapped the croissant in paper. "That was close. I don't fancy that one anymore. Would you like another?"

Hannah felt as though she meant their make-out session. "I'd prefer to carry on where we left off before we were rudely interrupted."

Suki shook her head. "I'm glad it was just a dog. I'd have been mortified if the woman had appeared first. Sorry I got carried away. I know that isn't how you normally do it. You just leap into bed at the earliest opportunity, but I can't do that. I need to have an emotional connection too. And I want our first time to be special."

Hannah tried to parse through the conversation. Did that mean Suki thought she was a player? With a shaft of discomfort, she had to admit Suki's accusation was probably true. After Megan, she'd had a series of one-night stands, as though she was trying on as many different new clothes as possible.

And she'd discarded them all.

"I don't do that anymore. And I do feel a connection with you. I'd love to explore more with you. Shall we go home?" What Hannah didn't say was "and continue what we started here," but the promise hung between them. "Thanks. This was romantic," she said and was awarded with a genuine smile. Hannah shook her legs out as she stood.

As they packed up and ambled back across the site of the fort, she glanced at Suki. It had been a great idea, and she'd been more relaxed than Hannah had ever seen her. Hannah was still amazed at this beautiful woman who surprised her nearly every day. It was a wonder that she was allowed to witness the sensitive soul beneath the feisty facade. Frustrating though it was to stop when they did, she respected Suki's wishes, and she would do what she could to make their first time special as Suki wanted.

At least there was a promise of a first time. Now she needed to burn off some of the sexual energy. "Come on then, I'll race you home."

But Suki was far faster than Hannah, and she'd already showered when Hannah finally made it home and flopped onto the sofa.

"Do you want a shower while I make lunch? Salad?"

There was something in Suki's tone that closed down any possibilities today, so much so that Hannah wondered if she'd imagined it all. But Suki definitely kissed her, and there had been the hint of so much more. Suki had retreated into her shell, but if Hannah wanted this to go somewhere, all she could do was wait.

And for a woman like Suki, Hannah was more than happy to do so.

CHAPTER TWENTY
Staffordshire, May 1941

THE FAMILY PEW seemed very empty during the service for Bill. For the first time ever, Maud sat beside her mother, and there was easily enough room for Violet to sit on the other side of the twins, but she wanted to snuggle into Maud, available to her for just the day.

"I miss everyone," Violet whispered to Maud, clinging onto her with a desperate grip.

"So do I." Maud looked away so Violet wouldn't see her tears.

While the vicar intoned about the sacrifice of the heir to the baronetcy, and the sadness felt by the entire town, Maud could not relate to the casket sitting in the centre, draped with a Union flag, as being her brother. She pictured him smoking as he worked on cars, the ash in danger of dropping into the engine and starting a petrol-fuelled bonfire. She pictured him as he danced with Ethel Porter, his expression animated in a way she'd never seen before. Maud stole a look at Ethel on the other side of the aisle, eyes red rimmed and trying so hard to be stoic. She glanced across at Maud, and they shared a tearful smile.

Maud's gaze swung two pews back to where Bea had always sat with her landlady, Miss Talbot. It was just another gap around the congregation, the community stretched to hold together like a net shopping bag. Bea had written to say she wouldn't be able to get away as they were working very long shifts and said she'd written to Maud's parents to pass on her condolences. Still, the pew seemed cold and empty without Bea's smile and wave to Maud and Harry. *Harry.* Maud took a deep breath in and muttered a prayer for him, wherever he was. She was so tired of constantly holding her breath and knowing that the entire country quaked with uncertainty.

She hated that the war made everyone put on a face, keeping secrets, trusting no strangers, and looking out for themselves. Yet they held out a twig of empathy to those who lost everything, whilst being grateful it wasn't their son, brother, or daughter. With so many people being caught in the Blitz, women were on the front line too. And those about to go to certain death, concertinaed life into as many brief moments as they could cram in. Marvell's time's wingèd chariot stampeded near.

She scanned the church. There were only old men, children, and taut-lipped women. There were a couple of uniforms, including Maud in her Land Army togs. The blue of the flyboys was probably the most attractive uniform. One chap at the back had actually turned up in his flying jacket. Maud did a double take and shot her head back to the front. George. What was he doing here? She had deliberately not said anything in her latest letter to him about Bill's funeral, as she didn't want to talk to him directly. She hoped to send him a letter separately, which was cowardly, but she couldn't get into why she was breaking off the engagement, and he was bound to ask.

"Why are you screwing up the paper?" Violet whispered.

She looked down at the order of service paper in her grip. "Sorry."

Finally, the vicar finished, and they all filed out to the family plot, where the coffin was to be lowered to join their ancestors, who had all been buried here since the time of the Norman conquest.

Violet gripped onto Maud's hand so tightly she thought the blood would be squeezed out.

"Is Bill really not coming back?"

Maud gulped and shook her head, not trusting herself to speak. In her peripheral vision, she was aware of George slowly making his way towards the main mourners. She couldn't escape. Finally, he stood beside Maud and stretched to kiss her on her cheek. Maud felt such a fraud, she would have to tell him. Glancing at her watch, she calculated she had three hours before she had to catch the train back to Derbyshire. She cleared her throat and was about to speak when another voice spoke.

"Ah, Mr Waites, thank you for coming. It's very touching that you got some time off to attend. I do hope you will join us at the hall afterwards," her mother said.

"Thank you, Lady Heaston. I'm so sorry for your loss. Bill was a splendid chap."

Mother nodded and turned to meet the next person in line.

George gripped Maud's elbow. "Can we go for a walk?" He scowled at Violet. "Alone."

Violet hid behind Maud's legs just as she had when she was a little girl. Mother glanced at the tableau and seemed to assess the situation.

"Violet, come and stand with me, dear. Let Maud have some time with her fiancé."

Violet reluctantly let go and returned to their mother's side.

"I'll see you later, Vi," Maud whispered. Sweat beaded on her forehead. She hoped to leave it to the last possible minute, but she couldn't see a way out of talking to him now. He offered her the crook of his arm, and they walked back over the fields towards her family home.

"Thank you for coming, but you needn't have."

"Why not? Bill would have been my brother-in-law. I was flying this way, delivering a Hurricane. I dropped into Abbots Bromley and hitched a lift here."

"You shouldn't be telling me that. Walls have ears." Maud quoted from the propaganda posters that were pasted on every village noticeboard.

"What walls?" George waved his free arm around. "I'm sorry about Bill."

Maud's stomach roiled. "Thank you. But George, there's something I need to tell you. I can't marry you."

He dropped her hand and spun to face her, frowning. "Why ever not? I've bought you a ring and everything. It's why I came."

He slipped his hand into his jacket pocket and brought out a small red box. His lazy eye caught up with the other one and he stared at her, his eyebrows furrowed. Her stomach turned to lead, but she pushed on. "George, you need to marry someone who will love you for who you are and make you a wonderful wife. I can't do that." Maud focused on the meadows below them. The flowers reminded her of walking this way with Bea only two years ago, but it could have been two lifetimes.

"Why not?" He thrust the box back in his pocket and picked out a cigarette.

He stopped to light it, shielding the flame with his cupped hands. Then he flicked the match violently to extinguish it and tossed it on the ground. Maud had never seen him do that before; he was always so considerate of his surroundings. "There's someone else. Who is he?"

"You're a great man. You deserve someone who loves you. I like you, but I don't love you, not in that way."

He gawped at her, the cigarette dangling from his open mouth.

"I can still write to you, if you want," Maud added, squeezing the last bit of courage she possessed.

"Fuck off."

She stepped back, surprised and shocked at his language. The vehemence of his anger covered his hurt and revealed her guilt, both raw and sharp. She reached out to stop him. "Where are you going?"

He shrugged her off and kept striding, stiff and upright. "Back to my plane. Goodbye, Maud."

She halted and withdrew her fingers, letting him go, unhindered. "Goodbye, George, I'm sorry." There was no point saying anything else. She should have been stronger in the first instance. Guilt and sorrow for George and Bill and anxiety about Harry mixed in a cocktail as toxic as hemlock. She doubled over and rested her hands on her thighs. The material of her Land Army breeches was rough, like sackcloth. She deserved no better.

Could she just go straight back and catch an earlier train? Maud checked her watch, but as she looked up, her family were in view, walking across the meadow towards the hall. Violet ran to her, and Maud bent to hug her sister.

"George left very abruptly," her mother said.

"Yes, he had to go back to his base," said Maud, hating yet more lies and secrets. She couldn't say she had called off the engagement.

"Come up to the house, refreshments are being served."

Maud followed but slipped out of the wake and wandered to the wood where she and Bea had kissed. She wished Bea was here. Everything would feel better, and the world would right itself instead of spinning out of control. Maud traced the deep fissures in the bark where they had picked up acorns only two years ago. Few acorns littered the ground today; it was too early in the season. There were just a few leavings from previous years, hard, brittle reminders of earlier, innocent summers.

Was all this subterfuge worth it? Would she have been better following her head and marrying George, as everyone expected? She closed her eyes and leaned her forehead against the rough bark. No, she loved Bea, and she would do whatever she could to reconnect and be with her after the war, assuming there was some normality after the war, and they weren't under Hitler's jackboot. She shivered.

"I thought you'd be here. It's horrible without everybody, and now you're going away again."

Maud clutched her chest, startled for a brief moment, before she embraced Violet, who clung to her with a desperate intensity. "Yes, I'm sorry, Vi. Next time I'll be here for longer." She brushed Violet's fringe from her eyes and kissed her forehead. "It's just I've made this for you." Violet unfurled her fist and handed over a handkerchief with crude embroidery of a violet on it. "One violet, by Violet, so you'll never forget me."

Maud swung her sister up and spun her around. She was so much heavier than before. "Oh, Vi, I could never forget you."

CHAPTER TWENTY-ONE
London, June 1941

MAUD STEPPED ONTO the concourse at Euston Station and was engulfed by a cacophony of sounds. Whistles blew, steam hissed from the engines, and a blue and khaki torrent of people swept past her. She made her way through the throng to check the whereabouts of Bea's train. It was due in half an hour, but passenger transport was often delayed to allow for troop or goods trains to come and go. She had no choice but to witness the people greeting each other, shouting, parting, crying.

A hollowed-eyed, bomb-crazed wreck of a man in uniform slunk into the shadows, trying to escape the terror of whatever was playing in his head. The war was bound to change Harry, but she hoped he wouldn't be like that and offered a prayer for his safety.

Maud clung to the pillars as each train arrived that could bring Bea. With each delay and disappointment, she worried whether Bea had been delayed on her overnight shift or hadn't been able to make it at all. Particles of soot drifted down like solemn confetti, reminding her how dirty and noisy the city was.

A woman with two children struggled and dropped two cardboard suitcases, probably containing all her worldly belongings. Maud stepped across the fast-flowing current of bodies. "Can I help?"

A mixture of fear and relief washed across the woman's face.

"Where are you going?" Maud said.

"Hemel Hempstead train. Platform three. Thank you, sir." Her eyes widened. "Miss."

Maud snatched up the cases, making light work of them as months of farm labour paid off. She strode towards the platform. Did she really look that masculine? Gawky and big-boned, yes, but enough so that she could be mistaken for a man? She glanced down at her best Land Army uniform, a mix of green and orange-brown, misfitting breeches, socks, and a shapeless overcoat; the woman had a point. What if Bea saw her that way too?

"Thank you, miss. Sorry about back there," the woman said in her broad East End accent.

She'd probably just lost her home, and Maud was worried about how she looked. She shook her head to clear her misplaced perspective. "No problem. Have a safe trip." Maud lifted the cases into the carriage. "Move along inside, please." Months of bellowing at the cows gave her the confidence to shout out. People squeezed together to let the family in, and Maud swung the cases onto the overhead racks and lifted the children into the carriage. The little girl was around Violet's age, but her expression was one of terror. Maud smiled and felt inside her pocket for the two boiled sweets she had meant to share with Bea. "Here you go." She placed one in the grubby palm of each child. "Good luck."

"Thank you, miss."

Maud nodded and re-entered the stream of haunted humanity. Returning to her place by the columns, she scanned the crowds, her heart jolting with everyone who had a passing resemblance to Bea. Then amongst a sea of bobbing berets and caps, there was a hat covering blonde hair scraped in a bun, a double-breasted jacket, and tie. The face looked pale but healthy, tired but radiant, and definitely Bea.

Maud whooped and focused in on her smile as she faced the stampede. And then Bea, beautiful Bea was in touching distance. A pang of shyness slipped in uninvited. Should she kiss her, hug her? Maud should have been elated, and she was, but a mix of anxiety and uncertainty bubbled below the surface. It had been nearly two years since they'd seen each other in person, and the war would have changed them both, the way it had distorted everyone else. She was no longer the naive girl she once was. She'd lost a brother and grafted for long hours in hard manual labour, she was contributing to the war effort and was earning her own money. It wasn't much, but it was the first strike for independence.

The radiance of Bea's smile dissolved her concern like the sun burns away the fog, and Bea threw herself into Maud's arms. Together, they laughed in delight as Maud swung Bea around in a tight embrace.

"Put me down, put me down, or I'll be sick." Bea laughed.

Maud let Bea slide down and pulled apart to reacquaint herself with her love, noticing minor changes and reassuring herself in the similarities.

"I can't believe this. I can't believe you're actually here," Bea said.

The years and distance slipped away, and they were staring intently, reading each other's faces as they had a lifetime away in Staffordshire. Suddenly remembering their surroundings, Maud said, "You must be starving. I'm afraid I don't have enough for an expensive restaurant, but I'm told the Communal Feeding Centres offer hearty grub at reasonable prices."

"I thought exactly the same. And I have the accommodation booked. But maybe we could take in the cinema beforehand?"

The thrill of sharing a room with Bea slipped down Maud's spine. Would she have asked for a twin room or a double? They would manage either way. Or maybe Bea just wanted to be a friend. She supposed they should have sorted this out before meeting, but it was so difficult to write in the letter, and who knew if the censor would check them.

Bea held Maud's hand so they didn't lose each other in the throng, and the warmth of her thrilled Maud. To touch her again, to feel her, had Maud's head spinning. As Bea headed towards the Underground station, Maud pulled back. "Do you mind if we walk rather than take the tube? I'm not used to all these people." She sounded like a country bumpkin, but Bea didn't seem to mind and shifted direction to the exits.

"Sure, we'll have to go on it later, but I'm happy to walk."

Their gazes met. *I wish I could kiss you now; you are so beautiful, so perfect.* Maud tucked a loose strand of hair behind Bea's ear, hoping that simple action would convey everything she couldn't say with words or a more intimate touch. A wave of politeness and small talk seemed to be all they could manage when a torrent of questions and longing to reconnect fizzed under the surface. Or maybe it was just the shyness Maud felt.

Bea linked her arm in Maud's and leaned in. "It's wonderful to see you again. I've dreamed of this day and missed you so much."

"Me too."

"I wish I could kiss you now in front of all these people," Bea whispered.

Maud caught the scent of lily of the valley, so familiar, and Bea's shampoo with a hint of rose, different from what she had used before. Maud's anxiety melted away. "Me too. Let's go."

***

On the tube, they deliberately squeezed close to keep the connection that had built in the cinema. Maud clung to the worn leather straps and pulled Bea tight, ostensibly to protect her from the swaying of the train and the lurching of the mass of bodies pressing against them. But all she could feel was the brush of Bea's fingers gripping at her coat. The dim overhead bulbs reflected the sparkle in Bea's eyes, her Cupid's bow lips stretching and pursing as she chattered about *Rebecca*, a rerun of last year's Oscar winner, but neither of them cared, as it meant the cinema was less packed and they could snuggle together, each secret touch a promise of more to come.

The tube train shuddered to a halt. As Maud leaned down to hear what Bea was saying, she caught the warmth of her breath caressing her cheek. If she just leaned down a little further, she could press her mouth to Bea's. The lights flickered and died, leaving a carriage of sweaty passengers in complete darkness. Maud dipped her head lower and placed the tenderest of kisses on Bea's mouth. Bea gasped but responded, open-mouthed. Maud melted a little inside, sure it wasn't just the stifling heat of the packed carriage.

The light bulbs hummed, and Maud retreated as the lights returned. There was a half-hearted cheer from a group of soldiers as the train juddered into motion, but Maud was drawn into Bea, who winked when she caught her eye. Bea nuzzled closer, and the scent of flowers and cigarette smoke wafted from her hair.

Maud wanted this journey to be over so she could kiss her properly. Twenty-two months was too long to be apart, and so much had happened. She blinked away the thoughts and put them in a separate box to look at later. Who knew when they could be together again? There was just this, now, clinging together in a fogged-up carriage with a hundred people whose lives they would never cross again.

Finally, they reached their stop and by the moonlight, they hurried down the pavements to their lodgings, out in the suburbs. Their footsteps thudded on the flagstones, and they passed a couple of gap-toothed buildings that had once been homes, heaps of bricks, and dust, and twisted metal seeping onto the street. A shiver slivered down Maud's back. "Do we need to go to the Anderson shelter?"

"No, there'll be no raid tonight."

In the moonlight Maud caught Bea's smile, her expression certain.

"Trust me."

And Maud wanted to but knew she couldn't ask *what* Bea knew and *how* she knew. She hated this war, with all its lies, and secrets, and clandestine whispering.

When the person they had been following turned into a blacked-out hulk of a house and shut the door, Bea pulled Maud close. She reached up to Maud's neck and drew her in to willing lips. Maud's breath hitched, a thrill of fear mingling with excitement. She closed her eyes and inhaled, almost tasting that summer of snatched kisses and wide-eyed wishes, and the rush of certainty washed over her, like it had before. This was so right. She pulled back for air.

"God, I've missed you. I've missed this, missed us," Bea said, her voice deeper and more raspy than normal.

Maud grunted in agreement. "I think we need to go inside before we get carried away."

"Come on, then. I don't think it's far."

Bea pulled at her arm, breaking into a run, laughing as she skipped over rubble on the road. Eventually they arrived at a three-storey terraced house, and Bea rang the doorbell. After a few minutes, they heard the bolts being drawn back, and the door opened a crack.

"Mrs Ramsbottom? My name is Miss Williams. I booked a room."

"Okay, come in. We're just listening to the wireless."

Maud was introduced but hardly noted anything as the landlady proudly showed them the internal bathroom and their room, with a double bed filling most of the space.

"I hope you don't mind if I take payment up front. It's just we've had a few who've rushed away in the morning without paying."

"Of course." Bea counted out the change and poured it into the woman's hands.

"We've got electric but with so many power cuts, I've left you a candle and matches on the mantelpiece. Breakfast is at seven thirty sharp."

"Thank you, Mrs Ramsbottom."

Bea closed the door, and they collapsed against it, diving into a frantic kiss, all tongues and passion, exploring and washing away the hard months of separation and loss.

"Shall we?" Bea nodded to the bed with a cast iron bedframe.

Maud hesitated a second. Her chest heaved, and she rubbed her chin. This was all she'd dreamed of in their time apart.

Bea scanned her features. "It's okay. If you don't know or you're not sure, we can just kiss, or just snuggle, or do whatever feels good."

Her gentle smile, so familiar and yet so different, confirmed she meant it. Maud gulped. "I want to. It's just I've never been with someone before, and I'm not sure what to do." The tingling heat crept up her neck and spread up her face. She didn't dare look at the mirror on the chest of drawers; she didn't need confirmation her face had turned scarlet.

Bea held out her hands as she sank onto the bed. The springs squeaked, and they both laughed, dissolving some awkwardness. Bea leaned forward and unlaced her shoes, placing them neatly by the end of the bed.

"Can I lie beside you?" Maud asked.

"Of course. Shall we slip under the covers?"

Maud tugged off her shoes, tucking them under the wooden chair. The bed springs protested as Maud joined Bea. The sheets were cool, starched so stiffly they almost crackled. The light overhead flickered.

"Should we use the candle for light instead?"

Without waiting for an answer, Bea popped out and lit the candle. She blew out the match, and the smoke curled, leaving a tinge of sulphur hanging in the air. With the electric lamp off, the shifting candlelight deepened shadows. The semi darkness gave Maud extra courage. This was it, their one chance for who knows how long and she wanted it. She swallowed, amazed at how dry her throat felt. "Can I watch you undress?" she asked. It felt so bold, so brazen and beautiful.

Bea's eyes flashed in the candlelight, and she nodded. "Of course."

Her fingers trembled as she removed first her jacket and blouse and folded them neatly on the chair so they didn't crease. As Bea turned around, Maud took a sharp intake of breath, her chest heaving.

"Can I help you?" Maud whispered, licking her lips. Bea nodded and held out her hands. Throwing back the bedcovers, Maud approached her, desire overcoming shyness. She trailed her index finger from Bea's shoulder to the hollow of her neck. Bea hummed with pleasure as Maud traced her finger along the skin between her breasts. Bea stiffened, and her nipples hardened to peaks through the fabric of her soft cotton bra. Emboldened by the sighs and the glint in Bea's eyes, Maud mapped the contours of her breast and stroked the summit. "May I?"

"Please," Bea half breathed, half spoke, her breathing getting faster, matching Maud's.

Maud slipped both of her hands behind Bea's back, unclipped her bra, and trailed the shoulder straps to her elbows before releasing the cups. The cloth fell away, and Maud admired Bea's breasts, so much smaller than her own, with much paler skin and delicate nipples. "You're beautiful," she said and reverently placed the bra on top of the folded clothes. As she turned to face Bea again, she was immediately behind Maud, close, as close as in the tube. Their breaths mingled as Bea twined her hands around Maud's neck and drew her down into a kiss. Gentler and measured, as though they had all the time in the world rather than one short night. Bea unbuttoned Maud's shirt and bra, and the garments fell to the ground like blossom. As they disrobed each other, Maud's heart beat faster, and the clothing dropped with less care until finally they came together, skin to skin, Maud's whole body burning from the touch, and Bea's nipples hard points against Maud, causing her breath to hitch.

Feeling too tall, she dragged Bea onto the bed, the springs squeaking as they lay back. Bea's eyes were now so dark, the blue was but a rim around the pupils, and Maud could see her reflection in there.

"Tell me what you want," Bea whispered.

She paused in her stroking of Bea's nipples. "I'm not sure what to do."

"Do you touch yourself?" Bea asked.

Heat burned Maud's cheeks, and she nodded.

"Why don't you just do to me what you enjoy, and I'll guide you in what I like. Do you want to be on top?"

Bea shuffled around, and with much sagging of springs, they manoeuvred themselves so Maud was staring down at Bea's petite form, lit by the dancing candlelight. Bea's hair was still constrained in a regulation bun, and Maud unclipped the pins, freeing her blonde locks to splay out on the pillow. Maud traced Bea's jawline with the back of her hand, aware how rough and dry her fingers were against the downy skin of Bea's face. "So soft," she murmured. "I'm almost too scared to touch you with my calloused hands."

Bea turned her head and kissed the flesh, lifting her own hands to turn Maud's and feathered kisses on the palms. "Your hands are so strong, doing honest work."

She took Maud's hand and sucked on her fingers, which had a direct effect on her core, and she writhed. But this was supposed to be about Bea. Maud withdrew her fingers and traced across Bea's perfect lips and tracked a direct line from her chin to her chest, pausing to cup her breasts.

Bea groaned and arched her back, pushing herself into Maud's palm. She placed kisses down to Bea's other breast and sucked her nipple, amazed how it became taut. She raised her head as Bea grunted, and she licked her way up to the cleft in her chin. Bea tasted salty and sweet, uniquely *Bea*. Encouraged by Bea's faster breathing, Maud traced her fingers lower to the coarser hair at the junction of her legs. She curled her fingers around and slipped them lower into Bea's luscious folds, deliberate and slow despite the quickening of her heart. Bea groaned again.

"May I?" Maud asked and at the sighed assent, tentatively slipped a finger inside, feeling the pull of Bea's muscles inviting her in. It was strange to be at a different angle to when she pleasured herself, but Bea arched her back, clenched her hands in the starched sheets, and stifled a cry.

"More."

Maud added another finger, thrusting and setting a rhythm, fast and staccato, listening for Bea to instruct her if she wanted anything different. She was vaguely aware of the accompaniment of the squeaking bedsprings, but she didn't care. Pleasuring Bea was her only desire. Sweat glistened on Bea's body as she juddered and flushed, obvious even in the yellowish light. Bea bit herself hard on her hand as she tightened around Maud's fingers, flooding and releasing as she dropped into orgasm. Maud felt a ridiculous sense of pride and delight that she had pleasured Bea. And Bea was so beautiful when she came.

Bea stretched like a cat. "Well, that was definitely worth waiting for. Thank you."

Maud smiled and cupped Bea's face in her hands and grazed her lips across Bea's. "No, thank you. You're amazing." She couldn't believe how lucky she was to be lying in bed with this beautiful, funny, kind woman.

Without another word, Bea flipped Maud over, surprising her with her strength. Bea wriggled down the bed, nuzzling between her breasts, licking her erect nipples, and breathing softly down her stomach and lower. Blood rushed to Maud's core. "What are you doing?"

Bea grinned, mischief gleaming in her eyes. "Something I learned at college. Do you trust me?"

Maud nodded and closed her eyes, tuning into the sensations where Bea grazed her skin and trailed a path of fire as her breath warmed the soft hairs under her belly button and nuzzled the coarser hair at the meeting of her thighs.

Then Bea licked her pearl. Maud gasped and almost bent double. "Oh, that there." She exhaled.

Bea raised her head. "My American friends call it clitty. And yours is a very pretty clitty."

She sucked and licked again, and Maud lost all words, thrusting herself up to give Bea more access to kiss, lick, and suck. Maud muffled her cries in the pillow. Her entire body fizzed, and heat radiated from her core, her heart pounded in her temples, and just when she thought she couldn't cope with the tension anymore, an explosion deep within rocked her. Every cell in her body seemed to dance as the orgasm took hold and transformed her, as if her cells dissolved into atoms, and all the atoms melted into particles and the space between particles merged into infinite space.

Still buzzing a few minutes later, she kissed Bea. Everything had shifted. Now she knew what the fuss was about. She snuggled up to Bea. "Dear God, that was fantastic. What a fabulous thing to learn at college."

"Ah, it was definitely extra curricula, Miss Heaston."

They laughed and clung on tight, painfully aware that this was just one brief night.

Bea rolled over, so she was sprawled across Maud and nibbled on her earlobe. "Thank you."

Her voice was drowsy, and Maud remembered Bea had come straight off night shift, so she must be exhausted. "Are you comfy?" Maud whispered, but her reply was just the soft breath of sleep. The thrill of this evening fizzled below the surface of Maud's skin; she couldn't possibly sleep. This was the best day of her life. Wow, just wow.

She felt like a bud relaxing into full bloom, glowing and heady. And all because of this wonderful woman draped on top of her, her quiet breaths warming Maud's chest as she slept. She gently brushed a strand of hair off Bea's face, tempted to kiss her, but she didn't want to disturb Bea's much needed sleep. Maud pulled the coarse blanket up to cover Bea as best she could and watched the candle guttering.

This night was like the candle, a single source of brightness in an entire room of darkness. And for being so isolated, it drew in the attention, brilliant and unforgettable.

CHAPTER TWENTY-TWO
Bristol, present day

SUKI AND HANNAH wheeled their bikes into the tiny hall. Hannah reattached her own less-used bike up on the hooks highest on the wall and rested Suki's near the door.

Their faces were flushed with the exertion, and Hannah was about to run up the stairs, but her aching thighs complained. She settled for heaving one leg up at a time. "What did you do to me? I'm knackered."

Suki raised an eyebrow. "It was only twenty-five miles. Wasn't it great riding through Ashton Court Estate?"

Hannah vaguely remembered seeing the parkland and trees but had been too preoccupied with keeping up with the ultra-fit Suki to enjoy it. "I guess I need to do this more often if I'm going to keep up with you." She would need to get fitter if she was going to do any other physical activity with Suki, too. *If only.*

"Tea?" Suki asked. "And are you up for reading more of your Gammy's letters?"

"Sounds like a plan, but I'll definitely need a shower first. You didn't even break a sweat." Fifteen minutes later, Hannah slid into her favourite seat on the floor in front of the sofa. Suki was already curled up with her legs tucked underneath her.

"Bunch up," Suki said and pointed for Hannah to settle in front of her. "I'll read." Suki picked up the first letter as Hannah took a sip from her tea. "This is dated September 1942. It's a letter from your great grandmother to your gammy."

Dear Maud,

I do hope this finds you well. and your blisters have improved. I will send you some more socks. Some women in the village are knitting them for the soldiers, and I thought, why shouldn't you have a pair? I'm afraid I write under difficult circumstances. The Hall is being requisitioned for the US army to be stationed here, so we are moving to one of the three storey Georgian houses near the centre of town. It is so annoying as we have planted all the formal gardens to allotments with carrots and potatoes and won't even have the benefit of them now. Still, we must all do what we can for the war effort, but it seems to go on forever. Things will never be the same.

I saw Mrs Waites the other day. She was distraught about poor George. I think they thought because he was in the ATA that he would be safe but foul weather can affect anyone out in it. I was rather irritated that she said at least I have other sons. I reminded her I have already lost my heir and eldest, and Harry is in a prison of war camp somewhere in the Far East. Not that we have heard anything more. I hope he receives better treatment than your father had in the Great War after he was gassed. I hope you are not too upset about George. He was a good man. Violet asked me to send you a picture she drew for you of the new house. She has already decided which room shall be yours, next to hers.
Your loving Mother.

Suki showed Hannah the faded picture of a doll's house and at the window a girl's face in purple, presumably Violet, and in the next window a much taller woman drawn in black wax crayon, Maud.

"That letter's so formal, isn't it? It reminds me of the way the elderly Japanese speak to each other. Polite, but not passionate."

"Is that what you are looking for, love and passion?" Hannah held her breath, waiting for Suki's response.

"Isn't everyone? My name means beloved."

"Really?"

"Yeah. It's an unusual name in Japan, but my mum insisted, and eventually my dad relented. Do you want to read the next one?"

Clearly Suki didn't want to open up about her hopes and dreams. She spoke about her early life so rarely, each revelation was like precious jewellery to be pocketed and admired later. Hannah reached for the next letter in the pile. She lay back as Suki stroked her hair, glad she didn't have any gel on. She felt like purring. Hannah sat as tall as she could to make it easy for Suki to reach, but Suki stopped and patted her on the shoulder.

"Come on." Suki nudged Hannah.

Hannah sighed. It was definitely two steps forward, one back with Suki. "Okay. This was about the same time, September 1942. It's from Auntie Bea to Gammy."

Dearest M,

Thank you for letting me know about George. I can fully understand why you would feel so guilty, but honestly, you have nothing to feel guilty for. You didn't love him. They put you into a difficult position to agree to marry him, and when you got the opportunity, you told him you couldn't go through with it. That was the right thing to do. You absolutely did not cause his accident; he was flying in foul weather. Nor did you deserve this as a punishment for loving me. Don't listen to what the rector says. I know we won't agree on our views on religion and the church, but loving you is the best thing that has happened to me, and I think you agree it feels so right. How can it be wrong to love?

Take care, sweetheart. I wish I could talk to you face to face and we could discuss this properly and I could support you through this. Alas, the war seems never ending. I must go, I am working the night shift.

Your loving B xx.

"That's tough, for both of them," Suki said, "to love but not to be together. And now, after all these years living in the same house, they're apart again."

Hannah twisted to look up to Suki. "I know. I heard what you said, and I've booked a train up on Saturday. I asked to speak to Amanda, but she's not there."

Suki draped herself round Hannah's neck. The hug sent heat ricocheting all around Hannah's body.

She nuzzled her chin on Hannah's head. "I'm so proud of you. I don't know why, but it feels so important that you go there and see for yourself. I don't trust your cousin, Amanda."

Hannah stretched to maximise the contact, with Suki's arms still wrapped around her. "Me neither. I think she's out for herself. I haven't heard from Matthew, but he's always a bit hit and miss with his replies."

"Sounds like someone else I know."

Hannah felt Suki kiss the top of her head. Hardly daring to breathe, Hannah placed her hand over Suki's. She didn't pull away, as expected, but interlaced her fingers with Hannah's. It felt like being around a skittish deer, waiting to see what it would do next. Suki stroked Hannah's hand with her thumb.

"Mm, that's nice," Hannah said, wanting Suki to know that she was open to whatever was on offer. But it was getting harder to sit comfortably in the friend and housemate category. Her fingers tingled, sparking to her core. She needed to move before she did something she shouldn't, so she turned, still holding Suki's hand, and kneeled in front of her, in Suki's space. Thinking Suki would pull back, Hannah primed herself to jump up and offer a snack as a distraction, but Suki stayed there, with Hannah at her knees. She stared at Hannah's lips, which had gone dry. Hannah traced her top lip with her tongue.

Suki leaned forward, her breathing shallow and fast, tracking from Hannah's eyes to her mouth. "May I?" Suki asked.

"Please."

Suki shuffled onto the ground, pulled Hannah to her, and sealed her lips over Hannah's hungrily, with a passion that took her by surprise. Hannah amped up to meet her, stroke for stroke, their tongues exploring each other. And the kiss was more than just the linking of bodies; it was the outpouring of months of repression and yearning, burning off disappointments and setting aflame potential for the future.

Dear God, she needed this. This was not like her series of one-night stands, slipping out before dawn, always destined to be a short, sweet relief but ultimately unfulfilling. Was it just a kiss or was it more? Hannah wanted it to be more, so much more.

Suki pulled back. "Wow," she said, "I didn't expect that."

"You're telling me." Hannah shuffled on her knees. "So where do we go from here?"

Suki stroked Hannah's scar where her lip ring had been. "Does it need to go anywhere?"

Hannah sank back onto her haunches, deflated like a three-day-old helium balloon. "Oh, I assumed it meant you like me, more than a friend and housemate, I mean." Her voice sounded almost as squeaky as if she'd inhaled the helium.

"I do like you, Han, you're very special to me."

That sounded like the kind of brush off a lover would give before breaking up. "So, is this just an experiment?" Hannah pulled away so they no longer had physical contact.

"No, but I don't know where we go or what we do." Suki reached out and stroked Hannah's cheek. Her fingers were soft.

"Shall we just see how it goes?" Suki asked.

Frustration, anger and yearning warred in Hannah. She unfurled herself and stood. "Fancy some crisps?" She needed a distraction and to rearrange her thoughts to hide her disappointment. Maybe Suki just needed more time, and Hannah should keep her libido in check.

CHAPTER TWENTY-THREE

Colchester Military Hospital, February 1946

It TOOK MOST of the day to travel from Derbyshire, even though Maud had caught the milk train. She fidgeted in her train seat with a mixture of excitement and trepidation. Mother had written to say that Harry was changed and not to expect him how he was. The fact that he was only just back in England showed how ill he had been.

She tried to read her book but couldn't get beyond the same paragraph. A baby cried. She stared out of the window at the broken landscape. Everything seemed grey: grey sky, grey smoke, grey people trying to rebuild a country crippled with debt and trauma. It was such a contrast to the jubilation of the victory celebrations. She tried to stretch her legs but her bag under the seat in front prevented her from getting comfortable. Ignoring the nuisance, she reminded herself she was staying with Bea this evening and licked her lips.

Now Bea had started a new job in London and was living there, Maud hoped she could escape, and they could move in together. Her mother was expecting her to go home, but she didn't want to. When she had a job offer, she could be demobbed from the Land Army, but they were releasing married women first. Understandable, but frustrating. Now Alice had left, it was dull at the Hardy's farm and the cold winter hit harder. Maud rubbed at her chilblains. Her hands seemed so much more gnarled and callused now than when she had first met Bea in London. Was that really nearly five years ago?

She took a bus to the hospital. Eventually, she found the ward and asked one of the Queen Alexandra nurses where she could find her brother.

"Down the row, about middle on the right." The woman pointed down a long ward of around twenty simple iron-framed beds either side.

As she passed, searching for recognition, each face was a mask of lines, etched deep with the horrors of war. But it was their eyes, some wild and haunted, following her every step; others were blank as though they still held visions of terrors no one should witness, of actions done to them, or by them. There was an all-pervading smell of disinfectant, and the floors were highly polished, as if they were trying to scrub away the pain and fear. She sucked in a breath and wandered down the row of identical beds, seeking for a mask to meld into her brother's face.

"Hey, giraffe, you've gone too far," a frail voice said as she passed halfway along the line.

Maud spun around and gazed in the direction of the voice. She felt dizzy and took a step back before forcing her legs to move towards the bed. A shrunken skeleton with greying hair stared back at her from the recuperation bed. Harry's skin was leathery, ochre coloured, and the whites of his eyes were yellow.

"Sorry you had to see me like this. I'm not quite there yet."

His voice was cracked and shrill like an old man's, not a twenty-six-year-old. A smile played on his lips, but his eyes seemed dull, as if someone had switched them off.

Mother had said he was changed, but she hadn't expected this. He didn't look or sound like Harry, and he must have been so hurt that she just walked straight past without recognising him. She put her hand to her thundering chest.

"Oh, Harry." Maud kissed his forehead. The smell of his stale breath rose to greet her, making her feel queasy. As she clutched his shoulder through his pyjamas, all she felt was bones. She pulled up a metal chair and cradled his emaciated hand in hers. Even his cuticles were yellow. She searched his face, desperately trying to see a glimmer of her brother behind this cadaverous mask. "What happened? What did they do to you?" she whispered.

He closed his eyes, his mouth a thin line, and wheezed in breaths. He paused so long she was unsure he was going to speak at all.

"We were diverted to Singapore just before they capitulated. Stupid idiots had all their defences pointing out to sea, but the Japs came overland via Thailand and Malaya. You'd have thought they would have learnt from the Great War, wouldn't you? Clearly not." He coughed, and his breaths came in shallow rasps.

She squeezed his hand. "Don't speak if it upsets you."

He shook his head. "The Japs took us prisoner, and we had to work on a railway in the jungle in Thailand over a mountain range, without proper tools and not enough to eat. There was so much disease, and the Japs

WARM PEARLS AND PAPER CRANES

were cruel; they would whip a man for not bowing." His hand gripped hers. "They didn't comply with the Geneva convention. Don't trust them, Maud."

"I won't, but I don't expect to see any Japs, anyway." Maud tried to smile as if he had made a joke, but she felt sick to her soul. How could anyone treat another human being like that? Harry looked like the Jews in the picture she'd seen of the Nazi death camps at Belsen last year.

Harry coughed and coughed, then fought to catch his breath. Through his wheezing, he turned to her. "You'll be the oldest now. Look after my car, and the twins, and Sprocket. I can't do that."

An icy hand had clamped around her heart. "No, no, no. You're back home now. You'll get better soon and can go back to your old job messing around with cars and pretending you're a mechanic. And you can finish your degree."

He shook his head through his next coughing fit. He sipped a little water through a straw. "I love you, little sis."

Tears bubbled up, and she tried to blink them away. He must be ill to be this nice to her. "I love you too, Harry. But no talk of this. You'll get stronger and pull through."

He grimaced and clamped his lips tight and tried to breathe more deeply, but his chest heaved in shallow, rapid jerks. She wiped away the tears that slipped down the side of his cheeks.

"Look after Bea for me. She loves you."

Maud's head shot up. "What? What do you mean?" A blush burned up from her neck to her cheeks.

"She told me. It's why she turned me down." He managed a lopsided grin.

For a fleeting second, he almost seemed to be her Harry again, not this spectre of a man. "I didn't know you knew."

He nodded. "She's a wonderful woman. I know these things are not the norm, but love is love," Harry said and coughed again.

Her shoulders relaxed, and the warmth of acceptance, gratitude, and love wrapped around her like a warm winter cloak. "Thank you for saying that," she whispered and held his hand, tears rolling down her cheeks for Harry, for Bea, and for herself.

He squeezed her fingers and cleared his throat. "Do you love her?"

She nodded, too full of barely contained emotion to speak.

"So do I. I know she's hoping to come and see me next weekend, but I can't see her. Not like this." He waved at his emaciated body.

"I'm sorry," she whispered, not sure what to say. Bea had chosen her, not him. If Bea hadn't rejected him, would he have still joined the Engineers, or would he have waited to be called up? But the road of what ifs was the road to insanity. She pulled at the thin, rough blanket. "I feel so guilty."

"Don't." Harry shook his head, the sweat trickling down his temples. He gripped her arm. "I want you both to be happy. Please, look after her. Do that for me. Promise?"

She gazed at him and wiggled her little finger as they had done as children. "I promise."

He shuffled and struggled to force himself upwards. "Help me sit up."

She gently lifted him up and propped the pillow behind him, but it was no comfort.

"I cough less when I'm upright." As if to prove himself wrong, he started coughing again. She offered him more water, but he shook his head. "Will you get my cigarette tin from my locker?"

She couldn't stop the gasp that escaped her lips. "You don't still smoke, do you?"

"No. I want to give you something. Look in there. There's a photo of you, Bea, and me by the car. Bill took it. It's been all around the world with me, and I'd like you to have it."

She withdrew the stained and battered gold tin, embossed with the red marque Wills Gold Leaf. She struggled to remove the lid from the warped tin and extracted the frayed, creased photo, browned and ripped. How had this survived? She traced the outline of their faces with her finger. A triangle had been torn off in the corner, cropping the slacks she wore. She could almost feel the coarseness of those slacks and see the olive green of them, the powder blue and white of Bea's summer dress. Both he and Maud were gazing at Bea. He had just related a story about a customer at the garage and they were all laughing.

"Thank you, I'll always treasure this. We looked so young and happy."

"We were… even if my foot was still sore where you trod on it."

His lopsided smile made a fleeting appearance, and she huffed, although she didn't mean it. What she would do to go back to then, to have Harry back to his best.

"So, if you're not getting married, what will you do with your life?"

She laid her hand on his arm and worked hard not to recoil at the texture of his bones draped in yellowing skin. "I've applied for articles to be apprenticed as an accountant, but they've got so many applications from men leaving the services they can't take me on yet. One firm, Gardener and Yarborough, has said if I reapply in six months, they may take me on as a bookkeeper, but I won't get qualifications. It's in London, but after I've paid for digs, I'll have less to spend than I do in the Land Army. And of course, because I was only engaged to George, I don't get a war widow's pension."

"Mm." He nodded, but his eyes began to close.

"Maybe you should lie down again. Obviously, I've bored you with my hopes and dreams." She tried to crack a smile, but all she could think was he might not get to see that, to share that. What a waste of youth and life, all the undone years, as Wilfred Owen said. And as she helped Harry shuffle down the bed, she had a vision of studying the war poets with Bea in the library at home, with the sunshine streaming through the floor to ceiling windows, when Bill and Harry were young and happy men. She kissed his forehead. "I'll come again, the next weekend I can get time off."

"Sure. Love you," he muttered, but his eyes had already shut.

She couldn't move, too caught up in conflicting emotions, glad to have had the opportunity to speak to him but hated that he had lost everything: his love, his youth, his health. What must he have seen and experienced, and yet instead of bitterness, he had given his blessing. She offered a quick prayer before she rose and kissed his forehead again.

When Bea met her on the station in London, all smiles and joy, all Maud could do was cling on for support and not howl like a banshee. "I walked straight past him. I didn't recognise him. It was awful." Maud tried to blink away the vision of him in the hospital bed. "How can anyone do that? To Harry? He said the Japanese were cruel and treated them like less than human."

"War is cruel—"

"This wasn't just cruel, it was sadistic."

Bea led Maud back to her shared London digs. As they lay in the small double bed in Bea's cramped attic room, Maud's visit to Harry replayed over and over.

"Sorry, Bea, will you just hold me?" she asked and shuffled down the cold bed so she could lay her head on Bea's shoulder. If Bea was disappointed that they didn't make love, she said nothing. She simply held Maud close and stroked her back, until Bea drifted off to sleep. She hoped Bea didn't think it a waste of their precious night together before Maud returned to Derbyshire. She listened to the noises from the street and the flicker of the occasional car headlights all night.

Two days later Maud finished the milking and was brushing out the stalls when Cecil Hardy appeared at the cowshed door, holding an envelope and fidgeting.

"Telegram," he whispered and handed it to her.

She knew what it was before she opened it, but a small part of her hoped it was something else. Anything else.

HARRY DIED IN HIS SLEEP. SORRY. MOTHER.

"No reply," Maud said, and Cecil mumbled his apologies before slinking out. She folded up the telegram and placed it in her pocket as if she could hide the truth. She snatched up the broom and attacked the cow stalls, tears dripping as she swept. What a waste of a life. Maud resolved she would never forgive or forget. The constant dripping of propaganda during the war, and the shock of seeing Harry, calcified her grief into rage against the Japanese.

CHAPTER TWENTY-FOUR
Staffordshire, present day

HANNAH WAS SHOWN to Gammy's room by a care nurse called Amy, according to the badge pinned to her ample breast.

Her pager flashed, and she checked the message. "Excuse me, duck, I need to go."

She bustled off, waddling down the corridor in her sensible black shoes. Hannah knocked on the door jamb of the ground floor room. Inside, Gammy sat in a wheelchair looking out to the garden. Gammy was more shrunken than she remembered. The last year had not been kind since they last met, and her hands had the constant tremor indicative of Parkinson's. So that was why she couldn't look after herself anymore. Hannah had the urge to flee. She forced herself to enter the doorway.

A stab of guilt shot through Hannah; Suki was right, she should have come before. But it was difficult to overcome the memory of constant criticism and judgement when she lived with Gammy and Auntie Bea. Had Gammy resented her coming to live with them? Hannah pulled at the neck of her university hoodie. It felt hot in here, and it wasn't just that the temperature in the home was cranked up high. Having read so much of her early life through her letters and diaries, she finally felt like she knew Gammy, not as this frail husk of a woman, nor as the domineering matriarch she'd encountered as a teenager, but as a dynamic, engaged person, full of life and love. She pulled the hem of her hoodie down further over her jeans and strode into the room.

Hannah crouched in front of the wheelchair. Gammy smelt of talcum powder, and her skin was mottled and leathery. Somewhere in another room, an inmate was groaning and calling out. She couldn't bear to be trapped in a place like this where she couldn't escape. Hopefully euthanasia would be legal before she got to that stage. "Gammy? It's me, Hannah."

Gammy tried to twist in her wheelchair. "Who?"

Tempting though it was to snark, "You know, Hannah, the girl you loved to torment," Hannah repeated her name. Gammy turned her constantly bobbing head and her eyes met Hannah's. She thought she might face the glitter of anger and contempt, but Gammy's expression was soft, red-eyed, and watery. All those assumptions she made, as Suki kept on reminding her.

"Hannah? My Hannah?" Gammy reached out from under a blanket and stretched to touch Hannah's face, as if trying to confirm she wasn't just a figment of her imagination.

Her eyes sparkled, and a smile curled her mouth, lightening her face and dropping years. *My Hannah?* Is that how she thought of her? Had she been misjudging her aunt all these years? "Yes, Gammy."

"We haven't seen you for a long time."

Seriously, she was going to give her a hard time? No, it was a statement of fact, not a criticism. "Yes, it's been too long. I've been working on my PhD." Even as she spoke the words, she knew it sounded like the excuse it was. "I'm sorry I haven't been up to see you, Gammy. Are you settled in your new home?"

Gammy's eyes misted up and the spark disappeared. She pulled a handkerchief from her sleeve. It was crudely embroidered with a violet on it. The colour was faded, and the handkerchief was slightly yellowing. Gammy dabbed it at her mouth with shaking hands, catching a glisten of drool.

"Your Nana Violet embroidered this for me," Gammy said, stroking the stitches as if she could conjure her sister by connecting with something she had made.

Hannah frowned at the sudden change of subject but rolled with it. "Did she? Nan tried to get me to do embroidery and knitting, but it's not really my thing."

Gammy chuckled. Hannah failed to recall the last time she'd heard it. But then, she hadn't been around her for a long time.

"No, I remember her being unable to work out how you'd made fifty-nine stitches out of thirty."

Hannah shrugged. "Skill, I reckon." She grinned. Their gazes met, and the shared joke seemed to melt some of the reserve that had built up between them.

"She was so proud of you. So was your mother."

Hannah sucked in between her teeth and blinked hard. They hadn't strayed into this topic since she had first moved in with Gammy, twelve years ago. She gulped. "I thought you didn't approve of Mum?"

Gammy sighed and looked down at the handkerchief. "I wasn't as understanding as I could have been. I couldn't see how she'd travel with her band for months on end and leave you behind, only to turn up and disrupt your routine for a few weeks. Bea always said I should give her a bit of slack. Despite her problems, she always adored you." She looked up at Hannah, her eyes even more watery than before, then her gaze dropped to her hands fiddling with the hankie.

Hannah didn't remember that much of her mum, snatches of being taken backstage at festivals, but it was all too loud, and there were too many people, either hyper or stoned. When her friends at school had been awed by Janice Jones being her mother, Hannah didn't like to say they probably saw as much of her as she did. Nan had been her rock, her maker of scones, and helper with homework. Now the only thing left of her nan was the hankie Gammy fretted with.

Was Gammy apologising? Now they'd started this conversation, Hannah needed to know, so she held Gammy's hand. "I thought you didn't approve of me."

Gammy's head shot up, her eyes wide. A tear rolled over the ledge of her eye, and she wiped it away with the handkerchief. She cleared her throat and tried to speak, but no proper words came out. She cleared her throat again. "Oh, Hannah, how can you say that? I'm so proud of you."

"But you don't like my blue hair, or piercings, or when I got my tattoo." She almost said first tattoo, but there was no point making the situation worse.

Gammy sniffed and dabbed at her eyes. "I only ever wanted the best for you. I wanted you to get a good job so you didn't have to depend on anyone. Bea said I chased you away. It seems she was right." Gammy placed her other hand over Hannah's with a grip that was surprisingly tight. "I'm sorry if you ever thought I didn't approve."

As she seemed about to weep, Hannah freed her hands and wrapped her arms around her. They didn't need any more words for now, and the years of judgement and misunderstanding began to melt in the warmth of the hug. Hannah blinked to stave away the tears. She should have been before. This frail woman in front of her was the vulnerable young woman as well as the strong matriarch. Hannah had judged Gammy, which was ironic, given that was what she had accused Gammy of doing, and they had wasted so much time. *She* had wasted so much time.

The carer, Amy, returned with a pot of tea and two porcelain cups and saucers on a tray. "Your aunt always insists on proper bone china," she said to Hannah. "If I leave it here, will you pour?"

"Of course."

Amy left, clearing up an empty glass as she did.

"It's not Staffordshire china, though," Gammy said when the door clicked shut.

That sounded more like the Gammy she remembered from her teenage years. "It's pretty though." Hannah smiled, attempting to dissipate the judgement. She placed the tea strainer over the cup. It was good that the home provided little extras such as milk in a jug and proper tea. She knew that would mean so much to Gammy. But then, from what Amanda said, it was a very expensive home, like staying in a luxury hotel. Gammy nodded assent, tucked her handkerchief back into her sleeve, and accepted the teacup. It rattled in the saucer with her shaking hands.

"Shall I put it on the table for you?"

"Yes, please. Damn hands. Today's not a good day."

Hannah put the saucer on the table and gave Gammy the cup. She realised too late that she'd filled it too full when it spilled on Gammy's lap. "Sorry, let me." Hannah took a clean tissue from the table and daubed at Gammy's lap. She almost expected to get reprimanded, but Gammy just sighed, exchanged her cup for the tissue and tried to clean the stain. Hannah sensed that suggesting a tippee cup wouldn't go down well with her proud aunt. "I filled it a bit full. I'll know next time," Hannah said.

Gammy looked up again. "There'll be a next time?"

Her expression was one of hope, yearning almost, and it broke Hannah's heart. "Sure, if you'll have me." The smile she received would have melted even the hardest heart, like a candle warming cold wax releasing a sweet fragrance. Hannah squeezed Gammy's shoulder as she stood. She made her way to the en-suite bathroom with Gammy's cup, poured some tea down the drain, and returned.

Gammy fixed her with an intense stare. "I'd love you to come again. Perhaps we can get Auntie Bea to visit too? I'm trying to see if I can transfer to her home, did I tell you? I'm not sure what the mix up is, as I was very clear with my instructions. Everything was set up. I just needed to organise all of my paperwork and disperse my things."

Hannah handed Gammy her tea. "I thought Amanda took over your home from you?"

"She did, and she had builders coming in the moment I moved out."

"If you were supposed to go into the same home as Auntie Bea, how come you're here?"

Gammy frowned. "I'm not sure. My solicitor, Katherine, is trying to chase it up."

"Do you want me to check with Katherine?" Hannah asked before she could stop herself. She vowed not to get more involved, but it did sound strange.

Relief flashed across Gammy's face. "Would you? I don't like to be a trouble, but..." She took a sip of her tea and managed to hold the cup to her lips without spilling it again. "Katherine's address is in the address book on the mantelpiece."

Hannah crossed to the ornate mantelpiece. She wasn't sure if it was marble or not, but it seemed expensive and uncommon for a specially built care home. Placed on top was a picture of Bea in her Wren uniform and Gammy in her Land Army uniform, a worn photo of them both by an old car with one of Gammy's older brothers, and the moving home card Hannah had sent. Maybe she did like Hannah then. Hannah sucked in a breath. That Gammy had kept Hannah's cheap card amongst her mementos was humbling and stripped down her armour and prejudice. She didn't deserve the honour; she hadn't been there for Gammy at what must have been a difficult time. It was just hard to believe after all these years when she thought Gammy didn't approve or like her.

Hannah picked up the book, a well-thumbed address book with an alphabetic index. "What's Katherine's surname?"

"I think it's under s for solicitor."

"Not l for lawyer, then?"

"Cheeky," Gammy said, although there was a glisten in her eyes.

Hannah found it and transferred the number into her phone contacts. "I'll call her on the train home," she said as she came back to the chair.

Gammy traced her finger in a jittery line over the arm of her wheelchair. "Did you look through any of the letters?"

Hannah leaned forward. "I did. Thanks for sharing them. I feel I know you better now." She wanted to ask Gammy if she was gay but didn't know how to come out with it. Maybe next time they met.

E.V. Bancroft

Gammy smiled, a sparkle of mischief in her eyes. "I wasn't always a grumpy old lady, you know."

"I never said..." Hannah's cheeks burned. She had thought that once. "Sorry, I might have implied that when I came to live with you."

Gammy chuckled and patted Hannah on the arm. "Don't worry, it was a long time ago and you were grieving. You were a lost soul. It's lovely to see you now, more relaxed and confident in yourself."

Hannah really wished she didn't blush so easily as she was sure her pink cheeks had now turned scarlet. "Thanks, Gammy, that means a lot to me."

"Now will you help me with the crossword? I'm stuck on five down."

Gammy gestured to the paper and Hannah picked it up, unclipping the pen attached to the fold. It felt like picking up her past.

"Do you still do it every day?"

Gammy's shoulders sagged. "I try, but it's not the same without Bea."

Hannah gulped down her guilt and sadness. She should have been there. "I'll contact Katherine and sort it out." She wasn't sure how, but she would do what she could. Her thoughts of not getting involved shattered as she made the decision.

"Thank you, dear. I knew I could rely on you."

Hannah wasn't sure what she had done to deserve this trust. Certainly, her past behaviour would not warrant it. Maybe it was the implied trust in handing over the letters and revealing her secrets. She asked questions about Gammy's time in the land army and Hannah's Nana Violet.

After some time, Gammy sighed and replaced her cup with a clatter onto the saucer. "What time is your train?"

Hannah glanced at her watch. "Wow, that time's gone quickly. My taxi's due in ten minutes."

"Oh." Gammy's face fell, then she smiled. "Thank you so much for coming, Hannah. I can't tell you how much it means to me."

"I'm sorry I left it so long." Hannah stared at the dregs in her teacup. "I need to hand in my next chapter in a fortnight, so it'll be around three weeks before I can get back here."

Gammy clapped her hands together. "That would be lovely, thank you."

She glanced at her watch again. "I guess I'd better go. It's been great to see you, Gammy."

144

Rising, Hannah stretched forward to kiss her and dragged herself away. She couldn't believe she had actually enjoyed hearing about Gammy's family and growing up in the thirties. Hannah felt she had to hold on for dear life. Her vision of how she saw the world was shifting. What had been raw and angry up close, with time and maturity, shifted perspective. She could see the context now with the knowledge of the letters. Suki was right; Gammy was a lonely old lady. Shame that she had been so judgemental shook her own sense of self. She would need to re-evaluate who she was in the world.

The taxi ride was uneventful, and the train was only five minutes late so Hannah scored that a victory. After she claimed her seat, she pulled out her phone and called the number she had plugged in earlier.

"Is that Katherine Braithwaite?"

"Speaking."

"Hey. It's Hannah Jones, Maud Heaston's great—"

"Hannah, I know who you are. It's lovely to hear from you. Haven't you just been to visit your gammy? How was she?"

The solicitor knew the family name for Gammy; maybe she was more involved than Hannah knew. But she had been avoiding all contact for over a year. Hannah shivered and squirmed in her train seat, as there was a draught coming from somewhere. "Okay, I think, but she's fretting that she's not in the same care home as Auntie Bea. She said she'd arranged it before Auntie Bea went in and that you were chasing it."

Katherine sighed. "Hang on, I'm just pulling over. There seems to be an issue, and I'm not sure how best to proceed as I don't have any powers."

"What do you mean?" Hannah flipped at the unread pages of her latest chapter, but it held little interest when a family drama was unfolding before her, one she should have been aware of.

Katherine cleared her throat. Hannah could imagine her doing that before she dealt with a serious conversation with her clients.

"How much do you know about the choice of home?"

Guilt prodded her, like walking with a stone in her shoe. She should have known, taken an interest, been there for Gammy. But she couldn't lie. "Nothing."

"Your gammy arranged for Bea to go into the home she did because they specialise in the deaf. Bea is both virtually deaf and legally blind. She planned to join Bea when she'd settled the rest of her affairs."

Alarm bells rang; she already didn't like where this was going. "But?"

"*But* your cousin Amanda arranged for your Gammy to stay in the home she is in now, which is a very nice home, I think you'll agree."

"It felt more like a five-star hotel but with extra sound effects."

Katherine laughed gently. "Precisely. It would appear the home is owned by the same company that own the exclusive golf and spa resort of which Amanda is a member."

Hannah didn't need long for the implications to percolate. "You think Amanda's getting some benefit or kickback?"

"I'm not sure what she would achieve, unless she receives a discount for the resort."

"Bloody money-grubbing—" Hannah muttered.

"Pardon?"

"Nothing, sorry. I don't suppose we have any proof?" Hannah asked, flicking at the pages of her chapter. So much for working on the train.

"No, none."

Something didn't smell right about that. Even if there was nothing fraudulent about it, it seemed to be a huge conflict of interest. "What if I phoned the resort and asked if there were any discounts for me, because my great aunt is in a care home run by their sister company?"

"Well, you could try."

Hannah stretched as best she could with her bag under the seat in front. Train seats weren't made for tall people. "I could speak to Amanda directly, but she'll just give me grief. I want to ask if I can claim any expenses on the train trips from the trust—I need to eat this month. Or I might try speaking to Matthew," Hannah said. "Could we take Gammy to visit Auntie Bea's home? Or vice versa?"

"You would think so, wouldn't you? But your gammy's home don't like their residents going elsewhere without the approval of the person paying the bill. They're petrified they'll be accused of facilitating kidnapping."

"As I'm a trustee, could I authorise it?"

"If you can get Matthew or Amanda to countersign the authority, yes."

"That's ridiculous. Okay, I'll definitely speak to Matthew and see if we can arrange it. Do you think Gammy could cope with a taxi?"

"No need. If it's a weekend, I can take you over and bring you back to the station."

"Are you sure? Won't your family mind you spending a day acting as chauffeur?"

Katherine laughed. "My wife will be out playing golf if she gets half a chance."

Wife? She hadn't expected that. All these queer women hidden away and she had no idea. Were they all part of some Sapphic Support Society? "In that case, great, thanks. What about bringing Auntie Bea over to see Gammy? If she's mobile, that could be easier."

"Unfortunately, the owners of that home won't deal with anyone who isn't the next of kin, and Bea has put down your gammy as next of kin."

Damn Amanda and her interference. If she had just done what Gammy had arranged this wouldn't be a problem. Hannah would bet her last penny Amanda was getting some benefit out of the deal. "Talk about catch twenty-two. If we could get a letter signed by Gammy to take to Auntie Bea's home, we may be able to take Auntie Bea to visit Gammy?"

"That's what I thought. I'm visiting next weekend, so I'll draft something for her to sign then."

"Thanks, Katherine. I'm sure they appreciate it, I do."

"It's the least I can do. They were both wonderful to me when I came out and was setting up my practice."

That didn't sound like the gammy she remembered. She had misjudged Gammy, again. And if that was an invitation for Hannah to spill the beans, she wasn't taking it. Not that it bothered her the whole carriage listening in, but it wasn't anyone else's business. "We're coming towards Birmingham New Street now, so the signal will drop out. Thanks for everything you're doing."

"You're welcome. Good luck with your thesis."

So Katherine knew about that too. Hannah picked up her chapter and her green pen. Her supervisor still wanted more historical case studies, but she was coming up blank on extra context.

Hannah stared out of the train window as it pulled away from Birmingham. Her phone buzzed with an incoming text.

ETA? Pizza? Suki xox

8:45ish. Perfect H xox

I've been reading more of your Gammy's letters. Hope that's okay?

Hannah assumed Suki was just being friendly and indulgent to Hannah. This called for more than a text exchange. "Hey, you can't read them without me."

"You want me to read them out to you?"

Suki's tone was soft. Hannah wanted to keep the connection going so she could nuzzle up to her phone. "Why not? I'm not going to get the corrections done. Where have you got to?"

"Okay, this seems to be after her brother Harry's death, and while your gammy was in the Land Army, but Bea had moved to work in London," Suki said.

"I don't think she ever got over Uncle Harry's death. She used to talk about him when I lived with them."

"Ahem, are you listening?"

Hannah's heart lifted at the sound of the smile in Suki's voice. She liked to be in charge, and Hannah was good with that. "Yes, boss."

September 1947
Dearest B,

Thank you for sending the details of the accountancy practices. Unfortunately, they responded the same as everyone else, that they are only taking on ex-service men for training—the key being men. I'm beginning to think I will never find a job in London. Unlike you, I have no skills, and with the food shortages, they want people to continue in the Land Army until the farm workers have all been demobbed. Then we'll be released. I'm feeling rather despondent about it all.

"In all the letters we've seen, that's the first time your gammy has admitted feeling defeated."

"I know, that's so unlike her. She's certainly a fighter. Even now."

"How exhausting, having to fight for everything you should just be able to have anyway."

Hannah smoothed out the papers in front of her. It was true, apart from losing her immediate family, she'd had it easy. But in a way, Suki had lost her family by choosing to work on the other side of the world, and she fought to be heard. Maybe that's why Suki seemed to think of Gammy as a kindred spirit. "A bit like you," Hannah whispered so the rest of the carriage couldn't hear.

"What do you mean?"

"Sooks, I've seen how you are when you feel people are disrespecting you or overlooking you; you get all feisty, so they can't help but notice you. It's got to be exhausting."

"Oh." Suki sniffed. "But you see me." She drew the phrase out as though realisation was breaking, like fog slowly burning off to reveal the sun.

"See you right now? Only if we used FaceTime," Hannah said, unable to keep the smart-arse grin off her face.

"Baka gaijin," Suki said, but it sounded affectionate. "Do you want to hear this?"

Hannah could cope with being called a stupid foreigner. She stared out the window at the houses flickering by like an old-fashioned movie film when it breaks. "Yeah, go on."

"Oh. She goes on a rant about the Japanese. The essence is that we're not to be trusted."

Shit. "Suki, I'm sorry. I've been skipping those bits. It's just she was so angry and upset about Harry, she blamed—"

"I get it. And I kind of understand it too."

"Really?"

"Yeah, if you're fed all the propaganda. When I see a patient coming in with a Daily Mail tucked under their arm, I know I'm in for a hard time."

"I'm sorry. But it becomes ingrained. Gammy wouldn't eat rice or buy anything Japanese. Yet at the home, she's given rice and they have a Yamaha piano, though I don't think she can play anymore because of her hands."

"What are you apologising for? My parents had a hard time being in a mixed marriage in Japan, so it's not unique. Besides, during the war the Japanese culture was you should never surrender, so as far as the Japanese soldiers were concerned, the Allied prisoners were dishonourable. Anyway, what's wrong with her hands?"

"They're not steady enough. Her Parkinson's is worse than I thought. It's hard to see. She got a lot of pleasure playing the piano although she said she was never as good as Nana Violet or my grandad."

"I'm sorry to hear that."

Hannah stared out at the fields, now bleaching into grey as the sun dipped down below the horizon. She slipped into a memory of her time living with Gammy and Auntie Bea.

Hannah had finished her homework and joined Gammy and Auntie Bea in the living room where they were working on a crossword, chatting, and reading the papers. They always took the Times and the Guardian, although Auntie Bea also read the left-wing intellectual paper, the Fabian Review.

Gammy huffed and shook her paper. "It says here that Nissan are making twelve hundred people redundant in their Sunderland plant."

Hannah groaned.

"I don't understand why anyone would buy Japanese."

Because they're not xenophobes like you. "Maybe the Japanese build cars people actually want. Not everyone can afford a Jaguar or Bentley." Hannah knew she shouldn't really wind her up, but she couldn't stand the bigotry.

"But the Japanese treated the prisoners as less than human."

How many times did she have to listen to this shit? "Just like the British slave owners treated their slaves then. You know, like our ancestors," Hannah said.

Gammy huffed and slapped her newspaper onto the side table. "That's ridiculous. The Heastons never had slaves. Get your facts right."

Hannah grinned. "But I've been researching for my project, and the Heaston Bank provided funding for the Birmingham gun manufacturers that were used by the slave owners, so that makes them equally culpable."

Gammy's eyes and mouth widened in large circles, like she was drowning in facts.

"Hannah has a point," Auntie Bea said.

Gammy glared at her. "You can keep out of this, Beatrice. I did not ask your opinion."

Hannah didn't remember Gammy and Auntie Bea arguing before. She looked from one to the other, unsure how this was going to unfold but was mesmerised anyway.

Gammy huffed again and stood, sweeping up her empty cup with a clatter. "I'm going to bed. Can you make sure the fire is out and all the doors are locked? Good night. I'll see you in the morning."

So, Gammy was going to run away rather than discuss the matter like adults. What a coward.

After she left, Auntie Bea sighed. "I think I might need to join you in the doghouse tonight." She put down her paper and tilted her head to one side. "Have you had any further thoughts about which course you're going to apply to?"

Hannah pulled at the frayed threads around the holes in her skinny jeans. She really didn't want this conversation but at least Auntie Bea listened. "I know you both want me to go to Cambridge—"

"I've never said that." Bea placed her hands on the arms of her wingback chair.

"Gammy does. But I really fancy the Politics and International Relations course at Bristol." Her burning cheeks were a dead giveaway.

"Aha. And does this happen to be because a certain Megan is going to Bristol?"

Shit. A thread unravelled from her jeans. It seemed fitting, as if her entire life was falling apart. There was no point trying to lie; Auntie Bea was as sharp as they come. "Please don't tell Gammy. I know she doesn't approve of Megan."

Auntie Bea raised one eyebrow. "Your secret is safe with me, but you know you can talk to us—"

"No, thanks. You wouldn't understand."

"I think you might be surprised."

Outside it had turned black, and all Hannah could see was her reflection in the carriage windowpane. She'd never realised there might be something in that comment. She relayed the last part of her memory to Suki.

"You came to Bristol to follow a girl?"

Hannah coughed. "Yeah, not that it lasted. Within six months, she met a guy who joined a merchant bank in London on graduation."

"You seem to fall for bisexual women," Suki said.

Hannah took the comment as curious rather than critical and shook her head. "I think Megan's definitely a has-bian. I'm sure she'd be horrified if you mentioned it now."

"Great for me. Now should I read more of this letter, or are you almost here?"

Hannah's heart skipped. *Great for me?* Did that mean that Suki was thinking they could be more, or just that she understood? Hannah peered out of the window at the glow of the city and necklaces of streetlights converging on the centre. "We're just coming to the outskirts of Bristol now. Let's have a look after supper."

And as Hannah stuffed her thesis into her rucksack, it occurred to her it was after that day that she knew Gammy no longer had any power over her. Thinking about it, it was also the day she started to pull away and strike for her independence. But why had she made things so difficult? With the perspective of time and understanding, Gammy had been trying her best, and it must have been hard to go back to secrets and lies about her relationship with Auntie Bea. How had she not seen the signs at the time that Gammy and Auntie Bea were a couple? Of course she hadn't. She was young and too self-absorbed to be concerned with what was going on around her.

CHAPTER TWENTY-FIVE
Bristol

SUKI PATTED THE seat next to her on the sofa. "Hey, come and sit here." Hannah wasn't going to turn that down. She hadn't approached the "where are we going with this" talk again, but Hannah was hopeful. She brought over their teas and placed them on the side tables. "I've got the last letter they exchanged for quite a while."

"Let me see. Come lie down."

Suki patted her lap and Hannah rested her head there, her body stretched out over the sofa and her legs dangling over the edge. Not the comfiest but definitely her new favourite position, looking up at Suki, smelling her sweet perfume, and feeling the rise and fall of her breath. They exchanged glances, and Suki gave her a shy smile. It was all Hannah could do not to break into a wide grin. She lifted up the letter and began to read.

"It's dated October 1947, in London from Bea to Gammy."

Dearest M,

I can't believe this time next week you will be here to live. It's my biggest wish come true. I hope you like the house. It's in the suburbs, and I confess I would not have got it at all if my father hadn't put down the deposit and my work hadn't said I needed it. They're not giving priority to single women. It's so much nicer than the digs I was staying in, constantly trying to avoid the landlady's husband. Why do men think it's their right to paw you as you walk past? Anyway, none of that from now on, except the welcome attentions of yourself, of course!

Perivale is a typical suburb and away from the main smog of London, which will be good for your asthma. As it's on the Central line, it will take you directly into Bank and your new job. I couldn't afford any furniture, not that there is much to have, just the utility furniture. I bought a new mattress, though, so that will have to be our bed and sofa for the moment. I hope you don't mind.

I cannot wait until you're here, and we can start our new life together. How were the Hardys with you leaving the farm? They've probably got used to having you around now. Have you seen Alice and her baby recently?

I will come to King's Cross to meet you on Sunday. I'm counting down the minutes.

88
Your loving B.

"What's with the 88 thing?" Suki asked.

"I googled it. Radio hams used it as short code in Morse for love and kisses."

"But isn't that two fat ladies?"

"In bingo, yeah. But I don't think either of them could be called a fat lady."

Suki stroked Hannah's hair. A groan escaped Hannah's lips before she could stop it.

"Neither can we," Suki said.

Her touch was soft and delicate as a light breeze on a summer's day and Hannah felt like purring. Suki swirled the short strands of hair around her fingers.

"I love your hair. It always smells so nice." She inhaled deeply. "Apples." Her lips grazed Hannah's forehead.

Hannah twisted her face to Suki like a flower following the sun, basking in the warmth. "I love it when you do that," she said.

Suki lowered herself further, kissing down Hannah's nose and eventually connecting with her mouth. It was tentative at first, then when Hannah responded, Suki opened her mouth and met Hannah's tongue with her own. A switch went on, exciting Hannah's whole being. Electricity zapped between them, and every nerve sparked and arced and tingled.

Finally, Suki pulled away. "Will you come to bed with me?"

Hannah registered the slight tremble in Suki's voice. She'd seen behind Suki's feisty image before, her cover so she wouldn't be taken for granted and would be respected. "Are you sure?" Hannah held out a hand to help Suki up. She put the crumpled letter on the side to sort out later.

"Uh huh." Suki switched off the side lamp, leaving only the borrowed light from the microwave to illuminate the hall.

Hannah half tripped over the bed in the unfamiliar bedroom. It filled much more of the room than she remembered from her occasional foray into it, but she didn't care as her heart raced in anticipation.

Suki switched on the bedside lamp that cast a soft glow, rippling shadows over the bedclothes. "Come," Suki said.

She clearly wanted to be in control, and Hannah was willing to comply. In her phase of flings and one-night stands, in her angry undergraduate days, she'd been the one to control and dominate, but it was different with Suki. This was more like uncurling the mainsail for the wind to catch and take her skimming over the water, exhilarating with the frisson of being on the tipping point of capsizing.

And she didn't disappoint. Suki dropped on the bed and observed Hannah standing in the half light. "Strip for me," said Suki.

Hannah whipped off her hoodie and T-shirt in one swoop, then paused as Suki's eyes focused on her. There was a softness there that Hannah had never seen before and the unmistakable glint of desire. Hannah opened the button of her jeans, not quite believing that her fantasy was finally playing out.

"Let me." Suki pulled Hannah close. She unzipped and hoisted down the material for Hannah to step out of. Suki snapped the elastic of Hannah's boxers. "I wondered what they looked like on. Very you, somehow, very androgynous."

Hannah began to take them off.

"Leave them on for now."

Hannah dismissed the unwelcome thought that maybe Suki didn't want to be faced with her lack of male junk underneath the cotton material. Suki trailed her index finger up over Hannah's belly button to just below her breasts, and the thrill of desire set off goosebumps all over her, making her shiver. In one motion, Suki traced her fingers out over the fabric of the bra across Hannah's nipples. Arousal flooded Hannah, and she moaned as her knees buckled.

Suki pulled up Hannah's bralette. Hannah shrugged off the straps, and it dropped in the puddle of clothes. Suki's eyes widened as she seemed mesmerised by Hannah's breasts.

"You're beautiful," she said and glanced up to meet Hannah's gaze, her expression one of wonder. "May I?"

"Of course." *Do whatever you want, but please do something now before I explode.*

Suki slid her hands to the front and caressed Hannah's breasts gently with her thumbs, then tweaked Hannah's hardening nipples. Suki kissed from the base of her neck down her chest, eventually replacing one hand with her mouth, and she licked and bit where her nipple rings had been. Hannah twitched and thrust her chest forward.

"On the bed, now," Suki whispered hoarsely.

Hannah spun around and flopped onto the bed, pulling Suki on top of her. The headboard banged against the wall. They needed to move it, but the thought drifted out of her consciousness as Suki sucked hard and with her free hand slipped it south over Hannah's stomach and skittered over the material of her boxers to caress her inner thigh.

Hannah arched her hips, but Suki ignored the invitation and traced circles on Hannah's leg and up to the meeting of her thighs. "You're killing me," Hannah said through gritted teeth, as Suki stroked her fingers over the fabric. Hannah could smell her own sex as Suki slipped her hand under her cotton shorts, now drenched with arousal.

"Mm, I think someone's a little excited."

Suki circled her finger around Hannah's clit, tantalisingly close. Hannah's body tingled to be touched, and she focused on the pulsing between her thighs. Suki's eyes were dark, searching. Her lips parted, and she pulled at Hannah's bottom lip with her teeth. It almost sent Hannah over the edge with desire, even though Suki had barely touched her yet. But she was so close. Suki's finger teased around her folds, then slipped in through the slickness, and Hannah's muscles tightened.

Suki's finger retreated, and a second joined the first, reaching deeper and wider. Her thumb brushed against Hannah's clit, and she bit at the pillow so she didn't scream out. Her pulse slapped in her temples as Suki thrust into her, deeper and faster. She paused only to circle Hannah's clit again, then resume her thrusting inside, curling her fingers upwards, till a cry deep in Hannah's throat unleashed itself, as she cascaded into a crashing, juddering orgasm. Hannah lay still, tremors coursing through her body, and tried to catch her breath.

"Oh my god, where did you learn that?"

Suki laughed and kissed her. "You're amazing when you come."

Hannah shook her head. "God, and you're not even undressed." She flipped Suki over, who squealed with delight. "I think we need to redress this," Hannah whispered. "Unless you'd like to go and read some more letters or play on my Xbox?"

"Don't you dare," she hissed.

"You'd like me to do this?" Hannah opened Suki's jeans slowly, and she lifted her butt so Hannah could remove them. Hannah looked up to see Suki biting her lip. "Hey, you okay?"

Suki worried her bottom lip some more. "I feel a bit shy now, after your display a few minutes ago. I very rarely have orgasms. I guess it's that letting go I find hard to do."

She flashed an apologetic grin and looked up at Hannah, an element of fear mingling with desire in her glittering eyes.

"It isn't a competition, Sooks. It's about enjoying it, and if you're not enjoying it, we'll stop now."

"No, no, I want it. I just..." Suki tugged at her top.

"Okay, but maybe if you tell me what you want, then you're in control." Where was the bossy, confident Suki who seemed to have multiple orgasms with Farty Boy? "Wait, it sounded like you really enjoyed sex with Connor."

A blush crept up Suki's cheeks. "I faked it, because it made him feel good."

Hannah brushed away a tear that glistened and trickled down Suki's face. She turned away, as though ashamed of her admission and her tears. What internal and external pressures did Suki feel to conform? She hated to see Suki like this, self-conscious and uncomfortable. Hannah cupped her face in her hand and gently pulled her head around so she could stare deep into her eyes. "Please don't ever fake it with me, or feel you need to. We'll only do what you like." Hannah wasn't sure Suki bought her plea completely, but she did trust Suki's openness and vulnerability. Suki was like a rose that was all prickles until it buds, then all Hannah could do was imbibe the scent and admire the beauty.

"I'd like you to undress me slowly. No, not that slowly."

Hannah pulled Suki's top over her head and revealed a lacy, delicate bra in royal blue that popped against the colour of her skin. "Stunning."

Hannah breathed and caught Suki's gaze.

"Are you going to get on with it?"

Hannah smiled, deciding to play along. "Yes, your ladyship." She traced her index fingers down to Suki's chest. "Hm, front fastening."

"Yeah, and push up, so there's not as much there as it might seem."

As the bra cups fell away to reveal Suki's small breasts and pert nipples, the sight poured petrol on Hannah's fire. Suki closed her eyes momentarily and shrugged off her straps.

"You're beautiful," Hannah said. Suki's body reacted as she brushed her fingertips over her hardening nipples and smoothed her fingers around her navel, then down to the top of Suki's knickers.

"Take them off," Suki said.

Hannah removed the fabric and inhaled the scent of sweet perfume and the musky aroma of sex. Hannah moaned at the sight of Suki's clit, engorged and inviting.

"Please lick me. Yes, like that." Suki shuddered, and her breath caught. "Yes, suck and... oh God, Han."

Hannah circled Suki's clit with her tongue and licked down her folds, causing Suki to buck.

"Please lick me, and go inside with your finger, no two."

Her next utterances were unintelligible, but Suki gripped Hannah's shoulders and pushed her hips forward to give Hannah more access.

"Faster."

Hannah struggled to maintain contact with her mouth as Suki writhed and bounced, causing the headboard to hammer against the wall.

"Don't stop, I'm almost..."

With an extra pull on Suki's clit, Hannah curled her fingers to the inner spot and glanced up. Suki threw her head back, shuddering and contracting on Hannah's fingers and trembling with aftershocks.

Suki didn't speak for a while, and Hannah enjoyed the beatific expression on her face as though a candle glass had been lit from within. Hannah clambered up the bed and wiped away the sweat from Suki's forehead. "Okay?"

Suki just peered at her through narrowed eyes. "Wow. Why didn't you tell me you were this good?" Suki asked.

Hannah grinned. "All I did was follow your instructions."

"I think I stopped instructing, didn't I?"

"Your body took over. Thanks for trusting me."

Suki stretched and smiled. "No, thank you. But I might need to check whether it was just a one off or whether you can achieve the same results again."

"Happy to oblige anytime. Purely on the grounds of science, of course."

Suki pulled Hannah to her and kissed her fiercely, as though she wanted to devour her. "Why didn't we do this before?" Suki asked.

"We're doing it now. Let's make up for lost time." Hannah felt as though they'd sifted through to the nugget below, not just the sex but to the intimacy, understanding, and respect.

CHAPTER TWENTY-SIX
London, 1949

MAUD'S SENIOR COLLEAGUE, Robert Berryman, entered the office reeking of alcohol after lunch. He slumped onto his chair and lay his head on his desk, pushing aside a pile of ledgers. When he acknowledged her, his face far too close to hers, his breath permeated the air like a thick malodorous fog and she tried not to inhale. She was determined to finish writing the general ledger this afternoon and check the double entry to make sure all the balances balanced before she neatly underlined the totals.

The clock ticked, and next door, separated by a high partition, she could hear Maisie, the receptionist and secretary, clacking on her Olivetti typewriter and answering the phone, taking messages for the partners. She was supposed to do the filing too but rarely had time to complete everything, so Maud did her own filing when she finished her tasks. She looked up at the sound of Berryman snoring. She hoped the partners couldn't hear. It was so gloomy in the room. The overall colour in the office was dark brown, and the only light was borrowed from the windows into reception. It seemed so Dickensian, she almost expected them to write with quill pens. But it was a job, and it meant she and Bea could live together, independently.

Berryman snored again, followed by a stuttering intake of breath. Maud couldn't decide whether it was better to wake him and be subjected to his tormenting or leave him where he could get into trouble and then take it out on her anyway. She was about to manoeuvre her way around the filing cabinets to rouse him when the door opened.

Mr Yarborough, the junior partner, entered, a pipe clenched between his teeth and a ledger in his arms. "What's going on with Mr Berryman?"

Maud sat up straight in her chair and smoothed the blotting paper, not sure how much to reveal. "He had a business lunch with the Ginger's Biscuits bosses."

Mr Yarborough shook his head and frowned and placed the ledger on her desk. "Why did he bother? There's no way they'll leave Mastersons.

What a waste of the new client budget."

Despite having a member of staff clearly the worse for drink, Mr Yarborough didn't seem too disconcerted. Maud felt embarrassed for Berryman, even though he was a pain in her neck. She held her tongue but could have added Berryman was best friends with the son and heir apparent to the Ginger's Biscuits fortune.

Mr Yarborough puffed on his pipe, but the few sparks glowed and faded. "Damn, I need this set of accounts to be drawn up by tomorrow lunchtime."

"I can do that, sir." Maud offered her widest smile.

"But you're just a bookkeeper."

Maud clenched her teeth and stretched the smile that was becoming more fake by the second. Mr Yarborough wasn't even aware of the insult, as he pulled on his pipe with a sipping noise.

"Perhaps, sir, but if you remember, I applied for accountancy articles and came top in the aptitude tests. And when Mr Berryman leaves his textbooks around, I've been reading up on the subject."

Mr Yarborough took his pipe from his mouth, pressed down on the tobacco, and rummaged in his pockets for his matches. He appraised Maud through narrowed eyes for a few seconds. "Why would you do that?"

He struck his match on the desk and puffed at his pipe to light it. Paper and other combustible materials covered the desk. His cavalier attitude toward fire reminded her of Bill and Harry. She gulped. Now was not the time to think of her brothers. Instead, she smiled again as though it was the most obvious thing to say. "Because I want to be articled and eventually become a chartered accountant."

Mr Yarborough sucked in and then blew out a fog of smoke. She would need to open the high window to the next office when he left. It was the thing she missed most about the Land Army, the fresh air and light. He had a twinkle in his eye and a kind expression.

"Miss Heaston, I admire your dedication, but no firm is going to article a woman. The training's too expensive, and I don't need to remind you that under the marriage bar, women have to leave when they marry."

"I won't ever marry, sir."

"Why ever not?" He looked her up and down. "A strong, young woman like you, the daughter of a baronet, I'm sure you would make a young man a nice catch."

Yes, that was what they always saw: her father's title. "My fiancé was killed in the war, sir, and I do not intend to get married." The two statements were factually correct, but hid all the crucial facts, a bit like the new bikinis that had just come out in France. Not that she would ever wear one, but Bea had talked about getting one. She fought to control the upswing of her lips, as she thought about how Bea would look in a tiny scrap of material.

"I'm sorry to hear that, Miss Heaston, and I admire your loyalty, but then you'd never have children."

Obviously, she was not to be viewed as anything but a breeding factory. But she wasn't going to back down, even if he thought she was being insolent, or speaking out of turn. "No, sir, but I have five—I mean three—brothers and sisters, so I will have plenty of nephews and nieces, I'm sure."

He stared at her, then at the ledger on the desk, and seemed to debate with himself. Finally, with a glance at Berryman's body, he turned to Maud. "See if you can draw up a set of accounts with profit-and-loss account and balance sheet from this set of books. Bring them to me by nine tomorrow morning. Tucked in the front are last year's accounts, which will act as a guide."

"Yes, sir, thank you, sir." Maud pulled the ledger towards her and extracted the previous year's accounts and accounting template, excitement and trepidation fizzing in her blood. He nodded and exited, his shiny black shoes clopping on the wooden floor.

In theory, Maud knew where most of the expenses were allocated. Now it was just a question of putting it all together. She chewed her bottom lip and sat at her desk undisturbed for nearly an hour before Berryman raised his head. He stretched.

"Hey, giraffe, any chance of a cup of tea? And have you finished writing up those books from yesterday yet?"

Maud clenched her teeth. How dare he use the same nickname as Harry had given her? Maybe he felt intimidated because she was a good two inches taller than him.

"I will make tea, but I'm doing some work for Mr Yarborough."

His eyes widened, as he perhaps realised Mr Yarborough would have seen him in a compromising position, certainly grounds for terminating his articles. He cleared his throat. "What, directly?"

E.V. Bancroft

She nodded to the ledgers and accounts in front of her, not meeting his eye. His ego would make him difficult to be around, and she didn't need any more tormenting.

He straightened in his seat and aligned his tie. "But he's supposed to come through me. I'm the senior articled clerk."

"You weren't available." It galled her that this wastrel should be given all the opportunities, especially as he seemed to squander everything he had. *It's a job* she repeated to herself for the umpteenth time that day, and it gave her the independence to live with Bea.

He coloured and tapped his pen on the blotter. "The client insisted we had another drink, but I think I'll be able to get him to come around and give us the custom." They both knew he was lying, but his job was secure, so he smiled and wiped some drool on the back of his hand. "Tea, thank you."

When she returned, he was looking over what she had been working on. Bile rose up her throat, and she banged down the cup and saucer, not caring if it slipped over the side. She had deliberately forgotten to include a biscuit and sugar.

"Well, you've been doing the easy bit so far, all the profit and loss accounts. I'll be interested to see how you get on with the balance sheet."

Berryman flipped over the sheets and followed the figures down with his finger, tallying the total in his head, and nodded. He wouldn't be able to challenge her arithmetic, as she had checked it twice. He fixed her with his bloodshot eyes, and she caught the whiff of stale alcohol as he snatched the saucer from the desk.

"Don't forget to amortise all the trademarks using a reducing balance method," he said. "Cheers. Damn, there's no sugar. Maisie, hello, Maisie, can you bring me in some sugar, sweetie?" he shouted.

"Of course, Mr Berryman," Maisie said from the other side of the thin wooden screens that carved up the office.

Maud's eyes narrowed. She didn't know what he meant but was determined to find out. Returning to the ledger, she entered the figures in pencil in the templates they had.

Berryman looked over from the newspaper he was reading and waggled his index finger at her. "Uh, uh, don't write in pencil. Surely you know that by now. Too easy to be manipulated."

She adopted the false smile and an overly bright tone, determined he would not get to her. "Of course, Mr Berryman, that's true for writing up the ledgers, but I'm drawing up the statutory accounts, and I only have one accounting template."

Nearly two hours later, she had completed most of the sections but needed to look up what amortisation meant. She had followed what she could from the previous year, but it appeared to be different. Berryman was just putting his newspaper into his leather briefcase. Should she just look it up when he left? But he would be livid if she touched his personal property. "Could I consult your financial accounting textbook, please?"

He grinned at her and tossed the book into his briefcase. "Sorry, no can do. I need this for revision tonight."

It was the first time she'd ever known him to take any books home. Ordinarily, he would get her to cover his work (with very detailed overbearing instructions, as if she was stupid) and then study in the office, except when the partners came through.

Swallowing her pride and the irritation crawling up her throat, Maud said, "In that case, can you tell me how I amortise the goodwill?"

He smirked again and cracked his knuckles, enjoying himself just a little too much. *Pompous git.*

"Okay, but I can only spare you two minutes; I'm meeting some friends at the club shortly."

Maud finally arrived home just before eight, tired but pleased. She had hardly stepped through the door when Bea approached her, all smiles. Maud's heart lifted tempo, and she reflected on the welcome. How she loved this woman. Bea relieved Maud of her satchel and pulled her into a tight embrace.

"Good evening, sweetheart. You're late." Bea slid her hand under Maud's jacket and tickled her nails down her back.

"I had to cope with Berryman being drunk on the job again. But it's given me an opportunity, because I have to draw up a set of accounts and present them to Mr Yarborough by nine tomorrow."

Bea gave her a kiss that said I love you no matter what you have to put up with, and the world shifted back into its proper place.

"What a lobcock, but good for you. Tell me all about it when I get back, but I need to dash as I've a meeting of the Wollstonecraft Appreciation Society. Would you like me to check what you've done, later?"

Maud chewed her lip. Although Bea had never done accounting, she was still a whizz at thinking through problems. It's why it was such a puzzle that she chose a job as a bilingual secretary rather than going back to Girton College. But it meant they were together. Maud couldn't help but smile. "Would you mind?"

"Of course. I've made supper. It's in the oven." She cupped both her hands around Maud's face. "I love you, and I'm so proud of you," she said and kissed her on the nose.

"I love you too." *Even though I have no idea what you really do at work.*

As Maud heard Bea singing on her way down the hall, it seemed incredible that this beautiful, vivacious woman chose to be with her. They revelled in their love making, and Maud was an eager student. She chuckled to herself. At work, they always accused her of being strait-laced. If only they knew what Bea and she had explored in the bedroom. She sighed. To work.

The following morning, she presented her set of accounts at eight when she first arrived. Mr Yarborough took them from her and looked them over, without a word. He cross-checked the figures with the ledgers, making little ticks and circles in coloured pencils on the accounts. He looked up from the papers. "Thank you, Miss Heaston, I'll get back to you. Now return to your work, please."

"Yes, sir, I will. Thank you for the opportunity, sir."

He waved her off, seemingly not as generous as he had the previous day. Was he displeased with what she had done? She glanced at her last view of green leaves and daylight for the day and returned to the cave of an office she shared with Berryman.

About half an hour later, Mr Yarborough came through, his pipe clenched between his teeth and his arms full of ledgers. He dropped them on her desk.

"Miss Heaston, this is pretty impressive. The only error I can find is that the company has a policy of amortising trademarks using the straight-line basis, not reducing balance method."

So, Berryman had deliberately fed her the wrong information, the bastard. Berryman gleamed at her, slouching back in his chair.

"I'm surprised that Mr Berryman didn't tell you." Mr Yarborough flashed a look at Berryman, who shuffled to sit up straight, "but he wasn't in a fit state to do anything yesterday afternoon." He fixed Berryman with a hard glare. "I had a word with Mr Gardener, and he agrees you should have an afternoon's pay docked, Mr Berryman. It would appear your lunch was not on authorised firm business."

"But, sir—"

"That will be all. I will expect the Marston Webber accounts on my desk by six o'clock this evening."

He swept out of the office, puffing at his pipe, leaving a trail of smoke signals to pollute the air. Maud got up to follow him out to go to the powder room and escape the wrath that was doubtless coming to her, but Berryman rolled his chair to block her way between the desks and filing cabinets. "Smug are you, missy?"

"I'm only trying to do my job, Mr Berryman. Now, please will you excuse me? I need to go. Would you like me to bring you a cup of tea on my way back?" There was no point poking an already angry bear, as he could do her too much damage.

"You'd better. And if you are so clever, you can draft the Marston Webber accounts. I'll need them by four." His lips twitched as he rolled to let her pass and rummaged in his drawer for his newspaper.

"You'll have them at five to six after I've finished my other work, and you'll have to trust me that I've done them correctly, rather than deliberately sabotaging them."

He shot out of his chair. "How dare you?"

She strode out of the room, smiling to herself, knowing she had won. This round, anyway.

Half an hour later, Mr Yarborough asked to see Maud in his office. Berryman smirked at her, obviously anticipating she was in trouble. She just smiled at him when she shadowed Mr Yarborough, hiding the trembling in her knees.

Mr Yarborough entered his office and shut the door behind her. "Please sit, Miss Heaston."

"Thank you, sir." It was the first time he had invited her to sit on the leather visitor chair in front of the desk, and she hoped it wasn't the last. From it, she could see into the square. The leaves were rustling in the trees, dappling the sunlight. A cooling breeze drifted in through the cracked open window. She inhaled, but the air was a mix of tobacco and musty books.

"Don't look so worried." He wiped his forehead with a handkerchief and tucked the square into the pocket of his suit. "Mr Gardener and I have discussed your situation. I understand that you will not marry, and there are not as many eligible men around anyway. I would hate to think my daughter was not given opportunities because of her sex. You have a gift for the work and an enthusiasm which has not gone unnoticed."

"Thank you, sir," she said, holding her breath, waiting for the inevitable *but*.

"We would like to address that. Mr Berryman is articled to Mr Gardener. I would like to ask you if you would be my articled clerk."

Maud was glad she was sitting as she might have collapsed otherwise. *Surely not?* She needed clarification. "You mean to become a qualified bookkeeper?"

"No, Miss Heaston."

Her whole body felt heavy with disappointment, but she tried to maintain a professional expression and straightened her shoulders.

His lips parted into what passed as a smile, revealing his yellowing teeth, discoloured from his constant pipe smoking. "I would like to offer you articles to become a qualified accountant."

Her heart turned somersaults, and she wanted to jump up and down. She battled hard to keep the smile from breaking out on her face. "Oh, thank you, sir, I don't know what to say. But I thought you were going to offer the clerkship to Mr Berryman's brother?"

"Don't you want the position, Miss Heaston?"

Her grin broke free, unfurled like a flag, and she failed to tether it down. "Yes, sir, more than anything in the world. Thank you, sir."

He puffed on his pipe and the leather on his chair squeaked as he leaned back. Maud followed the trail of smoke as it curled, rose, and disappeared.

"Good. You know it's at least a five-year commitment? Longer if you struggle with the exams. The Institute of Chartered Accountants has a few women members now. We are about to enter the 1950s after all. I don't say it will be easy though."

He could try to put her off as much as he wanted, but this was it; the first chink in the cave to let in light, and she would do whatever she must to make it shine. "Yes, sir, I won't let you down."

"You'd better not. I'm sticking my neck out for you. Now would you send Mr Berryman in, please."

"Yes, sir. And thank you again for the opportunity."

She left and skipped through the reception area before composing herself, hoping that Berryman would not be even more vindictive. She couldn't wait to tell Bea this evening.

CHAPTER TWENTY-SEVEN

Perivale, London, 1954

MAUD LET HERSELF into their home. *Home.* Every time she unlatched the gate, she gave a quick prayer of thanks for that. The lights were on in the front sitting room, which was unusual. In case Bea was entertaining, she didn't call out her usual loving greeting. "Hi, Bea."

The door for the sitting room shot open and Bea joined Maud, steering her towards the dining room. "Hi, honey, I hope you're okay if we have a visitor tonight? She may be staying one or two days." Bea hunched her shoulders, tension pulling her normally open stance tight.

Maud frowned. They'd never had guests stay overnight in nearly seven years. "Does that mean one of us will have to move into the other room?" she whispered.

Bea looked startled, as if she hadn't thought about it. She cocked her head to one side. "I suppose that might not be a bad idea."

"What's going on? I've never seen you this tense."

"It's just Lidia has nowhere else to go. And that was part of the deal."

Maud chewed at her bottom lip. "Part of what deal? I don't understand. You're worrying me."

Bea sighed and sat on one of the utility dining chairs. Maud sat on the one opposite and waited for an answer. She looked out at the garden, mainly laid to vegetables and vaguely observed that the carrots needed thinning.

"I can't tell you what I do because I've signed the Official Secrets Act, but part of me being eligible to buy a house after the war as a single woman was that I might occasionally have to take in guests, refugees if you will. Lidia is one of those refugees, originally from Poland, but she has nowhere to go. I'm sorry I couldn't let you know before. I thought about calling you at work."

Maud frowned and drummed her fingers on the table. She hated surprises. She liked things planned, organised, and scheduled. It's part of why she was such a great accountant. "I didn't know there was a condition to us living here."

Bea gripped onto the edge of the table. "Are you saying you wouldn't have moved in? You'd have preferred to share a house with a shared kitchen and toilet and the groping landlord."

Maud raised her hands, palm down. "No, sweetheart, I'm not saying that. It's just we've lived here for seven years now, and I didn't know. It would have been nice to have discussed it and not had it sprung on me when I walk through the door."

Bea's eyes closed off. "I can't discuss it."

Maud had never seen Bea like this before, her lips taut and the tension set around her eyes. Was she in danger? Were they in danger? "Is it illegal? Is she illegal?"

Bea picked up her box of Swan matches and tapped it on the table. It seemed as though she was deciding what to say. "I work for the government. You know that."

"The two are not mutually exclusive." Maud smiled but Bea frowned.

"True, but you'll have to trust me on this. Are you okay?"

"I'm not sure I have a choice. But yes, of course I trust you."

Bea's shoulders relaxed. "I'll see how supper is doing. I made stew."

Maud rose. "Thanks. I'll move my stuff to the box room. I assume Lidia will be in the front?"

"Yes."

Lidia appeared at the dining room door, looking anxiously between the two women.

Bea smiled at her and rose. "I'll finish supper," she said and addressed Lidia in Polish.

"I'll just lay the table then," Maud said, and Bea nodded, her attention still focused on Lidia. Polish was Bea's fourth language after all, and she didn't practise it much. At least, Maud assumed she didn't practise it as she really had no idea what Bea did at work. Bea went through to the kitchen and Lidia followed like a duckling trailing a mother duck, too timid to be out of her sight. She chatted in Polish, and Bea made slower responses.

Maud banged down the cutlery. She'd never felt so excluded from her own home or their joint life. *Get a grip.* Jealousy and anger were not attractive emotions. Bea would pick up her mood in an instant, but she couldn't help the resentment bubbling up. Why hadn't Bea told her before? Maybe she could have prepared better and not felt so mortified that she had to move her belongings from their room to the small box room she used to study. She stomped upstairs and made two extra beds, one for Lidia in the spare room and the other single camp bed in her box room. They didn't have extra single blankets, so she doubled over the pink material to make do.

"Supper's ready," Bea called.

Maud inhaled, straightened her shoulders, and went downstairs. She prepared herself to dig deep into her daughter of a baronet, country gentlewoman façade to be charming and set aside her internal churnings. She smiled as she entered the dining room and took her chair. If she'd looked in the mirror, she probably would've seen a replica of her mother's public smile. She could be polite, civilised, and set aside her own internal turmoil.

Bea handed out the plates and said something in Polish. Lidia nodded and stared at Maud.

Bea's own smile looked strained. "I told Lidia that you came in the top ten in the country in your accountancy exams. Lidia's father was an accountant until he disappeared in 1947."

"I'm sorry for your loss," Maud said, and Bea immediately translated it. Lidia gave Maud a watery smile, then flicked her eyes back to watch Bea as she ladled out the stew.

Maud couldn't remember reading much about Poland after the war, except it was now a vassal state of Russia. She studied Lidia carefully; her eyes were on the move constantly, as if she expected to be attacked at any moment. She seemed very young and vulnerable, and who knew what she had to deal with. Shame gripped Maud that she'd been so angry and judgemental. The poor woman had probably suffered so much already and here she was in a strange land, not yet able to speak the language. No wonder she was clinging to Bea as if her life depended on her. It probably did.

Bea laughed at something and clinked their water glasses as though they were drinking alcohol.

"Lidia said this looks like Polish vodka. I told her it tastes like the Thames."

Maud laughed then took a mouthful of stew. In all honesty, it was more like homegrown carrots and potatoes in gravy. Any meat was lucky dip. She saw Bea had given Lidia three pieces of meat, while Maud had two and Bea none. It was those little acts of kindness that Maud admired so. She placed one of her meat chunks onto Bea's plate. Bea looked as though she was about to object when Lidia said something else. It sounded all z's and no vowels. So different from the Italian opera Bea translated from the gramophone for Maud.

Bea was so smart, and she wasn't petty and resentful like Maud. They lived very different lives. Maud's life was neat, ordered, and methodical, and she loved the truth in numbers. At home, she was open with Bea and chatted about the frustrations and triumphs of the day. Nothing caused her more discomfort than having to hide who she was and pretending that Bea was no more than her landlady and friend. What did they have in common really? Bea was so sophisticated, learned, and multilingual, and she never spoke about her work. But Lidia sitting in their dining room, eating their meat ration, had something to do with Bea's work, but Maud had no idea what.

Maud hated herself for being resentful but struggled to pull herself out of the sinking sand. She cast her net wide into the sea of her emotions but didn't like her catch: a pink crab, all snipping claws out to defend her wounded heart, a bottom feeder sifting through the toxic dust of jealousy. Yet there, amongst the detritus, was a shell she prised open. Formed by grit and an accretion of love was the single pearl of trust in Bea. She would not harm a soul, and she loved Maud, for all her sharpness and insecurities.

"Are you okay?"

Maud raised her head and met Bea's gaze. "Fine, why?"

"I asked you if you wanted cake, twice, but you didn't reply."

Maud smiled. "Must have been miles away."

"Sorry, is it boring for you? Unfortunately, Lidia doesn't speak English. I'm going to try and set her up with lessons from tomorrow."

Maud took a deep breath and kept a retort buried deep.

"Don't worry, Lidia is only staying a day or two until she gets settled. Then I'll show you just how much I appreciate your patience and understanding."

Bea's smile was mischievous and seductive.

Yes, definitely a pearl.

CHAPTER TWENTY-EIGHT

Staffordshire, September 1954

AT HER FATHER'S wake, held at her mother's Georgian townhouse, Maud couldn't help remembering the services for her elder brothers. The whole world had moved on and it seemed they had never existed, except in her heart. Whilst everyone else had closed the flaps of skin and healed, she still had an open wound, raw and sensitive. Ethel Porter, who had been so sweet on Bill, seemed to have moved on quickly as she was married, with a baby on the way, judging by the way she was cradling her stomach.

Violet was nearly twenty-one. She'd been so shy and quiet before the service, with no hint of the little boisterous girl she once was, leaping into Maud's arms. Instead, Vi had held out her hand to shake Maud's, very politely, as though they were strangers. Which they were. Maud had ignored her hand and drawn her into a warm hug. Jack and Joe were both married now. Jack, the eldest twin by twenty-five minutes and now the new baronet, was lording it as the head of the family. He'd followed their father into banking and Joe had moved to London as a stockbroker, but Maud never met up with either of them.

"So, Maud," Jack said, as he helped himself to some salmon paste sandwiches being brought around for the guests, "are you still doing bookkeeping in London?"

She was sure this was his way of trying to put her down. He must know that she'd moved on from that, but maybe Mother never spoke about her or what she was doing. That was certainly a possibility. She stood straighter, her head high. "No. I've qualified as a chartered accountant. I came in the top ten in my exams across the country." A little pride seeped into her tone, but she'd managed it with a lot of help and exam practise from Bea.

His eyes widened. "Really? Given your haphazard education, I'm surprised you were even allowed to do it."

"You'd be surprised what a woman can do if she's given the opportunity. Take Vi, for example, I know Mother expects Vi to look after her now Father has passed, but I'm sure you could do the role just as well, especially now you've moved into Heaston Hall."

Jack gave just the briefest of nods, perhaps conscious that if titles passed down the female line too, it would now be Maud's home and title. He smoothed down his hair, which already seemed to be thinning on the top.

"It's so run down after the Yanks abused it during the war years, it will cost a fortune to return to its former glory. Besides, Elsie and I are planning to have a family soon."

He flashed her a self-satisfied smile of superiority. Maud couldn't believe her little brother had become this arrogant young man. The heat of anger caused the faint hairs on the back of her neck to rise. "Shouldn't Vi be given the opportunity to do what she wants?"

Vi sidled up to Maud and tucked her arm in Maud's elbow. "Oh, don't worry, Maud, I don't mind. Looking after Mother will be an honour. I can't spend my whole life making embroidery and playing the piano. I need to do something useful."

Maud clamped her mouth shut and counted to ten. Didn't Vi have any ambition at all? "But don't you want to do something more than caring for Mother?"

"I did think about becoming a nurse, so I'll just be caring for Mother rather than a stranger. I'm happy to do my duty."

Jack's eyes lit up and Maud pulled back the urge to do or say something she would regret.

"It's just as well Vi is happy, otherwise you'd have to come back from London, given you aren't married."

Maud grimaced in a pale attempt at a smile. "I have a profession now, and no-one can take that away from me."

"Surprised you didn't get married to George Waites while you could, before the war. His father's here. Have you seen him?"

Maud went hot and cold simultaneously and turned around so Jack wouldn't see the blush on her face. *Please don't let Mr Waites mention I broke off the engagement to George.* Beads of sweat dribbled down her spine. Maybe he'd said something already? He must be hurting, having lost his only son. Guilt twined around her chest like ivy, squeezing out her breath. Did they blame her for George's death? And would George's father know why Maud had called it off? George had been a good man, even though the war had changed him. Would Mr Waites say anything to her mother, or did she already know Maud had called off her engagement? She was sure her mother must have noticed Maud fled back to the farm after George's funeral service, not staying for the wake. She hadn't been able to face the hypocrisy of lies and guilt. *Please, let him say nothing.*

Maud stole a glance at Mr Waites. Too late. Her mother was talking to him and glared across at Maud, as though they were talking about her. Maud turned back to face her siblings. She needed a different topic of conversation before she had to take the train back home to Bea. "You must come up to London, Vi. I'd love to show you the sights: Big Ben, Tower Bridge, Buckingham Palace."

"Really? Could I stay with you?" Vi's eyes shone with excitement.

Maud felt the heat of a blush again. How could she say no? But then how would she explain that she and Bea shared a room, when there were two small but perfectly acceptable spare bedrooms? She glanced up at Jack, then back to Vi. "I'm sure we can arrange something. When would you want to come?"

"Soon would be good. Mother is going away for a couple of weeks with a coach tour to Scotland, so maybe I could come down next weekend?"

Maud sent up a silent prayer to forgive her for lying again. "Sure. I'll need to check with my housemate that she's happy too."

"Housemate? But I thought it was your house?" Vi looked puzzled.

Maud didn't want to have this conversation here. "No, I couldn't afford a place on my own." She steered Vi away from Jack and towards the back door. When she was sure they were out of earshot, she whispered, "Vi, nobody must know, but I share a house with Bea. You remember Miss Williams who came to tutor us before the war?"

Vi's eyes went wide. "Miss Williams? Vaguely. But I thought Mother had banished her from ever coming here?"

Typical that that story had been handed down. At some point it would be good to talk to Vi about what she remembered about her childhood before the war. Did she remember Bill and Harry at all?

There were footsteps down the hall. They both looked up to see Mother striding towards them, a grim line of determination set on her face. Behind her came the Reverend Davies. This did not look good.

"Maud, may we have a word with you, in private? Come with me."

Maud rolled her eyes and followed her into what had been her father's study, the place he would retreat to when he needed peace to read his books or newspapers. Her mother pointed to a chair and commanded one herself.

With the same dread she felt when her parents had cornered her about kissing Bea, Maud perched on the edge of the green leather captain's chair and gripped onto the polished walnut arms.

"I understand from Mr Waites senior that you broke off your engagement to George. Is this correct?"

Maud sat up stiffly, then shuffled back on the chair. "Yes, Mother."

"And can you promise me that you have had no further contact with Miss Williams or indeed other women who are similarly depraved."

Mother would not bully her. She was no longer the young girl who had no prospects, no means of support, and no other options. "No, I don't promise that."

Her mother made the sign of the cross and cast her gaze upward as if seeking strength from heaven. "Maud Heaston, you will be damned forever if you do not repent your sins. For the sake of your father and your brothers, I request you take this opportunity to confess your sins to Reverend Davies. He is happy to hear your confession."

Maud squared her shoulders and looked her mother directly in the eyes. "I won't make a confession as I've done nothing wrong."

Her mother unpeeled her long black gloves and smacked them in her hands. What was she going to do, challenge Maud to a fistfight?

"Do not compound your sins."

Reverend Davies cleared his throat like he did before delivering his sermon. "My dear child, maybe God is punishing you for your wickedness? Losing your brothers and your father and your poor fiancé George."

Maud gripped the chair arms so hard she thought she might crush the wood. Rage burned in her body, just a tweak more and she would explode in a wild conflagration. How dare he? "No, Reverend Davies. What is wicked is that the war happened, otherwise they would all still be alive. What is wicked is the way my brother, Harry, was treated by the Japanese, and my father being gassed in the Great War and taken prisoner, so he suffered with his health. It is nothing to do with me. I have worked hard to get a professional qualification, I live a good life, and I do not believe I am wicked because of who I love. That is simply who I am." It felt so good to speak those words out loud, even though she resented having to say them in the first place. She forced down some calming breaths, reminding herself that this man was not the mouthpiece of the God she prayed to. Her God did not judge or blame, her God was love.

He blessed himself, as though protecting himself from the vehemence of her reply. His eyes narrowed. "Dear child, you have clearly not been reading your scriptures. I will pray for you. And if you wish not to torment your mother and be damned forever, if you will not be cured, you must not act on your deviant impulses."

Her mother shook, her face an interesting shade of puce. She slapped her gloves on her hands in mock self-flagellation.

"Maud Heaston, if you do not promise to stop this behaviour, you will not enter this house again."

Calm coldness descended on Maud and stiffened her back as hard as steel. Nothing had changed in all those years, except now she had a choice. "I didn't want to have to choose, Mother. But as you give me no option, I choose my career, being in London, and my happiness. I will go to the station now. Reverend Davies." She nodded formally, glad to have made her point without showing weakness. The regret that she would be even more removed from her family weighed as heavily on her shoulders as her warm cloak.

Maud hugged Violet tightly on the way out and promised to contact her for a visit. She walked to the train station, her head high and too angry to care who saw her storm off. The only downside was she didn't expect Vi would be permitted to visit them.

CHAPTER TWENTY-NINE

Perivale, London 1958

MAUD WAS KNEELING in the garden, digging up the weeds. She didn't see the point of flowers, but Bea loved them so they had flowers in the tiny patch in the front and vegetables in the much bigger back yard. She had no lawn, which was a waste of good growing ground as far as she was concerned. For grass, they could go for a walk in the park.

Her knees were getting sore, so she thought she'd make a cup of tea. As she stood, she heard footsteps approaching.

"Maud, Maud, thank God I've found you."

Maud squinted as a woman ran along the pavement. The woman morphed and became clearer and recognisable. "Violet? What are you doing here?"

Violet staggered at the gate, her coat flapping and her kitten-heeled shoes slopping off her feet. Maud wiped her hands on her gardening apron and rushed to greet her. She flung her arms around her younger sister, who collapsed and held onto her.

"What's wrong, Vi? Come in." Maud closed the gate behind them with a snick and kicked off her wellingtons by the front door, leaving her gardening tools to put away later. Violet leaned on her heavily.

"Hello, sweetheart," Bea said. "I've put the kettle on, and I've just made you a coffee cake for tea."

Maud coloured up. Had Vi heard what Bea called her? She'd told Vi that they were living together though, when they had met up at her father's funeral. It was the last time she had seen any of her family. What was it, nearly four years ago? And despite a number of invites to Vi, she had never been able to come. "Bea, we have a visitor."

"Oh, really?" Bea popped her head out of the kitchen and wiped her hands on her apron.

"Violet, do you remember Miss Williams, Bea?"

Violet nodded, but her eyes were wild and unseeing, like a stampeding heifer.

"Hello, Violet. Why don't you two go into the sitting room and I'll bring you through tea and cake?" Bea said, her tone all honey and concern.

Maud helped Violet off with her coat and took her through to the sitting room. She picked up the newspapers and the open books of Shakespeare they'd been reading aloud last night and placed them on the Welsh dresser. "Vi, it's lovely to see you, but are you all right?" That was such a stupid question. Bea was so much better at saying the right thing.

Violet collapsed onto the sofa, her head in her hands, and sobbed. Maud sat beside her and put her arm around her little sister. Violet said something garbled that Maud didn't catch. Maud handed her a handkerchief.

"I don't know what to do."

The door opened, and Bea came in with a tray of tea and cake. "Oh," she said, catching sight of Vi. "Do you want me to go?"

"No," Vi said.

Bea placed the cups and saucers on one of the nested side tables. "Here you go, Violet. Would you like sugar?"

Vi nodded. "My friend Sally arranged for me to have an appointment in London tomorrow."

They waited to let her continue. Did she want to stay here the night? Violet's breath was coming in rasps, and she clutched onto Maud with the grip of a frightened animal.

"But I don't know if it's what I want to do. It might be dangerous."

Maud and Bea exchanged glances. "Do what, Violet?" Maud asked.

Violet blew her nose. "It's just that it will take all my savings, and they don't know if it's safe and it's illegal, and I love Ed; but we can't afford to get married now."

"Are you saying that you're expecting?" Bea asked.

Maud didn't trust herself to speak. Violet nodded, her eyes full of tears, her face scarlet. Maud stared at her, grim faced, her grip tight on the teacup. Stupid girl, why hadn't she taken precautions?

"And this friend of yours, Sally, has arranged for you to see doctors in London to what, have an abortion?" Bea asked.

Violet gave a slight nod.

"But you're not sure if you want to?"

A more energetic nod.

"And have you told your boyfriend, Ed?" Bea glanced across at Maud and raised her eyebrows.

It was clear from Vi's expression that she almost certainly hadn't.

"We took precautions, but the rubber slipped. I thought it was okay, but I've missed two monthlies and I've been feeling sick."

"So, you haven't had it confirmed by a doctor? But it seems likely you are pregnant." Bea placed her hand on Violet's shoulder.

How did she do that? Maud was trying to contain her rage. How could Vi be so careless? Violet swallowed hard and looked at Maud. She tried to tamp down her anger. "Do you want to keep the baby?" she asked, and it came out harsher than she intended.

"I don't know. Ed and I talked about getting married, but we can't afford it at the moment. He's just been offered a job at Lichfield Cathedral."

Bea frowned. "Is he a clergyman?"

"No. He's an organist and piano teacher...my piano teacher."

Maud put her cup down with a loud clatter. "I suppose it's a small mercy that he's not a man of the cloth."

"Do you love him?" Bea asked.

"Yes," Violet whispered and smiled.

"And does he love you?"

Violet nodded.

"So why would you want to have an abortion then?" Bea asked as though it was the most logical thing in the world.

Violet's eyes stretched wide. "What would Mother say? And the people in the town. I couldn't bear the shame. He might have to leave his job for not being a good enough Christian."

Bea glanced across at Maud, who nodded, happy for Bea to lead on this.

"Okay, I think the first thing is to have an open conversation with Ed and see how he feels about it," Bea said.

She did that sometimes, tried to fix things with logic, seeking extra information before deciding. Violet sat up straighter. She looked so young and vulnerable. Maud couldn't think of Vi being a mother. But she still didn't trust herself to speak.

"What if he says no?" Vi whispered.

"Well, you could keep the baby." Bea held up her fingers to count the options.

It would be a bastard. *Why Bastard, wherefore base?* The lines from King Lear she'd read out the previous night drifted through Maud's mind.

How ironic was that? At least Bea seemed to be calm and cool.

"Or give it up for adoption." Bea ticked off her second finger.

Vi twirled her hankie around her trembling fingers. "I'm not sure I could give it up. But I couldn't live with Mother. She would throw me out like she banished you, Maud."

Maud was about to say that she wasn't so stupid to get herself pregnant, but maybe sensing her thoughts, Bea touched Maud's forearm.

"Maybe you could have a quick wedding? It won't be the first or last time that's happened, and if it's just a question of timing, it seems better to do that than risk your health or go for an illegal procedure," Bea said. "Does Ed have a telephone you can call him on?"

Vi looked at her watch. "Yes, he'll have finished his piano lessons now. He'll be practising."

"Why don't you give him a call? When you've got all the information, it will be easier to make a decision," Bea said.

How could she be so reasonable? Maud stood; she needed to get out. If Vi got married, or if she had a baby, her mother would probably expect her to go and look after her. She gathered up the tea things and wandered to the kitchen and started washing them.

A few minutes later Bea joined her and picked up the tea towel.

"I'll need to look after Mother," Maud said, her voice a ghost of its normal contralto.

Bea picked up three saucers together and dried the top of the top one and the bottom of the bottom one then shuffled them. It always irritated Maud, who preferred to dry them one at a time.

"What do you mean?" Bea asked, wiping faster with the tea towel.

"Think about it. Whatever happens, Vi won't be able to look after her anymore and the twins won't do it. I'm unmarried. Mother will expect it."

Bea stacked the saucers in the cupboard and snatched up the cups, attacking the crockery with a vehemence Maud had never seen before.

"This is the same mother who told you never to come back to her house again?"

"Yes, but it's my duty."

"So, why doesn't your mother get a personal assistant? She can afford it. Your father must have had a pension from the bank, and she'll get a widow's pension. It's not like she has eight mouths to feed now. It's just her rattling around in that enormous house."

Bea's usual sunny disposition dissolved in her hard words and harder expression.

"You don't know, you've got no family," Maud said. Seeing Bea sag, hurt washing across her expression, Maud's anger curdled into regret, and she reached out a soapy hand to touch and connect. "Sorry," she whispered.

Bea shrugged off her approach. "We'll have this conversation later."

She snatched up her cigarettes and matches and let herself out of the backdoor. Although she was trying to give up, sometimes she needed to de-stress and found smoking the easiest way to do that. As she left through one door, Violet entered the other, radiating light.

"He said yes, he said yes. I'm going to get married." She did a twirl and seemed like a little girl again.

Maud tried to smile, but her mouth and eyes refused to cooperate.

"Thank you." Violet flung her arms around Maud. "Where's Bea?"

"Outside, feeding the rabbit," Maud said, using Bea's phrase.

"What? You have a rabbit?"

"No, she's having a cigarette. Go and tell her."

Violet skipped outside and Maud sagged against the tall cupboard, leaning against her hands. She felt like weeping. When they were still outside chatting, she finished off the rest of the drying, then put away her gardening tools and sat in the sitting room. She picked up her newspaper but couldn't concentrate on the crossword. She couldn't think of a way around it.

Violet chattered and planned her way through the evening. Bea and Maud responded to her but didn't talk to each other. As the clock ticked, the tension between them increased. Maud went upstairs and made up a bed for Violet. She walked to the main bedroom but decided not to take out her belongings and clothes ready for work the following morning. Damn Violet.

It was time Violet knew, so she would understand the consequences of her getting pregnant. Maud knew she shouldn't hold Violet responsible, but she couldn't help it. Everything she and Bea had struggled and worked for would be wiped out in an instant by Violet's carelessness. She returned to find Violet scribbling a list of everything she needed to do.

"I'm sure we could get married in the church. It is our church, after all. And maybe have a marquee at Heaston Hall, I'm sure Jack won't mind. We could get external caterers—"

"I've put you in the room at the front. Our room is at the back. I've put a clean towel on your bed."

Bea's head shot up.

Violet did a double take. "Did you say 'our room'?"

"Yes." Maud picked up the crossword, affecting an air of nonchalance, but couldn't rid the taste of ash in her mouth. All of their hopes of being together, living together forever were dying embers in the fire of their love now. Bea would never understand.

Violet looked between Maud and Bea as though she was trying to confirm what she thought she heard. "But when you said you shared a house, I thought you meant as housemates. You know, to share costs. Do you, you know, share a bed?" Vi giggled, although that might have been embarrassment. "Like man and wife?"

"Yes," said Maud, glowering at her and avoiding Bea's stare.

Vi stifled a snort and tried to cover it with a cough. How could she react this way when they'd been kind to her, when she had come here terrified just a few hours before? What happened to gratitude? "If you're going to be rude and disrespectful, I'm going to bed. You mustn't tell anyone. I have an early start. Will you go home tomorrow?"

Violet kept her face straight, but her eyes still twinkled. "Yes. Thank you. Thank you for everything. Both of you."

"You're welcome," Bea said. "It would be nice to get an invitation, even if we can't come to your wedding."

Violet frowned. "Why not?" She stared at Bea goggle eyed. "Oh, I see. Is that why you were...?" The glee drained from Vi's face as realisation hit, and Maud nodded. "I'm sorry. I didn't think of that." She gave a sympathetic smile. "We'll send you some wedding cake."

"That would be nice." Bea smiled at Vi, but the creases around her eyes didn't move.

"Good luck," said Maud, and she meant it, despite everything. "I'll go up now. Help yourself to anything you need."

As Maud stood, Violet rushed over and clung to her as if she never wanted to let her go. "Thank you. I've missed you. Sorry, I didn't think about why you might not come home. I assumed you didn't want to see us."

"Of course I wanted to see you, Vi. I've missed you too." She kissed her sister on the forehead and hugged her close.

***

Later in bed, Maud stared at the reflected light on the ceiling, unable to sleep. Their life together was about to change dramatically, and there was nothing she could do about it.

"So, you're going to sacrifice your own happiness, our happiness, for your sister and mother?"

Maud cleared her throat. "I have to, Mother can't manage on her own anymore."

"Don't we have a great life here? None of the drudgery of looking after anyone else. We go out, have fun. And great sex. I thought you loved your life, loved being with me?"

Maud took Bea's hand in hers. "I do." She turned her head to face Bea in the semi darkness, but Bea stared at the ceiling. At least she hadn't stopped all physical contact. "I need to do my duty, to my mother and to help Violet. I couldn't live with my guilt if I didn't go. You saw how Violet was this evening. I can't deny her that chance of happiness."

Bea shook her head, rustling her hair on the pillow. "Yet you'll deny ours."

Maud sniffed to stop the tears from welling up, and she squeezed Bea's hand. "I don't want to deny our happiness. I love our life, but I have to do my duty to the family and in the community. It's expected. As far as everyone knows, I'm a single woman. Nobody knows about us, nobody sees us. To the world, we don't exist. Our relationship doesn't exist or matter."

"It matters to me." Bea withdrew her hand. "You're throwing away ten years of our life for a family that have never cherished you the way I do. Where does that leave us?"

"I don't know, Bea. I love you, you know that, but this is something I need to do. Who knows, my mother may die in the next few years then we can be together. Or you could come with me and find a job in the Midlands?"

"I can't just drop what I'm doing."

A flash of rage snapped out of the hurt clamping around Maud's chest. "Why? You rush off to your job in Westminster every day. Occasionally we host a refugee or two, and sometimes you're so tense I can see the stress in your eyes, but you never tell me what you do." Maud knew she shouldn't be lashing out. It was unfair and unkind, but the upset was overwhelming. Bea turned to Maud. "I can't talk about it. Please don't ask. I can't just up and leave. It's important."

"I feel excluded from something that's such a large part of you." Maud took Bea's face into her palms. "If your job is so important to you, maybe you should stay here and make a career of it. I'll go back and look after my mother so Violet can get married and have a family. We can visit each other. And when we can, we get to live together again. We did it in the war and people were trying to kill us, surely we can do it in peacetime."

Bea swiped at her tears with the back of her hand. "But I love you," Bea whispered.

Maud kissed Bea on the forehead. "I love you too, but we both have to do what we have to do."

Bea snorted and turned away from her in bed. The cleft between them became a chasm. They would never agree on this. Maud placed an arm on Bea's waist, but she shrugged it off. If Vi hadn't been there, Bea might well have left to sleep in the spare room. They hadn't slept apart in years. Could she really do this? Was she being fair to Bea, to herself? For what? So Vi could get married and have her chance at happiness and have her baby? And Bea didn't have a family, so she couldn't understand. Now her father had died, she had no-one except Maud.

But Bea didn't have to be alone, lonely. That was her choice. Just as Maud was choosing family and duty over their relationship, their hidden, illicit relationship, so Bea was choosing her career, her "important" work. Maybe their relationship didn't have a chance with the attitudes and expectations of society. Maybe they should be grateful they had had ten years together, ten joyful, loving years.

"Is this what you wanted?" Bea rolled over to face Maud, sniffing away her tears that glistened in the half light.

Maud cradled Bea's cheek. "No. What I wanted was to become an accountant and be financially secure so I didn't have to rely on anyone, so I could choose to be with you, to live with you, to love you." She also wanted to be able to visit her sister, her family, be accepted in the family pew at church, to be respected for who she was, to serve in the town of her forefathers, but she didn't say that aloud.

Bea pulled back. "So why are you choosing to give that all up to look after a mother who banished you? It doesn't make sense." She dragged her body to the edge of the bed, away from Maud, staring at her as if she had never seen her before. "It feels like you don't love me enough."

Bea's eyes closed slowly. When she opened them again, there was a hardness to her stare that Maud had never seen before.

"Your mother can afford to get help. She could have a full-time nurse or a bank of staff to cater to her every whim."

"It's not the same, it's everything else." Maud wished she'd didn't feel obliged to not only look after her mother but also fulfil the roles her mother could no longer manage: the charity work, the shows, being the hub around whom the wheel of the society ran. Not the trappings of office, that was always the men, but the ones who made everything happen, who did the work behind the scenes, who took the notes, who baked the scones, and made the tea.

Maud couldn't bear to look into Bea's face, crumpled in hurt and anguish, knowing she'd caused it. No. She'd not caused the hurt and anguish, society had. The church had with their norms of what was acceptable.

She tentatively traced her thumb to swipe away the tears on Bea's cheeks. She didn't want to be the one to cause those tears. The guilt, and hurt, and longing for everything to be as it had this morning churned inside her like the cement mixers that were in evidence everywhere building new homes. It was thirteen years since the end of the war and every bombed gap was being filled with steel and concrete. And like concrete, her resolve solidified. For once in her life, she had to do the right thing and do the duty that she had shirked for years and left for Vi. "Can't you come and get a job there?"

"I can't." Bea's voice was clogged with tears. "You know I can't. I can't tell you what I do, but it's important, and I'm in the middle of a project."

"Something to do with the stream of foreign women who stay here for a night or two who later move on?"

Bea nodded. "Exactly."

"Maybe I can get Jack and Joe and their wives to care for Mother at the weekends, maybe once a month, and at least now we can phone."

Bea scoffed. "How can I hold you on the phone? Or kiss your handsome jaw? How can I make love to you over the phone? Or do this?" Bea slid her hand down Maud's chest before fondling her breast. "Or this?"

Bea tweaked Maud's nipple that always made her squirm with delight and trigger the heat and desire at the junction of her thighs.

"Or this?"

Bea stroked Maud's clitty and Maud moaned. "Oh Bea, I know. I want you," she said in no more than a hoarse whisper that tickled her throat. "I love you. But we can meet up when I can get away."

"Except your mother will ensure you have umpteen charity calls to make, just to keep us apart, and she'll never let me anywhere near the house."

"We could stay in a hotel."

"Where everybody knows exactly who you are. How long do you think it will be before the whole town knows you're sharing a bed with me?"

The band around Maud's chest tightened till she thought it would crush all the breath out of her. She didn't want to have this argument, and she hated seeing the anger in Bea's eyes.

"Since my dad passed, I've had no one. No, not no one, you. I thought I had you forever. You're my love, my life, my family, and now you're leaving me to do your duty for someone who cut you off. I don't understand."

Bea clenched her eyes tight. Maud reached out to touch her but stopped before she made contact. "You can't just do duty for people you love; it doesn't work like that."

It was pointless arguing. Bea would always out argue her, but Maud's conscience reminded her of her Christian duty, something Bea would never understand. The space between them became an unbridgeable void. "I'm sorry," Maud said.

"Fine." Bea leapt out of bed and dragged on a nightie and dressing gown. Then she snatched up her cigarettes and matches from the dresser as she slammed her feet in her slippers.

"Where are you going?" Maud asked.

"Out."

The door closed with a final click and the stairs squeaked as Bea made her way downstairs. A few minutes later, Maud looked out of the curtains. By a sliver of moonlight and the glow of the cigarette end, she could make out Bea's shape sitting on the bench amongst the carrots and potatoes. At least she'd put a jacket on. The moon highlighted her nose and forehead in pale silver. It reminded her of the night of the dance so many years ago, when love was young and all encompassing.

Maud leaned her forehead against the windowpane and placed her palms against the glass. The condensation was cold and damp. She felt as far removed from Bea as ever as she did then. She would miss all this. Waking up with Bea, making love to her, talking about politics, sharing the gardening and crossword puzzles.

"I love you," Maud whispered into the dark.

She shivered, anticipating how this was going to go. She would load her two suitcases into a taxi and be carried off to Euston station. She would turn away so she wouldn't cry, so she couldn't see Bea crying, and the sadness and anger in her eyes.

Bea couldn't leave because of her job, and Maud couldn't stay because of her duty to family.

It felt like splitting firewood. At first the axe doesn't seem to make an impression, then it cuts in between the texture, and each successive blow splits a wider cleft. Her heart was cleft in two. She hated seeing the sorrow in Bea's eyes, but couldn't unhear her words, "You don't love me enough."

It shouldn't unsettle her so much, but a splinter of truth burrowed into her heart. A tiny part of her wanted the acceptance of being the dutiful daughter and a person of status and consequence in the town of her roots where her family was known and respected, where people would tell her a story about her father, or Bill, or Harry, usually something naughty or funny that Harry had said or done.

In London, they were anonymous and hidden. Like they were just two more of the unknit women who clung together like a ball of wool, because they had no mate or had lost a mate in the wars. Their anonymity gave them choices and some freedom to be themselves, but she wanted freedom, love, *and* Bea. Underneath it all, Maud felt a sliver of guilt clawing at her, because she wanted to be accepted by her family and respected in the community too.

Bea didn't care. She would have walked hand in hand in the parks if Maud had let her, would have shouted it from the rooftops, and put an advert in the Times. For all her intellect, Bea was the romantic, and Maud the practical one. They would be together again, she would ensure it.

It was surprising how quickly her whole life changed. Within a week, her mother had secured a position for her with Baker, Hope, and Talbot, the top accountancy firm in the town. Her mother had called in a few favours and Maud hated that, the privilege of connection, but was grateful too. Her mother was delighted, as if she had planned Vi's pregnancy to bring her eldest daughter back into the fold, into the heart of the family, and out of the path of sin.

Maud didn't even have to work her full months' notice as she had holiday owing. She dreaded leaving Bea. In the last week, after the arguments and the patched-up reconciliation, they had touched and kissed each other whenever they could, to say I love you without the need for words. But she felt Bea withdrawing, like a hedgehog curling into a ball to protect its soft underbelly.

As the taxi pulled away, Maud couldn't look back. Her head throbbed from trying so hard to hold back the tears. She had promised to be back in a fortnight at the weekend, but she knew this was a real parting, the ending of their wonderful life together, for now.

It seemed like the whole of her life was a compromise, trying to balance competing needs, with no one ending up happy. As the taxi was about to round the corner, she looked back. Bea was standing, unashamedly weeping in the street. Bea looked as miserable as Maud felt. She raised her hand against the glass and the world blurred. Her heart was ripped in two and the largest part, she left behind.

CHAPTER THIRTY
Staffordshire, 1959

ALFIE AND CHARLIE Baker were the bane of Maud's life. They reminded her so much of Berryman, except they didn't have his brains. Yes, Berryman had turned up drunk after lunch about once a fortnight and played golf one afternoon a week, but he brought in more clients and worked hard the rest of the time and had eventually come to respect Maud. Alfie and Charlie worked in the accounting offices of Baker, Hope, and Talbot on the sole recommendation of being the nephews of the senior partner. And BHT was the prime accountancy firm in the town, dealing with all the accounts of the wealthy, the three main industrial companies, and a range of farmers. It was this latter area in which the firm wished to specialise more and expand so Alfie and Charlie had decided Maud should be the one to charm the farmers.

"Who should she go to first, do you reckon? Jenkins or Abbott?"

"Well Abbott will let his bull roam, so that should shake her up."

"Yeah, but Jenkins just throws all his receipts in a cupboard, this year's, last year's personal and business. That takes forever to sort out, and they're all covered in cow shit."

Irritated with them talking about her as if she wasn't standing beside them, Maud put a stop to their speculation. "Gentlemen, as I have been qualified the longest, surely I should decide. I think the Knot & Castle bank would be the client for me."

"No," said Charlie. "That would give you an opportunity to size up the opposition."

Maud shook her head. "I don't have anything to do with my brother's bank."

"The clue's in the name: Heaston bank. Oh, and what's your surname? Heaston."

Maud clenched the pen she was holding so tightly the clip dug into her palm. "You mean like your names are Baker and the firm name is?"

"Smart arse. Anyway, we're going to recommend to Mr Baker that you do Jenkins' accounts. He's grumpy and hates women too, but that's okay, because you're not a real woman, are you?" Charlie smirked.

The insult hit home, and despite feeling the burning in her cheeks, she squared her shoulders, lifted her chin, and returned to her desk. She couldn't let them see she was hurt by their comment. What did they mean? Did they know about her, or did they just mean she wasn't married and producing a child a year?

Two days later, Maud stood in a draughty barn in a crude office carved out of a corner of the cowshed. It was open to the metal beams, pock marked by swallows' nests, and splattered with guano. There was an underlying smell of cow shit and hay. Surprisingly, it was comforting and familiar and took her back to the time in the Land Army, of loving Bea… when Harry was still alive.

Mr Jenkins held a large container of fly spray in his hands and gave it a squirt as she approached, as if warding off the evil spirits.

She offered her hand in welcome, but he didn't take it, presumably not wishing to sully himself by touching a woman.

"Everything's in there." He pointed to a tall, stained cupboard. A string was looped through the hole where a knob should be. "Don't take too long at it neither and charge me the obscene rates you charge. And I don't take kindly to you having breaks."

"Mr Jenkins, I assure you that you won't be charged for my lunch break."

"And don't go wandering round the farm neither. I don't trust you townies not to leave gates open or smoke in the hayricks."

"I promise I will sit in my car." Maud looked out of the barn doors across the farmyard at Harry's A7, relieved it still worked and that she'd learnt to drive tractors during the war, as the old car was just as temperamental. She was glad she'd worn her breeches and thick jumper, given the bitter cold in the barn office. She settled down to sorting the cupboard full of receipts that Mr Jenkins had just thrown in. As the Baker boys had said, some were covered in cow shit. Maud had hoped she wouldn't smell that again, but there was an overpowering stench of urine and manure. How long did he spend in this office? It was unpleasant and cold, and the open beams were laced in cobwebs. As she looked down, she heard the tell-tale scampering of rodent feet. Although she'd worked on a farm for seven years, she had never got used to rats, the dirty clever little creatures getting into everything and spoiling the grain stores. Shivering from disgust as well as the cold, she put her jacket over her shoulders.

Maud had bought a concertina file with her and started by sorting the receipts into months, business, and non-business. As she worked through them, she noticed that where a signature was required there was an inconsistent squiggle. There were no written notes anywhere, no books, or catalogues, or Farmer's Weekly, unlike in most other farm offices. Mr Jenkins had a calendar on the wall and by certain days he had applied different marks but no writing.

Maud had planned to leave the file with him, but the tabs written Jan, Feb etcetera may as well have been written in hieroglyphics. Presumably he could read numbers, so she retrieved a 6B pencil from her pencil box and added the numbers one to twelve. She further sorted the receipts into date order and held them together with bulldog clips.

This really should be a summer job, due to there being no heating and only a naked light bulb dangling from the solid roof beams. By four o'clock, she couldn't feel her feet or fingers. She was about to pack up for the day when all the lights went out, and she heard swearing from the cow shed side of the barn, then shouting.

"What have you done, girl? Have you touched something?"

"No, Mr Jenkins," she called out and grabbed the solid rubber torch from her case and switched it on. She went outside to the other entrance to the cowshed, the beam illuminating the way in the rapidly dying light. "Are you all right, Mr Jenkins?"

"No, I'm bloody not. The fuses have gone, and I don't have spares. How am I supposed to get the milking done with no electric? The milk board is coming this evening. Bloody hell." He kicked at a bucket, and it skittered across the straw.

"You could milk by hand."

He thumped the side of the barn with his fist. "And how long's that going to take me?"

"I could help if you like. I'm a bit out of practise, but I spent seven years in the Land Army, and we milked by hand night and morning."

He huffed. "I'm not paying your charge out rates, missy."

Patronising git. She was trying to help him. But he was a client, and if she wanted to win his favour, she needed to bring him on side.

"I'm not going to charge you, Mr Jenkins, but if I go and get my car coat and wellies, we can get this sorted together. In fact, do you want to go into town and get some new fuses while I make a start on these beautiful Friesians?"

He gawped at her, as though he was not sure whether to believe her or not and slid open the gate to the milking parlour. "No job for a woman."

He slapped the cows that were lowing and waiting to be let in. Was that a yes or a no? Maybe he didn't believe she could do it, and she hoped she still remembered how to milk a cow. It must be like riding a bicycle surely, they say you never forget.

Maud took her briefcase and the file and stored them in the car and changed her smart blazer for the car jacket and her shoes for boots. When she returned to the shed, he'd already started to milk the cows by hand. She washed her hands under the icy water in the dairy, then grabbed a cobweb covered stool and cleaned out a bucket. A cow stood in the stall, patiently waiting, chomping at the hay and flicking at a fly with her muddy tail. "Do you have any disinfectant?"

He nodded at the iodine and handed her some cloths. He stood up, regarding her, ready to pounce if she did it wrong. Maud felt down the cow's engorged udders, talking to the cow softly to keep her calm. She hadn't had an audience like this since she was in training at the agricultural college. She cleaned the teat, discarding the first streams of milk and tidying up using a dry cloth, before pulling and twisting to release the milk into the metal bucket. It all came back to her, the smell of cow and rough texture of the flank as she leaned in. She could be eighteen again.

"Aye, you'll do," he said when she finished the first cow. "I'll get some more fuses."

He returned in less than an hour, and was accompanied by his neighbouring farmer, Mr Archer. Not, it transpired, to help—he only had poultry and pigs—but to observe the spectacle of a girl, the accountant no less, milking the cows.

Mr Archer secured the cattle so they couldn't move around, but the cows picked up on his anxiety and Maud worried they'd be less likely to release their milk.

"Thanks, Mr Archer, shall I do that? Would you mind taking this bucket and pouring it into the tank? Thank you." Maud smiled at him, to look as if she was genuinely grateful but tried not to grit her teeth.

Around half six, Mr Jenkins got the electricity back on, so it was a quick job to complete cleaning down the shed. As they finished, she sprayed her wellies with a hose to wash off the worst of the cow shit. "I'll be off now, Mr Jenkins," she said. "I've taken your receipts so I can write up the books and accounts from the office. I'll bring them all back later in the week."

"Aye, all right."

No thank you for your time or sorry for ruining your jacket, that now reeked of manure. She doubted it would ever be fresh again. Maud sighed and banged her torch, which glowed a dim cream now rather than a bright white, and made her way back to the car.

She arrived home at seven thirty to her mother pacing at the door.

"Where have you been? I telephoned your office, but they said you'd gone for the day. And what on earth is that smell?" her mother said before Maud had even stepped into the hallway.

"It's a long story, Mother. I'll tell you after supper, but I need a bath. I'll go and switch the immersion on. Would you be happy with sandwiches and cake tonight rather than a full meal?"

"But Tuesday is cottage pie night. Would it take too long to prepare?"

"Yes, Mother, we don't want to be eating at nine. Besides, I have my phone call then."

Her mother stiffened and pursed her lips. They had come to an uneasy truce: her mother could pretend that Maud was the dutiful daughter, if she made no mention of Bea or her fortnightly visits to London. She still complained that Jack's wife, Elsie, did not know how to look after her whenever Maud went up to London for the weekend. But Maud was grateful for her sanity break and to see Bea again, even though leaving her on Sunday afternoon was hard. Each absence stretched in time, distorted by yearning like a lifetime between each coming together. And each coming together was intense, compressed to an instant, before they were kissing goodbye. Every time seemed to magnify the impact and make it harder.

The following day Maud went to the office of Chuttons and Dale, one of their new clients.

"What do you know about the new subsidies to improve productivity?" Mr Dale asked.

"At the moment, nothing, sir, but I'll research it and come back to you."

Mr Dale grunted, clearly not impressed. "Don't bother, we've already done the research."

He then explained how the agricultural policy had changed over the fifties from being just price support, to direct grants and subsidies to improve farm productivity. She listened and made a mental note to check whether all the farms she was dealing with were making such claims. If not, she would help them make their applications. She realised it was the job that a land agent would do, but most of her farmers couldn't afford those services and therefore could miss out, especially if they couldn't read like Mr Jenkins.

She filled in the forms for her five farming clients in the next few months. Other farmers appeared at the BHT offices and demanded they get the accounting services of the "posh, tall woman who looks like a man." Not terribly flattering, but it meant that the firm was getting noticed, and she was respected. That was a win and evidence that she would make an excellent partner in the firm. It was heartening to be accepted for who she was and what she did, and to make a real contribution. If only Bea was here, life would be perfect.

CHAPTER THIRTY-ONE
Staffordshire, 1960

WHEN MR BAKER, Sr called her into his corner office, Maud hoped he might discuss the new partnership that had been mooted.

"Sit down, Miss Heaston."

"Thank you, sir." She smiled, slid back on the chair, and placed her feet flat on the floor, her hands laid demurely in her lap. Out of the window, through the open venetian blinds onto the river and the 11th century church, she watched crows thermalling up.

"I'm sure you know why I've called you in, Miss Heaston."

She shook her head but tried to hide the grin that tweaked at her lips.

"We've been very pleased with the work that you've done and the extra business that you have brought in."

"Thank you, sir." Now she did allow herself a smile.

"So, we'd like to promote you to senior manager."

The full beam smile she had prepared, slipped. She hoped she didn't make a whining sound. "Oh. I thought you were talking about partnership?" she asked before she had chance to couch it in more polite terms or not say anything at all.

He shifted in his seat and pulled at his collar. "Ah, Charles has been offered the open partnership role."

She gripped the arms of the chair and inhaled deeply to give herself time to respond rationally. "Charlie? But why, sir, apart from the fact that he's your nephew? I have more experience, I passed my exams in the top ten in the country, and I've brought in nearly two hundred thousand pounds a year extra income."

"Yes, yes, and we appreciate all that, which is why we're offering you senior managership."

She unclenched her teeth that were so tight her jaw ached. "But why not partnership? Are you saying you don't think I'm partnership material?"

He tugged at his shirt collar and looked everywhere but at her. "Well, it's just that a lot of business is done in the golf club and the Conservative club, and you're a member of neither."

"No, sir, because the golf club doesn't allow lady members, and I don't subscribe to the Tories."

"And that's precisely my point. Almost all of our clients are members of one or both. To be a partner, you have to be able to mix with them. I know your father was well known in the town, as is your brother, but you cannot live on your name alone. I'm sorry, Miss Heaston, but as a woman you'll never be accepted by the great and the good of the town, and that is what we need in a partner."

Maud blinked, trying to grasp at the coattails of reason and fairness. The porridge she'd had for breakfast felt leaden and roiled in her stomach. "So, you're saying no matter what I do, you'll never promote me to partner?"

"It's not me, Miss Heaston, it's our clients. We have to do what they will accept."

The oxygen of prejudice mixed with the fuel of rage, and the missile launched. Her heartbeat rushed in her ears and all she saw was red. The headache that had been threatening swelled into a tempest and she shut her eyes. She deserved that role. She'd earned it. He knew it, and she knew it, but Mr Baker was not like Mr Yarborough. Mr Baker was not one to take a chance on anyone. He was a coward and was quite happy to promote his idle, stupid nephew over her. She clenched her hands so hard on the arms of the chair, her knuckles went white. She fizzed with fury, and her choice became obvious. With a serenity she couldn't quite believe, she squared her shoulders and looked Mr Baker directly in the eye.

"In that case, Mr Baker, I tender my resignation. I need to give a month's notice, and I'll ensure I leave all of my clients in good order."

His eyes widened, and he blinked a few times. "Miss Heaston, if you're foolish enough to think that you can set up in competition, I should remind you that you signed an anticompetition clause that says that you will poach none of our clients."

Maud's smile was tight, polite and false. "Correct, Mr Baker. I won't poach your clients. However, if they decide to follow me, then I'm not obliged to turn them away. Now if you'll excuse me, I need to visit one of our most lucrative new clients, the Whistford Estate. A client that I brought in." She stood, holding her head high and he rose too. She was a good couple of inches taller than he was, and could see the balding patch on his head, that he covered with an overcomb. Not quite believing she had just changed her life completely and thrown away everything she'd worked for, she strode out of the room.

Later that evening as she served the egg and bacon pie, she explained to her mother what had happened.

"What on earth possessed you to hand in your resignation? You were doing so well. I saw Mrs Talbot at the Conservative Ladies Club, and she said they were considering you for promotion."

Was nothing a secret or confidential in this town? It was interesting that her mother had said nothing before. "Yes, Mother, that's precisely the point. They were going to promote me to senior manager and one of the Baker boys to partner."

"Well, that's only right. His uncle is the senior partner."

Maud slammed down the spoon, and it clattered in the Pyrex dish. "Why should it be right? No, don't answer that. I've earned my practising certificate, and I just need to write to the institute to get it. I just hope I don't need the partner's approval."

Her mother smoothed down her skirt, always black now as she remained in mourning as every good Edwardian lady should do. "You should have thought about that before you argued with Mr Baker. Maybe if I had a word with his wife at the Parish Council meeting, she might persuade him to let you back in."

"No, Mother. Thank you, but if there's a problem, I'll ask Mr Yarborough to vouch for me since I took my articles with him in London."

Her mother brushed an imaginary crumb off her long silk skirts. "Maud, I don't understand why you're so headstrong and fight against the status quo."

"The world's changed. A woman's role is no longer limited to homemaking and producing babies. The work in both world wars has shown women can do all the jobs men can do, and often better."

"But why do you want to change? Don't you want a man to treat you like a lady?"

Maud rolled her eyes and huffed. "You know I don't. All I want is to be treated with respect for what I do and what I've achieved. I'll set up my own firm. I'm hoping I can persuade Jack to give me the bank work, and I know some farmers will follow me."

She hadn't thought about asking Jack, but she hoped she'd be able to persuade her brother.

"But Jack has a professional long-standing arrangement—"

"*I* am a professional." Maud listed it off on her fingers. "I work hard, I've brought in new clients, I've never claimed expenses that I wasn't entitled to, I've never been drunk on the job, or gone to play golf and charged it to the client—"

"The golf club isn't open to women members."

Her mother picked up *The Lady* magazine and flipped past the adverts for domestic servants. Clearly, she considered the conversation finished. Maud snatched at the magazine to close it.

"I know. I'm fed up with the nepotism between mates who all happen to be male."

Her mother retrieved the magazine and uncreased the cover. "Nobody will want a woman as their accountant; they'll be a laughingstock."

Maud leaned forward and rested her elbows on her knees. "Thanks for the support. I was hoping you might use some of your influence to help me." Her mother raised an eyebrow but didn't reply to the sarcasm. "And on a practical level, I hope I might use the parlour as my office."

"You want to do what?" she asked.

"It would save me any office rental costs until I'm established. Most of the time I'd be going out to clients, especially the farmers. I'll keep the old A7 going as long as I can, but as soon as I can afford it, I'll buy myself another car. I guess the money I was saving to buy myself into the partnership can tide me over until I make my own way." She scribbled down a note on her growing list of things she needed to do to set up in business.

"You've clearly thought about this," her mother said.

As she'd grown older, she seemed to have mellowed somewhat and added a little honey to her tartness.

Maud smiled. "Well, only since coming home. Can I use the parlour? We never use it."

Her mother pursed her lips. "And have people traipsing through the front door?" Maybe still more lemon than honey.

"It's perfect. We can put some chairs in the hall as a waiting room." They could use the old WC if they need facilities, she thought, but didn't say that as it might have elicited a definite no.

"Please, Mother, I'm asking you to support me as you would support the boys. I know Father helped both Jack and Joe secure their jobs."

Her mother sighed. "I suppose I could try, but I don't think it's very ladylike."

Maud gestured at her gangly, oversized body. "Look at me, I've never been ladylike."

"You'll never find a husband."

Maud's eyes rolled at her mother's wistful and disappointed tone, and she counted to ten under her breath. Not this conversation again. "I've told you before, I don't want a husband. You know I'm never going to marry. I know you don't approve but I—"

Her mother raised her hand sharply. "I don't want to hear what you're going to say. But yes, you may use the parlour as long as you ask anyone who comes in to clean their shoes properly."

"Thank you, Mother." Maud walked over and did what she never did, placed her arms around her mother's neck and gave her a peck on the cheek.

"There's no need for that, Maud," her mother said, but her cheeks pinked up with pleasure.

Maud grinned as the grandfather clock struck nine. She went out to the hall to wait for Bea's call and closed the door behind her. Thirty seconds later, the bell rang and she snatched up the receiver.

"Hello, beautiful," Bea said.

Hearing her light and bubbly voice stirred many delicious sensations in Maud's body. "One of these days it won't be me who answers the phone, then you'll be stumped. And hello to you too."

"But it was you, and I've got some exciting news to share with you."

Maud curled the phone cord around her fingers. "I have news too. What's yours?"

"I've finished the project I was working on for the last few years, and I can finally seek part-time employment elsewhere. As long as I attend a meeting once a month in London, they're prepared to pay me a small retainer and expenses. I'll be able to apply for a job close to you, maybe in the same office? And we can see each other more often, have lunch together, and maybe I could sneak into your house when your mother's not looking." Bea giggled.

"That's wonderful, but I thought you wanted to continue with your career. I think my news complicates things. I handed in my resignation today, after they didn't make me partner and have no intention of ever doing so. I've decided to set up my own accountancy practice."

"Wow. Congratulations, sweetheart. I always knew you could do it. If I sell the house here maybe I could buy something there, or better still we could move in together and save—"

"There's still Mother to consider. And she's just agreed I can use the parlour for my office."

"That's great news, saves on all the overheads. Wait. Why don't I come as your personal assistant and secretary? I could help you establish the business. Maybe we could specialise in helping women who want to set up their own businesses, that really ties in with your need for financial independence—"

"That's really exciting, but you're forgetting one thing; Mother will never let you into the house."

Bea sighed. "Even after twenty odd years?"

"I could tell her you will be my personal assistant and you need to come in, but honestly, she was more forgiving of Violet having to get married. I suppose them moving to Lichfield immediately after the wedding was the opportunity for them to become the perfect happy family. I'm glad she's settled now, but I still wish I hadn't had to give up living with you. It's been a long twenty months."

"And sixteen days."

"You've been counting?" Maud couldn't keep the surprise out of her tone.

"Of course. I love you. I miss waking up to you, chatting about anything and everything as we prepare supper and split the household chores, reading Shakespeare and Dickens and working in the garden. I'm afraid the vegetables haven't done anything as well without you, and I really miss making love with you."

Maud leaned against the wall, her head back. "Me too, sweetheart, me too." If she closed her eyes, she could almost smell Bea's scent, and she loved to hear her breathing on the other end of the phone.

"Maud, we need more logs for the fire," her mother called from the sitting room. Maud was surprised she didn't still use the little bell she'd had for poor, overworked Daisy before the war.

"I'd better go. Duty calls. Eighty-eight."

"Maybe duty should be grateful for everything you do and the sacrifices you've made—*we've* made. Don't worry, sweetheart, we'll make it work.

Have some more thoughts around the assistant idea."

Maud wound her fingers tighter around the telephone cord. That would be wonderful. To be with Bea and not have the dread of the impending departure dangling over their weekends together like a sword of Damocles. She picked at the corner of the telephone directory with her free hand. "But what if I don't get enough clients to support us both?"

"Then I'll get an office job. I know we can make it work. I love you, and I want to be with you."

"Maud. The fire's going out."

"Me too. Night night and thank you for making it happen at work. It makes me feel cherished," she whispered.

"You are," Bea said.

The sitting room door handle rattled, so Maud replaced the handset and rushed to collect more wood from the scullery.

"The fire's gone out now," her mother said.

Her irritation was clearly settling in again. Maud imagined it like those bead curtains that rattled if they were caught by the breeze. Her mother was still a force to be reckoned with and having her support could make all the difference to her business succeeding or not. Maybe now was not the time to bring up the thorny question of Bea being allowed back in the house. Perhaps she would announce she needed a secretary to answer the phone. Would her mother allow her to carve up the parlour into two rooms or better still convert the music room with its ancient grand piano? Neither of them played anymore. Violet had always played. Along with playing with her piano instructor, of course.

CHAPTER THIRTY-TWO

THE FOLLOWING EVENING Maud was calculating a budget, factoring in Bea's costs as well as her own. If she could keep the car going for another year, or maybe two, it was doable. She looked up from her calculations to watch her mother frowning as she read. Maud stood and switched on the standard lamp. The light cast colours and shadows in the formal sitting room, signalling their established evening routine. It still seemed incongruous to see the antique furniture from Heaston Hall in her mother's house, but it had to fit in with the new, like her mother was having to adapt to modern practices, and Maud was about to challenge again. There was still plenty of room in the three storey Georgian townhouse that resembled a doll's house Vi had drawn so many years ago, but her mother could jump either way.

Maud cleared her throat. "Mother, I plan to have an assistant join me and will need to split up the parlour into different rooms so I can have private conversations. I was wondering if I could take over the music room as well? I'll pay rent of course."

Her mother looked up, the frown still fixed on her face. "No, I use that for my sewing because the light is good. Besides, if you have the parlour, I'll need somewhere to bring acquaintances whom I do not wish to bring into my sitting room."

While understanding where her mother was coming from, she'd hoped for a little more flexibility and support, like her brothers had always received.

Her mother put her bookmark into the book, closed it, and placed it on the side table. She straightened and smoothed her skirts. "And I don't want any of your clients hanging around in the hallway, especially not market stall holders."

This felt like her mother's spite as well as snobbery. If Maud didn't need to save on rent, she would have told her mother what she thought about her vindictiveness, but she stilled her tongue.

"So, if you're going to make a mess and noise in the parlour, you had better factor that in."

At least she had permission to split up the parlour, but she'd have to replan it. Maud consulted her drawings, wondering how she could rearrange it so both she and Bea could see outside and get real light.

Mother picked up her book again. "If you're looking for an assistant, Mrs Talbot's niece is looking for a suitable position," she said.

"Mrs Talbot, the chair of the Conservative Ladies Club?" And the biggest busybody in town. Even if the position wasn't already taken, she would never allow Mrs Talbot or her relatives to have that power and influence. This was about her independence. Her mother peered over her book, obviously waiting for a reply.

Maud knelt to put another log on the fire, probably the last one of the night. She poked at the embers and coaxed the flame to erupt, debating how best to approach the conversation.

"No, the position is already filled," Maud said and placed the poker back in its holder. She stood and watched her mother in the mirror over the mantelpiece.

"Who? Someone local?"

Maud met her gaze in the mirror, wondering how to broach this to elicit the most favourable response.

Understanding seemed to flicker across her mother's face, then she scowled. "No. Absolutely not. Miss Williams is not welcome here."

Maud spun to face her. "Miss Williams is perfect for the role. I want her here, and she's accepted the position."

Her mother slammed her book onto the side table, rattling the Tiffany lamp. "This is just a farce. Why would a Cambridge graduate settle here when she can get up to her perverted little ways in London?"

Maud wiggled her jaw to release the tension building there. "Firstly, Bea is not a pervert. Secondly, she didn't return to Cambridge as she did important war work for the Government. But more than that, I love her."

Her mother looked as though she would snort but refrained.

"If she stays in London, I'll go and set up my business there. Who would look after you and do all your civil and charity work then? I put my life and happiness on hold for you, and I would appreciate some respect and gratitude for both of us."

Mother clutched her skirts so tight she crumpled the silks. "I do not want her in my house."

"She'll be coming to work here." Steeled with righteousness, Maud outstared her mother, who finally looked down.

"Fine, she can work in the office—"

"And use the facilities, so she can make tea for my clients and use the bathroom. And if she wants to take a break, she can relax in the snug."

"Don't be ridiculous. I will not have sinners in my house."

"No. You're the one being ridiculous, your hypocrisy is obscene. How many times did Violet get off with Ed in the music room while supposedly practising Beethoven, and now she's the perfect daughter?" Maud offered up a prayer for sacrificing Violet, but the occasion demanded it.

Her mother picked up her book again and split it open with a force sufficient for the spine to crack. "She can use the facilities and the office. That is final."

Maud clamped her teeth together hard so she didn't respond. Maybe better to stop with the concessions she had won. Then she smiled and a thrill shimmied through her. After all these months they might actually be together again as they should be, in the same place, seeing each other every day. Now they just needed to work out how to live together.

CHAPTER THIRTY-THREE
Bristol, present day

HANNAH LAY IN her new favourite position, stretched out with her head resting on Suki's lap. They seemed to be settled into a new routine. After supper, rather than Hannah playing on her Xbox and Suki reading manga, they would read one or two of Gammy's letters. Hannah picked up a letter and snuggled in, inhaling Suki's perfume and the scent that was just Suki. Suki curled her fingers around Hannah's hair, pulling slightly.

She pushed away the desire to throw the letter down and take Suki in her arms. Later. "This is just before Bea joined Gammy as an employee, dated 1960."

Dearest M,

Thank you for your letter. It was lovely to hear from you, and I enjoyed our chat on the telephone last night, despite duty's interference. As to your concern, I know the work won't be as stimulating as I've had, but I really don't mind, if by being your secretary and assistant I can be with you, it's worth it and is so exciting. I do understand what you say about the village busybodies, and your duty, but we will deal with them. I will be the perfect assistant, and nobody will suspect. I can't wait to see you next week when I've sorted everything here.

88
Your loving B xx.

"So, they clearly decided to keep their affair a secret."
"How exciting."
Suki was such a sucker for a romantic story. Hannah glanced up at her, a dreamy look on her face. "Is it?" Hannah sounded sharper than she intended. "I had no idea when I lived with them. I just feel so sad I didn't know, then. We could have had a very different relationship. She could

have helped me when I was struggling to come out and find out who I was." Hannah shrugged and carefully put the delicate letter back into the envelope and replaced it in the pile. "Or, we would have spoken about things that matter instead of her scolding me for everything I did wrong. All I remember when I lived there is having blazing rows with her, like when I had my tattoo done."

"Oh yeah, didn't you have that mockingjay emblem from *The Hunger Games*?"

Hannah was pleased Suki remembered and touched her upper arm like a talisman. She had so related to Katniss Everdeen, the girl who kept battling despite having lost everything. And at the time it had felt like a battle for survival, and she'd been determined not to be beaten. "Gammy was livid, but Auntie Bea was brilliant. Looking back now, I think Auntie Bea was trying to tell me. She was great at encouraging me to aim high, and I'd never have gone to university if it hadn't been for her. I was such a bitch to her, to them." Hannah lay down on Suki's lap again, and Suki resumed threading her fingers through her hair.

"You'd just lost your mother and your beloved Nan Vi; it's not so surprising you were angry," Suki said.

"But if I thought I could have spoken to them, maybe I wouldn't have spent years trying to escape their influence. The secrecy was like a sore eating away at all of us. I hate all the lies. I don't want to be like that anymore." As she spoke, she realised what she and Suki had was hidden away. They hadn't even informed Hannah's best friends, Jess and Ash, and Hannah was sure Suki hadn't told anyone at work, and certainly not her parents in Japan. "Maybe we should go out in the evenings sometimes? Join Jess, and Ash, and the others after ultimate training at the pub."

Suki stopped stroking her hair, and her leg muscles tensed. "Why? I thought you liked this?"

"I do. I love it. But I'd also like to acknowledge you to my friends, and maybe go out on a double date with Jess and Ash and hold your hand in public." Hannah tried to pick her way through the minefield carefully.

"I don't do PDAs."

"Okay, maybe not hold hands in the street, but at least let me tell Jess, she's my best friend."

"I don't understand why you have to announce it to everyone."

Hannah sat up on the sofa. "Are you ashamed of me? Of us?"

"No, of course not."

"It feels like it." Hannah didn't want to have this conversation now. It was her fault; she shouldn't have started it. Could they just smooth it over? She loved being with Suki. What they had together warmed her soul, and she'd yearned for this for so long, but she wasn't sure she could deal with the secrecy. She needed to retreat and sift through her emotions before she said anything else stupid or something that would antagonise Suki. "I think I'll get started on my conclusions." She snatched up the pile of letters and tucked them back into the boxes behind the sofa.

"Sure." Suki picked up her manga book, removed the bookmark, and placed it on the side table.

Her intense absorption seemed too quick, like she didn't want to argue either. Hannah sat in her old room, which had become her study since they slept together in Suki's room every night. Suki's room was much bigger than hers and felt more open as it looked out over the rooftops of Bristol. But more than that, sharing Suki's room signified the strength of their relationship, like gaining access to some exclusive club.

She picked up her stress ball and tossed it against the wall with a satisfying thwack. Untangling their argument, she didn't want to pull at threads to their logical conclusion—they wanted different things from their relationship. She hoped it was just a knot that needed unpicking, and they could continue as they were.

CHAPTER THIRTY-FOUR
Staffordshire, 1960

MAUD'S MOTHER WALKED into the new office. The parlour had been split into a long reception area overlooking one of the front windows so that Bea had a view. Maud planned to use the small room off the reception as a meeting room and eventually, for an articled clerk. The reception was the largest room set up with filing cabinets, two waiting chairs, and a desk.

Her mother never bothered to knock. It annoyed Maud, and she'd discuss it with her sometime soon, though maybe when Bea arrived, her mother wouldn't pop in so frequently anyway.

"I'd like you to take these food baskets to Beckley. I promised Mrs Smith you would take them this morning."

Maud looked up from her papers. "Mother, I'm working."

Her mother made a big show of scanning the room for other individuals. "I don't see any clients."

"Yes, that's because I have to work on the accounts and marketing when the clients aren't here. I'm trying to design handbills to hand out at market day."

Her mother sniffed, as though mention of the market stall holders would taint her sensibilities. "How many clients do you have now, apart from the Conservative Ladies' coffee morning?"

Maud hung her head. That question was so difficult to answer. Some people had said they might take a risk with her but none had actually confirmed yet. She tried not to think of the cost of it all, especially with Bea joining her. Although she was excited about being with her, part of Maud was also concerned about her mother's reaction and that of the people in the town and the church. She needed it to be kept a secret. But Bea was especially good at secrets.

Mother pursed her lips. "I told you, you should have stayed with Mr Baker. People in this town hate change, and they don't trust a woman to look after their finances."

"Which is why I'm looking to new businesses, especially those run by women, like the market stall holders."

"I don't want those people in my parlour."

"All of my clients will be welcome here. This is my office, Mother, and I will be paying rent for it. "

"Eventually."

Maud sighed and counted to ten. "Yes, I really appreciate you delaying payment until I'm established. That's what I'm working on at the moment, trying to get established."

"You can work on getting established in the evening rather than phone that woman."

Maud rattled her fingernails on the desk. "I will contact Bea as often as I like, and no, not on your phone bill—"

"Mrs Smith needs the food today; her aunt is really unwell."

As expected, her Mother always cut across the conversation whenever Maud mentioned Bea, as if saying her name out loud would bring the devil himself out of hiding. "All right, but I'll leave it half an hour until the frost has burned off. It's very icy and the old jalopy struggles."

Her mother looked at her watch very pointedly.

Maud sighed. Some battles weren't worth fighting, and this was not the hill to die on. "Okay, I'll go now. The sooner I get it done the better." She picked up her jacket, scarf, and gloves from the hall table. Her wellies were already stowed in the back of the car, ready for anything, like milking cows when the electric went down.

She shivered as she crunched her way through the icy puddles to the car, and her breath formed mists around her. The crank handle was finger-biting cold even through her gloves as she rotated it to start the car. A new car would need to be the first major purchase. This old beast was being nursed along by Albert, the local mechanic as a favour because he had always been fond of Bill and Harry, both of whom had worked with him during their university holidays. He said the least he could do was to help their sister.

After the third try of cranking the engine, the car revved, and she leapt inside to alter the mixture. She clapped her hands together to warm them, slipped the car into gear, and slowly manoeuvred it over the skating rink that had manifested overnight.

To get over the Whiston Bank, a short but steep hill that the road builders had decided to climb rather than build in the flood plain, Maud needed to build up momentum around a sharp bend and hope the car didn't slide down again. Fortunately, there was no-one else around as she approached, so she could get a good run at it. Once safely over the other side, she enjoyed the view of low-lying mist snuggling into every nook and cranny of the valley and the bright sunlight above. The beauty made her breath catch.

Mrs Smith welcomed her into her tiny damp cottage. Maud felt guilty that she had argued to delay going when she saw the palpable relief on the old lady's face.

"Thank you, Miss Heaston, we are very grateful. We're so glad that you are taking over where your mother left off. We're all suffering from rheumatics and can't move around the same. The weekly bus service is none too reliable. My, aren't you tall? Mind your head as you come through. Would you like a cup of tea, Miss Heaston? I would have made a cake, but I'm trying to make sure we have enough to pay the coalman who's coming tomorrow. Did I hear right that you have left Mr Baker's employ? Is it true that you made a mistake—"

Maud's cheeks burned, despite the cold. "No, I did not make a mistake. Who told you that? That's completely untrue." Maud took a couple of breaths as the old lady flinched. "Sorry, Mrs Smith, I didn't mean to raise my voice, but that's not the case. I resigned because Mr Baker made it clear they would never promote me to partner just because I'm a woman."

"I didn't mean to offend, Miss Heaston. As I said to Mrs Talbot, that didn't sound like you, as you are always so precise. And here you are coming over on a frosty day to help us out and all I can do is upset you. I'm so sorry. Now, do you take milk and sugar?"

"I'm not offended, Mrs Smith, but I'd be grateful if you'd correct Mrs Talbot and anyone else who's been spreading those incorrect rumours. I can't really stay for tea, thank you. I need to get back to work."

Mrs Smith's gnarled hands flew to her mouth. "Oh dear, no tea. I really have offended you. I am so sorry."

Maud raised her hand to placate her. "Not at all. And if you insist, I'll have tea with milk, no sugar—I'm trying to give it up." She glanced at her watch; it would be at least half an hour before she could escape but she didn't want Mrs Smith to tarry under the impression she was offended. The poor woman would worry about it for weeks and she had enough to contend with.

E.V. Bancroft

Maud looked around as Mrs Smith bustled out to prepare tea. Frost traced patterns on the inside of the windowpanes and if Maud huffed, her breath formed mists of condensation. Mouldy wallpaper hung off the walls, unable to stick against the water seepage. Lots of spills had been made in the laid fire with a few meagre lumps of the brown coal, lignite, that would smoke with a sulphurous stench and give off little heat. But it wouldn't be lit until the evening, however cold it was during the day. On the mantelpiece were photographs of Mrs Smith's husband, who died in the 1919 Spanish flu epidemic, and her three sons, who died in the Second World War. For many years she had managed to make ends meet with her sewing business, repairing her grief one stitch at a time. Eventually her arthritis had stopped all that. But at least she and her aunt didn't have to pay for the doctors anymore thanks to "Mr Bevan's wonderful health service," as Mrs Smith would say on any occasion she could introduce it.

The tight band around Maud's chest and the wheezing caused by the mould spore convinced Maud to talk to the landlord about repairs and decoration. She hoped her brother wasn't the landlord. He owned a number of houses down here, and she'd always hoped he would treat his tenants well, like their father had always done. But Jack was not like their father.

On her way home, Maud made a slight detour to the old hall, now Jack's family seat. His wife, Elsie, never made her very welcome but fortunately, there was only Daisy's granddaughter there polishing the brass doorknobs. Maud left a message requesting that Jack send a load of logs over to Mrs Smith's so they could keep warm during the day.

As Maud drove down the potholed lane, she recalled walking down here with Bea and Violet. Turning a corner, she had a vision of meeting Harry driving home from work in this car, a cigarette hanging out of his mouth and singing Jack Hylton's "We'll Meet Again" at the top of his voice just before he went to war. She smiled at the bittersweet memory. It was such a long time ago, but Bea would be here soon. A thrill thrummed down her back, and she tapped the leather steering wheel and hummed the tune.

Most of the mist had lifted, but there were still patches of ice in the shadows. Maud gathered the momentum to get up Whiston bank and the car seemed to be flying over the top. She dabbed her brakes but nothing happened. *Damn.* She ground the car into a lower gear. The bottom of the hill and the sharp left-hand bend were coming up fast. She pumped the brakes—still nothing, so she changed down to second, and the engine screamed in protest. The acrid smell of asbestos filled the cabin. *Please God, let nobody be coming.* She changed down to first and pulled the wheel hard. If it stayed upright, she should be fine. Then the narrow tyres hit the ice. She was instantly propelled towards the ditch and a huge tree filled the windscreen. She yanked the steering wheel, praying she wouldn't spin on the ice. Then blackness.

Knocking. Maud opened one eye and felt only blinding pain. She stared at her cut and bleeding hands. Her head throbbed, and her other eyelid refused to open. Her glasses were still on her face but twisted at a drunken angle with the nose pads gouged into the side of her nose. The metal taste of blood filled her mouth. Pushing her tongue gently around her mouth, it stung like an open mouth ulcer. She must have bitten the inside of her cheek.

A judder went through her. Could she move? Her head hammered, demanding attention. Raising her hand to her forehead; it was sticky and wet, and stung like a thousand needles. Tiny shards of glass prickled her fingers. Lord, would she be scarred for life? Her breathing came quick and shallow, accompanied by a pain in her ribs. She tried to slow down her breaths. *Don't panic. I'm alive.* When she waggled her toes, a jagged bolt of pain seared through her left leg, and she sucked her breath in through her teeth to stop from crying out. Sweat trickled down her forehead, but it was falling at forty-five degrees. How weird. The engine was still going, so she turned the key and slipped it in her pocket. Everything was at a strange angle and there was knocking again. She carefully twisted herself around, gasping at the pain along one side. The man's face at the window was blurred and out of focus.

"Miss Heaston, is that you? Are you all right?" She held her hand up to squint. The face flickered and morphed before melding into one she recognised. "Mr Jenkins?"

"Aye, we need to get you out, now. Might be easiest out of the window. Can you unwind it?"

He looked at her from above. He was right. The door was probably too crumpled, but there was the window handle. Pain shot through her arm as she gradually turned it. She gritted her teeth and tried not to cry with the exertion.

"There you are. It's coming. I can get my hand in now and do the rest."

She relinquished control and put her head back against something rough. The tree was in the car. She eased her head to her left. The tree had crushed the whole of the passenger side. If she hadn't steered away from it at the last moment, she would have been under there. *That was close.* She offered a prayer of thanks.

"Miss Heaston, please. You need to get out, now."

A look of anxiety crossed his tanned, lined face. Was there a problem?

His calloused hand came towards her as though offering her a dance. "Can you climb out?"

She tried to lever herself out of the seat, but the jagging pain in her leg elicited a scream. "I think I may have broken my leg." She tried to catch her breath against the agony of her ankle. She thought she might pass out and forced herself to breathe slowly. She needed to stay conscious to get out of here. *Breathe in and out.*

Mr Jenkins shoved his greasy tweed jacket through the window. "Loop my jacket round you, and I'll haul you out."

Maud pulled and tucked it under her armpits, handing the second sleeve back to Mr Jenkins. She could smell vinegar and eggs on his breath as he grunted to free her; he must have eaten pickled eggs. That was always Harry's favourite. Had he been trying to get her to join him in heaven? But then her mother said she was going to hell. She didn't believe that.

Pain radiated from her ankle, and she twisted her body to manoeuvre round the steering wheel. Once she was out as far as her waist, she used her arms, even though her hands were lacerated and dripping blood, to pull herself out. As she emerged, she could also see the extent of the damage. Nausea bubbled in her throat, and she fought not to vomit. Someone had to be looking over her to have escaped that alive.

The car was a wreck, a distortion of metal, fabric, and collapsed tree, and now she understood Mr Jenkins' concern. Amongst the smell of soil, and blood, and brakes, there was the distinct smell of petrol, pungent and slightly sweet. A hissing sound came from the engine, indicating the radiator must have punctured.

She gave a last push and almost screamed again as her foot flopped. She clawed at the side of the crumpled vehicle and its maroon paint came off in her hands. Harry had always been so proud of the car and polished it weekly. *Sorry, Harry.*

"Best if I carry you to my van. I'll pull the car out later if it hasn't gone up in flames. Can I lift you?"

She nodded assent, and he flipped her onto his shoulder like she was a sack of potatoes. Although he was gentle, as he placed her in the passenger seat, she still wanted to scream with the pain. The cold nibbled at her nose and stung the scars on her face, but her armpits were hot and beads of perspiration trickled down her back. The nausea was getting worse too. Don't be sick, don't be weak. What would Mr Jenkins think, weak woman can't be trusted to do anything? She inhaled deeply. "Can you get my handbag?" she gasped between breaths.

"Where is it?"

"Passenger side." As she spoke, it registered there was no passenger side anymore. "Don't worry, let's go before I faint."

"Right-ee-o, better belt you up then. What a bloody mess you've made to your face. Good job you weren't a looker."

His comment hurt almost as much as the bruises covering her face, and her tears fell. Salt stung her cuts, so she swallowed hard to hold them back and raised her eyes to the roof of the van. Cow dung on the fabric...how strange. How had it got there, or was it some other mark? Maud raised her hands, now smeared with the drying blood, and traced the planes of her face. There was swelling over her partially open left eye, and it was tender to touch. She sucked in through her teeth. She couldn't face Bea looking like this; she'd run a mile.

As the van manoeuvred to return to the hospital, she looked at the wreckage of the car and she could swear she saw her brothers looking it over and tutting at the state of it, cigarettes in their mouths. "Don't have lit cigarettes near the fuel tank. You'll blow it up," Maud mumbled. Harry looked at her, grinned and waved his cigarette perilously close to the fuel tank, taunting her. "Sorry I crashed your car, Harry," she whispered.

CHAPTER THIRTY-FIVE

MAUD OPENED HER eyes, and everything was bright. By the smell of disinfectant, the echoes of footsteps on polished floors and the uniforms, she must be in hospital. The long ward of identical iron beds reminded her of where Harry had been. She tried to move her left leg and groaned. It was in some sort of cast. Everything hurt, and her head, arms, and hands stung. Whatever they had given to her to make her sleep had clearly worn off.

"Good morning, gorgeous. Glad to see you're awake at last."

That voice, she would know it anywhere, it was guaranteed to make her feel better and bring a smile to her face. Maud swung around, then regretted it when her head banged like a threshing machine. "Bea?" Her tone was hoarse, as though she had been shouting all night, and her throat was sore. She covered her face with her hands. The bandage on her forehead didn't help how she looked. "Please don't look at me. I feel like the monster from *Beauty and the Beast*."

Bea stretched out her hands onto the sheets. "Sweetheart, you look like you've been in a fight with Sugar Ray Robinson, but it'll mend. You're here and you're alive, that's what matters."

Maud carefully reached to touch Bea. Of all the wonderful things to see on waking, it was Bea. Her heart expanded in her chest. If ever she needed proof of Bea's devotion and love, this was it. She tried a tentative smile, knowing it would be lopsided and probably ghoulish. "How come you're here?"

Bea raised an eyebrow and interlinked their fingers. "I've never been so frightened in my life when I phoned and your mother said you'd been in an accident. I wasn't entitled to any information because I'm not family. She was polite, but I had to push her about where you were and your condition."

Bea would have had to use all her persuasive skills to get past her mother. It warmed Maud's heart that Bea would be so persistent but hardened her anger that her mother would resist. Sadness that Bea would never be accepted as family settled in her lungs.

"How did you manage to get away? You had things to sort in London."

"It's amazing how something like this puts what's important into perspective." Tears dangled on Bea's eyelashes.

This wasn't the usual, bubbly Bea. She looked so pale and uncertain, like someone had drained her of blood.

Bea cleared her throat. "I thought I'd lost you," she whispered. Then she straightened in the wood and metal visitor's chair. "I've already told your mother I'm coming to look after you as you heal and that can either be in her house or in a separate lodging. She's grudgingly allowed me to stay."

Maud stroked her thumb across the back of Bea's hand. "She has? You mean you'll be under the same roof? That's my silver lining."

"Hmm, I don't think we'll be making love anytime soon—"

"Shh." Maud looked around, but no-one was paying attention. She chewed at her bottom lip. Bea had given up everything, and now she couldn't even… "I'm not sure I can continue in business on my own. I don't have any real clients to speak of, and it could take months before I can work again."

"I've been thinking about that. There's a little surprise for when you're discharged. I was going to save it, but I'll tell you now. I've bought one of those Morris Mini Minors that everyone is going crazy about. It's small, but I'll be able to transport you around and pick up books as necessary."

"I didn't know you could drive."

Bea stroked Maud's hand. "I learnt during the war, but there never seemed much point paying for a car when we lived in London."

Bea had sold the house to buy a car? Maud should be grateful, but it was all too much. Bea had sacrificed everything she held dear: her house, her career, her social causes, and now Maud couldn't even afford to keep them both, and they'd be forced to live with her ungrateful, disapproving mother.

Maud closed her eyes and the threshing noise in her head seemed to get louder. One of her nostrils was blocked, so she'd probably been snoring earlier. How embarrassing. Yet, despite how she looked, how they'd been apart for years, Bea was there. She'd never given up on them, on her. As sure as a pendulum in an old grandfather clock, Bea was the fixed point around which she pivoted, the rhythmic marking of time and serenity. But was this too much even for Bea? "I feel so guilty. You've given up everything to come here, and now I'm not sure I can give you a job."

Bea shook her head slightly and smiled. "Sweetheart, we'll do it together. And if you need to work for someone else and I do too, it's fine. The main thing is to get you better again."

Maud's heart pulsed hard. Bea didn't seem angry, or resentful, or repulsed. Maud wasn't sure she could've been so magnanimous, but Bea was so wonderful. A crooked smile was all she could manage through the swelling in her face, but she hoped it conveyed her relief, gratitude, and love. The scars on her face tightened at the movement, reminding her that she probably looked a sight. "But how will I go out and market the business like this?" She indicated her bandages and plaster cast.

"I thought I might do some marketing for you. For a start, there's the local Fabian society."

"In Tory held rural Staffordshire? I've never heard of it."

Bea grinned and the twinkle in her eye returned. "I'm going to set it up. And a women's group, of course."

"Stir the pot, you mean."

"That's the plan."

Maud laughed and wished she hadn't. "Don't make me laugh. I'm useless in a hospital bed, and I can't concentrate for long with only one eye and a pounding head."

"No, of course not. You need to rest, and you can tell me what to do."

Bea glanced around then grazed her lips against the back of Maud's hand. She turned it over and kissed the scars on her palm. She'd automatically lifted her hands at the last second to protect her head. The image of the tree hurtling towards her flashed like the same piece of news reel going over and over. "I was heading straight for a tree but somehow I shifted the steering wheel at the last moment; otherwise, I would've been dead. The tree crushed the passenger side. It sounds crazy, but as I was being carried away in Mr Jenkins' van, I was sure Bill and Harry were watching, smoking and teasing me."

Bea palmed away a tear, and she seemed as if she was trying to cover her shock, as she was trembling. "Well, maybe they were watching over you. I for one am very grateful. Sweetheart, I don't want to be apart from you ever again. These last two years have been really hard. Even when we're together, I'm constantly watching the clock, calculating how long it will be before you have to go. Do you promise we won't be apart again?" Bea squeezed Maud's hand, who flinched involuntarily. "Sorry, I didn't mean to hurt you."

"I don't want it either. And maybe Mother will come around, if you can charm her. But it will have to be a secret to everyone else, including the rest of the family."

Bea sighed, her expression seeming to portray both frustration and understanding. "I know. Maybe things will change over time."

Someone coughed behind them. Bea gently replaced Maud's hand on the bed. She looked up to her visitor. "Mr Jenkins, thank you for rescuing me."

"Aye, well, you helped me milk my cows once and got some grants for me, so I guess that debt is settled now."

"From what Mother said, the car caught fire only a few minutes after we left."

He shrugged. "Right enough."

"So, you saved my life. Thank you. That sounds so inadequate. How can I ever repay you?"

Mr Jenkins cleared his throat, looking uncomfortable. "I came to ask you a favour."

Maud braced herself, wondering what was coming next.

He looked down, wringing his flat cap in his hands. "Can you do my accounts?"

Maud flashed a glance at Bea. "Of course. I'd be delighted."

Bea rose and held her hand out. "Sorry, we haven't been introduced. My name is Beatrice Williams. I'm Miss Heaston's personal assistant."

The phrase rolled off her tongue so expertly it was as if she said it every day of the week. Mr Jenkins' eyes widened. He wiped his hair down with his hands then rubbed his hands on his trousers and gave Bea a beaming toothy grin.

"How do. Fred Jenkins. Pleased to meet you, Miss Williams."

"How do you do? May I ask why you decided to ask for Miss Heaston's accountancy service?"

He glanced around then leaned forward. Maud caught the whiff of vinegar and eggs and immediately she was back in the car, shocked and in pain. A bead of perspiration trickled down the side of her face. She swallowed and tried to focus on the present.

"That young Mr Baker, he's not really interested in doing the work. Said he wanted everything sorted before he looked at the accounts, then left me the forms to fill in for the grant. I don't go doing any forms."

Bea turned up the wattage of her smile, the one that had first captured Maud's heart and still dazzled everyone around her.

"Of course, Mr Jenkins, we'd be happy to oblige. I can pop over and collect all the paperwork and ask you to sign the agreement later this week." She shook hands with him again. "I won't be able to help with the milking though. I don't know one end of a cow from another."

He nodded as if it was a serious issue and turned to Maud. "Will you be well enough? You could take months to get better."

"Thanks for your concern, Mr Jenkins, but Beatrice will assist me, very ably. She was educated at Cambridge, you know." Maud attempted to put on her professional voice, but it sounded thin and slightly slurred, so maybe she was still drugged. Her whole body felt like lead and her head too heavy for her body. She hoped she was intelligible and tried to fix Mr Jenkins' gaze, but he was ogling at Bea, the admiration dancing on his features.

"I didn't know pretty girls went to university."

"Thank you, but I'm not a girl anymore."

He studied Bea. If he drooled, Maud wouldn't have been surprised. The tug of jealousy mingled with pride. He was their first proper client.

"No, you're not," he said, slightly breathy. "When will you come over? Do you have transport now Miss Heaston's car, well, you know?" He glanced at Maud again, as though anxious to refer to the accident.

"I do have one of the new Morris Mini Minors, thank you."

"Do you? I'd like to see that." He observed her for a few seconds, then looked down at his cap twisted in his hands. "Well, I'd best be going. The cattle auction starts in an hour."

He bowed, which seemed slightly comical in his tweed jacket and baggy trousers and departed after further thanks from Maud.

"Your first real client." Bea's skin creased at the corners of her eyes.

"Hmm, I think you may need to be careful with him. He's rather smitten with you."

Bea laughed. "He's no problem. His heart's in the right place."

"It's not his heart I'm worried about."

"Ooh, is that the green-eyed monster mocking the meat it feeds on?" Bea prodded Maud, playfully.

"Except I've got black eyes at the moment."

Bea's joy faded. "Oh, sweetheart, I know." She kissed Maud lightly on the cheek.

"Please, not in public."

"You were lucky, I was going to kiss you on the mouth. Those kissable lips. I'm sorry you're in pain, but I keep thinking, what if? I don't believe in a god, but I prayed and thanked her anyway."

"I've prayed too, and I do believe."

Bea stroked Maud's cheek. "I know you do."

Their eyes met, and searching deep within Bea's pupils, Maud could see their connection, feel their love, and touch Bea's very soul. Her eyelids drooped, and despite struggling to stay present, the exhaustion and drugs started to take effect.

"Would you like me to read to you or do you need to sleep?" Bea said.

Maud yawned. "Could you read to me till I fall asleep?"

"Okay, the choices are Shakespeare or a new book called *The L Shaped Room* which I haven't started yet."

"Too much death and violence in Shakespeare."

"Because you've had a knock to your head, I'll ignore that comment and read you the novel instead."

Maud didn't even hear the opening sentence of chapter one.

CHAPTER THIRTY-SIX

THE FOLLOWING DAY, Maud was getting listless in the hospital when her mother arrived for evening visiting hours. She brought a basket, like she used to do on her charitable missions. "Hello, Mother. Do you know when they're going to let me out? When I spoke to the doctor earlier, he said they were still concerned about concussion and that I needed supervision for a few days."

"Yes, I spoke to him too. I'm getting the music room adapted so you can sleep in there, so you don't have to struggle with the stairs."

Maud's position softened, and she shuffled back against the pillows. A glow warmed her heart. Since her accident, her mother had been thoughtful and concerned. Maud basked in it, however long it lasted, like a cat stretched out in front of the fire. "Thanks, that's kind. And what about Bea's room?"

Her mother's expression sharpened as if she had just tasted a lemon. Clearly the consideration did not extend to Bea. If only her mother could see Bea for who she was: a funny, intelligent, and caring woman.

"I've had another thought about that. As you no longer have a car, I believe we can adapt the old stables garage into a small bed sitting room since you insist she works for you. The builders are working on it now. They're fitting a kitchenette and small bathroom in there. I've already spoken to her, and she's agreed to pay rent from when it's ready."

"So not in the house then? And can't you let her have a rent holiday until we have the business established? It's not as if you need the money."

"No. She's not family. And I've already told her that nobody in the church or community must know about her as anything but your employee."

Maud pulled up the bedcovers as a shiver went down her spine. "That's a good way to make your point and a profit at the same time."

A faint smile twitched her mother's lips until her expression became more neutral. "I thought it was a very suitable arrangement. And before you say anything, she agreed to the terms."

Maud sighed and looked up as the doors at the end of the ward swung open, but it was no one she knew. "I'm surprised she's not here. She said she'd bring me some puzzle books to do. Reading makes my headache worse."

Her mother nodded and pulled two puzzle books from her basket. "I told her I was coming here this evening and you shouldn't have too many visitors. She asked me to give you these."

Her mother presented the books with an unmistakeable gleam of triumph in her eyes. Maud clenched her teeth at her mother's conniving and tried not to slip into anger. It would achieve nothing. This way, Bea would be close by. As Maud flicked through the pages, she noticed there was a neat paragraph of dots and dashes on the inside back cover. She concealed her smile at Bea's subtle subterfuge. They hadn't used Morse code for so long, she hoped she could still remember it.

Her mother rose and squeezed her hand. "I need to be off. I said I would call in to see Mr Wilson while I was here, as his wife can't make it. Goodbye, my dear, I'm glad you seem to be on the mend."

When her mother left, Maud stared at the message and reached for her glasses and a pencil. The swelling under her eyes made the glasses sit strangely, making it difficult to focus. After a few missteps, she deciphered the message.

Dearest M, change of plan but we won't be kept apart. More conditions. I have to go to church, have to deny us. I want to sing it from the steeple, I love you. And if it's what we have to do to be together, I will do it willingly. Just been banned from seeing you tonight. Think a family only rota is being organised. I will come when I can. Thinking of you. 88
Your loving B xx.

Maud reread the message and carefully tore the back cover off the puzzle book. Bea would hate to go to church, yet another sacrifice to be together. How could she ever repay her? She read the message again, clutched it to her heart for a few moments, then tucked it under her pillow.

Jack and Elsie arrived seconds later with baby Matthew. The baby pawed at Elsie's face and hair but Elsie ignored him, looking exhausted and tight lipped. Motherhood did not suit her. Maud always thought Elsie was more interested in the title, the money, and Heaston Hall than in Jack.

She'd expected a bevy of servants and a nanny, but Jack was unwilling to have that expense. Elsie had asked Maud to look at their domestic accounts, but Maud said she would only do so with Jack's agreement. She wondered if she had betrayed a fellow woman but didn't feel too sorry for her. Elsie wasn't interested in any of the moral duties or obligations of her title and had done nothing to help their tenants. She was one of those modern women interested only in what she could make and take, not contribute to society, and did not subscribe to *noblesse oblige.*

Maud looked across at Jack. He had an unhealthy pallor, not that she could comment. She'd avoided all mirrors but could tell her bruises were morphing to purple and yellow, so her face must be hideous. As if to prove the point, Matthew took one look at Maud and screamed. "Thanks," Maud said.

"I'll see you outside. We'll wait by the car," Elsie said.

"I hear you're still planning to go solo," Jack said.

He sat at the edge of the chair, pristine in his Jermyn Street suit, looking every inch the banker. She preferred the wild boy who was nothing but mischief, back when the twins had been real. She struggled to sit as upright as she could. Everything hurt, and exhaustion clawed at her consciousness and willed her to rest. But every time she closed her eyes, she was in the car again. "Yes. Although I've taken on an assistant."

"Mother said. Our old tutor, bit of a surprise."

Not that old, if you don't mind.

"It's like she's got a soft spot for our family. Just as you lost George, she seems to be clinging to the memory of Harry. Bloody waste if you ask me. I know lots of chaps who'd be happy to have her."

Maud wiggled her jaw to release the tension. "She's not a piece of meat to be handed around."

"Okay, keep your hair on. What I meant is, if you're still looking for extra clients, I could put a good word in for you at the Conservative Club."

She bit her lip. She hated to ask and didn't want to be beholden to him, but she needed some support. "What about bringing Heaston's bank across to me?"

"No offence but banking is a very specialised area, and there'd be a conflict of interest for the audit."

He gave her the fake smile he adopted for his customers. It had been a bit of a long shot since he was a golfing buddy of the partner at the current auditors.

Maud returned his smile with equal insincerity. She needed more clients, even ones against her political leanings. "If you could put in a word with the Conservatives, that would be helpful."

***

A couple of Sundays later, Bea drove them to church in her Mini Minor, Maud's first outing since leaving hospital. It was hard to swing her legs in and out as the seats were low and the crutches seemed too long. With a bit of juggling and treating it like a spatial puzzle, Bea arranged the crutches between them and could access the gear stick, just.

"See, I told you we could do it." Bea grinned.

"Is it safe?" Maud asked, not wanting to admit fear clamped her heart. Being brought home in her brother's Rolls Royce had felt so solid and secure. This car was so tiny that she'd to dip her head to avoid the ceiling. The car was bright red, and it would certainly be noticed, just like Bea.

"Of course it is. Are you saying you don't trust my driving?"

How could she explain her fear of feeling vulnerable and exposed? Maud inhaled and tried to calm the tremor in her hands. "No, it's just..."

"Oh, sweetheart, seat belts, see." Bea reached over to help fasten the belt and took the opportunity to plant a quick kiss on Maud's lips. She locked her eyes on Maud's. "I promise I will drive as safely as I can. I have the most precious cargo."

"I could really do without church today. Everyone will stare, and my face still looks bruised and scabby."

Bea stroked Maud's cheek. "You're beautiful."

Maud huffed out a breath. "You're biased."

Bea started the engine with the ignition key, and it was wonderful not to have to use a crank handle in the cold and wet. "True. Now are we all set?"

Maud gripped the door handle the whole way to the church. As they drove Bea sang "Kiss me, Honey, Honey, Kiss Me" as loud as she could. Maud joined in on the chorus, laughing and grateful Bea was distracting her from her fear. She didn't want to admit she'd had nightmares and sweated most of the night, dreading the journey. Fortunately, it wasn't far; Bea was more enthusiastic than tuneful, unlike the fabulous Shirley

Bassey.

"You'll be too hoarse to sing the hymns if you go on like that." Maud sounded grumpier than she intended, but Bea didn't seem to care.

"I'll just mouth the words then."

Bea parked in the parking spot reserved for Baronet Heaston by the entrance to the church. "You can't park here."

"I don't believe in all that nonsense. Besides you are supposed to be resting that leg as much as possible, not doing a two-mile hike on your crutches." Bea must have seen the look of concern on Maud's face. "I'll help you into the church and then go back and park."

Maud sagged with relief. This was definitely not worth having an argument with her brother about, so she just smiled at Bea. "Thanks, honey, honey."

Jack and his family had reserved the prime seats in the family pew, followed by her mother and then Maud. There was plenty of room for Bea, but her mother made it very clear that Bea wasn't welcome in the family pew. Bea shrugged and placed Maud's crutches beside her and moved across the aisle a few pews down.

The new vicar, Reverend Johnson, was very much in the mould of Reverend Davies with his first sermon about the evils of promiscuity and the way of the flesh. Although it was still painful to twist, Maud couldn't resist looking across at Bea. Bea blinked repeatedly, and Maud realised it was Morse code. Dah dah dah diddit, dah dah dah diddit. Maud grinned and knew what it would be without translating it: 88. She winked.

There was a crash on the pulpit as Reverend Johnson brought his hand down hard on the old wood. "Hell and damnation await all sexual deviants."

Maud rubbed her neck. She had snapped back too quickly and felt slightly nauseous.

He glared at Maud. "No homosexuals will ever get into heaven or into my church."

Great, so her mother had already spoken to him. Her mind drifted towards the afternoon tea her mother had set up with an eligible gentleman, not subtle in her intentions. The man was wealthy, supposedly good looking, and single, and spent most of his time in London.

Maud had refused, but her mother smiled as if she was about to play the winning card in bridge. "Roger Manley is also looking for an accountancy practice to take over his large estates."

"All right, I'll have tea with him."

Not to be thwarted in her plan, half an hour before Roger Manley was due, her mother wandered into the music room that was also acting as Maud's bedroom. Maud and Bea looked up from their budget calculations.

"You're not working on a sabbath, are you?" The accusation was as sharp as if she'd caught them in bed together.

"We're just planning what we need to do next week and have just finished." Maud smiled, hoping to recapture the warmth her mother had shown when she was in hospital. But those times were rare like the family pearls she'd given Maud.

"Good. I need Miss Williams to take a basket of food to Mrs Smith—"

"But—"

"You clearly can't go." Her mother fixed Maud with a hard stare, almost willing her to challenge her authority.

They all knew it was an excuse to get Bea out of the way. But Maud wasn't that stupid to play into her mother's games. There would always be some other plan she had in mind, even if they could find a legitimate reason to delay.

Bea rose. "It would be a pleasure, Lady Heaston. Do show me where the basket is, and I will go over right away." Bea held out her hand to indicate for Maud's mother to lead the way and winked at Maud as she slipped through the door.

Maud sighed. Some battles were worth fighting, others were not, and if Roger genuinely wanted accountancy services, it wasn't like she could afford *not* to see him. She pushed herself across the bed and grabbed her crutches. She'd better make herself presentable or her mother would dress her like some Edwardian dowager.

Half an hour later, Roger Manley was shown into her mother's best sitting room. Maud had wanted him to come into the offices, but her mother was clearly out to impress and showed him into the high-ceilinged, elegant room with French doors leading out onto the formal garden at the back. But if he was as wealthy as her mother thought, he surely wouldn't be impressed by the room that doubled as a library.

Roger Manley was tall and wore a pale cream three-piece suit with a maroon cravat. He floated across the carpet and sat down delicately on the wing-backed chair, the picture of elegance. "Lady Heaston, thank you so much for inviting me here. I've heard so much about your family." He crossed his legs and swung the free foot up and down, his hands clasped around his knee.

"We're very honoured, Mr Manley."

It was then that it struck Maud that his name was ironic: he was probably the least manly man she had ever met. He dabbed at his lips with a handkerchief before scooping up the best china teacup with the grace of a ballerina. Her mother could not be more obvious if she tried as she fussed and flirted. Her mother droned on with banal chat, and Maud took the opportunity to observe him. He was probably in his early forties but seemed out of his time, as though he should have been around in the twenties, discussing fine wine with Bertie Wooster, or maybe in the thirties, chatting to Noel Coward.

Mr Manley replaced his teacup and saucer on the coffee table. Taking this as a cue, her mother rose. "I know you wish to talk to my daughter, Maud, about accountancy services, Mr Manley, so I will excuse myself. I don't get involved in business," her mother said and left.

When the door shut, Maud turned. "I hope my mother hasn't brought you here under false pretences, Mr Manley."

He stretched his legs out in front of him and leaned back in his chair with an air of confident casualness. He arched his eyebrow and his eyes twinkled with mischief. "Oh, call me Roger, please. I can't stand all this stuck-up formality."

Maud couldn't believe the transformation. It was as if he had shed a sheen of expectation and was now revealing the man beneath. She was unsure what to make of him. "I don't know if you are genuinely looking for accountancy services or not, but I'm more than happy to ask what your needs are and how we can meet them." She fiddled with the teacup, turning it around and around in the saucer. The scraping sound was enough to put her teeth on edge, so she stopped and placed it on the side, trying to gather her courage to speak the truth. "If, however, that was just a ploy on my mother's part, and she intimated to you I am single and looking, I apologise, for I am not in the market."

His eyes glinted with amusement. "If you mean, do I think your mother is trying to set us up, the answer is yes, definitely. She told me how your fiancé was killed in the war. My condolences, by the way. She also explained how that was a long time ago and you're looking to settle down."

Maud groaned and burrowed her head in her palms. "I'm so sorry."

"Don't worry about it. I'm not in the market either. I am however looking for some accountancy services."

A knock at the door raised Maud's head, and Bea's smiling face peeked around the door.

"Am I disturbing anything?" she asked.

Maud's heart sung as it always did when she set eyes on her. "Not at all. We were just about to discuss accountancy services." She twisted towards Roger. The movement was still uncomfortable, but it seemed to get easier each day. "This is my assistant, Beatrice Williams. Bea, this is Mr Roger Manley."

Roger stood and crossed the room, a broad smile on his face. "Beattie, it's lovely to see you again." They shook hands.

Beattie? Maud frowned. "Do you know each other?"

Bea grinned. "Roger is a fellow Fabian, and he said he was looking for some accountancy advice, so I suggested he make contact."

"I see what you mean about Maud's mother. No offence, dear, but icicle doesn't cover it. Just as well she's not my mother-in-law." He and Bea chuckled and shared a look.

Maud stared from one to the other, feeling she was missing something vital and wasn't sure what. She gestured for them to sit. Roger reclaimed his previous seat, and Maud caught a whiff of delicate aftershave. Bea perched herself on the arm of Maud's armchair. It wasn't very professional but perhaps that's how they were in the Fabian society meetings. Bea placed her hand on the back of the chair behind Maud's head, so close Maud felt the warmth on the back of her neck.

"Roger, please tell Maud what you told me."

He sat straighter and cleared his throat. "Maud, I think we all have a lot more in common than you may think. Though, of course, we all have to be discreet. Through no fault or favour of my own, I inherited a large pile in this part of the country. I also have a house in London, where I live with my *assistant*, Anton."

Maud reflected their smiles, and her shoulders relaxed as she realised what he was confessing, although it was so much riskier for men. It was illegal for men to be together, despite the Wolfenden report being published, as the Tory government had blocked the bill at every turn. "So, my mother was barking up the wrong tree on more than one count?"

"Precisely. Needless to say, I'll be the last in the direct line of Manleys, and I have no intention of leaving my wealth to the money-grubbing cousins, so I would like to set up a trust with the idea of Manley Hall being used either as a school or possibly as a hospital or home for the elderly, and if it's not suitable, maybe selling it and raising funds to set up some sort of foundation to help the poor."

Maud smiled at him. She really liked this man and could see herself working with him. "We can definitely help you with that, Roger, and we'd love to get involved."

Bea squeezed Maud's shoulder. Yet another client Bea had conjured out of thin air. She was a godsend in so many ways, as well as being adorable. "Thank you," Maud whispered.

CHAPTER THIRTY-SEVEN
Staffordshire, December 2007

THE CAR WAS sliding towards the tree. Maud pulled the steering wheel at the last moment, and her heart raced as she had to get out of the car before it set alight. Where was Mr Jenkins? The smell of pickled eggs and vinegar drifted into her awareness, and she gagged. She couldn't push herself out of the car. Violet was sitting on the hedge with Harry and Bill, cadging a cigarette from them and swinging her legs like she did as a little girl. "Vi, I didn't know you smoked. You shouldn't do that; it's bad for your health."

Violet gave her a watery smile, passed the cigarette to Harry and blew out a perfect smoke ring before turning to Maud. "It doesn't matter now, Maud, I'm dead."

Then Vi's daughter, Janice Good-For-Nothing, was propped up against the hedge, looking stoned on something, as always.

"How can you not know who Hannah's father was?" Maud asked.

Janice shrugged in that way she had that Hannah seemed to have adopted too. "It could have been three of them, although I don't think it was Kabali, 'cause Hannah's white." She snorted as though she had just made a hilarious joke. "They all buggered off though when they knew I was pregnant. Don't look at me with all that judgement, Auntie Maud, you're not exactly perfect either. I know your secret now." She waggled her index finger and tried to wink, but it came out as a blink. She laughed again. "All those lies, Auntie Maud! What would the vicar say, and the county set ladies, if they knew you were fucking a woman? Do you think they would still let you do the flowers in church and be deputy mayor? I think I might tell them you're a—"

"Janice, that's enough," Violet said.

She looked older now, as she had been the last time they'd met, a sprightly old lady who was looking forward to a trip to Birmingham Christmas market.

"Thank you," Maud said, grateful that Violet had never judged her.

Vi's eyes teared up. "Please, Maud, look after my little Hannah."

Panic gripped Maud's heart and squeezed it like a lemon. "But what about Ed, can't he take her? I don't know how to deal with teenagers."

"No, love, he's too heartbroken. But little Hannah, she's a lost soul. She needs love, and help, and guidance, and I can't give it to her now."

Then the car ripped into flames and Vi's face contorted into a silent shout. Maud screamed, knowing she couldn't save her.

"Hush, sweetheart. Wake up, you're dreaming again," Bea said. "It's just a nightmare."

Sweat poured down Maud's face, despite being cool in the bedroom. It was the same nightmare every sleep since they'd learned about the accident that had killed Violet and Janice. And today, Hannah was going to come and live with them after the funeral. If only someone else would take her, but Hannah didn't know who her father was, so they had no hope of tracing him.

Maud wiped away her tears with the back of her hand and snuggled into Bea, laying her head on her shoulder. Bea wrapped her arms around her. The neon red from the clock alarm caused a red glow around their bedroom: 2:32 a.m. She didn't dare go back to sleep again but being awake was just as much a nightmare. "I'm not sure I can do this," Maud whispered unnecessarily. "I don't know how to deal with teenagers, never mind a grieving, angry teenager. I'm too old for this—we're too old. What if she turns out like her mother? Vi would never forgive me."

Bea kissed her tenderly on the forehead. "The only thing we can do is to love her," she said, soft as liquid honey.

"I don't understand why her Grandad Ed said he couldn't look after her. She gets on really well with him."

"He's not well either, though, is he? And he's grieving for his wife and daughter."

"I'm grieving my sister." Maud sounded harsh, petulant almost.

"I know, sweetheart, but grief doesn't have hierarchies and people need to deal with grief in their own individual way. Ed says he can't look after her, and Matthew or Amanda won't have her. Since the twins died, none of the rest of the family have had much to do with Hannah."

That's because nobody approved of Janice. Maud didn't say it aloud. "But it makes sense for her to be with her cousins, with people her own age. She's always looked up to them."

Bea brushed the dank hair off Maud's face, cupped her cheek in her hand, and gently stroked her thumb over Maud's lips. "Hannah won't think of them as her own age. They're a generation older than she is."

"I don't know anything about sixteen-year-olds. It was so different in our day."

By the red glow of the light, she could see Bea smile. "That's true. We'll manage between us. I've been looking up this thing called YouTube to find out about the culture of the young. They upload video clips. The most popular seems to be of a child complaining about having his finger bitten by his younger brother."

"I have no idea what you just said, it sounds insane. I don't understand."

Bea chuckled. "I don't think we're supposed to understand. Poor girl, she's lost everything." Her expression was serious. "Just love her."

"I do love her."

"Well, that's a start."

Maud swallowed hard, the truth of what she was about to say sharp in her mind. "We'll need to sleep in separate rooms again."

Bea stopped caressing her face and pulled back, a frown furrowed deep between her eyebrows, shadows created by the red glow, giving her an almost sinister feel. It was not an expression Maud had seen very often and never wanted to see again.

"No. You promised me. After your mother died, we agreed we'd never sleep apart again."

Maud stroked Bea's cheek. "I know, my love, but we can't traumatise the girl anymore. Nobody knows. She'd be disgusted."

"She's sixteen. The world's changed, and she'd probably accept it."

Maud sat up. "No. I wondered if we could refurbish the old stables again—"

Bea shot up too, and it created a distance between them on the bed as wide as a chasm. "I'm not going in there."

"I didn't mean for you, I meant for Hannah, then perhaps we could share a bed."

"No, she needs to feel surrounded by love, not be isolated in another building."

Why was this so difficult? She'd hoped Bea would see it was the only logical conclusion, and they would make it up to each other while

Hannah was inevitably out at all hours, like teenagers were wont to do. Maud closed her eyes to give herself strength against the hurt and anger sharpening Bea's eyes, like a knife honed on steel. "In that case, we need to have separate rooms. If you take the other guest room on this floor—"

"I disagree completely. We promised each other. The poor girl probably won't care. She's grieving and has enough to worry about. I want to sleep with you, to be with you properly. It's only in the bedroom that we can be who we truly are. I'm not complaining, it's just after so many years, it would be nice to be out and be able to live openly. You don't need to worry about your homophobic clients anymore—"

"Just my homophobic family."

"Who gives a shit what they think?"

Bea's anger showed in the profanity she rarely uttered. Normally her arguments were logical and calmly delivered. Anybody else would think she didn't care, but Maud knew Bea was upset. But it altered nothing, and it couldn't happen. "I do. And how do you think the church and other councillors and town notables will react?"

"It's about time we had some diversity in this town. I detest its small-minded bigotry."

Bea slapped back down onto the bed and turned away, pulling up the bedclothes and shutting Maud out. She stared up at the ceiling, blinking to stop the tears. This was all too much, but she couldn't come out. Hannah would tell her friends at school, and she would be the laughingstock. The trouble with secrets is that the lying never stops.

The lies that had once seemed just a glossing over and malleable had hardened over the years and fossilised till the imprint was all that remained. She couldn't retract them and say they'd been a couple all along. Surely Bea could see that. And Hannah had enough trauma to deal with now without the extra upheaval of discovering a secret about her great aunt. Maud glanced across at Bea muttering some Shakespeare. It sounded like Portia's speech from the Merchant of Venice. So she wasn't too angry. She was just trying to recalibrate herself.

Maud trailed her index finger down Bea's back. She would miss this closeness too, but it was the right thing to do. They had kept the secret so long, it couldn't be acknowledged now.

Eventually, after a third repeat of "the quality of mercy is not strained, it droppeth as the gentle rain from heaven," Bea sighed and turned over in the bed.

"I disagree with you. She's young and she'd take it in her stride, but I understand if you think the timing isn't right. We'll do what we can to make her feel at home." She shuffled to Maud and lay her head on her chest. "Do you promise when Hannah is at school that we make time in the day to do this? Lie in bed together. So, I can be with just you, my love, my life?"

Maud inhaled Bea's lily of the valley talc and her shampoo and relished the warmth of their bodies cuddled together. "I promise, and if she stays overnight anywhere, we'll sleep together that night. Thank you. I love you." Maud lowered her head to meet Bea's and traced a line of kisses from her hair, her forehead, and down her nose. "You have very kissable lips," Maud said and planted her own mouth over them. Bea responded, and they reconfirmed their love, like they had thousands of times over the years. Through all the pain or parting, hiding, and having to fight to be together, this one solid bond always pulled them together. It was right. It had always been right and worth every one of the hardships and compromises, however hard it had been.

When they came up for air, more quickly now as their lungs were not what they were, Maud raised her head to gaze at Bea, softness in her eyes. "You're beautiful, my precious Bea."

Bea snorted. "I thought it was me losing my eyesight, not you. I'm an old woman now."

Maud interlaced her fingers with Bea's. "When I look at you, I still see that wonderful tutor who bounced into my life with the light shining through the library windows, casting a halo around your head."

"I must have been in silhouette, then." Bea chuckled and snuggled closer. "If this is our last night together for a while, maybe we should make the most of it? I think I need to be re-acquainted with pretty clitty."

Maud giggled like she was fifty years younger and stretched out to welcome her. "I love you," she said again. Not that they really needed words anymore, but it was so liberating to be able to speak its name.

CHAPTER THIRTY-EIGHT
Staffordshire, 2008

THE DOOR BANGED, and the tornado arrived. Hannah threw down her school shoes and backpack, which splayed over the floor like storm debris. Maud came through to the hall, wiping her hands on a tea towel. "You're late, did you miss your bus? Don't leave your things where Auntie Bea will trip over them. You know she can't see very well."

Hannah huffed, adding in an eye roll for extra effect. Why did she have to behave like the stroppy teenage stereotype? It was exhausting.

"I haven't even got through the door, and you're already on my case."

That was fair enough. Maud inhaled, what had Bea said? *Give her some slack.* "Sorry. Good evening, Hannah, it's lovely to see you. I hope you had a good day at school, and now will you please put away your shoes and bag. Better still, take your bag upstairs and start your homework now before supper."

Hannah exhaled noisily, then stooped to throw her shoes in the shoe rack. She flung her bag on her shoulder and flinched, sucking in her breath through her teeth.

Maud frowned, trying to hide the anxiety gripping her chest. "Are you hurt?"

"No, Gammy, it's nothing."

She stared up at Hannah. Maud had shrunk from her five feet eleven, but Hannah was nearly six feet already. She would never get used to having to look up to her great niece. They shared the same dark hair and dark eyes, and Maud had to catch her breath. It was like looking at a younger version of herself sometimes, except Hannah was too sassy by half. Like her mother, God rest her soul.

Maud didn't blink and simply waited. Hannah glared back.

"Don't lie to me, Hannah Jones, you've hurt yourself. Let me see."

Hannah's hand flew to cover the top of her arm. A flush crept up her neck. Had she been fighting?

"I'm fine."

Maud sniffed, realising she used the same reaction as her own mother used. She'd hated that so much when she was Hannah's age. Her shoulders sagged. "You're clearly not fine. Come into the living room and let us have a look at it."

Maud made her way down the hallway, complete with pictures and mementos from all over the world on shelves lining the walls. Not that she'd ever been, thank you very much. She didn't understand this desire to travel. Most were from her nephews and nieces, although she didn't display the one from Japan that Amanda had brought back from her travels, as that would dishonour Harry's memory. Hannah still hadn't moved. "Hannah." Why did she always have to repeat her instructions? She didn't know it was going to be this hard. Maud sighed for the umpteenth time that day. Everything was a battle. An angry sixteen-year-old was not what she had bargained for. Poor Violet would be turning in her grave.

Bea looked up from her puzzle as they entered the sitting room. Her eyebrows met in a frown as she sensed the tension between them. "Hello, Hannah, is everything okay?"

Why was Bea siding with the girl? It undermined her authority.

Hannah straightened to her full height, her chin up, defiant like her mother. "I'm fine. I had a tattoo done after school." Her mouth twitched in a smirk, although she tried to hide it.

Maud's hand flew to her mouth, stifling a gasp. What would Violet have said? She wasn't setting Hannah on the right path. What would be next? She said a quick prayer and crossed herself. "A tattoo?" she whispered. "But why? Why would you ruin your beautiful skin? What will people think? That you're some working class slob?"

"Don't be so fucking superior."

"Hannah, don't swear at your aunt, please." Bea put down her crossword to make it clear she was giving the matter her full attention.

"You keep out of it. I don't know why you're always hanging around; it's creepy."

Bea sagged in her seat, and her features crumpled downwards. The hurt flashed in her eyes before she regained her neutral expression. Maud felt hot and cold simultaneously, rage shooting up her throat. "Hannah, apologise to Auntie Bea at once. She lives here, and it was her home before it was yours." She raised her hand as if she might strike Hannah but let it fall and curled it into a tight fist. She hadn't felt so angry since she was fighting for her partnership. Why did Hannah have to press all her buttons?

"Sorry, Auntie Bea."

That tone was half sing song, half mocking. Sometimes she wished she could... no. The girl was still grieving, give her some slack, as Bea kept reminding her. But why did she have to be so angry and rebellious? And now she'd got herself a tattoo. Maud inhaled and took a different path. "If you want to get a professional job, you need to look the part. People will judge you on how you look. A tattoo may be fine for footballers and sailors—"

Hannah snorted.

"But if you want to be a lawyer, or an accountant, you have to look respectable."

Hannah seemed as if she was about to sneer. "I don't want to be a lawyer or an accountant."

Maud fidgeted with her pearls, fingering them as if they were a string of rosary beads. "But you need a good profession behind you, something you can always fall back on. You need to be financially free, so you aren't beholden to anyone. Sadly, a university degree isn't a guarantee of a good job anymore."

Hannah bit her bottom lip. "I don't want to go to university."

"Sit down, Hannah dear, and let's talk about this properly and rationally."

Maud glared at Bea. Why was she interfering? This was her responsibility. Maud sighed and released her grip on her pearls. Bea was only trying to help, and Maud didn't know how to deal with this. It was like slipping into sinking sand, the more she tried to wrestle a way out the more she was sucked into arguments with Hannah. When the twins had been naughty, they always respected Maud's authority as elder sister, eventually, but Hannah didn't seem to respect her at all. She felt so helpless, and there were no operating instructions for grieving teenagers.

Maud stared up at the ceiling and blinked back tears forming in her eyes. She must not be weak now, otherwise how would she deal with it if Hannah did drugs or slept around? She was her mother's daughter after all, God rest her soul. Hannah installed herself on the armchair on the opposite side of the hearth, back as stiff as starch, and her hands clenched on the arms, knuckles white.

"Why don't you want to go to university?" Bea asked, her tone gentle, as though she was genuinely interested in the answer.

Hannah scuffed her Converse against the Chinese rug, which was curling up at the edges slightly. Maud wished Hannah wouldn't do that on her rather threadbare heirloom from her own childhood. Hannah's kicking would only make it worse.

"What's the point? I hate school: pointless rules and regulations, and why get into debt and not get a job at the end of it?"

Maud's cheeks burned as she remembered staring at the same rug on that awful night when her parents coerced her into marrying George Waites, when she was just a little older than Hannah was now. But this was different. This was her trying to give Hannah the best opportunities to be independent. Maud would have loved to go to university. Couldn't Hannah see how fortunate she was? "But most professional jobs need a degree—"

"I don't want a professional job." Hannah spoke through clenched teeth.

Bea put her hand up to still Maud. "What do you want to do?" she asked Hannah.

Maud wished Bea wouldn't interrupt. They would clearly need to have a conversation afterwards.

Hannah shrugged. "I dunno. I want to travel, see the world, volunteer for a charity, do something important. I haven't decided yet."

Bea nodded as though she was considering Hannah's point of view. Was she serious, or was she just putting on an act to calm Hannah down?

"That makes sense," Bea said, "and you can certainly do that after university. Travel is such a great broadener of the mind. I was very fortunate to be taken around Europe with my father when I was a teenager. Not that we called them that, then." Bea smiled at Hannah, ignoring Maud's scowl.

A look of triumph flashed on Hannah's face, and she stole a glance at Maud. "Anyway, I want to go to sixth form college, not stay at school."

Maud clutched at her pearls. "What? But it's an excellent school with a great reputation. They get a high percentage of people going to university from there." Wrangling Hannah was like trying to catch the soap in the bath, with it constantly slipping away and sploshing in the water.

Hannah sat up straighter, squaring her shoulders and holding her head high. It was an action Maud recognised in herself. "But my friends are going to the college."

There was something about the way she said friends and the slight pink around her cheeks that set off Maud's warning bells. "Oh, is this about some boy?"

Hannah's pink cheeks turned scarlet. That seemed akin to a confession. "No."

Maud huffed out a breath. This conversation was going off track. "Don't they just do BTECs at college?"

Hannah shrugged as if she hadn't bothered to research the topic at all, adding to Maud's conviction that she was looking at college for the wrong reasons. Bea stepped across to the desktop computer and jiggled the mouse to activate it. The font was so large you could read from the other side of the room. Maud made a mental note to tell her not to leave any of her lesbian or radical web pages open. In fact, wasn't there somewhere you could delete all the history? She'd talk to Bea about it later, Bea would know.

"You can do A levels at the college and they do proper two-year courses too, not just cram it in to one year, where the maximum you can attain is a C. Most universities require A grades."

Hannah's knuckles whitened on the chair arms, and her legs jiggled up and down. "I don't want to go to university and get a boring job. I want to make a difference."

Bea twisted away from the computer and stroked her chin, as if debating options. "Ah, I see. You want to help people?"

"I'm interested in politics." Hannah's body stiffened, as though confessing what she really thought made her vulnerable and open to being mocked.

Bea's eyes sparkled, as if she had just found a soul mate. It surprised Maud that Bea didn't clap her hands together in glee.

"There are some great courses in politics and international relations. Would you like me to help explore the opportunities with you?" Bea asked.

Hannah's eyes shone and she nodded, then perhaps remembering she was not supposed to show enthusiasm, she affected nonchalance.

"It's about keeping your options open," Bea said and beamed, resuming her seat in the wing back chair.

Maud stifled the irritation, and maybe envy, that Bea had broken through Hannah's defences where she couldn't. She sighed. The girl wasn't trying to be difficult, but they just came at things from the different end of the telescope. "So, what did you get as a tattoo?" Maud asked.

"It's a mockingjay."

"Ah. Katniss Everdeen," Bea said and picked up her crossword.

Hannah's and Maud's heads shot up in unison, and they gawped at her.

"You've read the Hunger Games?" Hannah asked.

Bea chuckled and gestured at her iPhone. "I can't read very well now, so I listen to Audible as I walk and work in the garden. I thought I'd see what all the fuss is about. I really enjoyed it. It was well written."

"Wow, did you? It's my favourite book."

"Well, I should hope so if you've tattooed her symbol on your arm."

Bea grinned, her face creased in a million laughter lines, grooved deep from years of joy. Maud stared at them both as if they were talking gobbledegook. Typical that Bea could relate; she was always so good with people.

Maud had failed. Hannah was getting more and more like her mother every day. Violet would despair at the job Maud had done. She couldn't even talk to her great niece without causing a volcanic eruption. And the horrible thing was she didn't know how to fix it. Bea seemed to have a tenuous link, but Hannah was getting angrier with them. Maud had never felt so hopeless in her life. *Forgive me, Violet, I'm trying my hardest, but it just isn't good enough.*

CHAPTER THIRTY-NINE
Staffordshire, 2009

THE BORING ROUTINE of daily life with Gammy and Auntie Bea was driving her insane. It was so unfair. She desperately missed her mum and Nan. Her mum wouldn't have cared where she went and what she did. She'd have thought Hannah was cool. Why did she have to go and die, in a stupid car crash of all things. At least if she'd taken an overdose, it would have been a fitting rock and roll death, instead of in Nan Vi's Nissan.

Hannah so wanted to talk to Nan. She would've understood her infatuation with Megan. Nan knew about passion and the complete overriding, all enveloping, yearning desire of wanting to be with someone, to breathe their air, to follow their scent and walk for miles in the hope of catching a glimpse. Not like the two desiccated strait-laced husks she lived with who had never known love and wouldn't know what it was if it slapped them on their arses.

She'd no interest in coming home from college to study until supper, and collaborate on the crossword, when she could be out with her mates being a normal seventeen-year-old. If she needed the internet, she had to use the PC in the sitting room, and most times Auntie Bea was using it.

She wished she had one of the new iPhones like Megan had. Hannah always got an earlier bus so she could meet Megan as she arrived at college. The trouble was Megan's popularity with the boys who crowded her out. But Megan had kissed her, just the once, and Hannah kept hoping she would do it again. At least they could sit together for classes.

Auntie Bea read out the clues from the Times crossword, and Hannah looked at her watch. "Can I watch *Gavin and Stacey*?"

"Not until we've finished the crossword," Gammy said.

Hannah wanted to hurl. Who cared about the fucking crossword? She banged her fist on the arm of the chair. "Why all these stupid rules? Why can't I watch my programme, like everyone else does? Most of my friends have TVs in their own room, or at least their own PC."

Gammy stared at Hannah over her glasses like a disapproving head teacher. "It's a question of consideration for all the people in the house. What was the clue, Bea?"

Auntie Bea peered at the clue through her magnifying glass that distorted her eye. "Who is the Egyptian Goddess of war and healing, seven letters?"

Hannah rolled her eyes. The sooner she got out of here, the better. They were relics from a different century, in fact they probably remembered the bloody pharaohs. She inhaled sharply. Better to comply, then at least she might have a chance of catching some of it. She counted out on her fingers. "Pharaoh?" she said.

"No," Gammy said. "Why don't you look it up online?"

That was it. She tried, but they never let it go. Hannah slammed her fists on the arms of the chair. "I don't care who the sodding Egyptian goddess of war and healing is. I just want to watch my programme and do normal things like others my age." She ran up to her room and slammed the door. She kicked and flailed at the wardrobe door until it dented, and there was a rather ominous cracking sound. It split, so she tried to splice it together and breathed a sigh of relief when it seemed to hold. Hannah threw herself on her bed and the mattress squeaked.

Half an hour later, Gammy knocked on the door. "Hannah, we need to talk."

Hannah pulled the duvet around her shoulders. "Go away."

"You are seventeen, not seven. We need to have a discussion about what just happened. I'm coming in."

She opened the door and stood in the doorway, filling the frame like a silhouette in one of the old crime movies. Hannah pulled her knees up to her chest and shuffled to the side of her bed by the wall. "Why can't I have any privacy in this house? Tomorrow wouldn't be soon enough to leave. I hate being here with your stupid rules; it's like living in a bloody old people's home."

"Hannah Jones, don't be so rude. I will not have you speak to me like that. It's about time you thought about other people apart from yourself. For that insolence, you'll take the evening meal around to Mr Hobbs for the next week."

Hannah pictured the last time she had visited the disgusting kitchen Hobbs sat in and how he had to lock his growling bulldog in the other room so the brute wouldn't attack. "He stinks, and his dog scares me shitless."

"Nevertheless, that's your punishment. Perhaps you'll think about others who are less fortunate than you." Gammy sighed. "I know you don't want to do the crossword but it's important to limit TV time. Maybe we need to schedule it in along with time on the PC, so you get access. Now if you want to watch your programme, come on down."

Hannah kicked at a cushion on her bed. "It's probably finished by now."

"Suit yourself, but the option is there if you wish to take it." Gammy turned and left.

"Fine." Hannah tramped down the stairs behind her since she needed a drink anyway, and her programme would already be over. She strode back to the kitchen and was tempted to return upstairs with her juice.

"Do you want to finish your personal statement, Hannah?" Auntie Bea called as Hannah passed the open sitting-room door.

She stood at the threshold, the glass of orange juice in her hand. "No Shakespeare reading this evening?" She cast a glance at Gammy to see her reaction, but she was engrossed in the sudoku. "You know that sudokus are Japanese, Gammy?"

Hannah grinned to herself as Gammy huffed and shook the newspaper. Auntie Bea smiled faintly as she turned to look at the PC.

"It's been set by The Times, a British Newspaper, presumably by a British journalist," Gammy said.

Hannah stepped into the room and placed her glass on a crocheted doily coaster, before sitting in her normal armchair. "Ah, The Times. That paper that's owned by an Australian-born American who uses his power to influence and manipulate UK politics?"

"Hannah, shall we look at your statement?"

Auntie Bea intervened to avoid an argument, but Hannah was determined to challenge Gammy's xenophobic bullshit, who scowled as she returned to her paper. Hannah grinned as she stood by Auntie Bea at the computer and caught the amused sparkle in Auntie Bea's eyes. She shook her head at Hannah, as if saying, "Don't tease your great aunt." Hannah shrugged. The only power she had was to tease, so she was going to use it as often as she could.

"You need to come across as enthusiastic about the subject you're going to study. Why do you want to do International Relations? At the moment this reads as if it's just a list of what you do at college," Auntie Bea said.

Ouch. Go for the jugular, why don't you? Hannah slumped into her chair and picked at the frayed piping on the cushion. "But it sounds naff if I say I'm interested in current affairs."

The landline phone rang. "Answer that, would you, Hannah?" Gammy asked.

Hannah gave a mini mock bow and picked up the receiver on the table by the door.

"Hello, is that the home of Miss Beatrice Williams?"

Hannah covered the mouthpiece. "Auntie Bea, it's for you."

"What do they want? If they're trying to sell us anything, tell them we're not interested," Gammy said.

"I'm Emily Cooper-Smythe. I work as a researcher for the BBC. We're putting together a documentary about the people who worked at Bletchley Park during the war, and we'd like to speak to Miss Williams about her war service."

"Wow," Hannah said before she could stop herself. "It's the BBC. They want to talk to you about the work you did in the war at Bletchley Park. Did you work on the enigma machine?" Hannah had to laugh as both her aunts stared at her, like meerkats on guard at the edge of their burrows, alert and whiskers twitching.

"I can't speak to the media as I signed the Official Secrets Act," Auntie Bea said and turned back to the computer, "and it wasn't just breaking the enigma code." She sniffed.

Hannah spoke to the posh woman on the end of the line. "Um, she says she can't talk to you because she's signed the Official Secrets Act." Hannah put the phone on loudspeaker so they could all hear the reply.

"Oh dear, so many of the potential participants believe that. The information has been in the public domain for many years and the general public is fascinated by it, especially as the government is finally going to recognise the contribution made by the code breakers. It would be really helpful if Miss Williams could tell us about her experience."

"Tell her to send me her questions by email, and I'll think about it," Auntie Bea said, her attention still on the computer screen, although she had cocked her head to hear the conversation.

When she finished the call, both she and Gammy stared at Auntie Bea, waiting for an explanation.

"You worked at Bletchley Park?" Gammy whispered.

She seemed surprised. How could she not know that's where Auntie Bea had worked? They'd spent most of their lives as best friends from what Hannah could gather.

Auntie Bea shrugged. "Yes, but I wasn't allowed to speak about it. I'm still not sure it's appropriate."

"Awesome," said Hannah. Megan would be so impressed when she told her the following day. They'd been talking about the enigma machine at college the other day.

"But I thought you were a bilingual secretary?" Gammy asked. She rubbed her sternum with a trembling hand. "You never told me. After all these years you never breathed a word, even to me?"

The shock seemed to have morphed into something else, and her eyes glittered with tears. Was the Great Maud Heaston actually crying?

Gammy stood and placed the newspaper by the wood burner for it to be made into spills the following day. "I'm off to bed. Goodnight, both."

And she swept out of the room. After the door clicked shut, Hannah turned to Auntie Bea. This was much more intriguing than writing about herself. "What did you do there?"

Bea twisted to face her. She blinked twice, as if deciding what to impart. "Eventually, I worked on the Colossus computer, which was the first programmable digital computer, whatever the Americans claim." She chuckled.

Gammy could be heard moving around upstairs, readying herself for bed banging wardrobe doors and stomping around. *Ha.* Hannah could hardly keep the smirk from her face. She knew something that Gammy didn't.

"All those secrets we had to keep," Auntie Bea said. "The trouble is, there always seems to be an impact. For something like that, national security was at stake, which is fair enough. But other times..." She shook her head. "I think it's better to talk about what's on your mind. Share the burden, so to speak."

"What was it like at Bletchley?"

Auntie Bea's gaze shifted to the middle distance, as if she was reliving the experience. "Exhausting, pressured, exhilarating, and heart breaking at times."

"Why heart breaking?"

Auntie Bea blinked. "Because sometimes we knew something was targeted but nothing would be done to stop it, because that would give away that the enigma codes had been solved. One chap I worked with had a brother serving in the merchant navy that was targeted by the U boats. He never got over knowing beforehand and not being able to do anything about it."

She indicated towards the open personal statement on the computer. "Have you decided which university you wish to put down first? We'll need to tailor the personal statement to their particular course."

By the rapid change in subject, Hannah realised Auntie Bea didn't want to talk about it. Maybe she would ask some further questions later.

"Bristol," Hannah said and felt the heat in her cheeks. Damn, talk about a giveaway.

"Ah. And is that because a certain person is going to Bristol?"

Hannah thought if she glowed anymore, they'd need to call the fire brigade. Megan had put Bristol first, and as the college's star student, she should get an offer. Hannah hoped they'd be able to share lodgings and Megan had hinted at that if Hannah could get in. "I...well..." How could she say anything? Firstly, the two old biddies would be nosey; secondly there was nothing concrete to say, unfortunately; and thirdly, Megan was a woman. Her pulse quickened and her belly stirred just thinking of her.

"That's fine but think about the consequences if you go somewhere for love or do something for love."

"I didn't say it was love." Hannah realised she'd just been trapped into confirming she was going because of someone else.

"All the more reason to think about the consequences then. If it all falls to pieces in a few months or years, will you regret the choice you made? If not, then go for it."

"You're just saying that because you want me to go to Cambridge. I don't even know if I'll get in, especially as I have no idea who the Egyptian God of war and healing is—"

"Sekhmet."

"I was being sarcastic."

Auntie Bea smiled, her eyes full of glee. How could she be so good-natured all the time, especially living with Gammy?

"I know, but it doesn't harm to increase your general knowledge. And we have no preference where you go. She just wants you to be happy and to do something that you enjoy that will give you financial independence."

Hannah snorted. "Right."

Auntie Bea prodded her. "I wouldn't adopt sarcasm as a response if you get offered an interview, if I were you."

It was all right for them in their cosy little world. They'd probably never been in love. They didn't know what wonderful anguish it could be.

CHAPTER FORTY

THE FOLLOWING MORNING, Hannah left for college earlier than usual. She said it was to study, but Maud wasn't sure she believed her. Bea knocked and slipped into her room with two cups of tea on a tray. Maud smiled, her heart nourished with love's demonstration. "Good morning, beautiful. You spoil me."

Bea handed her a china cup and saucer and put her own down, before flipping up the duvet to climb into bed. Maud placed her cup on the side table and snuggled up. She loved the smell of Bea's hair and her warmth, and the frisson of lying in bed on a weekday morning. It was so deliciously decadent.

"This is the best moment of the day," Bea said, "when I have you all to myself before you go and do all your good deeds."

Maud kissed her. "Do you think she knows what we do when she's not here?"

Bea canted her head. "She's a teenager; she doesn't think about anyone except how they relate to herself. But I do wonder if we should tell her."

Maud sat up straight, rolling Bea off her. "What? No."

"It's just she's clearly infatuated with someone at college, and I suspect it might be her friend Megan that she talks about."

How had she missed that? Maud's heart jumped in excitement, then calmed. "Really?"

"Yes, but I think she's too embarrassed to talk about it, well, to us anyway. I just thought if we told her about us, she might open up a little and be less defensive all the time."

Maud picked up her cup and took a sip to give herself time to ponder what Bea said. It would be wonderful to be open, to lie in bed like this every night and not worry. But Hannah would be disgusted by the thought of the two old ladies in bed, especially her great aunt. She could almost see the sneer on Hannah's face, and she'd probably be even more desperate to run away. What would poor Violet say? Would she be disappointed and think Maud hadn't done her job properly, or would she think Maud had turned Hannah gay? Cold shivered down Maud's back, and ice hardened in her heart like the wind-whipped tundra. "Even if she was a lesbian, she'd be repulsed about us two old ladies having a physical relationship. And if she's not, dear God, she'd have even less respect for us than she does already. Besides, she might say something to her friends or her cousins. No, it won't do. It will be hard enough standing for Mayor again next year because of my age, without adding that into the mix."

Bea sipped her tea, then replaced it on the side. "Don't you think it will help Hannah, if she's struggling with her own sexuality?"

Maud put her cup down with a clatter onto the saucer. Clearly Bea thought it would help, but she couldn't countenance it. "I don't see her struggling."

"Oh, sweetheart, are you sure you're looking, or are you just pushing up your defences against her jousting with you?"

Maud sighed and replaced her cup and saucer on the coaster. She leaned against the upright pillow. "Why does she deliberately needle me? I find it so hard. I tried to tell her about Harry and the Japanese, but she didn't want to listen."

Bea laid her head in Maud's lap and fiddled with the hem of her pyjama top. "It's history to her. And looking back, knowing the outcome, she won't have the same perspective of someone who lived through the anxiety, uncertainty, and exhaustion."

A jab of pain whittled away at Maud's heart. "Talking of the war, why didn't you tell me you worked at Bletchley Park?"

Bea sighed. "I could see that upset you, but they drilled into us about not revealing what we did—"

"During the war, yes, I understand that. But afterwards? You've never breathed a word." Maud knew she wouldn't be cross for long, but she couldn't quite climb over the hurt yet. Bea stared up at Maud with her intelligent gaze. She reached up a hand and traced Maud's jawline with gentle fingers.

"After the war, I still worked for GCHQ before helping set up the Refugee Council, but it was all still secret and covered by the Act. And they drilled into us we mustn't tell anyone, not even our spouses."

Maud swallowed back tears, feeling foolish as she did. It shouldn't matter now, but it stung. She hated all the lies, and secrets, and with Bea it was the one area of her life characterised by honesty and openness. "I thought we had no secrets between us. I feel really hurt, as if I didn't know a big part of you and your life."

"Come here." Bea pulled Maud down under the covers. "You know all about the important parts of me. That was just the job I did. It isn't who I am and frankly, most of the work was long, stressful, and boring. You're the most important part of my life, always have been and always will be."

"But I feel excluded from that part of you. I told you all about my time in the Land Army and fighting to get recognition professionally."

Bea stroked Maud's cheek. "I'm sorry you feel that, but I've always given you all of my heart."

Maud sighed. "I know." Guilt crept up her spine, like a snake uncoiling, slithering around her chest and squeezing out her breath. She couldn't begrudge Bea her lie by omission when Maud had insisted they both lie about their relationship for so long. Each lie or secret was like a drop of water corroding their joy. Over time, what should be shiny and beautiful had become tarnished with rust. Bea had been denied and their relationship trivialised, yet she was still here in her bed, by Maud's side. Tears pricked the back of her eyes. "You sacrificed so much to be with me."

Bea shook her head, mussing her hair on the pillow. "I sacrificed nothing. I made a choice, willingly. Yes, there were consequences, but I'd do it all again, despite all the dissembling. I'd love to be as open as the kids are nowadays, but I get where you're coming from, and I know you're scared."

The snake seemed to crush the air from Maud's lungs, denial forcing its way through her lips. "I'm not scared."

Bea pulled away so she could look Maud in the eyes. "Sweetheart, you don't want it to come out about us. You don't even want to tell Hannah, the girl you love most in the world."

Maud clamped her mouth shut, not wanting to argue, and not just because Bea would always win, but also because they both knew Maud wouldn't budge. Bea called it stubborn, Maud called it being clear. "This conversation is going in circles."

Bea grinned and twirled her index finger around the button on Maud's pyjamas. "Maybe it's time for less talking. How long until you need to do the brasses?"

"I'm meeting the vicar at ten as he wants me to do the reading this

Sunday. Will you come along?"

"If you'd like me to come, yes, of course."

Bea kissed her, and her body relaxed at Bea's touch, the kiss tasting of tea and home.

CHAPTER FORTY-ONE
Bristol, present day

W<small>HEN</small> S<small>UKI</small> <small>RETURNED</small> from work, she sidled up to Hannah and wrapped her arms around her. "We need another member on our quiz team tonight. Alyssa's had to do an extra shift. Will you come?"

"Really?" The last thing Hannah needed was to waste an evening with strangers. She wanted Suki to herself and her own friends, but Hannah knew she couldn't say no to Suki's doleful eyes.

An hour later, Hannah followed Suki through the noisy pub. They squeezed onto a bench seat with four of Suki's colleagues, all nurses or radiologists, calling themselves the X-ray Specs.

Suki indicated the raucous group on an adjoining table. "We don't really fancy our chances against the doctors, but we're going to try. They've been taunting us all week."

Some of the doctors looked half cut already, apparently assured of victory, and were trying to claim the hamper as the winning prize. Over three hundred pounds had been raised for the children's hospital, the majority coming from the X-ray Specs team with their patients generously contributing before their appointments.

"This is my flatmate, Hannah," Suki said.

Flatmate. Nothing more, despite them sharing the same bed. Hannah's hopes of finally being acknowledged crumpled like discarded paper. Introductions were made, but Hannah wouldn't remember their names. Suki rushed off to grab a round of cider and beer for the team, and Hannah went with her to avoid being alone with a bunch of people she didn't know. As Suki predicted, the server completely overlooked her and addressed Hannah behind. Hannah motioned to Suki, who had turned scarlet and was gripping her purse with white knuckles. Suki shouted the order, and the bartender apologised, shrivelling under the sharpness of her stare. By the time they made their way back to the table, the quiz master was tapping on the microphone and asking for quiet. There were probably seven teams, but the only one that mattered was their Wot's Up, Doc? rivals.

"Round One, General Knowledge. Pencils ready. We will collect the answers after each round. Question one," the quiz master said.

The captain of the X-ray Specs, Ramesh, was clearly a very intelligent guy and answered most of the questions without having to confer. Hannah sipped her cider and scanned the seething mass of humanity, thus far unable to contribute.

At the end of the round, Ramesh leaned closer to Hannah and his thigh touched hers.

"What do you do?" He fluttered his long eyelashes at her.

Was he seriously trying to hit on her? Hannah glanced at Suki, but she was talking to another colleague. Normally, Hannah would just set someone straight about her sexual orientation. She couldn't have been more obvious if she had a neon sign above her head, but she had a feeling Suki would be really unhappy if they thought she lived with a lesbian. And she was upset already because of the bar incident. Somehow, she always took it as a personal slight when she was overlooked.

Hannah inhaled deeply, catching the smell of stale beer and steamy, sweaty bodies. Maybe he was just being friendly. She gave him the benefit of the doubt. "I'm doing a PhD at the university," she said.

"Ah, we have a doctor on our team."

He dazzled her with a smile so brilliant Hannah almost needed sunglasses. "Not yet." The thought of the work waiting for her when she got home made her cringe. It would be another late night and her deadline was looming.

He fiddled with the pencil and gazed at her intently. "We'll surprise them with our secret weapon then."

Suki nudged Hannah with her leg. Relieved to break contact with Ramesh, Hannah bent to listen to Suki.

"I should have warned you that Ramesh might try to chat you up. He's desperate for a girlfriend."

Hannah leaned forward and inhaled Suki's perfume. "It's all right, I'll just say I'm a lesbian."

Suki jerked back and flashed her a warning look. "Please don't, they might think I am too."

Hannah gripped her glass tightly. "You've already introduced me as your flatmate, so why would they make any assumptions about you?" Hannah shook her head. She sounded sharp, but she'd hoped Suki would acknowledge her openly and stop this farce. But she just turned away and chatted to the person next to her, whose name Hannah couldn't remember and at this stage frankly couldn't care. She shouldn't be surprised. She knew how Suki felt, so why had she expected anything different? Well, she hadn't expected to be hit on by a straight man. He must be blind as well as being desperate.

She had another slug of her cider as they waited for the second round and thought about skipping out early. Hannah glanced at the exit and all the bodies and chairs that impeded her escape. It would be a major feat to hack her way to the door. She hoped there wouldn't be an emergency.

"After round one, we have three clear rounds, from The Double Entries, What's Up Docs, and X-ray Specs. Well done, those teams. Now round two: food and drink."

Jana was the X-ray Specs superstar in this round, and again Hannah wasn't able to answer any questions. She felt a little silly, sitting here trying to avoid the advances of a man and pretending she wasn't sitting by her girlfriend who wouldn't acknowledge their relationship. She stole a glance at Suki, desperately trying to fit in and laughing at the in-jokes.

As they waited for the next round, Jana leaned across the table. "Is Connor not around this weekend?"

"No, he's at a gaming convention."

Hannah hissed through her teeth. So, Suki hadn't told her work mates she was no longer with Farty Boy, even though it was six months since they'd split up. Hannah's stomach churned. Maybe she should have eaten something more substantial than crisps before drinking. She felt as invisible as Suki at the bar, denied and unimportant. Even now Suki was ignoring her. Hannah pulled at the label on the cider bottle and ripped each shred of paper into tiny pieces. They'd been sleeping together for four months now, and Hannah thought they were on the fast track to something solid. Although Hannah was placid and had learned diplomacy, this was getting too much even for her. She glanced at her watch. This was a waste of time, and she wasn't sure if she didn't mean their budding relationship as well as the evening.

Suki squeezed Hannah's thigh under the table and left her hand there. What was she trying to do, buy her silence? Hannah sipped at her cider, debating whether to make her escape now anyway and hang the consequences. Her free leg bounced up and down. She needed to calm herself, so she inhaled deeply and focused on the quiz.

The next round was geography, and at the conclusion, they were neck and neck with the doctors and the accountants.

"It helps we have a team member from every continent," Ramesh said.

He was still trying the charm offensive but with less enthusiasm now. Maybe because he could sense the steam rising from Hannah.

"So do the doctors," Hannah said, not caring if she sounded rude. Suki stroked her thigh under the table, but Hannah stopped her hand. Her silence couldn't be bought by physical affection.

"Round four, art and literature. Are you ready?" the quiz master asked.

Hannah's team groaned.

"You can tell the quiz master's a retired doctor. I bet we don't get a round on entertainment," Jana said.

Just as well. I'm rubbish, and all we do is watch Friends reruns.

"In which Shakespeare play does the protagonist give away his property to his relatives, then find himself banished and eventually go mad?"

Hannah grinned. At last, something useful from all her time with Gammy and Auntie Bea. It reminded her to check up on Gammy. She scribbled King Lear on a piece of paper and handed it to Ramesh. He nodded and copied down the answer onto the answer sheet.

Suki bumped her arm. "Sounds like your gammy," she said.

"Yeah, I know," Hannah whispered. "Look how Lear ended."

At the end of that round, the doctors had a two-point margin over the X-ray Specs. Their mocking and jeers grew louder.

"Yeah, yeah, wait till the next round," Ramesh said.

Ramesh looked genuinely annoyed as he turned to face his teammates. Competitive much? It was only a quiz. And yes, they were raising money for charity, but it was supposed to be fun. Hannah stared down into her drink, wishing for the ordeal to be over, but focused anyway.

"The next round is myths and legends."

The X-ray Specs moaned and muttered. "Oh, come on, we didn't all have a classical education."

"Question one. In Greek mythology, which Titan held up the world?"

"Atlas," whispered Ramesh and scribbled it down. He also got the next two.

"Question four. What is Thor's hammer called?"

Suki and Hannah knew that one, as Hannah had asked to watch the

Marvel movie two nights ago, rather than yet another Friends rerun.

"Mjolner," Suki whispered, "but I'm not sure how to spell it."

She leaned against Hannah and stroked up Hannah's inner thigh. She took a sharp intake of breath as her clit responded. Her body had clearly not got the memo that she was annoyed with Suki, and it was very distracting.

"Question five. Who was the Egyptian goddess of war and healing?"

"Ha! I know this one," Hannah said and gave the answer to Ramesh. Suki's stroking was getting more insistent, and Hannah bit down on her bottom lip. Her body buzzed in response. "Stop it. We need to talk," Hannah whispered in her ear to be heard above the din in the pub. Suki pulled her hand away, and Hannah missed the warmth and pressure seeping through her jeans. Traitorous body.

"Sorry," Suki whispered.

"How long does this go on?" Hannah asked as yet more questions were called out.

The quiz master asked for all of the answer sheets in before Suki responded. Ramesh rose and offered to buy drinks. Hannah put her hand over the top of her glass.

"No, thanks. I've got to work this evening. Nice to meet you all, but I need to get on." She stood and snatched her wallet, keys, and phone from the table. "I'll see you back at the flat."

"No, wait. I'll come back too." Suki pulled her bag from under the table. "Bye everyone. See you at work tomorrow."

Before they reached the steamed-up glass paned double doors, the quiz master announced that the winners were the X-ray Specs to a cheer and more raucous booing from the doctors.

"See, you made all the difference," Suki said, as she followed Hannah out into the weather.

Hannah shrugged and pulled up the collar of her jacket. The rain would muss up her hair, yet another thing wrong with this evening.

"Hannah, wait for me, please."

Hannah huffed and turned, her hands deep within her jacket pockets, but she stopped.

"I know you're cross with me, but—"

"I felt humiliated. You haven't even told them about Connor—"

"I was going to tell them after this weekend when I've got a week's leave from Wednesday."

"So?" Hannah wasn't even going to bother to work out that logic. She started striding again, not caring if her Doc Marten's landed in puddles and splashed Suki behind her. "And when would you tell them about me?"

Suki slipped her hand through the crook of Hannah's arm. "Soon, Han. I just need a bit of time. It's not easy for me to be open."

"Why not? We're in the 21st century, for fuck's sake."

They turned into Redland Park, Suki now half running beside Hannah, still clinging onto her arm until they reached their flat. Once in, she unlaced her boots and left them on the mat. Without saying another word, she skirted round Suki's bike and swept up the stairs two at a time. On reaching the living room, she shrugged off her jacket and hung it over the low back of the kitchen stool to dry out and slipped into the bathroom to sort out her hair.

She leaned her forehead against the mirror and exhaled, causing a circle of condensation to form on the glass. She thumped her fist on the sink and inhaled sharply. She had to get a grip if she wanted to salvage whatever she had going on with Suki. The glass squeaked as she wiped it clear, as if she could clean away her hurt and humiliation. *Damn Suki.* She needed to think.

She barged out, brushed past Suki and into her room. The door banged as it shut behind her, and Hannah pushed her clean laundry to the side so she could lie on the bed and throw her stress ball against the wall. Suki would hate it, but she didn't care.

Thwack. Hannah tried to unpack her jumble of emotions. She hated feeling humiliated and insignificant, but below that was the realisation that she was a lot more into Suki than Suki was into her. How stupid she'd been to think that Suki might introduce her as her girlfriend.

Thwack. In Hannah's experience, in a relationship one party is more involved than the other, but if Hannah waited, would Suki catch up or would they always be like this, locked away in a private vault?

Thwack. If a relationship wasn't acknowledged in the world, was it real or was it like a holiday? Wonderful and appealing but all too soon the laundry needs sorting and the waste recycling.

She placed the stress ball on the bedside table and folded the clothes, ready to put away in the Marie Kondo method, but she doubted it would spark joy right now. It didn't seem to matter as one T-shirt was much like another, but Suki insisted. What did Hannah want with a relationship with

Suki? She wanted to go out together as a couple, with friends, and for Suki to be her someone special at graduation. At the moment, she seemed to be the only one likely to hand back her visitors' tickets to her graduation ceremony. Talk about Billy no mates.

She closed the shirt drawer. If this was going to work, she needed to understand what Suki's objections were. Stropping and stomping about wouldn't help. Maybe she needed to see it from Suki's point of view. Just because Hannah wanted them to be out and proud didn't mean Suki was as confident in her standing within her team or in society. Suki had said her father was very traditional. Perhaps she didn't want it to get back to him, although there was no chance of him meeting her work colleagues.

Hannah tried to picture herself living in the gossipy, judgemental society surrounding Gammy. Would she also be loath to come out to those around her? The truth was, she'd fled to Bristol and rarely ventured back because she didn't want to face the contempt of her relations and a small-minded rural society. Was she being a hypocrite?

She sighed and went to the lounge, where Suki had turned on the lamps to give a warm, ambient glow.

Suki carried mugs of tea and sat on one end of the sofa. "Please, sit down. I'm sorry I denied you in the pub. I'm just not ready to come out to them yet. I know we're in the 21st century, but when you face 20th century prejudice every day, you don't want to heap on more. Or I don't. Does that make sense?"

Hannah took a sip from her tea, hot and not too strong, just as she liked it. "It feels like a slap in the face, as though I don't matter."

Suki walked her fingers along Hannah's arm. "Of course you matter, Han. You matter so much to me. I love you."

She extracted the mug from Hannah's fingers and placed it on the side, so she could straddle her. She rested her hands on Hannah's shoulders. Despite her resolve, Hannah melted. Suki's words made her fizz beneath her skin, and her proximity triggered Hannah's heartbeat to change gear, like she was cycling downhill fast and slightly out of control.

"I'll show you how much," Suki whispered.

The warmth of her breath sent goosebumps down Hannah's spine, and she moaned as Suki kneaded her tight shoulders then kissed her neck. While Hannah's body was a willing recipient of the proclamation, her mind still needed convincing.

CHAPTER FORTY-TWO
Staffordshire

KATHERINE JOINED HANNAH as she hurried down the corridor. "I'm so sorry I'm late. Bloody trains," Hannah said.

"Never mind, you're here now."

"How was the big reunion?" Hannah asked.

"Lots of tears. Wonderful, heart-warming, and heart breaking knowing that I need to take Bea back this afternoon. I'm going to find the manager of the home and see what can be done."

Hannah entered the large ground floor room. The care workers had placed a seat next to Gammy's wheelchair so she could look out over the lawns. Gammy and Auntie Bea held hands on Gammy's lap. Gammy put their linked hands on the arm of her wheelchair.

"What are you doing?" Auntie Bea asked.

Maud tapped her hand three times sharply with hers, hardly a tremor showing on her fingers. If Hannah didn't know any better, she would have said that Auntie Bea had been massaging Gammy's inner thigh. She thought the sight would have made her a little queasy, but it was sweet and warmed her. She went over to Gammy's other side and kissed her on the cheek. "Hey, Gammy."

"Hello, Hannah, it's lovely to see you again. Thank you for coming."

Hannah squeezed her free hand and saw the spark back in her great aunt's eyes. It touched her to the core.

"What's going on?" Auntie Bea asked.

Gammy tapped some more on Auntie Bea's hand.

"Company?" Auntie Bea looked up through her thick lenses as if trying to make out shapes. "Who is it?" She held out her gnarled fingers. "May I touch your face?"

Hannah manoeuvred herself to kneel in front of Auntie Bea's chair, so she could trace over her spiky hair, features, and twenty-three piercings—it'd take her a while and Hannah hoped she wouldn't tear any out.

A broad smile slowly crept over Auntie Bea's face as recognition set in.

"Hannah. You came." She cupped Hannah's face in her hands. "Did you read the letters and documents?"

"Yes."

"She won't hear you," Gammy said. "Take her palm and tap on it one long, one short and two long. I can't do it much before my wretched hands shake. No, it needs to be more evenly spaced than that. That's it."

Auntie Bea nodded. She grinned and patted Hannah's hand. "I told you she'd read them. You didn't believe me, yet here she is." She turned back to Hannah. "Your great aunt is so glad you've come. She thinks about you every day, you know—"

"Silly old fool," Gammy said, but there was affection in her tone. "Now she's started, you won't be able to shut her up. Hold her palm flat if you want her to stop."

"I'm sorry I didn't organise for you to see each other before or come up more often," Hannah said, feeling she needed to get it out.

"What's she saying?" Auntie Bea asked.

Hannah bit her lip. "How do I do sorry?"

Gammy rattled off some instructions.

Hannah frowned. "That's only three letters."

"Yes." Gammy cracked a smile. "It's easier to do text speak. That's soz."

"Seriously? What is it again?" Hannah laughed, tempted to say OMG, but she restrained herself. Gammy repeated it, and Hannah tapped it out for Auntie Bea.

Gammy held out her shaking hand. Hannah knelt in front of them, linked palm to palm, and they both squeezed her hands.

"I'm sorry if I pushed you away. Auntie Bea said I did. I only wanted the best for you. I wanted your Granny Violet to be proud of you—"

"What are you talking about?" Auntie Bea asked.

Gammy's hand shook more. "Tap out, Vi, dit dit dit dah, diddit."

"Oh, V for victory?" Hannah remembered from being forced to listen to them explaining about news broadcasts starting with the Morse for V for victory during the war.

"That's it." Gammy repeated it for Hannah to tap out.

"Oh Violet, lovely little Violet. She caught us kissing once, you know?"

Auntie Bea chuckled, and Gammy smacked her on her forearm with some force, but Hannah saw the look of adoration in her gammy's eyes.

How had she missed their affection all those years ago?

"Ow, what's that for? It's true. If Hannah's read the letters, she must know. Do you know about us, Hannah dear?"

Auntie Bea withdrew her hand and made a big thing about rubbing where Gammy had hit her. Gammy stroked the same place, then stroked her cheek.

It was like watching an intimate dance. "What was yes, again?" Hannah asked. Gammy repeated it and Hannah tapped it out, then held her breath as the enormity of what she'd just said struck her. Her heart sped up. Still holding onto Auntie Bea's hand, Hannah faced Gammy. "I know about you. Do you know about me?"

She looked deep into the watery eyes, still clear, still bright.

"Are you..."

It was as though Gammy stumbled at the word, and it wasn't one she could bring herself to say.

"Yes. I love women, or at least one woman: Suki." A clammy hand covered Hannah's and Gammy gazed at her, wonder in her eyes. An unspoken nod of understanding passed between them, like repairing a gaping hole in tapestry one thread at a time.

"You do? We wondered."

Hannah cleared her throat. "That's why I didn't come or phone you because I had to hide more and more of my life. Or assumed I did. I'm sorry, Gammy." She choked around the lump that settled in her throat.

Gammy shook her head and cast her gaze down. "All our secrets, all our lies. I didn't call you because I thought you'd be disgusted by an old woman...."

Gammy's trembling became more intense. Hannah patted Auntie Bea's hand and released it to lean over and hug her gammy. She blinked to keep back the tears and kissed her on the forehead, conscious of how frail her aunt was. Hannah then pulled Auntie Bea into the hug and kissed her too, so they were doing an awkward three-way embrace.

As she pulled back, no longer able to stop the tears, Hannah dropped her hands to wipe her face. Auntie Bea stretched over and picked up Gammy's hand and brought it to her lips. Gammy smiled and with her shaking index finger, traced her lips. Auntie Bea kissed it.

How had Hannah never noticed this tenderness between them before? Was it there when she lived with them? Or was she just too angry and grieving from losing her own family and working out who she was, that she didn't notice? Or maybe they were so used to covering up, they disguised it well? "I didn't know. Were you together when I lived with you?"

Gammy turned to face Hannah again. "Yes, it was a secret. I was ashamed. Tell Bea about you. Tap out dit dah diddit."

"That's just one letter. Don't tell me, is it L?" They shared a grin. Why had she cut this woman off for so long? Gammy repeated it so Hannah could tap it out on Auntie Bea's free hand.

Auntie Bea seemed to ponder it, then faced Hannah with her opaque blue eyes. "Love? London? You're a lesbian?" she asked, a knowing grin shaking out the laughter lines.

Hannah nodded, then realised she wouldn't be able to see, so she tapped out Y, pleased she remembered it.

"Good. Thought so. With all that spiky hair and piercings and your interest in gender studies...set my gaydar pinging."

Auntie Bea chuckled, and Gammy joined in. Hannah could never remember Gammy chuckling. It wasn't something she did. Or maybe she did and Hannah never witnessed it, too caught up in her own selfishness. "How did you know about my studies?"

Gammy raised an eyebrow. But the archness did not strike fear in Hannah, as it had once done.

"You mentioned your supervisor several times, so we looked her up on the university website. Her specialism is gender and international relations, so it wasn't that difficult to put two and two together. What's your PhD on?"

"Impacts of migration of sex and domestic workers from Eastern Europe."

"Interesting. Bea wondered if it was something like that. She did a lot of work after the war, helping refugees to flee Europe. We even housed some refugees occasionally. She continued her campaigning until she lost her eyesight and couldn't be active."

"Really?" Hannah was genuinely intrigued. Maybe she could interview Auntie Bea as part of her research? That would make an interesting historical case study and please her supervisor.

Katherine knocked on the door frame and entered. "Hannah, may I have a word?"

"Sure." Hannah squeezed both Auntie Bea's and Gammy's hands and crossed the room to join Katherine in the corridor.

Katherine frowned. "I spoke to the manager of the home, and they won't do anything without Amanda's approval."

"Shit. I guess I'd better speak to Amanda and see what we can do to get Gammy into Auntie Bea's home." Hannah pulled out her phone and wrote out a reminder.

"They belong together, they make a lovely couple. Were they open with you about their relationship?" Katherine asked, holding Hannah's gaze.

"Yes, and I told them about me." Hannah felt herself getting warm but didn't know why since she'd come out many times. But there was always that decision, to be explicit or let someone gather as they went along.

"Oh, you are too? How delightful. Are you with someone?"

It was starting to feel like a cross examination. She guessed that made Katherine a good lawyer. "I am."

"Fabulous. Why don't you bring her along next time?"

"I can't."

Hannah glanced through the open door at Gammy, who was straining to hear their conversation, while still holding Auntie Bea's hand. She dragged Katherine out of sight. "Suki's half Japanese."

Katherine nodded. "Ah, I see. Leave it with me. Maybe I can approach it."

"Okay. Let me know and I'll ask Suki, if you come back with good news." She turned to watch them looking out of the open window, hands entwined. "I'd better go in and say goodbye. They both look tired."

"Please come again. It means the world to them. Thank you for sorting that Bea could come over here," Katherine said and picked up her handbag from a spare chair.

"I will. I'm just sorry the train was late so I couldn't come with you to pick up Auntie Bea."

"If you like, I could drop you off at the station then take Bea back."

"Would you? If it's not out of your way."

"It's no trouble."

Katherine went over to Gammy. "I'm glad you've had a lovely afternoon, but I need to take Bea back now."

"No, no." Gammy clung to Auntie Bea. They clutched each other, and Gammy cried as she communicated with her index finger.

"You promised we'd never be parted again. What's stopping us?" Auntie Bea asked.

Gammy tapped something on Auntie Bea's hand, but her fingers had a more pronounced tremor in them now, and it wasn't just the Parkinson's.

"Amanda," Gammy said as she tapped out the name on Auntie Bea's palm.

Auntie Bea balled her hand into a fist. "That selfish little homophobe will never do anything to help."

Hannah couldn't remember seeing Auntie Bea so angry. She was normally such a placid peacemaker.

"I'll speak to Amanda," Hannah said as she kissed her goodbye.

Gammy looked defeated, her head too heavy for her shoulders as she reached for her handkerchief.

***

Hannah sat in the back seat of Katherine's car with Auntie Bea. She'd seemed to shrink as the car travelled away from the home. Her mouth fidgeted in a taut line as she mouthed words Hannah recognised from King Lear. That wasn't a good sign.

"I'm sure that was Roger's hall," she said. "It had the same feel about it, right sort of dimensions too. I'll ask Maud next time."

Hannah glanced at Katherine in the driver's mirror. "Who's Roger?"

Katherine shrugged. Auntie Bea blew her nose on a tissue and tucked it in her pocket. Maybe she thought there wouldn't be a next time. If only it was easier to communicate with her. Tears streamed down her cheeks. Hannah reached out her hand to comfort her, but Auntie Bea flicked it off with more strength than Hannah would have expected. Her legs jiggled up and down as though she wanted to run, and she wrung her hands together.

Hannah caught Katherine's eye in the mirror. "I'm not sure if this is worse torture, tearing them apart at the end of the day," Hannah said, feeling awkward talking about her as she sat beside her, unable to hear the conversation.

"If they get used to regular visits, it might be easier." Katherine slowed for a red light. "The text to Braille reader should arrive next week, so at least Bea can read from a laptop or iPad."

"So Gammy will be able to send her emails? Or we can?"

"Yes, and there's an app that converts Braille input to text, although Bea is still learning Braille at the moment."

"I'm sure she'll master it quickly; her brain is as sharp as a razor." Hannah turned to face Auntie Bea, who seemed the picture of misery. She touched her hand and this time, she wasn't shaken off. She stroked the back of her gnarled hands to stop the constant wringing. This craziness was because they'd kept everything secret—just like she and Suki were doing. Was this her future? She looked at Auntie Bea's profile as she stared with unseeing eyes out of the window, her head held high, despite the tears running down her face.

"We'll have to get the right apps or software for your gammy to send emails, because her shaking is getting worse. Do you think that could come from the trust fund?"

Hannah wrote a note in her phone. "At least if they can communicate, it will help, but that's not a long-term solution. I'll call Amanda when I get on the train."

Fear churned in her stomach. She couldn't bear to see the misery of Gammy's and Auntie Bea's faces or see history repeating itself. All the lies and secrets that had caused distress for both of them, and the friction between herself and Gammy. It wasn't what she wanted for her future. Times had changed. She wouldn't be hidden; it caused too much upset in the long run. Better to suffer discomfort for a short while, than be subjected to misery for a lifetime.

CHAPTER FORTY-THREE

THE TRAIN PULLED away from the station. She should do some more work on the corrections, but she needed to speak to Amanda first. Hannah consulted her notes to ensure she'd written down the points she wanted to make so the conversation didn't go off track. She took a deep breath and called her. "Hey, Amanda, it's Hannah."

"Oh, the prodigal great niece. If you're calling about reclaiming your train and taxi fares, I'll send you an electronic form I've designed which automatically feeds into the accounting system once I've approved it, of course. No, Andrew, you cannot see Mark now, supper's almost ready."

"Great," said Hannah. It would certainly be easier if she didn't have to beg to be given reimbursement. In fact, she shouldn't have to beg at all. Gammy had set up the fund to benefit the entire family, and that included her and Gammy. "We need to get Gammy a computer or iPad with voice recognition software so she can send emails to Auntie Bea."

There was an intake of breath on the other end of the call. "I'm not getting anything for Beatrice from the Trust before you ask."

"I wasn't asking. Katherine has already ordered and paid for it." Hannah wished she had spare cash to buy what was needed, so she didn't have to go through this tortuous conversation. She was sure Amanda was a brilliant accountant and a worthy successor to Gammy's business, but she was tighter than a duck's ass. She smirked to herself as Amanda reminded her of a duck. With her long body and short legs, she hadn't inherited the tall gene and resented it like hell. She pulled herself back into the point of the conversation. "It's cruel to keep Gammy and Auntie Bea apart. Although they had a lovely afternoon visit, they were distraught when they separated. They've lived together for years and organised it so they would be at the same home. That's what will make them happy. Then you changed that, for no apparent reason."

"Gammy is in a much nicer home. Beatrice doesn't have the funds to move into the same home. Ian, will you leave Andrew alone? Go and set the table, please. Listen, Gammy enjoys the best in life. Beatrice may be a dear friend, but the trust is only for family, and it's much more expensive in Gammy's home. Bea has the specialist deaf-blind care she needs where she is."

"She gets one hour a day to teach her braille," Hannah said, clenching her fists. "That's hardly a huge amount of specialist support. Extra support could come from the trust fund."

"It's for *family* only."

Hannah gripped the seat in front of her so tight her knuckles glowed white. "Auntie Bea *is* family." She couldn't out Gammy and Bea, but this was ridiculous. She would ask Katherine for a copy of the original trust document to double check the rules.

"No, she's not. Anyway, you're organising visits now. They'll get used to it. I need to go, it's supper time and with two hangry teenagers—"

"Wait. How long have they got left, realistically? We owe it to them to carry out their wishes, and who cares if there's less in Gammy's trust fund for us?"

"That's easy for you to say with no children to provide for or school fees and such."

"So, get Gammy into the same home as Auntie Bea, which is what they originally planned. Or do you lose your discount on your exclusive gym and golf club if you do that?"

Amanda cleared her throat. "It's a much nicer home for Gammy."

She seemed to have perfected the same tone of disapproval that Gammy had had when Hannah was younger. "Where they're both miserable because they're separated. As trustees, we have to do what's best for the beneficiaries. I know Matthew agrees. You need to do what you can to get Gammy into Auntie Bea's home."

Amanda gave an exasperated sigh. "Fine, I'll have a word with the other home."

"Good. Let me know what they say."

"My, you're getting bossy. Or don't you trust me?"

No, I don't trust you, you egotistical bint. "And this is about what's fair and right."

"How naive. Life isn't fair."

Hannah drummed her fingers on the pull-down table, breathing sharply to calm herself down. "In general, maybe, but if we can do something specific, we should do it. It's Gammy's wish, and it's her trust fund."

"It's a bit late for you to get all noble. Where were you all those years when she longed for you to call?"

"She could have called me," Hannah said without thinking; this wasn't about point scoring. She rubbed the back of her neck. "Just sort it, Amanda. And soon. Like tomorrow. Thanks." Hannah ended the call and laid her head back against the coarse fabric of the train seat. *Selfish git.*

She still couldn't grasp how she'd missed the affection and love between Gammy and Auntie Bea when she stayed with them. She'd almost outed them to Amanda, but that wasn't her story to tell. She probably needed to see if Gammy would be prepared to tell Amanda herself. They might accept Auntie Bea as family then. But knowing how traditional they all were, maybe they wouldn't. But she shouldn't make assumptions, as Suki kept telling her.

Hannah stared out of the train window at the passing fields and snippets of people's lives. A dog walking a couple, straining at the lead. Why didn't they let it wander? A family on their bicycles, the little girl wobbly without stabilisers. In an isolated farmhouse, an older woman was hanging out her washing.

Hannah set down the thesis chapter she was supposed to be correcting and reclined against the seat, unable to concentrate. It seemed like the continuing delay in getting Gammy into Auntie Bea's home was affecting Gammy's health. Each day a swirling undertow dissolved the sand beneath her. After the discussion with Amanda, decisions and action should be taken soon.

She sighed. Poor Auntie Bea had been unbearably distraught. The woman was living in a black hole, trying to cling to sanity by reciting poetry. That was no way to live when her love was ten minutes' car journey away. Next time she'd order a taxi so she could take Auntie Bea to see Gammy again. Sod what Amanda thought.

Hannah picked up the red marked pages. This was her last chapter. She should be delighted, but a stone weighed in her stomach. What next? The fields skipped past faster. She'd considered applying for a role at London or Cambridge University, both of those seemed really interesting and prestigious. But the dean was really keen for her to stay in Bristol. She sighed and smoothed the edges of the papers.

She wanted Suki to come with her, but she suspected the answer would be no. There was no logical reason to give up where Suki was and move to another city doing the same job, except to be with Hannah. The possibility that Suki didn't love her enough, or even at all, turned her mouth to ash.

With the clarity of a camera snapping into focus, Hannah knew Suki would never leave Bristol, would never come out to her parents, and would never admit to being with Hannah. *Shit.* As far as the world was concerned, they were flatmates, and not even their closest friends knew they shared a bed every night. Now they were the ones making noisy sex. Hannah's lips twitched into a wry smile, and she leaned back to stare as the blurred fields morphed into buildings. The train dropped into a tunnel and slowed as it approached the bowels of Birmingham New Street station.

The doors swished open, allowing the sounds of announcements and people moving and talking to seep into the carriage. A cute girl entered and winked at Hannah as she passed by, searching for her seat. She clearly clocked Hannah for what she was, out and proud. She'd left Staffordshire so she could be her authentic self. She didn't want to be like Auntie Bea, who'd given up everything to remain a secret, even in the family. She couldn't pretend or live with all the secrets and lies. Even if she let her hair grow out and removed her ear studs, she still looked like the lesbian she was proud of being.

Hannah shuddered at the vision of her future. To be out and proud, or pretend and live a lie, like Auntie Bea and Gammy had done. It was heart breaking to see them as they had to separate. She couldn't hide away and didn't want to be like that, but Suki would never come out.

It wasn't going to work. She loved Suki, but as sure as winter followed autumn, the time would come when they would argue about the secrecy, being hidden, and having to lie. They had already had a couple of skirmishes and retreated to continue another day. Surely it would be better and kinder to both of them to finish things now. She wiped her face with the back of her hand. She hadn't realised she'd been crying. How would she tell Suki? She would probably throw her out. No, Hannah would leave. Maybe she could sleep on Jess's couch until she found somewhere else.

Hey Jess, how'd the game go today? Can I crash with you for a few nights x?

Sure, babe UOK xox?

I'll explain later. X

Escape route sorted, all she needed to do now was face Suki. As the train pulled out of Birmingham station, she felt sick as she sent a quick text to Suki.

Train should be on time, 8:35. I'll catch an Uber. X

Better to get it over and done with.

Pizza? Looking forward to hearing how you got on. Missed you. Xxx

Hannah gulped and wiped her face again. Could she do this?

***

Hannah fumbled with the key in the lock and trudged upstairs to the flat. As she entered, Suki flung her arms around her and stretched to kiss Hannah on the lips.

"Perfect timing. I've put the pizzas in the oven to keep warm and the cider is cooling in the fridge." Suki pulled Hannah into the kitchen area, where she had already laid out cutlery and place mats. "Can you get the plates down? How was it? How were Gammy and Bea?"

Hannah retrieved the plates from the cupboard. "They were lovely together, but they were distraught when Auntie Bea had to leave. It really cut me up." She distributed the plates with a clatter on the place mats. "They need to be in the same home. Amanda's going to make the case at Auntie Bea's home, hopefully tomorrow, for Gammy to transfer." She hoped that Amanda would be as good as her word.

Suki put the pizza on the chopping board and used the pizza cutter wheel to carve it into slices. Now Farty Boy was gone, there was a much fairer allocation of food and leftovers for breakfast. "Auntie Bea was angry and so upset when she left. Katherine said all she's doing at her home is wandering around the yard quoting Shakespeare. She's bored and frustrated. Katherine's got her a braille reader and writer, but she seems to have difficulty learning the code because she can't hear the instructions, and it takes ages to get the sensitivity in the fingers."

They sat at the kitchen bar and Suki grabbed a slice of pizza and plopped a couple of pieces onto Hannah's plate. Her stomach was in such a tight ball, there was no way she'd be able to eat. She felt like a coward, but thought if she explained about Auntie Bea's woes, Suki wouldn't notice she was not being overly affectionate.

She wanted a relationship with a stunning, sassy woman, but she wanted it on her terms. Suki swooped up a mushroom that had dropped onto her plate and gracefully placed it in her mouth in a way that was so sexy. Was she crazy to do this? They loved each other, but Hannah needed to be out and proud. She hated the scurrying around, redistributing clothes if friends came around. At least they only had one bathroom, so didn't need to change all the toiletries. But she couldn't—and wouldn't—do that forever.

"Are you not eating, Han?"

"Hm?"

Suki pointed at the slices of pizza congealing on the plate. Hannah picked up a piece that sagged in the middle, in danger of dropping the mushroom topping. *Tell her*. She put the pizza back down. "I was thinking on the train. I can't bear that Gammy and Auntie Bea are in separate homes—"

"Yeah, that's harsh, but hopefully you'll be able to do something about that." Suki touched Hannah's arm in a warm and gentle caress.

It was all she could do not to flinch. She gulped, unsure why her throat felt so dry. She took a swig of Adam's Fall cider. "And reading through all their mail. I can't be an Auntie Bea and an unacknowledged secret. I can't keep hidden and pretend. I hate dishonesty and lies." Her eyes prickled, and she blinked, but the weight of the tears spilled over the dam of her lower lid.

"What do you mean?"

"Suki, I love you, and I know you can't come out to your parents for cultural reasons and family is critical to you. I won't insist on you coming out to them, but I can't go on pretending. I want to be with you for all to see, to introduce you to my friends as my girlfriend, and for your work colleagues to know who I am. And I might have to look for another job soon, which might be in London or Cambridge, and I'd love you to come with me, but I know you won't do that. And even if you could, people would wonder why you'd changed your job."

A mushroom slipped off Suki's pizza and dropped onto the counter, but she didn't wipe it up. She slumped and looked so tiny, Hannah wanted to sweep her up in her arms and take back the words that seemed to have slashed Suki one syllable at a time.

"What do you mean?" Suki whispered.

Hannah couldn't bear the look of confusion and sorrow on Suki's face. Her eyebrows flickered up and down, betraying a range of emotions.

"You're finishing with me?"

Hannah couldn't find the words to explain, and they withered before becoming solid and formed.

Suki slammed the pizza on to the plate, knocking an unused knife onto the floor and it spun with a grating noise. "Well?" Her stool scraped on the tiles. "You say you love me, but how is that love?" Suki fled to their room, her room. "Get out, get out of my house."

The door slammed, and the sound reverberated around the kitchen. Hannah rested her hands on her knees to stop her legs wobbling, and she had to breathe deeply to control her lungs from fluttering in panic. Everything had crumbled; this was much worse than she envisioned. She had hoped they could have a civilised discussion about it all, and Suki would agree it was for the best, but the pain on her face would haunt Hannah for a long time. She needed her stress ball.

There was silence from their room. Should she go in? She needed to pick up some clothes anyway. She braced herself outside the bedroom door. "Suki? Can I come in? Can we talk about this?"

"There's nothing to talk about. Just go—"

"But all my things..."

She heard the sound of a drawer being pulled out of the chest, a grunt, and footsteps. The door opened, and without looking at her, Suki tossed the contents on the floor. Hannah stepped back as her clothes cascaded on the wooden floorboards. Her tin of lip balm rolled and rattled before settling upside down. Hannah stooped to pick it up. "Please don't be like this. Can't we talk?"

"And get those bloody boxes out of here too," Suki said as she spun around and slammed the door shut in Hannah's face.

"Can I pick those up when I've settled somewhere?" Hannah asked.

"You've got two weeks then they'll be burned."

No. Hannah banged the door jamb with her fist. "You can't. They're precious." Hannah glanced across at her boxes, still jutting out behind the sofa. They'd been the opening of their relationship, but now they just felt like Pandora's box, scattering mayhem and misery.

"I thought you didn't want them?" Suki's voice was more muffled now, so she must have moved away from the door.

She hadn't wanted them before, but that was before she discovered they contained the history of her great aunt's secret life, her true self. Now she knew how much they had in common, the letters had opened a whole new perspective, not just about Gammy and Auntie Bea, but also about herself. "Suki, please open up so we can talk. I do want them, and I'll pick them up as soon as I can." Nothing but the sound of Suki blowing her nose. "Please talk to me," Hannah said.

"Just go."

Hannah crouched to pick up her clothes, bundled them into sports bags, and snatched up her Xbox. She scanned the flat. Would this be the last time she was here? She couldn't just go without saying goodbye. She scribbled a note on the pizza box. *Suki, I'm really sorry. I love you, but I can't be your secret. H xox*

As she left, she heard sobbing coming from the other room. If only she could fix this. Tears flowed down her cheeks as she wheeled her overladen bike out of the front door.

CHAPTER FORTY-FOUR

The following day, it really hit home how life had changed. Cycling into Bristol and up to the university through the grasslands of Ashton Court estate was a much harder climb and twenty minutes longer than the ride from Suki's flat. Okay, it was getting her fit again, but her knees still twinged as she pedalled. That pain was nothing to what she felt in her heart. Sorrow, guilt, and anger against the world and prejudice stewed inside like a bubbling cauldron of distress. If only she had a wand to whisk away her problems, but there was no simple solution.

She kicked her burning legs harder on the pedals and tried to take in larger lungfuls of air to combat the clamping around her chest. Swiping at the tears, Hannah locked her bike in the bike rack. She removed her rucksack from the pannier and slung it over her shoulder. When she arrived at the department, everything else was normal. Her store cupboard that masqueraded as an office with its old-fashioned radiator and tiny desk was still stuffed with papers. Checking her emails, she could almost forget the vast hole in her heart. And when she thought about Suki, wondering what and how she was doing, she wondered what she could do to ease the blow. And realised there was nothing, unless…

Hannah called a florist, who said that white poppies represented an apology. She blanched at the cost of a bouquet and delivery. Her credit card would creak with the extra cost, but she gave her details anyway. She wanted Suki to know she didn't mean to hurt her. Part of her hoped she would get a reply but knew that wasn't really Suki's style.

That evening, she sat at Jess and Ashley's kitchen table. Ashley was a fabulous cook, and each week tried to replicate her favourite delicacy from the *Great British Bake Off.*

After a simple but tasty sea bass recipe with lime and coriander that Hannah pushed around her plate, Ashley produced a sumptuous lemon drizzle cake which she placed on the table along with two plates and mugs of tea. Hannah suspected the cake had been made specially in her honour as it was her favourite.

"I'll just take Scraps for her walk." Ashley said.

Normally that was Jess's job in the evening, so they had arranged it so Jess and Hannah could have time to talk. Scraps, an adored mid-brown cockerpoo, tilted his head as if to say what's going on? Sensing Hannah's upset, he laid his head in her lap and looked up at her with mournful eyes. She stroked his fluffy ears and head, and every time she stopped, he tapped her with his front paw, reminding her she was his servant.

"Come on, Scraps, let's go check peemail."

He raised his head, tail wagging, and rushed to the front door of the cottage, his claws skittering on the stone flagged floor. Hannah couldn't help being drawn to watch as Jess and Ashley kissed goodbye. They seemed to have the perfect life, both set in their careers, deeply in love even after a couple of years, with a lovely home and adorable dog. Tears welled up, and she affected fascination with her mug of tea to take control of her emotions flip-flopping between envy, guilt, and sadness. The stupid thing was that she'd never wanted to go into the commercial world, but the consequences of her career choice were very evident in the different trajectories she and Jess were taking.

When Ashley had exited with a very excited dog, Jess turned to Hannah. "Shall we make ourselves comfortable?" She picked up her mug and cake and made her way to the sofa, sitting on one end and waiting for Hannah to sit on the other. "Okay, Han, tell me what's going on. I know we were all too knackered to speak properly last night. But why did you split with Suki if you love her?"

"Because she isn't *out*. It's wonderful when we're in our little bubble, but I don't want to be her secret. She hasn't even told them at work that she finished with Farty Boy about six months ago, and she'll never tell her parents." Hannah picked at the lemon drizzle cake, but her appetite deserted her. "When I see what's happened to my Auntie Bea, who has been my gammy's partner in secret for years… She's going insane in a separate care home. I don't want to be like that."

"But the world is very different now—"

"Exactly, but Suki doesn't seem to see that." Hannah crumbled the cake into smaller pieces. "Has Suki ever openly come out to you?"

"No, but I don't really know her that well, only when she's subbed for an ultimate game or training."

Hannah laughed, despite herself. "You wouldn't believe the fuss she made about us being called the Bristol Gold Stars. She said, 'I'm bi, and I've been with men, so I can't play for you.' I told her in her honour we'd call ourselves the Bristol All Stars when she played for us."

"We've had some straight women play as well over the years. Maybe we should consider changing it anyway. But that's really not the point. Are you saying you can't go out with her because you'll never be able to hold hands in public?"

Burning crept up her neck. It sounded so trivial when Jess put it like that. Typical lawyer, wanting to get to the crux of the matter. "It's much more than PDAs. She'll never come out to her family as her father is very traditional Japanese and a homophobe, and she'll never go against the family.

Jess arched an eyebrow. "And that's different from you hiding in Bristol and not coming out for years, how?"

Sometimes Hannah hated Jess. She raised her hands. "Okay, okay. It's just Suki will never come out to her family and probably not at work, either. I don't want to be invisible or unimportant. I want to be special to Suki, so special she's prepared to be open about us."

"Are you saying you believe her coming out at work and to her family is evidence she loves you?"

"I guess so. And I know she loves me, but I want other people to know she loves me too." It felt so inadequate when she said that, and so superficial, but Hannah couldn't articulate it further so she took a nibble out of the lemon cake. It was delicious. The flavours zinged around her palate, and she wished she could bake as well as Ashley.

Hannah's phone buzzed with a message, which she ignored, and she licked a few cake crumbs off her index finger.

"Maybe just give her time? You know how Ash was when we first went out. She took ages to come out to her dad, and he was fine in the end."

They reminisced for a while, but Hannah kept circling round what she could have done differently, like a washing machine on an endless cycle, never able to wash away the misery.

A few minutes later Hannah's phone rang.

"Do you need to take that?" Jess asked.

Amanda. What did she want? Maybe it was to give a date when Gammy would move to Auntie Bea's home. "Yeah, I'd better." She swiped to accept the call. "Hey, Amanda."

"Did you get my message?"

"Sorry, I'm with a friend. What is it?"

"Gammy's in hospital."

"What?"

"I did ask about her being able to transfer, but she can't go in Auntie Bea's home, because they can't deal with her Parkinson's—"

Why was Amanda telling her this now? And was that really true anyway? Her already knotted stomach twisted harder. "What happened to Gammy?"

Amanda sniffed. "They've let her room go now anyway. But Gammy decided she was going to try and get there on her own and was found on the footpath on the way to the bus stop. She might have fallen, or had a seizure, and who knows how long she was lying there—"

"Oh God. Where is she?"

"Wolverhampton hospital, she's not regained consciousness yet, so they're not sure what the long-term impacts are."

Hannah's stomach wrung itself inside out. *Please let her be okay.* "Can she take visitors?"

"Now you want to visit her? She's been desperate for her favourite niece to come to her for years, and now when she's taken ill, you decide you'll drop everything to come."

The sneer in Amanda's tone was unmistakable. Clenching her fists so she didn't say anything she would regret, Hannah asked for the details.

"Visiting times are in the afternoons and evenings, so you may as well come up in the morning to visit in the afternoon."

Hannah did some calculations. If she stayed at a local hotel, she could write up her thesis corrections when she wasn't visiting the hospital. In fact, it would mean she had no distraction.

"I thought I might draw up a rota for visiting," Amanda said.

Hannah could imagine the multicoloured spreadsheet that would be produced, complete with instructions. "I'm going up and will work on my thesis when I can't be there."

"But they may only allow one or two visitors at a time."

"So? You can fit around me since I'm the favourite niece." She was tempted to flick her cousin the bird, but as the only audience would be Jess, the gesture would be pointless. "I'll see you up there. If you hear anything else, please text me."

"Will you bother to pick it up?"

"'Bye, Amanda." She closed the call and threw her phone down. "What a cow."

"Your gammy?" Jess looked puzzled.

Hannah unclenched her hands and jaw. "No. My cousin Amanda. It seems Gammy was serious about trying to escape. She slipped out, I've no idea how, because they've got locks on the external doors, but they found her in the road, unconscious. She's not regained consciousness yet." She gnawed at the scar on her lip.

"And you'd like to visit her?"

"I thought if I took my thesis corrections I could work around visiting and stay at a local B&B, or maybe stay with Matthew."

"Have you got enough cash?"

Hannah felt her cheeks tingle. She hated thinking about money, or rather the lack of it. She would ask the bank if they could extend her credit. "I'll just stack up the credit card."

Picking up her phone, Jess was already searching online. "You absolutely will not, Hannah Jones. You'll never pay it off on your postgrad allowance. Let me sort that out. A hotel near New Cross Hospital, Wolverhampton then? For a week?"

Hannah looked up from her phone. "I can't let you do that." Even she could hear the lack of conviction in her tone.

"What's the point of having friends if they can't help you out when you need it? How many times have you come to dog sit when we've been away?"

"That's different, that's fun. I love spending time with Scraps, and Ashley always leaves a few fabulous treats. Plus you've got all the sports packages." Hannah grinned despite herself.

"Do you know how expensive doggy day care is, plus overnights? And Scraps loves you. It's booked. I'll email the reference and details and if you need longer than a week, let me know." Jess reached across the sofa and squeezed Hannah's hands. "Sorry you're having such a tough time, Han Solo," she said.

Hannah's mouth quirked up with a wry smile at Jess using her old nickname. "Seems very apt at the moment—"

"Oh shit, sorry, that was insensitive of me." Jess clapped her hand over her mouth.

"Hey, if you stop taking the piss out of me, I'll get very worried. Thanks for arranging the hotel. I owe you at least a fortnight of dog sitting."

"You're on. Now, do you want to watch the England game, I think it's on ITV4."

Jess had the superpower of knowing which channel any women's sport was on, particularly for football. She switched on the massive HD screen that almost filled one end of the open plan lounge. Hannah could almost see the pores on their faces when they took a closeup. At half time she sent Suki a quick text to tell her about Gammy. She would want to know.

When Hannah picked up her phone later, her heart skipped at Suki's text.

Hi Han, sorry I shouted, I was upset. Please come back home, I miss you. S XOX.

I miss you too.

Relief and joy cascaded over her, mingled with frustration that nothing would change if she went back. She wanted to go back home, and she couldn't impose on Jess and Ashley for long, and it was hard to witness their happy couple routine when her insides were wrung out. Maybe she would need to think about it all when she was away, but her priority had to be Gammy.

She sent a quick text back to Suki and hoped Suki didn't think she was using Gammy as an excuse.

CHAPTER FORTY-FIVE

GAMMY HAD REGAINED consciousness but seemed very confused. She spoke about Harry but didn't seem to know who Hannah was. It was difficult to understand what she was trying to say, so Hannah simply held her hand. She wasn't really the praying kind, but she sent up some requests that Gammy be okay anyway. Entwined with the guilt was a helix of grief twisting in her stomach. She couldn't have just reconnected with her, to get to know and understand her more only to lose her again. All the wasted years when she was too angry and proud, fighting to be independent when she could have been connected and loved. She could see that now, how Gammy struggled to be around a stroppy teenager, but how she'd tried. Hannah brushed away Gammy's pure white hair from her face, and she murmured something about Auntie Bea.

They were still like that when Matthew arrived. He gave Hannah a peck on the cheek and Gammy a kiss on the forehead. Gammy had slipped into a fitful sleep, and her hands were trembling again. She was so frail and powerless, a shadow of the former matriarch Hannah had both feared and loved. A tight band clamped around Hannah's chest. If she'd been to the meetings, maybe they could have avoided this scenario entirely. She wouldn't have let the trust go against Gammy's wishes. Clarity came to her mind like floodlights on a dark night. "We need to get Auntie Bea into the same home as Gammy, otherwise she'll just try to escape again." She waited for his response and was heartened when he nodded. "Did Amanda tell you Gammy can't transfer into Auntie Bea's home?"

"Yeah." He pulled up a chair and sat on the other side of the bed.

Hannah fixed him with a stare. Not for the first time, she wished she'd paid more attention before and looked at the accounts for the trust, although she wouldn't understand them. "It'll cost more for Auntie Bea to go to Gammy's home, especially if Auntie Bea needs special help, but I understand the trust fund is very wealthy. Isn't this exactly what it's for?"

Matthew shifted in his seat. "Amanda's against any change," he said, as though that was final.

He was so weak she wanted to shake him and tell him to grow a backbone. No wonder Amanda got away with everything. But if Hannah had come to the meetings, this mess might never have happened. "Yeah, but if we act together, we can fix this and honour Gammy's wishes."

"Not for changing the trust being only for family members, that needs 75% approval."

Damn. Hannah really needed to get the original trust documents. "Then we appoint another trustee who will act in Gammy's best interests. I nominate Katherine."

Matthew frowned. "The solicitor?"

"Yeah, she's perfect for it."

"Hm. Rather you than me trying to get Amanda to agree to that."

What a coward. She banged her hands on her thighs. It was too late to change the past, but she could try to make amends now. It seemed like the logic puzzle from a video game. This was about how to defeat the monster. She smiled at the thought of Amanda as an animated monster. Maybe that wasn't too far from the truth.

Later that evening, Hannah was sitting by Gammy's hospital bed when the ward door swung open. Katherine entered with Auntie Bea, who looked frail and was gnawing at her bottom lip. She made her way to the bed with her red and white cane clearing the way like a minesweeper. Hannah moved her chair out of the way and helped Auntie Bea to sit down on the side of the bed. It hardly sagged at all with her weight. She seemed to have shrunk since she'd last seen her. Hannah kissed her and felt her hands tremble as she mapped Hannah's face.

"Hello, Hannah dear. I'm glad you're here."

She squeezed Auntie Bea's shoulder and looked to Katherine. "How do I say, Gammy's sleeping?"

"Sorry, I've no idea. My Morse is pretty basic," Katherine said. "That was a good suggestion for me to be there when you emailed Bea about Gammy so I could bring her here immediately."

Katherine nodded toward the bed and smiled. Auntie Bea had slipped off her shoes and swung around to lay beside Gammy. Gammy didn't move or wake. There wasn't much room on the narrow hospital bed, so Auntie Bea shuffled herself to lay half on, half off Gammy's body. She brought her hand to Gammy's face and traced her fingers across it, as if she was tracing out her love. She stretched to kiss her on the mouth, and Gammy sighed.

"Bea?" Gammy murmured.

"I'm here, sweetheart."

Gammy opened her eyes and blinked a few times. A look of pure delight inhabited her expression. And just as they were kissing, Amanda and Matthew entered the room. The look on Amanda's face defined the word disgust, and she coloured from her neck upwards.

"What are you doing here? Matthew and I are scheduled to visit this evening, not…not this." She gestured wildly toward Gammy and Auntie Bea and reached inside her handbag.

Well, that's one way of coming out. Hannah chuckled when she inspected the paper Amanda thrust at her. "Who cares what it says on here? It's not like there are a hundred of us trying to visit at the same time. We need a conversation as trustees."

Amanda scowled. "Katherine is not a trustee."

"Let's get coffee," Hannah said and strode off, giving Gammy and Auntie Bea some precious time together. They needed the comfort of reconnection, and Gammy had brightened up completely. It seemed all that was needed was the physical contact of one person against another, the touch of a loved one.

They waited in awkward silence for their coffees to be prepared. The wind hurled raindrops at the glass and people huddled like tortoises in their coats as they hurried to their destinations. Hannah directed them to the small tables by the edge of the atrium, away from anyone else. There was a slightly awkward pause.

"I'll wait over there." Katherine pointed at another table and carried her coffee over.

The chairs scraped along the polished floor when they pulled them out, setting her nerves on edge. She was nervous enough, aware that what she said and did could affect both Gammy's and Auntie Bea's lives.

Hannah inhaled and sat up straight, lifting her head as she had seen Gammy doing when she wanted to show authority. "Under the trust agreement, another trustee can be appointed, one who will have the welfare of the beneficiaries at heart. Katherine Braithwaite has been a great friend and solicitor to Gammy for many years, and Gammy trusts her completely."

Amanda's mouth was a thin line. She could also look formidable. It was part of what made her successful in expanding Gammy's practice to one of the largest in the region.

"Fine, but that doesn't mean to say that she should be a trustee."

Hannah placed her hands on the table, determined not to reveal her nerves at this confrontation. She inhaled deeply and centred herself. She was doing this for Gammy and Auntie Bea, for all the prejudice they'd had to fight throughout their lives. And because she needed to expunge some of her guilt at not being there for them. They deserved this now, and she would do what she could to make sure they were together. "A trustee is supposed to act on behalf of the beneficiaries. You've not done that, and yet *you're* a trustee. Gammy was very clear she wanted to be in the same home as Auntie Bea. From what you've just seen, they're more than friends and companions. You said they can't be in Auntie Bea's home so Auntie Bea should join Gammy in her home."

Amanda added sugar to her coffee, presumably pondering her reply. Hannah didn't think she'd be one to add in extra calories, but maybe she was just stalling. Hopefully she was unsettled. She deserved to be. Hannah couldn't believe she'd looked up to her cousins all her life. Now it was clear they were nothing but grasping and self-serving.

Amanda churned the froth of her cappuccino into a homogeneous brown sludge. "Gammy's home is now full, and there are no spare single rooms."

"Again, you've now seen the nature of their relationship. They don't want separate rooms. They can transfer into one of the large double rooms or simply have a double bed put in Gammy's existing room." Given how close Gammy and Auntie Bea had been upstairs, she couldn't imagine that would be a problem. She tried to cover her smile, recalling the look on Amanda's face when she'd seen them together.

"But that's condoning—"

"What?" Hannah leaned forward across the metal table, knowing her extra height could intimidate. "They've been a couple for longer than you and I have been alive. They weren't able to be open about their relationship for decades, but they deserve to have their remaining time together as a couple, and not hidden away to protect your homophobic sensibilities."

Amanda shifted in her chair, and it made a God-awful sound against the floor that went right through Hannah.

"But Gammy's always been such a stalwart in the church—"

"Believing in God and being a lesbian are not mutually exclusive."

Amanda's expression soured. "I do not agree to this."

"You don't agree to letting them live *their* lives? Who are you to stop it? As a trustee, you're there to ensure Gammy's best interests are served. And it's in her best interest to have her lifelong partner transferred to her home as soon as it can be arranged." Hannah felt almost as surprised as Amanda looked at the strength of her conviction, and it gave her a glimpse of pride she had rarely experienced before. "I also propose, and Matthew seconds, that Katherine is appointed a trustee. While we're waiting for the move, Katherine will be able to bring Auntie Bea to see Gammy."

Amanda flashed a look at Matthew that could shrivel him, but he shrugged and said nothing. "Appointing Katherine would give you the power to amend the rules so the trust does not have to benefit the family. I strongly object and do not wish to take this any further until I've spoken to my solicitor."

The harder Amanda fought, the more Hannah honed her own strength, like sharpening her sword ready for battle. "If you want to do that, you'll have to pay for it from your own money. We won't agree to using trust funds for that. And if you wish to consult a solicitor, we have one sitting over there."

"Oh, for heaven's sake. As chair, I have casting vote in the event of a gridlock and I'm blocking all of your proposals. Now I need to get back to pick up the boys from their music lessons, so I haven't been able to visit Gammy at all, thanks to you." Amanda snatched up her half full takeaway coffee cup.

"I think Gammy's much happier as she is," Hannah said, not bothering to hide her smirk. Matthew nodded and looked morally superior despite having contributed absolutely nothing to the meeting. Still, it was useful to have a witness. She would need to fall back on Plan B then.

Hannah shook her head at Katherine, who rolled her eyes. Amanda deposited her cup and napkin in the flip-top bin as if they were contagious and bustled out of the café area. Matthew took a sip of his drink, then glanced at his watch. Hannah raised her hand to stop him from leaving. "Before you go, I need you to agree that the trust will fund Auntie Bea coming into the same home as Gammy. I'll organise it, and you can authorise it."

He wiggled his eyebrows and his lips trembled as though he might giggle. "Did you know about them?"

"Only recently."

His fringe flopped over his eyes, which might have been appealing when he was a young man, but in middle-age, he simply looked ridiculous. "I'm gob-smacked. But I guess it makes sense." He grinned. "I can't imagine them—"

Hannah held up her index finger. "If you're going to say anything homophobic, keep it to yourself."

He raised his hands in surrender. "Don't bite my head off. I'm not the homophobe in the family. But I guess Amanda will need a bit of time to come around."

"Do you think she will? Sod it. It's Gammy's fund, and it should be used for her benefit. If Amanda doesn't like it, that's tough."

Katherine came over and placed her hand on Hannah's shoulder. "I've just discovered something interesting," she said. "I found out who Roger was that Bea talked about. He was Roger Manley, who owned Manley Hall, which was the previous name of the home that Gammy is in. The Manley trust was set up in the sixties by Roger Manley, Anton Reynard, Maud Heaston, and Beatrice Williams."

"Who?" Matthew asked.

"Surely we can use it to our advantage. Can you send me the details? I'll talk to the owner of the home and see if we can get a discount or something."

When she got back to her hotel room, Hannah tried to go through the corrections on her thesis. Her thoughts drifted to Suki, and she wondered how she was doing. They'd exchanged a few texts, and Hannah had told Suki that Gammy was improving and would leave hospital soon. She wasn't sure what to do. It would be too hard, having enjoyed Suki's affections and bed, to return to being friends and housemates, and she didn't really want to. That complicated relationship would have to wait until she'd sorted things out for Gammy and Auntie Bea and *their* complicated relationship. Unable to focus on her corrections, she sent a text to Suki.

Hey S, thanks for looking after the boxes a bit longer. Still in Staffordshire, trying to sort out Auntie Bea coming to Gammy's home. Hope UR ok. H x

Miss you. Been reading rest of letters and diaries. Pls sort it. They need a happy ending, even if we don't get one. S xo

Talk about a knife to her heart. A whorling wave of emotions engulfed her, her heart and head warred within her, and her misery was all consuming. She couldn't bear to think of Suki sitting alone in the flat, too scared to come out. What right did Hannah have to insist she do so? If anything was going to have to change, it would have to be Hannah. But she wasn't sure she could live a secret life, even for Suki. She would have to cope with never holding hands in public, never being invited for family celebrations or Christmas, never meeting Suki's family or being acknowledged as anything beyond housemates and friends.

Gammy and Auntie Bea had sacrificed so much, yet they still found a way, and although it was funny to see two old ladies being intimate, it was sweet too. Yet they had had to sacrifice their own happiness at times and done their duty elsewhere. If Hannah didn't compromise, would she end up on her own? Surely a relationship was about being able to live with another's fears and foibles? She needed to talk to Gammy about it when she was discharged. She'd be able to make sense of it for Hannah. The thought stirred melancholy. If only she'd realised who Gammy and Auntie Bea really were, living with them would have been so much easier. Coming out would've been easier too. But she had to focus on the present and the future, for her and for Gammy, for the happiness of both of them.

CHAPTER FORTY-SIX

MAUD WHEELED HERSELF around in her room again, glorying in the thick carpets and wooden floor, instead of the squeaky linoleum, and inhaling the smell of potpourri rather than strong disinfectant. The primroses were out, necklaces of yellow in a decolletage of vibrant green. It was wonderful to be back home, but best of all, Bea would finally be joining her soon. The room was a bit small for both of them, but Lorraine had promised her they would be able to squeeze in a double bed. She hadn't raised an eyebrow at the request. How the world had moved on.

A king-size would be nice, but it wouldn't leave much room. When she felt stronger, she would get on her sticks again and walk the corridors to the library. But for now, she was glad to escape the sterility of the hospital and wait for Hannah to arrive. *Hannah.* How joyous it had been to see her every day, even though she had to return to Bristol later. She would miss her popping in and sitting by the bed. Vi would be so proud of her. She was proud of Hannah and grateful for everything she'd done to facilitate getting Bea where she belonged—by her side. Bea had been right, as she often was, and they should have come out to Hannah a long time ago. But there was no point dwelling on the past. Now it was time to be grateful for every day.

Maud daubed at her mouth to check she hadn't dribbled when there was a knock at her door. "Come in."

Hannah popped her head around the door frame. Her dark roots were showing through. Was she growing the colour out? Maud was used to the blue that seemed to suit her so well.

"Are you decent?" Hannah asked, hiding something behind her back as she stepped into the room.

"Not if you ask most of the world." Maud's eyes twinkled. She loved this banter they'd established.

"No, Gammy. We are members of a very exclusive club." Hannah produced an enormous bouquet from behind her back. "I brought flowers that had a strong perfume, so Auntie Bea could enjoy them too when she comes, although I wasn't sure about lilies as I know some people don't like them, so I got tiger lilies instead—"

Maud's heart felt like it could burst, and tears prickled the back of her eyes. "That's such a lovely thought. Thank you. I should be giving *you* flowers for everything you've done." She held her hands out, and Hannah came in for a warm hug and kissed her on the forehead.

"You're welcome. I'll put these in water. Do you have a vase?"

Maud pulled her knuckles to her lips. "I can't remember if we bought one or not. But I'm sure if you ask the manager, Lorraine, she'll fix you up."

"In that case, I'll just pop them in your sink for the moment." Hannah disappeared for a couple of minutes, then re-joined Maud at the French windows and pulled up a chair.

Maud bit her lip, shame squeezing the pit of her stomach. "They've locked the doors now. They said they can't trust me not to escape, but I said I was only trying to get to see Bea."

Hannah took Maud's hands in her own, an earnest expression on her face. "Oh, Gammy. Please don't try that again. You gave us all a huge shock."

Maud sighed. "I know, I know. I'd like to have the doors open, but they might think I'm trying to escape again. It looks like a beautiful spring day."

"There's quite a strong wind, so it's not as warm as it looks, but I can open the window. That way, you get some fresh air and stay warm, and you don't frighten the staff."

Maud canted her head so she could look at her great niece. "You're quite the diplomat, aren't you?"

"Well, I am doing a PhD in International Relations, so I guess it goes with the territory."

Hannah smiled, but the skin around her eyes didn't crinkle, and her pupils seemed dull. Something was off. Maud squeezed her forearm. "Are you all right, dear?"

Hannah dropped their joined hands, and her shoulders heaved. Eventually she looked up. "I don't know what to do, Gammy."

Maud nodded and waited for her to continue.

"I'd moved out of my flat and had been staying with friends until I heard of your fall, and I've been here ever since. I'll have to do so much dog-sitting to repay Jess."

Hannah took a deep breath in, as if she was considering how much the hotel and taxi costs would be. "Reclaim it from the trust fund. Have a word with Amanda," Maud said. Hannah shook her head. "But that's what it's for. I appreciate you coming to see me every day. It's really helped my recovery." Maud studied her great niece. She looked as though she was blinking back tears; there had to be more to this story. "What's really troubling you?"

Hannah rolled her shoulders. She probably spent way too long hunched over her books and computer, but Maud bit back the comment. Hannah didn't like being told what to do, Bea always said, and it meant she was working hard to be financially independent, which was all Maud ever wanted for her. That, and to be happy.

"I split up with Suki because I couldn't stand hiding our relationship. I saw what it did to you and Auntie Bea. But I really miss her, and she's sent me a text every day asking me to move back in. I don't know what to do."

Hannah was such a strong young woman; it was quite a shock to see her like this, but it was also so wonderful to talk about the things that were bothering her. Maud wished Bea was there; she was so much better at dealing with these kinds of things. What would she say? "Do you love her?"

"Yes."

A blush lit up her face. It was like she was sixteen again, except she no longer boiled with anger.

"And things are different now. You don't have to hide."

Hannah put her face in her hands. "She feels she's got to. She faces enough prejudice at work as it is. And her family's homophobic, at least her dad is, and her mother does everything he says."

Maud hated to see Hannah wound up and suffering, like a starfish tossed up by the storm and stranded above the waterline. "I won't tell you what to do, Hannah—not anymore—so what does your heart tell you?" She reached across to squeeze Hannah's forearm, and she met her gaze. Maud sighed. "I don't know if it's any help, but for me, despite all the secrets and lies—which I hated—I wouldn't be without your Auntie Bea." Shame, anger, and regret bubbled up like a pan on the hob, threatening to spill over, spitting and hissing. "All the secrets were my fault. I was too cowardly to be open. Auntie Bea wanted to tell the truth, including to you when you lived with us. I'm sorry I lied to you." She may not have said it out loud for so many decades, but freedom lifted her voice on its wings now, and the truth tumbled through the air, blowing away all the mistakes of the past. "Life's not perfect. We've had to make do and mend, to snatch what joy we've had and sew it into a quilt to cover us in the tough times. It's so hard to be without her now." Maud's hands trembled, and she held onto the arms of the wheelchair for support. "But you're going to sort that. I can't wait till she comes here." She felt strong inside, as though her thirty-year-old self was looking through her eyes. An understanding passed between them, across the chasm of years and incorrect assumptions. All those wasted years when she could have been there for Hannah.

"Thanks, Gammy. I'll talk to the manager now and see if I can get you a vase." Hannah rose and tapped the door jamb as she exited.

Out of Gammy's room, an underlying scent of disinfectant was more noticeable rather than the strong potpourri Gammy favoured. The corridors were carpeted in a raw umber striped carpet, presumably to reduce the noise level, but it still looked institutional. It reminded Hannah of university halls, and she was relieved to escape those as soon as she could. And she was so glad she did as that's how she met Suki when she applied for the flat share.

Behind reception, the door to an office was open. The sign on the door announced Lorraine Appleby, Manager. Hannah cleared her throat and knocked. A gaunt woman with grey streaking through her auburn hair looked up. "Are you Lorraine? My great aunt, Maud Heaston, said you might have a vase she can borrow?"

The woman's expression morphed into a smile. "Of course." She crossed the room to a cupboard, took one from a shelf, and brought it to the door. She tilted her head. "Are you Hannah?"

"Yeah, how do you know?"

Lorraine nodded. "The blue hair's rather a giveaway. Your aunt is really proud of you and talks about you all the time."

Hannah's cheeks burned. She glowed with the warmth of acknowledgement; it was the first time she heard and believed it. "I also wanted to check that everything's set for Beatrice Williams to move in?"

The sparkle dropped from the woman's eyes, and she gripped the vase to her chest. "Ah, there's a problem. We've not received the deposit yet.

Amanda Dixon has put a block on the additional funds for Miss Williams to come."

Hannah slammed her fist on the doorjamb. "Damn her. Gammy's expecting Auntie Bea to move in next weekend. Do you know why Amanda's blocked it?"

"Sorry, no."

"Please don't say anything to my great aunt. I'll sort it." Hannah paced across to the waiting area. She called Amanda, who picked up after two rings.

"Hannah, what can I do for you?"

"Don't act the innocent with me. I've just spoken to Lorraine, the manager at Gammy's home, and she said the money has been blocked for Auntie Bea moving in."

"Well, if you bothered to turn up for trustees' meetings, you'd know there's no cash budgeted for that."

"What? I'd like to call an emergency meeting then because that doesn't make sense. We need to get this sorted as soon as possible. Gammy is expecting Auntie Bea to move in next Saturday. I know she's not been in charge of the fund since she moved in, but she was always meticulous about money—"

"There's been expenditure, and Matthew agreed to it."

Hannah kicked at a chair leg. Why didn't he mention that the other day when she said she'd arrange it? "You mean you steamrollered him. Can we meet this afternoon?"

"No, I'm busy with the boys. The earliest I can do it is tomorrow after ten."

"Okay. I'll stay here another night and we can meet then. This needs sorting. I'll call Matthew and Katherine—"

"Katherine is not a trustee."

Hannah inhaled and replied in an even a tone as she could manage. "Only because you blocked it. She's a solicitor."

"Well, you can pay for her fees then. It's not coming from the trust."

Hannah clenched her fist. "I'll text you the details." It took all of Hannah's control to be civil and not scream at her. Why was she being so bloody difficult? The money was there. Was she just being homophobic, as Auntie Bea thought? She called Katherine and relayed her conversations with Lorraine and Amanda.

"You can hold the meeting at my offices. I'll send out invites. Will you need a lift?"

"I can get a taxi from the hotel," Hannah said and ended the call. She then left a message for Matthew and extended her hotel reservation for one night, hoping Jess was okay with funding it for now. She returned to Lorraine's office to pick up the vase. Her heart was still pounding, and she took a few cleansing breaths. "We're going to have a trustee meeting tomorrow morning and sort the money then. Did you know that my great aunt and Beatrice Williams were the original trustees of Manley Hall? They were friends with Roger Manley. I would have thought that would be worth a discount." Hannah tried her cheekiest grin; you could get away with most things with a smile.

"Roger Manley, our Chair?" Lorraine looked puzzled.

"Yeah, but he must be quite old now, in his nineties—"

"He's one hundred and two and still likes to keep his hand in. Let me call him now and see what he says."

Lorraine put the phone on speaker, pressed a number on her speed dial, and the phone was answered immediately.

"Good morning, young Lorraine. How is my favourite manager doing?"

"Roger, you say that to everyone. It's a business call—"

"Alas, I thought you were going to agree to elope with me. Anton might be disappointed though. Shoot."

"I have a young lady here who says that the original founders both wish to stay. Maud Heaston is already here, but there's a temporary problem with funds for her companion, Beatrice Williams."

Hannah held her breath, wondering if the old man would remember people he knew sixty years ago.

He chuckled. "Beattie? Good heavens, I haven't spoken to her in years. What's the problem?"

"The funds are controlled by Ms Heaston's trust, and the main trustee won't release the funds yet. We can't agree to a new resident coming until a deposit and the first month's rent is paid."

"Well, if it's just a question of timing, I'd be delighted to stand as guarantor until it's sorted. And is the old library suite still available?"

"Yes, that's been kept for you as requested."

"I'll never stay in the country, too many bugs. Let them have it. That would be a fitting suite for Beattie and Maud to stay in."

"Of course. Thank you."

"You're welcome. Tell me when they're settled, and Anton and I will make a foray into the deepest darkest Midlands to visit them."

He hung up, and Lorraine grinned.

"I'm so pleased that's sorted. The old library suite is on the ground floor, overlooking some beautiful lawns and the sensory garden."

Hannah felt like doing a happy dance and couldn't keep the smile from her face. "Thanks. It seems fitting. They met in a library, and now they'll get to live in one."

"Just sort out the funds, and we'd be honoured to have them."

Hannah picked up the vase. She just had one more call to make before she returned to Gammy. She phoned Suki and said she'd come home the following evening. If Suki would still have her, Hannah would try again. Better to have secret Suki than none at all.

CHAPTER FORTY-SEVEN

AMANDA LOOKED PARTICULARLY sour when they met at Katherine's office the following morning. Katherine volunteered to take the minutes.

"As chair, I dislike being required to attend an emergency meeting when not all trustees have been present for most of the previous meetings."

Hannah clicked the complimentary ballpoint pen provided by Braithwaites. She didn't need this passive-aggressive bullshit. "I live over one hundred miles away, and I've been studying for my PhD. As a student, I don't have the financial resources to travel up regularly, and I don't drive. My travel costs have only been subsidised recently, so it wasn't easy for me to attend. And yeah, I know I should have made more effort, but that's changed now, and I want to be involved and make sure Gammy and Auntie Bea have the care they expect and deserve. "

Her lips curved upwards, but the smile didn't reach Amanda's eyes. She could play as dirty as she wanted, but Hannah wouldn't be bullied.

"Ordinarily, agenda items need to be submitted fourteen days in advance—"

"This is an emergency meeting because Gammy, who set up the trust for the benefit of the whole family, is expecting and hoping her lifelong partner, Auntie Bea, will join her at the care home this weekend, and the manager of the home says that you haven't paid the deposit." Hannah gripped the pen till her knuckles went white. She carefully placed it on the table and stretched her fingers out.

"Bea is not a family member—"

"Except she's been Gammy's partner for over seventy years. If she were a man, this wouldn't be an issue."

Amanda sucked in her lips. "But none of us knew that, until we saw them canoodling in the bed at the hospital. Talk about lack—"

"We don't need your homophobic opinion. Gammy provided for and desired to be with Auntie Bea. As trustees, we're obliged to ensure this happens. Gammy cannot go to the same home that Bea is currently in, and the only objection to Auntie Bea moving in is from you." Hannah pointed at Amanda, who blinked.

Amanda straightened up. "The funds are not available," she said.

Fuelled by anger, like a steam train burning coals, Hannah was determined not to be derailed by this poisonous woman. "What do you mean?"

"As I said. The budget has been made for Gammy's stay at the home plus a living allowance, a small amount for admin costs and incidentals, including trustee travel costs, educational costs for family members, and investment in property. There's nothing left in the budget. Matthew approved it."

Hannah flashed a scowl at Matthew, who shrugged. God, he was such a spineless git. How had she ever looked up to him? "The educational costs are for which family members? I haven't seen a penny of that."

"You could have looked at the minutes. The education costs are school fees for Matthew's two sons, and daughter, and my two boys."

Now they were getting somewhere. "How much does that cost each year?"

"If you looked at your accounts, you would see that the costs are about £250,000."

Hannah whistled. "A quarter of a million pounds? A year? So, you're both looking after your own children, but not me? Did you have criteria for electing these amounts?"

"They were stipulated in the set of rules. It's only up to secondary education."

Hannah was tempted to add until your own children get to college age, when it will presumably be extended to cover tertiary education. But that was a side-track. "And what's the property investment?" Hannah asked and detected a tell-tale flush on Amanda's cheeks.

"Rather than earning diddly squat on investments in the bank, the trustees decided, in a quorate meeting, that funds should be invested in the Manor House property to increase its value, which will be realised by the trust when the Manor House reverts—"

Hannah slammed her fist on the table so hard the water glasses rattled. "Hang on. Let me understand this. You've used the funds to do the renovations and upgrades to the Manor House you live in?"

Amanda reminded Hannah of a cornered rat, eyes glittering and mouth twitching, as if debating whether to attack or run.

"Which will revert to the trust when I die."

Hannah balled her hands into fists. "You crooked, selfish bitch. You get the benefit of all that extra work in your personal home and Gammy is left to rot, alone and separated from the love of her life?" Hannah bit the scar on her lip to stop herself exploding into a stream of curse words.

"Please strike the profanity from the record, Katherine," Amanda said.

Hannah turned to Matthew. "Did you agree to this?"

He shuffled his papers and wouldn't look her in the eye. What a waste of space.

"Interest rates are very low. It seemed very plausible," he muttered.

Hannah's blood rushed in her ears, and she struggled to keep her voice calm. "You're using Gammy's trust fund to feather your own nests? This is despicable. I want a proper independent audit done of the trust. Is it legal, Katherine?"

Katherine looked up from her laptop. "I haven't had the opportunity to look at the trust minutes, so I can't give you an opinion, Hannah, sorry."

"But you personally are getting the entire benefit of the work done. How much was it, a hundred grand?" She pulled the ridiculous figure from the air but had a feeling it could be more.

Amanda went pale but held her head high to stare at Hannah. "If you looked at the accounts, which *have* been audited, you would see the property investments were three hundred thousand with the expectation that in thirty years' time, the value of the property would have increased by six percent per annum. That's a much higher return than any other investment. The investment was made for the maximum long-term benefit of the trust."

"Long-term? What about the benefit to Gammy now? She won't be around for your long-term plan, Amanda. But you don't care about that, do you?" Hannah pushed herself up from the chair and started to pace, trying to fight back the tears threatening to fall when she thought about losing Gammy. That money could have bought a flat in Bristol, but this wasn't about her. "That amount would pay for Auntie Bea being in the home for six years."

"But that's not an investment and at the time the decision was made, we didn't know of Beatrice's...*friendship* with Gammy."

This woman was unbelievable; she was clearly unrepentant. "Don't belittle what they share by calling it a friendship. You've twisted Gammy's intentions and misused her trust for your own benefit. I'm sure the local newspaper would love to know the details. I wonder what your clients would think. Or your professional body." Hannah gripped the back of the chair and looked directly at Amanda, deliberately towering over her. "Sell the house and use the cash to pay for Auntie Bea's stay in the home with Gammy. That's the right thing to do, and it's what they want."

"You will not sell my house."

"But as you've just pointed out, it's not your house. It belongs to the trust. If we sell it, it will cover Gammy's and Auntie Bea's living fees, and any balance could help with my costs too. It might even buy me a flat since I've not received anything towards my education."

Katherine raised her hand. "Rather than sell the property you're living in, Amanda, what if you were to pay monthly rent for the use of the property which would go into the trust fund to cover the costs of Bea's accommodation?"

"That works," Hannah said before Amanda could object. It'd be easier on cash flow and would retain the house in the trust.

Amanda huffed and did some calculations on her phone. "That's a huge amount of money each month."

"But still cheaper than paying out for your property alterations upfront," Matthew said.

Finally, he had something useful to say. Hannah was delighted he was siding with Gammy. She took out her phone and did some calculations too, determined not to be outmanoeuvred by the weaselly Amanda. "Yeah, but in six years' time, the education needs for one of your boys and one of Matthew's will be finished since it only covers secondary school. Then we can divert the money from the education pot to cover Auntie Bea's fees."

Amanda tapped her teeth with her pen. Her eyes glittered like a crocodile with its jaw clamped, livid but powerless. She'd been caught stretching the legality of her position, and she knew it.

"Fine," she said. "I'll make a monthly contribution to the trust, to cover Beatrice's accommodation costs—"

"And her specialist support." Hannah wouldn't let her wheedle her way out of full recompense.

"That's ridiculous."

Hannah waved her hand as if swatting an irritating wasp. "No. She's de facto family and is entitled to it. Also, I'd like my hotel and transport costs covered for coming up here."

"Fine. Use the electronic form I sent you."

"Are we all agreed?" Hannah asked. Matthew nodded. He was such a waste of space, but of course as the oldest male of his generation he had the baronetcy title. How farcical and anachronistic. Still, he'd sided with her when it mattered. Katherine recorded that it was passed unanimously. "Amanda, you'll pay the deposit and first month's care into the home tomorrow so that Auntie Bea can move in on Saturday." Hannah held her breath as Amanda's expression seemed to cycle from fear to anger and then to resignation.

"I'll need to do a transfer from my investment account, so the earliest I can get it in there is Thursday."

Hannah exhaled. Despite Roger's guarantee she was relieved she didn't need to tell Gammy that Auntie Bea would be delayed again. She wasn't sure what effect it would have on their mental health. "Good. I'll tell Lorraine to expect the bank transfer by Thursday at the latest."

Amanda seemed to visibly deflate, but Hannah had no sympathy for her. She hated the oiliness of self-serving greed. Hannah couldn't wait to tell Suki what she had pushed through. She'd be impressed that Gammy and Auntie Bea would get their happy ending. Hannah grinned, and a thrill ran down her spine at the thought of seeing Suki again, but it was quickly followed by the clamp of concern that they might not be able to work something out so they too could have a happy ending. Witnessing how Gammy was in the last week, observing how she was devoted to Auntie Bea and the strength of their love, even in difficult circumstances, warmed her soul. Hannah wanted that, needed that even. If she and Suki could share half of the love Gammy and Auntie Bea had, they were sure to be happy.

She dragged herself back to the present and addressed the meeting. "If that's everything, can I cadge a lift to the station? It'd be a shame to have to make an extra claim on the tight budget."

"Sure." Matthew nodded and collected his briefcase.

With no goodbyes, Amanda stomped out, her bangles jangling and her expensive heels clattering on the wooden floor.

Katherine smiled and shook Hannah's hand. "Well done. That was impressive. You've done your gammy proud."

Hannah grinned with the jubilation of the victor. One victory chalked up. She just hoped the next challenge could be resolved too.

But that might be more tricky.

CHAPTER FORTY-EIGHT

I<small>T WAS STRANGE</small> to unlock the door to Suki's flat. It didn't feel like her home anymore, and it was chilly. Suki must have changed the heating timer so it would be off during the day to save money. Hannah glanced at her watch and decided she had time to prepare the vegan cheese and vegetable casserole Suki had said she liked last time Hannah made it.

She sent a text to say she'd arrived home, although it seemed strange to write that word. Looking around the living room, nothing had changed much, except it was impeccable. Every book had been rearranged by colour, Suki's preference, not subject and author, which was Hannah's, and the sofa was pushed against the wall.

Wait, where were her boxes? Hannah's heart sped up as she zoomed around the apartment. In her old room she didn't find the boxes, but she did find two extra shelves had been mounted with new box files, labelled in Suki's neat handwriting in date order. Suki had read and organised them all. Hannah grinned.

On her way home on the train, she'd decided to sleep in her own room until they'd figured out what the future looked like. She wasn't sure whether her concession would be appreciated. Was it a concession or capitulation? She shrugged.

The key turned in the lock, and the tell-tale click and buzz of the bike being brought into the hall jangled Hannah's nerves. This could be a new beginning or the beginning of the end.

"Wow, someone's been busy. Smells delightful."

Hannah had dotted candles around the living room, and they filled the space with a warm scented richness of clean cotton and clove.

Suki dropped her bag and threw herself at Hannah. "Oh, Han, I've missed you. I'm so glad you're back."

Hannah saw the hope in Suki's almost black, almond-shaped eyes. She loved those eyes. She sighed. "We need to talk, Suki, but shall we eat first? Do you want a shower while I finish supper?"

The sparkle dimmed from Suki's eyes, and she blinked a couple of times. "Sure." She picked up her bag to take into her bedroom, but before she reached the door, she swung around to face Hannah. "Do you still want to stay?"

The catch in her breath tore at Hannah's resolve. Sod waiting. She strode across the room and captured Suki in her arms. "Of course I do. I love you. That was never in doubt. I've been thinking, and I also had a talk with Gammy. She said that even though it was tough hiding themselves and who they were, she's never regretted being with Bea. It's better to have snippets of love than not at all. Do you forgive me? Will you take me back?" It all came out in a rush, no sign of the carefully constructed sentences she'd written out and rehearsed on the train. All she sounded was needy and desperate.

Suki squeezed harder and pulled at Hannah's neck so their eyes met. "Of course I'll take you back."

They reconnected in a kiss, tentative at first, then with a passion fuelled by the electric charge, scorching all that had come between them. It was a kiss that tasted of forgiveness, potential, and Suki's cherry lip balm. Hannah buzzed with delight and anticipation as everything clicked back into place. She pulled back for air.

Suki's smile blossomed and her eyes gleamed. "I've got something to tell you, too and I think you'll be proud of me, but it can wait until later. I'm glad we've got that sorted. Now I'm having a shower, and you can tell me all about how Gammy is over supper." Suki unhitched herself and bounced to her bedroom.

A pulse still throbbing between her legs, Hannah returned to preparing the meal, humming to herself as she pulled down the plates. The whole domesticity of laying the table grounded her. Everything seemed to slip back into place, like a bike chain clicking onto the teeth of the chain rings. Curiosity and excitement wondering about Suki's announcement caused her heart to skip.

Suki joined her for supper and sat facing Hannah on the other side of the kitchen bar. She pulled Hannah's hand to hers and kissed her knuckles. "Do you want to hear what I've got to tell you?"

Dread crept over Hannah, and her heart raced. Had she misread the situation? She nodded.

"I listened to what you said, and I called my parents in Japan. It's not the easiest thing to say over FaceTime, but I told them I'm bisexual and that I'm in love with the wonderful woman I share a flat with."

Hannah snapped her jaw shut. That Suki had gone against everything she had said before, taken her courage into her hands and faced her fear of rejection by her family was amazing. Hannah felt very humbled and loved that Suki would risk all that for her. "Wow. That was brave, and big. How'd it go?"

Suki shrugged. "I guess, kind of how you'd expect. Mum was shocked but quickly came around to the idea. She said to leave Dad for a while, and she'd talk to him. They're hoping to have a conversation with you now you're back from sorting out your great aunt. You got a big tick in their books for standing up to your cousin and making sure your gammy's going to be settled. And in my books, too."

The endorsement washed over Hannah in a warm wave of pleasure. "Thanks. Did you tell them about Auntie Bea moving in with her?"

Suki raised an eyebrow. "No. I thought one bombshell was enough for one evening."

"Wimp." Hannah interlaced her fingers in Suki's. "Talking of bombshells, shall we clear up here and reconnect in the bedroom?"

Suki was already off her stool and opening the dishwasher. "I thought you'd never ask."

So much for the resolution to stay in her old room, but this was a much better plan. Hannah grinned to herself. Home didn't sound so out of place now.

CHAPTER FORTY-NINE

"IT WAS A shock on FaceTime last night when Hannah said that her girlfriend is half Japanese. I think she was cross when I just stared at her. I know it's stupid, but I felt betrayed or rather, that Harry had been betrayed," Maud said, not looking Katherine in the eye. She picked up an ornament from the bedside table and tried to ignore the tremor in her traitorous hand. Outside, the rain splattered against the windowpanes. Everything was grey. It wasn't the best day for moving into their suite if the movers weren't careful about traipsing dirt in on their boots.

"I understand, but that was a very long time ago, and Suki wasn't even born then," Katherine said.

Maud passed Katherine the trinket, a plaster cast of a seagull from Newquay. Katherine wrapped it in plain paper and deposited it in the open box. She had very few belongings left and only kept them because she didn't want to offend her relatives. "I know, I know. It doesn't feel very Christian of me not to forget and forgive." She checked her large watch with the big hands and a stab of panic seized her. "They'll be here any minute. I'm not sure what I will say to her...Suki, I mean."

"How do you feel when someone judges you for loving a woman?" Katherine asked.

She was clearly trying to be diplomatic, as she seemed to choose her words carefully. She should know, she'd faced enough prejudice herself. But that wasn't why Katherine was asking, Maud knew that. "I know it's hypocritical. You don't need to spell it out." Maud winced with irritation, then caught herself. She needed to do this for Hannah or she would push her away for good. "I'll try to be open."

Katherine nodded. "That's a good idea. Suki has hired a car to drive all this way to help move Bea."

Maud dabbed at her mouth with her handkerchief. "Am I being ungrateful?"

"She's doing you a kindness. I know the movers are doing the heavy lifting, but it was a kind thought to collect Bea and bring her fragile goods in a car. I volunteered, but Hannah and Suki were adamant they wanted to help."

"You've already done enough."

Katherine laughed. "I've already told you, Olivia plays golf at the weekends, so I may as well come and enjoy your company."

Maud stretched out a hand. "Thank you. You're a good friend." The knock at the door made Maud's heart jump a beat. "Come in," she said, annoyed her voice trembled slightly.

Bea entered on the arm of a small woman who looked Japanese. Maud wasn't sure if she expected her to look more English. But that was just prejudice, and she'd promised to be open. Hannah towered above them from behind, carrying a heavy box by the look of it, and she set it down on the floor by the door.

"Hey, Gammy," Hannah said, "I thought it better to bring these here while they take the rest of the furniture to your new room. Good thing it's a large suite; I didn't know Auntie Bea had so much stuff."

Katherine stood from her kneeling position by the box and helped Maud onto her feet. Maud and Bea embraced, Bea's small frame slotting into her arms perfectly, just as if she was made to hold her. She inhaled the comforting smell of Bea's lily of the valley perfume and the scent that was just Bea. She was here. A thrill zipped down Maud's spine.

"At last," Bea said, "we're together. I've been so excited I didn't stop chatting in the car. I'm sure Suki is fed up with me already." She broke from the embrace and twisted to Hannah and Suki. "Doumo arigatou gozaimasu, Suki," Bea said and gave a brief bow.

Hannah rolled her eyes and flashed what looked like an apologetic glance at Suki. Suki replied to Bea with a reciprocal bow. Not that Bea could see.

"Gammy, this is Suki, my girlfriend. She's come to help you and Auntie Bea move into your new room."

In other words, behave because she's doing something nice. Maud smiled and put out a hand, willing it not to tremble too much. She could be polite if she tried. "Sorry, I don't speak Japanese," Maud said.

Suki gently shook her hand. "That's okay. English is my first language. My mother is English."

Maud tilted her head to one side. "But you lived in Japan?"

"As a child, yes, until I came to university in Bristol where I qualified, and I've stayed here ever since."

"Oh," said Maud, unable to think of anything else to say.

Hannah introduced Suki to Katherine, who hugged her.

"Thank you for coming to help on your day off, Suki. It's very kind," Katherine said.

It was as if she was trying to compensate for Maud's polite but cool response. She sniffed, not happy they were all dancing around her.

"Now, what needs to be done in here?" Hannah asked.

"We started on the boxes but haven't got very far," Katherine said. "I thought we'd let the movers take Bea's things into the new room first and keep Bea and Gammy here, out of the way. I was hoping they could sit outside, but it's too wet."

"Sure. I'll bring the rest of the boxes from the car," Hannah said.

"I'll help," Suki said and spun around.

Was that an air of desperation in her tone? Maud needed to make an effort. Hannah said she loved Suki, so she must be a good soul. "No, you stay here with me, dear, it'll be nice to get to know you. Katherine, perhaps you could give Hannah a hand when you've settled Bea down?"

"Okay, that sounds great," Hannah said and retreated from the room.

"What needs to be packed up here?" Suki asked, pointing to the wrapping paper and boxes.

"Maybe you could do the books, my dear?"

"Of course. Are they organised in any particular way?"

"By author, or subject then author if it's non-fiction."

"That's how Hannah has her books organised. I love it done by colour so they're like a rainbow when you enter the room."

"Hm." Maud didn't think much to this modern way of arranging things but kept her opinion to herself. She placed her trinkets and photos in a box to be taken down the hall to their new room. Hannah had secured them the biggest suite in the house. It had its own private sitting room as well as an en-suite bathroom and a tiny kitchenette with a microwave and an on-tap boiler for hot drinks.

Maud picked up her tatty photo of Harry leaning on their car with her and Bea all looking happy. It was her favourite picture. She looked from it to Suki carefully dusting, then stacking books into a box in order. "What do you know about the war?" Maud asked Suki. She flinched. Perhaps that wasn't the best opening gambit on her quest to be more understanding.

Suki looked up from where she was kneeling and brushed her jeans. "At school, we had a trip to Hiroshima. It was very sad. The amazing thing was seeing all the paper cranes made by schoolchildren from around the world. Cranes symbolise harmony and long life." She bit her bottom lip. "Since I've been in the UK, there seems to be a war movie or TV show on most weekends, plus all the video games of course. So, I guess I've picked up the British view of the war."

Maud let Suki's comments percolate. She needed to be more open, as she promised. She blinked and picked up another photo and stashed it in the box. This young woman was not even alive then, and Hannah loved her. "Tell me about the paper cranes," Maud said.

"From what I remember, a girl who contracted leukaemia from the atomic bomb wanted to make a thousand paper cranes in origami, because that's supposed to grant you a wish. She didn't survive the radiation effects of the bomb, so her classmates finished off the cranes. It seemed to catch the imagination and children across the world make cranes and send them to Hiroshima as a symbol of peace. I think even Barack Obama made one when he visited."

Maud listened and nodded. All those innocent lives cut short, on both sides. How did her prejudice honour Harry? It didn't. What a waste. Tears prickled the backs of her eyes. "Will you help me make a paper crane?"

"Of course. I'll need to remind myself how to do it by looking online, but I'd love to."

And this time they shared and held a genuine smile.

Suki returned to the books and picked up a musty leather-bound tome. "Ooh, you've got the Barchester Chronicles."

Maud looked up. "You've read them?" she asked, unable to keep the surprise mixed with admiration from her tone. This young woman was quite a revelation.

"My mum and I watched the TV series, and then I read the books. I loved Obadiah Slope, he's a great character to hate. Mum always says she doesn't understand why Trollope hasn't been as popular as Dickens."

"That's an interesting point. I love Trollope but the only Dickens I really love is *Tale of Two Cities* even though it's not an easy read."

Suki nodded with apparent enthusiasm. "Right. Maybe we should have a reading aloud session?" she said.

A thrill ran up Maud's spine as she could imagine sharing some time with Suki and Hannah in one of her favourite activities. "That would be lovely. And now Bea has her reader, maybe she could join in."

Suki placed the next book into the packing box. "Perfect. I'm not sure Hannah would though."

Katherine and Hannah burst into the room as though they had hurried back from their task to rescue Suki.

"Hannah would what?" Hannah asked.

"Have a reading out loud session of Trollope," Maud said with hardly a tremor.

"Suki loves all that old stuff." Hannah ran her hand over Suki's shoulder.

"Cheeky, or does that mean you're old too?" Suki asked as she picked another book to dust.

"After lifting all those boxes, I'm knackered if not old." Hannah pulled Suki into a full body hug and looked over Suki's shoulder. "I hope you've been nice, Gammy."

Maud sniffed. She *had* behaved and they'd been getting on fine. "We've been talking about books and the war—"

Hannah groaned and whispered something to Suki, who shook her head.

"And Suki is going to show me how to fold paper cranes. They're a symbol of peace and longevity."

The conspiratorial smile she shared with Suki warmed Maud's heart. Hannah gaped from one to the other as if she'd just witnessed a miracle. Anxiety seemed to slip off Hannah's shoulders like a winter coat on a summer day, and Maud felt a stab of guilt that her fear and judgement had kept Hannah out in the cold for so long. All her prejudice had done was alienate Hannah, and all her lies and secrets had pushed her away and hurt Bea. How was that love? Heat burned up her chest and face. All the wasted years, the un-lived joy and connection because of what? Some judgement that did not honour Harry and gave them no comfort. She shook off the feeling, determined to make the most of now and stop looking back to a past long gone.

These were the people she loved most in the world. What a joy to be in her nineties and surrounded by love. The surprise was that she could see herself loving Suki, for who she was, not just because Hannah loved her. She would do what she could to bridge that gap and she would learn to make paper cranes, even if she struggled with her hands. She would try and earn all of their forgiveness and be worthy of the love and patience they showed. It was far better to love, to live in joy, than to clutch the chimera of righteousness.

EPILOGUE

Three months later

Maud looked over to Bea, dressed in a simple ivory silk dress with her hair brushed out around her shoulders. She'd grown it longer especially for the occasion and still retained her natural wave, now silver, but she remained equally alluring. Maud was tempted to run her fingers through Bea's locks but that would probably interfere with Hannah and Suki, who were helping them to dress. Now Hannah was quicker at Morse, she was with Bea, tapping out comments and making her laugh.

"Close your eyes," Suki instructed, her brush poised to apply eyeshadow.

Maud obeyed, trusting Suki completely. Her breath was warm on her skin and as gentle as the light strokes on her eyelids. She never thought she would see this day and wished they'd done it long ago. If Maud had been a man, they could have, but equally, she would have gone to war and, like Harry and Bill, may never have returned. Instead, she'd had a wonderful life with Bea. She'd been the constant, her sun, drawing Maud into her orbit. Even when she'd done her duty to her family and country, Bea was always on her mind.

She didn't regret any of it. Her only real regrets settled around Hannah. She should have trusted Hannah with their secret earlier, but if she hadn't chased her away, Hannah may not have escaped to Bristol and may not be there now with the lovely young woman who made her so happy.

Maud fluttered her eyelids open and stared directly into the concentrated expression of Suki. "Thank you, dear," she whispered. "You make Hannah very happy, and you will always be special in my heart for that."

"Thank you, Gammy. And thanks for letting us see your letters. It made me realise how important love is. More than outward appearances and expectations."

Suki placed her hand on Maud's shoulder, and she covered it with her own shaking hand. They'd been experimenting with the meds to get the right balance between calming some of the worst tremors and not spacing Maud out so she could enjoy this special day.

Her wedding day.

It had a wonderful sound like a peal of church bells: loud, strong, and jubilant.

Ruth, a non-denominational pastor, was to officiate, and she'd been lovely when they spoke to her, with no hint of judgement or damnation. She was so different from the Reverend Davies and his successors. Ruth had even joked with them whether she needed to have the conversation about procreation.

Maud chuckled at the memory and turned to watch Bea being made up. Her chest heaved at the sight. Never in her wildest dreams had she thought this day might be possible. Suki followed Maud's gaze and she frowned.

"Swap over, Hannah, you can't do make-up to save your life." Suki squeezed Maud's shoulder. "Be with you in a moment. I need to rescue your bride from looking like a painted doll."

"Hey, I resent that." Hannah tapped out something on Bea's hand, probably to announce Suki was taking over.

Bea held out her hand and Maud took it. "Today I make an honest woman of you…even if it is seventy-five years late." She chuckled.

Maud sighed. "That's so true. No more lies or pretending, no more omission." She tried to tap out 88 on Bea's hand, but her own shook too much.

"You'd better bloody love me, Maud Heaston, after all this time. I don't want you jilting me at the altar."

Maud patted her hand, as Suki tilted Bea's face to apply some foundation.

Hannah slid her arms around Maud's shoulders. "How are you doing, Gammy? All set?"

"The best day of my life." She sniffed to hold back the tears as her heart expanded and love blossomed within it. "With all the best people in the world."

Hannah stooped to kiss her on the forehead and fastened the necklace around her neck. The double string of pink pearls felt cool to the touch.

"Sorry, Gammy, maybe we should have warmed them beforehand."

"They'll soon warm up, dear." Maud remembered when she had first worn them, just the single string when Bea had helped her get ready for the dance before the war. Did she fall in love with Bea then, or was it when they were doing maths problems, or reading Shakespeare? She smiled to herself, then glanced at her watch, only two minutes had passed since the last time she looked. She gnawed at her bottom lip. "Have you got the rings?"

Hannah tapped at her jacket pocket. "Yep. Are we all ready? You both look beautiful." Hannah paused to tap out Morse on Bea's palm. She must have spotted Suki pout slightly, as Hannah stretched over to feather a kiss on her lips. "And you too, of course. But today is all about these wonderful women."

Katherine knocked and entered with her wife, Olivia. They presented the bouquets to the brides, chosen primarily for scent, gardenia, white roses, and lily of the valley. Maud's had a violet. Violet would have loved this; she was such a romantic. And Maud would have loved to have Violet here.

Bea accepted her flowers and inhaled deeply. "That's wonderful, thank you."

Maud patted Bea's hand. Hannah led the way, pushing Bea through the French doors, down the ramp and across the lawns to the waiting marquee. Suki followed, pushing Maud.

"Faster," Bea said. "We're going to get married. This is the best day of my life. Feel the warm sun on our faces. Isn't it wonderful to be alive?" She inhaled deeply. "Smell the new mown grass and the flowers..." Bea sniffed her bouquet again. "Lily of the valley, my favourite. And I bet the birds are singing in the trees. I imagine I can hear warblers, and blackbirds, and a woodpecker." She tapped on her wheelchair arm like a woodpecker and chuckled. "Sweetheart, can you believe we're going to get married?"

Maud laughed and caught hold of Bea's hands. Controlling the tremor, she lifted Bea's hand to her lips.

Bea twisted to face her and stroked her chin. "Thank you for making me the happiest woman in the world. Thank you for being brave and open. I love you," Bea said.

Maud gulped and sniffed away a happy tear. She tapped 88 on Bea's hand.

Hannah turned to Suki. "I could say the same to you."

Suki reached out and stroked Hannah's cheek.

"Thank you for waiting for me to catch up," Suki said.

Hannah smiled. "You're worth waiting for."

It was delightful to see Hannah so happy. No longer the angry rebellious teenager, she had done so much to get them to this day and Maud would be eternally grateful.

Bea banged the arms of her wheelchair. "Come on, come on, we've got a wedding to go to."

The other three women laughed.

"Let's go, Suki," Maud said. "I don't want to keep my future wife waiting."

A gentle breeze caught the brides' hair, and Bea laughed as she was pushed along. "Shall I compare thee to a summer's day? Thou art more lovely and more temperate. Rough winds do shake the darling buds of May, And summer's lease hath all too short a date."

As she continued, Maud joined in for the lines she could remember, "But thy eternal summer shall not fade, Nor lose possession of that fair thou ow'st."

"At least it's not King Lear. That didn't end well," Hannah said.

It was warm in the marquee and smelt slightly stuffy. Maud buried her nose into her bouquet. The smell of lily of the valley took her back to the days in the library at home, reading Shakespeare with Bea before the war, when they were young and in love. And now they were old and still in love, and warmth radiated from her heart, shrivelling all the prejudice and condemnation of so many years battling for acceptance. That glow would be with her for the rest of her days. Bea, *her Bea*, was going to marry her. A thrill shivered down her spine. For the first time in a very long time, Maud breathed deeply, fully as though breaking free of the last bindings of secrets. All the lies, cold and brittle, melted with the heat of truth and love.

She waved at the residents from the home and all her nephews, nieces, great nephews, and nieces. Even Amanda was trying to smile, but it looked more like rigor mortis had set in rather than an indication of pleasure. She scanned the marquee for her friends. Too few in number now, but the daughter of her Land Army friend Alice had come, and Anton had brought Roger in a wheelchair. She wondered what they would think, coming back to Manley Hall.

Ruth called everyone to order, and Maud realised she hadn't even heard the music. "In the Mood" by Glenn Miller, not your usual wedding march, but it was played loud enough for Bea to feel the vibrations. She began to sway in her wheelchair as they took their places. She didn't need the chair, but they decided to conserve their energy so they could do the first dance together.

They'd been trying to practise, but Bea was still the nimbler of the two of them, and danced with abandon, even though she couldn't see where she was going. Maud had been terrified they were going to crash into the furniture and had danced even more stiffly than she would have done ordinarily. Or maybe it was the damned disease. She sighed.

Ruth welcomed everyone. She spoke of their respective war services, and the audience were understandably more impressed by Bea's record as a code breaker than Maud's as a humble land girl. The Land Army always was the Cinderella service, as though their contribution to the war effort had been lesser. It had certainly been less glamorous. But then Bea had only been acknowledged and received a medal less than twenty years ago. She didn't bother to go to the presentation, and Maud had hidden her disappointment. She would have loved to meet one of the royals, even a minor one, but Bea said it would've been hypocritical given she was not a royalist.

Still, it would have been a nice day out. But this was a nice day out. This was the most wonderful day out, and the best day of her life by far. She looked across to Bea, whose face radiated a glow of pure delight. It seemed unreal, and yet here they were, sharing in their moment.

Someone cleared their throat, and she looked up. Ruth was asking them to exchange rings to say their vows. How had that happened already? They'd only just come in.

Maud held Bea's hands in her own and caressed them as she recited her more traditional vows, before adding her own lines. "We could have walked the easy path, the one that was expected. Instead, we toiled the mountain route, our love, still whole, at last respected."

Bea's vows included Shakespeare. "Love is an ever-fixed mark, that looks on tempests and is never shaken; It is the star to every wand'ring bark, Whose worth is unknown, although his height be taken.' Maud, you are my star, my ever-fixed mark." Bea's eyes watered slightly. "We've had to weather many storms in getting here, but now, we can shore up and bask in each other's warmth until the close of day."

Maud clasped Bea's hands, complete with shiny rings, and when they were invited to kiss, Maud stole a glance at the joyful tears amongst the congregation. As she bent to share a meaningful kiss, an "ah" breathed out around the mass, like blossom settling on the ground. The plan had been for a swift kiss, but Bea clung on, clearly wanting to savour the moment. Someone blew a wolf whistle, and a ripple of laughter went around the congregation. She chuckled and pulled back. To be this loved and accepted for who they were was unbelievable, and she couldn't keep the joy from her heart or laughter from her lips.

Maud began to shake, and Suki helped her into her chair. Hannah assisted Bea to hers and they turned them around so they could be wheeled out to the accompaniment of "Jupiter" from Holst's The Planets Suite.

The great thing about being older was that they didn't have to have a drawn-out affair. A few photos were taken, including by the local newspaper, but they didn't want people to be hanging around waiting for their lunch, so the main photographer was asked to take candid shots throughout. They had organised photos to be printed on raised paper, so Maud could describe them to Bea later.

The care home provided lunch followed by bananas and custard, because they were only allowed one banana when they were reintroduced after the war. Suki and Hannah had made table decorations of Origami paper cranes, plus a few Maud and Bea had folded. If anything, Bea's were much neater than those Maud had made as Bea had committed the method to memory and did everything by feel. Every crease was a coming together, every fold a sign of love. They had made enough cranes to give to everyone in the home and the carers, even if they weren't coming to the ceremony or reception.

After the ceremony, the local rag wanted to take a couple of photos to add to the interview they'd conducted a few days ago. Evidently, waiting seventy-odd years to get married was a big news story. Maud wondered if any of her old clients would read it and be shocked that she was marrying a woman. She thought of Mr Jenkins and how he had saved her. If he hadn't pulled her from the car, she would never have seen this day. She offered up thanks and a silent prayer.

"What's with the paper cranes?" the newspaper reporter asked, just before they packed up to leave.

"My great niece's girlfriend, Suki, told me about the significance of cranes in Japan and how they represent peace and long life. It was a joy to share making the cranes with two wonderful women, and we're grateful for the time and effort they've made for us."

Suki caught Maud's eye and bowed her head in acknowledgement. She was such a polite young woman and so good for Hannah.

The marquee was cleared to make a dance floor. This was the moment that Maud had been equally excited and nervous about. She hoped they wouldn't stumble, as she could feel tiredness sucking her energy. Everyone cleared a wide space, and Bea led Maud to the centre of the dance floor, with Maud correcting her navigation with a slight tug of her arm.

"I'm leading," Bea said. "Just don't let me go careering into the crowd. Don't forget, slow, slow, quick, quick, leading off on your right foot, backwards and small steps."

Laughter rippled around the onlookers. Most people hadn't seen Bea in this authoritative mode before. Maud would've said bossy, but she loved Bea for it. Butterflies fluttered in her stomach. Their hands fit snuggly together, and Bea settled her hand on Maud's back. A spark travelled around her body, as the clarinet and saxophone notes started on the track, "Moonlight Serenade."

Maud was ultra-aware of all the guests as they moved around, until they settled into a rhythm and she was drawn into Bea's orbit, and it was as if they were the only couple there, foxtrotting around like they had in the drawing room at her childhood home.

Bea tapped out I love you in Morse code on the back of Maud's hand. In the misty periphery of her vision, Harry and Vi looked on. As they finished dancing both of them clapped and Harry called out, "Do you need me to check for bruises from your trampled feet, Bea?"

Maud swallowed against the lump in her throat.

"Do you remember when we first danced together to that?" Bea murmured and tears trickled down her face.

Maud swept them away with her thumb. She must've been thinking back too. Forehead to forehead they clung to each other in the middle of the temporary wooden flooring, their warm breaths mingling.

Suki and Hannah brought over the wheelchairs, and Maud sagged into hers as the wedding guests joined the dance floor.

Later that evening, it was balmy enough to sit outside in the extensive gardens of the care home without jackets. The guests had left, the hired chairs and tables were stacked and wheeled away, and the marquee was being taken down.

"The wedding went really well," Suki said to Maud who sat opposite, but close to her, within easy hearing distance.

"Yes, it did." Maud caught Bea's left hand. She studied the simple gold bands on their ring fingers and her heart thumped. They looked so shiny and new, almost too bright for their old skin. She rubbed the metal as though she expected a genie to appear, but she had already received her three wishes, being surrounded by these wonderful women.

Bea paused from her Morse conversation with Hannah, cleared her throat, and turned to Maud. "I can't believe I can call you my wife after all these years. You've made me the happiest woman alive."

Maud glowed with pleasure. "Tap out thank you and I love her, please, Hannah."

Hannah nodded.

"Why didn't you get married when it first became legal?" Suki asked.

Maud sighed and tucked her free hand under her thigh, trying to control the shaking. The tiredness was really beginning to show now, but she wanted to answer Suki's question. She knew she owed her the truth, even if it didn't reflect well on her. "A mixture of guilt, shame, and fear. I had this image of myself, who I had to be and how I had to behave to be accepted in my community. I insisted Bea keep us quiet, even though she would have been open and didn't care what people thought."

"I understand that," Suki said. "I felt the same and almost lost Hannah. She told me you encouraged her to follow her heart. Thank you. It must've been so much harder for you both."

"Most people don't care though, as long as it doesn't affect them," Maud said, then chuckled as a thought crossed her mind. "Actually, Amanda may care. She thinks Bea is a gold digger and that Amanda won't get any inheritance. But we've both agreed we're going to leave any money left to the care home. They're lovely here."

"What changed your mind about getting married?"

Suki held her gaze intensely as though she was genuinely interested. Maud inhaled, wondering how much more to reveal to Suki. But she owed it to her, to Hannah, to prise open the oyster shell and reveal the pearl of truth. "It was Hannah and you. I realised what meant most to me is people. Bea has been constant, agreeing to the subterfuge for too many years to count and even agreeing to be separated in the home for six months so the family wouldn't suspect. The coldest lies are the ones that hurt the most, just because they're so old. I'd put our happiness at the lowest priority. I almost lost her, and I almost lost Hannah." Maud smiled at Hannah, who looked up when she heard her name. "We didn't talk for too long. I was too harsh with her. It was little wonder she rebelled. But I was too cowardly to admit I wanted her in my life." She patted Suki's hand and smiled. "Thank you for encouraging her to visit me. She's the closest I have to a granddaughter, and now I have two. I can't tell you how happy and touched I am that you came to our wedding."

Suki leaned forward. "Well, you're famous now on both the local and national news."

Maud dabbed at her mouth with her embroidered handkerchief and clutched it tightly in her grasp. Hannah was busy having a Morse conversation with Bea. She seemed quite proficient now. "I'm glad your dad has accepted your relationship."

Suki nodded and broke into a wide smile. "He could see how much I love Hannah, just as you and Bea love each other. He went against tradition, marrying for love, so as my mum said, he couldn't really complain. After all, love is love."

Maud nodded, and for a minute she was back in the hospital talking to Harry in the last week of his life. She stroked the embroidery on her handkerchief. What would Harry have said to know she was talking to a young Japanese woman on her own wedding day. He would understand, she was certain of it. "How strange. I haven't heard that expression in years. My brother said that to me a long time ago. Looking back, I realise now he was giving me permission to be with Bea. He loved her too and wanted to marry her. She was so lively; she loved to dance, and sing, and have fun. Everybody loved her. I'm so lucky to have her in my life, and so grateful."

"You both stole the show when you danced the foxtrot together."

Hannah slid Suki's hand into her own. They kissed. "Hey, beautiful, are you about ready to go back to our hotel room?"

"I think so, soon to be Dr Jones."

They kissed and hugged Maud and Bea goodbye.

Hannah grinned a cheeky grin. "Be good, you newly-weds. No breaking the bed tonight."

"Hannah." Maud feigned shock, although she wasn't really cross. She loved that Hannah bantered with her. In some ways, Hannah reminded her of Harry. Why hadn't she seen that before? She knew it was because she hadn't allowed her in, but that had changed now.

"I bet you used to be ravers in your day," Hannah said.

Maud shook her head. She was definitely not getting into that conversation. "Hannah, that's not something to be discussed."

"Don't worry, I'm only teasing. Can't have you approving of me too much. Next you'll tell me you love me."

Maud grasped Hannah's sleeve, the banter gone. "I do love you, Hannah, and I love your girlfriend too. She can come up anytime. You both can, you know that. I'm hoping we'll be invited down for your graduation."

Hannah returned Maud's smile. "For sure. You'll both be my guests of honour."

Maud's heart fluttered, joy sparking lights where there had once been darkness. "Thank you for everything you've done. We wouldn't be here now...." She paused for a moment, acknowledging her gratitude was tinged with the regret at the wasted years. "When you're as ancient as we are, every morning is a miracle and every day together is a blessing. It wouldn't have been possible without you both. It doesn't really express it all but thank you for doing your duty by a crusty old woman who probably doesn't deserve it."

Hannah leaned forward and looked deep into Gammy's eyes with a fierce intensity. "I didn't choose duty, I chose love."

When she and Bea lay together in their bed that evening, sleep did not come. Bea caressed Maud's cheeks. Though their main communication was through scent and touch, through frail fingers on fragile skin, it still held the power to ignite comfort, care, and love. Bea traced her fingers over Maud's face on the scattering of scars from the shattered windscreen, so many years ago.

"I almost lost you," Bea said, a catch in her throat, "and we would never have had this lifetime of love. We would never have got the chance to marry."

Maud trailed her fingers across Bea's lips, thinner now with a less pronounced Cupid's bow, and stretched down to kiss her, returning that love still burning bright and strong with certainty. Maud inhaled Bea's scent, the comfort and familiarity of soap and lily of the valley. Words just skimmed the surface, but touch, and taste, and smell transported her into the depths of Bea's love.

And love is everything.

Author's Note

Invariably, when you write an historical piece it is so easy to slip in anachronisms, and when you do research, there may be inconsistencies of memory etc. In addition to reading lots of books etc and claiming it was research, I interviewed both my dad and my ex-father-in-law, both of whom are in their nineties. It was a delight to delve into their experiences and actually capture a nugget of what each of them said to thread into the story, but also to connect with them and get a different perspective on them as people.

I conflated two incidents into the thistle field scene. One was from my research into the Land Army, the other was from my dad's experience watching a raid on Derby. The raid in Derby didn't take place until 1942 when the Rolls Royce canteen was bombed, and the German plane actually escaped after shooting down a British plane, but I've changed the details to what worked with the story. Apologies if that offends any sensibilities.

Also, although Girton college was established in 1869, Cambridge University did not issue women with degrees until 1947, despite women sitting the university exams. I didn't include all the details as it wasn't pertinent to the story.

If there remain any inconsistencies or anachronisms the fault is all mine.

I really hope you enjoyed reading *Warm Pearls and Paper Cranes*. If you did, I'd be very grateful for an honest review. Reviews and recommendations are crucial for any author, particularly one just starting out. Just a line or two can make a huge difference.

Thank you.

What's Your Story?

Global Wordsmiths, CIC, provides an all-encompassing service for all writers, ranging from basic proofreading and cover design to development editing, typesetting, and eBook services. A major part of our work is charity and community focused, delivering writing projects to under-served and under-represented groups across Nottinghamshire, giving voice to the voiceless and visibility to the unseen.

To learn more about what we offer, visit: www.globalwords.co.uk

A selection of books by Global Words Press:
Desire, Love, Identity: with the National Justice Museum
Times Past: with The Workhouse, National Trust
World At War: Farmilo Primary School
Times Past: Young at Heart with AGE UK
In Different Shoes: Stories of Trans Lives

Self-published authors working with Global Wordsmiths:
E.V. Bancroft
Valden Bush
Addison M Conley
Emma Nichols
Dee Griffiths and Ali Holah
Helena Harte
Dani Lovelady Ryan
Karen Klyne
AJ Mason
James Merrick
John Parsons
Ray Martin
Robyn Nyx
Sam Rawlings
Simon Smalley

Other Great Books
by Independent Authors

Music City Dreamers by Robyn Nyx
Does following their dreams mean losing out on their new love?
Available on Amazon (ASIN B08WR5ZMN6)

Scripted Love by Helena Harte
What good is a romance writer who doesn't believe in happy ever after?
Available from Amazon (ASIN B0993QFLNN)

Come Dream with Me by Karen Klyne
When your past and your future collide, who do you become in the present?
Available from Amazon (ASIN B096PB3HMF)

Nero by Valden Bush
Banished. Abandoned. Lost. Will her destiny reunite her with the love of her life?
Available from Amazon (B09BXN8VTZ)

Judge Me, Judge Me Not by James Merrick
A memoir of one gay man's battle against the world and himself.
Available from Amazon (ASIN B09CLK91N5)

That Boy of Yours Wants Looking At by Simon Smalley
A gloriously colourful and heart-rending memoir.
Coming November 30, 2021 (ASIN B09HSN9NM8)

Rock My Heart by Emma Nichols
What will it take for her to stay?
Available from Amazon (ASIN B09G1YNHQC)

The Proud Weed by Sam Rawlings
Children's picture book about discovering your place in the world.
Available from Amazon (ISBN 9798728860617)

The Women and The Storm by Kitty McIntosh
Being the only witch in a small Scottish town is not easy.
Available from Amazon (ISBN 9798654945983)

Printed in Great Britain
by Amazon

15463742R00200